MW00630153

THIS DELUXE ILLUSTRATED FIRST EDITION OF

STORYKILLER

IS LIMITED TO THIRTEEN HUNDRED INDIVIDUALLY

SIGNED AND NUMBERED COPIES BY THE AUTHOR

522/1300

Kelly Thompson

KELLY THOMPSON

Josh.

Thanks for all
the support, yo.
I know how you despise
chicks & chick
creators, & YA stuff
you old man.

xo Kelly

ADVANCE PRAISE FOR STORYKILLER

"*Storykiller* is a sweeping fantasy grounded by sarcastic wit and a modern twist on age-old characters that is great for any fan of *Buffy The Vampire Slayer*. No author has ever made me care so much for the villains, but Thompson does it again in *Storykiller* with Snow and Fenris."
- ERIN JADE LANGE, author of BUTTER and DEAD ENDS

"Tessa Battle saves the world from Stories, wielding a double-bladed axe and rocking a red mohawk. The Snow Queen, Bluebeard, Robin Hood, Romeo, Trolls…every classic Story you can possibly think of create the ultimate monster mash within the same pages, and it works. Tessa, Micah, and Brand give Buffy, Willow, and Xander a run for their money. Except this isn't an undiscovered Whedon story, it's Kelly Thompson's second novel – and she kicks the idea of a 'sophomore slump' firmly in the balls. Tessa Battle-style."
-KAREN MAHONEY, author of THE IRON WITCH TRILOGY

"Even though it's really about killing off fictional characters who aren't that fictional after all, it has that 'family is what you make it' message at its heart, because the main characters seem like such a ragtag bunch that don't belong together, but by the end, you couldn't imagine it any other way."
-CAANAN GRALL, Creator of CELADORE and MAX OVERACTS

"In a world filled with adaptations I adore (*Fables, Once Upon A Time, The Eyre Affair Series*) it can be a bit hard to write another version that doesn't smack of familiarity. Thompson does it like gangbusters though and man what a trip."
-POISONED RATIONALITY

"Rich, fast paced, and instantly enthralling. The fact that this takes place in a world where every single story ever written exists, leaves one anticipating any twist or turn with each page and Ms. Thompson does not disappoint! There are so many possibilities!" -GOODREADS

"Thompson has really outdone herself this time! In *The Girl Who Would Be King* she tipped the superhero genre on its head and it's hard to see how she could up the ante. But with *Storykiller* she does. She breathes life into characters old and new and sucks you into a world both Real and Fiction." –AMAZON

"Dangerously addictive!" –AMAZON

KELLY THOMPSON

WITH INTERIOR ILLUSTRATIONS BY:

KRIS ANKA   THOMAS BOATWRIGHT   BEN CALDWELL

ROSS CAMPBELL   RENAE DE LIZ & RAY DILLON

MING DOYLE   CAANAN GRALL   STEPHANIE HANS

REBEKAH ISAACS   CASSANDRA JAMES

STACEY LEE   MEREDITH MCCLAREN   DUSTIN NGUYEN

DECLAN SHALVEY & JORDIE BELLAIRE

MATTHEW SOUTHWORTH   NOELLE STEVENSON

KYLA VANDERKLUGT   BRETT WELDELE   JAKE WYATT

NEW YORK, NY

Limited Edition Hardcover with illustrations © 2014

All rights reserved, published by 1979 Semi-Finalist, Inc. Printed by Four Colour Print Group.

Illustrated Hardover ISBN – 10: 0991649249
Illustrated Hardcover ISBN – 13: 978-0-9916492-4-2
Printed in USA

Cover Illustration by Stephanie Hans
Cover and Book Design by Kelly Thompson

Interior illustration Section: Kris Anka (fig. 6), Thomas Boatwright (fig. 7), Ben Caldwell (fig. 22, 23, and 24), Ross Campbell (fig. 2, 4, 5, and 18), Renae De Liz & Ray Dillon (fig. 28), Ming Doyle (fig. 20), Caanan Grall (fig. 11, 21), Stephanie Hans (Cover, fig. 1, 30, 31, and 32), Rebekah Isaacs (fig. 29), Cassandra James (fig. 19), Stacey Lee (fig. 13, 14, 15, 26, and 27), Meredith McClaren (fig. 9), Dustin Nguyen (fig. 3), Declan Shalvey & Jordie Bellaire (fig. 12), Matthew Southworth (fig. 16), Noelle Stevenson (fig. 8), Kyla Vanderklugt (fig. 10), Brett Weldele (fig. 17), and Jake Wyatt (fig. 25).

"Itties" by Meredith McClaren. Manticore Logo by Caanan Grall

The type is Garamond. Also used is Beast by Hydro74 and You Are Loved by Kimberly Geswein.

www.1979semifinalist.com
www.storykiller.com

For Mom, Dad, Scott, and Dave—your support and patience have been endless and I couldn't have done much of anything without you.

For Joss Whedon's exceptional Buffy, for without Buffy there would be no Tessa Battle and so many other wonderful women (fictional and not) that I've come to love.

& for Adam, as ever.

STORYKILLER

The Slow Knife

ONE

'There's something wrong with me,' boomed through Tessa's head on repeat. She nearly shattered the flimsy stall door as she kicked it in with her combat boot, getting over the toilet only seconds before she vomited what felt like everything she'd ever eaten. A pair of girls at the sinks behind her groaned and got bitchy.

"Ewww."

"Gross. Way to go, new girl."

Tessa stepped on the flush with her boot and staggered out of the stall, glaring at them.

"Double ewww," the blonde said, looking Tessa up and down and making a gagging sound. Tessa thought for a moment about punching her in the throat, but the pinch of pain in her stomach made her feel strangely kittenish. Instead, she just moved to the sinks and turned the tap, which immediately snapped off in her hand as if she was The Hulk.

"Balls," Tessa muttered, tossing the broken knob to the floor. "Piece of junk," she said, squinting her eyes shut through a wave of sharp pains while the cool water gushed from the faucet. Tessa leaned over the sink and rinsed out her mouth as the girls slid from the bathroom giggling and calling her names. She washed her face, not caring that her hair or the heavy black make-up around her eyes was getting wet.

She glanced at her watch.

2:25 pm.

She'd been 17 for three minutes.

What an awesome start to what was sure to be a banner year back in Lore, Oregon.

 TWO

After the first two stops the school bus was almost empty, not that it had been full to begin with, but now they were only three. Tessa in the very back and a pair sitting a dozen seats in front of her that seemed like the kind of best friends you only read about in books. The boy and girl had a laughter and intimacy that rivaled the closest brother and sister. It had Tessa so envious she thought beams of jealous green light might come out of her eyes.

She felt weird.

Nothing had been quite right since she'd thrown up in the bathroom. Actually, it had all gone wonky just before that, but she wasn't sure why or how.

Also, someone was following the bus.

And not the kind of person that you think of when you think of creepy people that follow school buses. She'd been behind the bus since it left the school. She was obvious as all get-out and not just because she followed too closely. It was more the fact that she looked like some kind of albino supermodel in the most expensive-looking vintage silver jaguar convertible Tessa had ever laid eyes on. Big black sunglasses covered the woman's eyes, but her pale skin glowed as if lit from within. She was also wearing the lowest cut sweater anyone had ever bothered to design. It was thin silvery fabric, unreal in how it moved and caught the afternoon light—glittering like a damn sparkly vampire. It plunged, *literally* to the woman's belly, showing off even more porcelain-like flesh and defying all kinds of laws of physics in how it didn't expose, well, *everything*.

Tessa knitted her brow. The lady wasn't exactly trying to blend in. Bizarre outfit be damned, she was also the kind of beautiful that didn't seem real—almost as if she had been shaped from stone and born of imagination, not the messy business of flesh and reality. The bus slowed to a stop and Tessa stood, watching the woman curse at the bus when her hair—white as the driven snow—blew across her face as she was enveloped by a burst of dirty bus exhaust.

Tessa stepped off the bus and glanced at the two friends who had also gotten off and who were now looking at her curiously. Tessa turned for home and began walking.

"Hey!" the boy called out. Tessa knew he was talking to her, but she ignored him, she still didn't feel well and wasn't in the mood. "Hey. Don't I know you?"

Tessa turned around and was surprised to see the boy and his friend just a half dozen feet behind her, as if they'd followed her. Tessa narrowed her eyes at him. He was on the tall side, shorter than Tessa, but she was tall so that wasn't particularly notable. He was lanky and lean, a bit disheveled. Cute in a kind of 'mad scientist that doesn't know what to do with himself' kind of way. His brown hair was slightly mussed and he wore a Flash t-shirt and jeans. Tessa didn't recognize him.

"I don't think so," Tessa said honestly, turning back around to continue her walk.

"No, I think I do," he said, and Tessa could tell that he and the girl were still following her.

"Brand," the girl said, a warning tone creeping into her voice. "Leave her alone."

"You used to live here, right?" Tessa didn't stop walking but he was right. Maybe he had known her a million years ago, back before her mom left, before her dad shipped her off to the first of many, many boarding schools in Europe. "I think we used to go to school together. You have a cool last name or something. I swear, I remember, it's like—" he trailed off, as if it was on the tip of his tongue.

Tessa stopped and turned around. The boy and girl were so close on her heels that they crashed into her. They both fell back awkwardly onto their butts. Together, they looked up at Tessa from the sidewalk, apologetic.

"Sorry. Our fault," they said, almost as one. Tessa smiled a little bit. They were kinda funny.

"What are you sorry for? You're the ones that fell down." Tessa reached out her hands to help them up.

"Thanks," the girl said, brushing herself off as the boy continued to scrunch up his face trying to remember Tessa's name.

"Battle," Tessa said, filling it in for him.

"Excuse me?" the boy said.

"Battle. My name. It's Tessa Battle."

He pointed his finger at her. "Yes! That's it!"

The girl rolled her eyes at him and even groaned. Tessa smiled again. They *were* funny, like a little comedy troupe. The girl reached up and her small hand poked out of her giant sweatshirt to adjust large black-framed glasses on her face.

"I'm Micah Chen."

Tessa smiled at Micah as the girl blew at her black bangs, lifting them briefly away from her eyes. "Tessa Battle." Tessa repeated.

Micah smiled back, shy, and thumbed over at the boy, who was examining Tessa as if she was a bug under a magnifying glass, "This is Brandon Ellis."

Tessa nodded at Brandon.

"Uh-huh, but people call me Brand," he said, barely acknowledging the conversation, his eyes narrowed and his mouth screwed up contemplatively. "Your hair is different."

Tessa looked up at the unnaturally bright cherry-red strands falling across her eyes. "Yes, Brand, you're right. I did not have a borderline mohawk when I was in the fourth grade." Tessa and Micah shared another smile.

"No, no. Not that," he said, ignoring them. "The color. That's not your natural color."

Micah elbowed him. "Brand. That's not anyone's *natural* color."

Tessa stifled a laugh. "Correct. It belongs only to Manic Panic. Technically I'm a blonde. I think. I can't really remember. It's been a long time since I saw my real hair."

Micah chuckled and Brand nodded knowingly, "I thought so. I think we were in Miss Castle's fourth grade class together."

Tessa reached back into the vault of her memory, most of which she'd tried to block out since it reminded her of her mother. It all felt so long ago. She *had* been in Miss Castle's class. Did she remember a tiny version of this kid running around in superhero t-shirts? She didn't.

"Yeah, maybe, you do seem kind of familiar," Tessa said. Brand beamed and Micah cast a knowing look at Tessa, as if acknowledging that Tessa had done Brand a kindness and appreciated it.

"I knew it!" Brand said. Tessa turned and began walking again. It was actually impressive that he recognized her. Tessa hadn't thought anyone would or would bother trying. Brand and Micah fell into step behind her and Tessa wondered if their houses were even in this direction. There weren't many houses this way.

"Brand is great with faces," Micah said. "In fact, he's got a great memory in general, especially for people, names, history, stories—less so for math." Brand elbowed her.

"Hey, I do just fine in math."

"Is a C fine?" Micah asked.

"A C is totally average. That's like the *definition* of a C,"

"So fine means average?"

"I don't know but you're, like, embarrassing me here, Mike," Brand complained under his breath.

"Okay, okay," Micah said, giving up.

"Hey, it's October, why haven't we seen you before today?" Brand asked.

"I just got back to the States yesterday," Tessa said.

Micah hissed at Brand. "Stop being so nosy!"

Tessa chuckled as they jostled about, arguing behind her. They seemed so genuinely nice. That was rare in Tessa's experience and it intrigued her. Just as she was softening up and going to ask a question of her own, she caught a glimpse of the silver convertible in her peripheral vision and stopped suddenly. Micah and Brand both crashed headlong into her back and fell down again.

Tessa crouched down to help them up, again, one eye locked on the woman in the convertible. "Sorry, sorry, my fault this time."

Brand rubbed his head, "Jeez. What are you, like, made of adamantium?"

Micah reached for her glasses, which had gone shooting across the sidewalk. Tessa handed them to her. They all stood up again and Brand adjusted his backpack on his shoulder. "Adamantium is what Wolverine—" Tessa cut him off.

"I know what adamantium is," she said and then nodded to her house. "This is me."

Brand and Micah looked up at her, almost like puppies. Adorable, funny puppies.

"Oh. Yeah." Micah scratched her head and pointed back the way they had come, almost as if confused. "We're actually that way."

"Guess I'll see you tomorrow then," Tessa said, trying not to make it sound too abrupt, and keeping one skeptical eye on the woman in the car across the street. Brand and Micah headed back the way they had come and Tessa, from her front lawn, watched to make sure that the albino supermodel didn't do anything to them. She would hate it if the first nice people she'd met in just about ever got *something'd* by the sharp-looking supermodel. But the woman watched them go and then promptly returned her attention to Tessa, never more than swiveling her head. Tessa sighed and gave up, turning to her front door.

 THREE

There's something in the house.

The thought crashed through Tessa's head so loud as she put her hand on the front doorknob that it almost knocked her over. And as startling a thought as that was, she was more freaked out by why she thought some*THING* instead of some*ONE*.

That was weird, right?

Tessa paused, her hand on the door, fear rippling through her. She felt her fear so solidly that she suspected it of radiating off her, like some kind of stinky cartoon character. She didn't *have* to go inside. She could just not go in. But where would she go? Her mind raced for a moment, possibilities and options rifling through her head and then she felt a prick of anger.

This was her home, even if she hadn't lived here for the last eight years.

She wasn't going to be scared away from her own home. Besides, she didn't know anyone in town. Like, not a soul, except for Brand and Micah, but she didn't think two kids her own age and half her size counted as anyone that could help her. Besides she didn't want to get them into trouble, if there was indeed trouble behind her front door.

Tessa heard thumping inside and stepped back, startled. She stepped back to the door and pressed her ear against it. It sounded like something was in the kitchen. Tessa stepped back again. It was the middle of the day, horror-movie-type things didn't happen in the middle of the day, right? She imagined for a moment that maybe it was her dad. She'd arrived last night, after a very long flight from London, to an empty house, a white envelope full of crisp twenties, and a short note telling her he'd be back next Tuesday and to stay out of trouble. He hadn't even mentioned her birthday in the note. Maybe he'd remembered it and come home early?

Yeah, right. He'd missed the last eight, no reason to be here for this one, even if she was back home.

Besides, her dad was a some*one*, not a some*thing*.

Tessa edged open the door and the increased noise made the hairs on the back of her neck prick up wildly. The crashing sounds in her kitchen vaguely resembled massive footsteps. But like the way a mountain might sound if it had feet and began walking around on your hardwood floors. "Balls," Tessa breathed before sliding into the foyer, her eyes on the kitchen while she reached into the hall closet for her father's old baseball bat, right where it had always been as though it hadn't moved once in the years Tessa had been gone. She rested the bat on her shoulder, grateful for her father's perfect predictability.

She caught just a glimpse of the mountain lumbering from one side of the kitchen to the other and her jaw dropped open. This wasn't your run-of-the-mill suburban burglar, this thing was covered head to toe in brownish green scraggly hair. This thing had a shoulder span wider than a doorway and must have been nearly seven feet tall. Its shoulders were stooped so that gnarled hands attached to arms as wide as tree trunks nearly dragged across the floor. Tessa raised an eyebrow. It appeared to be opening cabinets and drawers as if searching for something. Tessa shook her head hoping to make the sight go away, but the monster remained. A jagged tremor of fear ran through her, settling deeply and nauseously in her stomach, and she bit her tongue to quell it. She turned for the front door. This was way over her teenage pay grade, no matter how long she'd been on her own.

With her hand on the door to escape, the noise behind her suddenly stopped. The thing said something under its breath that sounded like *"whore killer,"* but that couldn't be right, could it? Tessa turned to look toward the kitchen, and the thing stood there, giant and terrifying, but also kinda funny-looking, filling up the massive opening to the kitchen, one hand holding an empty kitchen drawer, its contents all over the floor. Its nose was like a misshapen light bulb, its mouth long and thin with sharp teeth poking out, and the eyes were black and small like shiny beads. When it spoke again, Tessa expected a growl or a roar, but instead she got broken but polite English, slightly accented. It sounded…Norwegian?

"Scion. You are it?" the thing said more than asked.

"Huh?" Tessa asked, dumbfounded.

"You are it. Scion," it said, dropping the drawer it was holding. Tessa stared at the drawer.

"What are you looking for?" she asked, and then bit her lip, unsure why she cared.

"You is what I am looking for," it said simply.

"You thought I'd be in a drawer?"

"I do not know your size. Mortals come in all sizes, I think," it said, explaining itself, and then added, "Like goats."

"Yes, well, I suppose, but few fit in drawers, or would want to," Tessa said, blinking stupidly, feeling as if she'd stepped into a *Twilight Zone* episode.

"I don't know of such things. But now you are here."

"Yes. Now I'm here." Tessa repeated back while looking around her house at all the destruction the thing had caused. Books pulled from shelves, furniture tipped over, a plant toppled, soil spilling across the floor. Looking at the mess she realized how pissed her dad was going to be and she found herself suddenly very angry and unable to stop herself from popping off. "Thanks for destroying my damn house. What do you want?"

"Now you are here. Now we fight," it said simply.

"Um. No?" Tessa said more as a question, simultaneously gripping the bat in her hand more tightly, preparing for anything.

It came at her much faster than she anticipated considering its size, and Tessa was so startled that she wasn't able to do anything except squeal a little and dodge out of the way, escaping into the dining room. She stood gaping at where the thing had clearly gotten into the house—the massive picture window that looked out onto the back lawn was smashed to bits. "Dammit!" Tessa shouted but before she could say anything else, the thing tackled her from behind. They both tumbled through the already broken window and rolled onto the lawn outside.

Tessa got to her feet and looked around. Better at least to be out here where there was less fine china, she thought. She looked at her arms and legs, surprised that nothing was broken. In fact, she felt pretty good. Like, a lot better than you should feel after being hit by something that must weigh 500 pounds and going through the remains of a broken window. She turned to look at the thing on the grass only to find that it had already gotten up and was in mid-swing. It clipped her across the face with its giant fist, and the force sent Tessa flying partway across the yard. She landed painfully on her back.

Okay, so, whatever was going on with her she could definitely still feel pain. But a blow that probably should have killed her hadn't.

"Not so tufffff," the thing grumbled as it lumbered toward her and then stood over her, preparing to punch her again while she was still down. Tessa drove her foot up into the thing's groin area. She didn't know if it actually had a groin, but she figured it couldn't hurt matters. And indeed the thing fell to its knees and then rolled away from her with a sighing groan of pain. "Mean though," it said, as if narrating its thoughts on her to itself as it slowly climbed back to its feet. Tessa popped herself into a standing position and they stood there looking at one another, about eight feet of bright green lawn between them.

"Yeah, well, I didn't break into your house now, did I?" Tessa said, eyeing her bat, which lay on the ground too far away to easily reach. Tessa had been in her share of fights before, well, okay, way more than her fair share of fights, but this was ridiculous. And she didn't even know what they were fighting about.

"Suppose," the thing said, grumbling a bit and taking a long armed swing at her, apparently not caring one way or another about the bat on the ground. This time, however, Tessa saw the punch coming. While she didn't have time to get out of the way, she squared her shoulders and anchored her feet in the dewy grass, raising her arms defensively, preparing to take the hit. It hurt like blazes when the punch landed but she didn't go flying across the yard this time and slight surprise registered on the creature's mossy face as Tessa took her turn at a punch. She connected with its general jaw area and the thing reeled back. It looked at her while massaging its face. "Strong," it said, still narrating. Tessa looked at her fist, more shocked than the creature was. She couldn't believe she'd actually connected, let alone hurt it.

"Thanks," Tessa said, distracted, wondering how her hand wasn't broken. The creature lunged at her and they went down together in a pile of arms and legs, rolling across the lawn, jockeying for position, until they crashed into some heavy cast-iron lawn furniture, Tessa on top, straddling the thing. Tessa drew back her fist and punched it three times in the face, trying to stun it, which worked, like, not at all, and instead just seemed to annoy it. Plus it oofed out a breath of foul air from somewhere deep inside that made Tessa wince in horror. The creature returned her punches, and Tessa felt her jaw nearly slip out of joint on the last one. She tried to say "ow" but it came out more like a growl. Tessa reached up to the top of the nearby patio table and pulled down a pair of massive hedge clippers. She spun the clippers in her hand like she was possessed by some kind of Kung Fu weapons master and drove them pointy side first at the creature's head. It jerked to the left, and the clipper blades buried themselves in the grass and dirt. The creature growled at her.

"Mean and strong and fast," it said and then pushed her off with a powerful blow to her chest. Tessa toppled backward off the creature but rolled into a crouching position, and when it came at her again, she reached for the legs of the heavy iron chair nearest her. Digging deep within herself, she swung the chair upward as she lunged forward into standing position. Whatever bizarre strength she was sporting plus her momentum was indeed a force to be reckoned with, and when the chair connected, the creature flew a good dozen feet into the air and almost seemed to pause there for a split second before crashing down again. The weight of it hitting the ground sent a tiny shockwave through the yard. The thing stayed down for a moment. Tessa watched to see if it was dead.

She wasn't sure if she wanted it to be dead or not.

She'd never killed anything that wasn't some kind of bug before, and she didn't feel great about it. At the same time, she thought it might eventually kill her if she didn't kill it first.

Tessa's heart hammered in her chest as she waited for it to move. Or not.

Finally she saw it take a breath, and it lumbered to its feet but didn't come any closer to her. She watched it, unmoving, still holding the chair by one leg. "Mean and strong and fast and smart," it said and then turned away from her and ran at full speed toward the tall wood fence at the back of the yard. When it was a second from crashing headlong into the fence, it reached long arms up, grabbed the fence tips and pulled, launching itself almost gracefully into the woods behind the house. Tessa saw a rustle of trees and a few birds fly into the sky, crying out in protest, and then nothing. It was as if nothing had happened at all. Just Tessa and the stupid, torn-up yard.

And then a small cough behind her alerted her to someone standing there.

Two adorable someones, in fact.

FOUR

Tessa turned around, knowing even before she did so that it was going to be Micah and Brand.

Sure enough, they were both standing, just on the other side of the wooden gate, staring at her with their mouths hanging open like fish.

"Um…hi?" Brand offered.

Micah looked at him like he was insane.

"What…what was that?" he asked, not even missing beats. "Am I, am I having a stroke?" He looked at Micah now who turned back to face Tessa. "You saw that, right? Tell me you saw that!"

Micah just nodded, her eyes wide.

"Tessa?" they asked as one, as if her name itself was the question.

Tessa looked at them. She had no idea what to say. Her mind was utterly blank. She didn't know how much they had seen, and she didn't understand a lick of it anyway so what could she say?

Her mind raced, but somewhere deep down she felt sure that the best thing she could do for them was to get them away from her.

Something was happening to her.

Something bad from the looks of it.

And they didn't need to end up as collateral damage. Innocent bystanders. And super nice ones at that. All she could think was that she had to get them out of there and away from her no matter what, and if boarding school had taught her anything it was deny, deny, deny. Admit nothing. Oh, and how to be mean. She'd learned that too.

"I have no idea what you're talking about. And you're on private property, kindly get off it," she said, a cruelty in her voice that made her cringe inside. But they didn't move. They just stood there, gape-mouthed and confused. So she looked at them for just a moment, making her eyes hard. "Get out of here, right now." She didn't even watch to see their shoulders sink, their expressions fall, she just picked up the bat, stepped through the broken picture window, and disappeared into the house.

Tessa sat on the kitchen floor for a while listening to them argue in hushed tones. They finally gave up and left and then Tessa burst into tears. She curled up on the hardwood and sobbed into a dishtowel until she fell asleep.

Tessa woke to the sound of the doorbell buzzing. Disoriented and confused, wondering if perhaps she had dreamed the entire bizarre incident, Tessa stumbled to the front door, tripping on overturned furniture that suggested it had not been just a nightmare. Tessa peeked through the window to the side of the door and then yanked herself back at the sight of the albino supermodel standing on her front porch. It was still light outside, but several hours had passed, the sun low in the sky. The woman called to her through the door.

"Scion. Bluebeard has your minions."

Tessa crinkled up her nose. What in seven hells did that even mean? Tessa spoke back through the door.

"What's a Scion?" Tessa asked and then, furrowing her brow even more deeply, she raised her voice, "Exactly who are you and what do you want?"

The woman sighed, clearly irritated. "I am The Snow Queen. I've simply come to tell you that Bluebeard has your minions."

Tessa scrunched up her face and unlocked the door, but kept it mostly shut, peeking through the crack, "Who has my what?"

"Bluebeard. He has your minions."

"Lady, I don't understand like…ANY of the words in that sentence."

The woman sighed even more deeply. "Those two small Mortals I saw you with before—your minions—"

"Micah and Brand?"

The woman looked offended, "I don't learn minion names, Scion. Those two small Mortals have been taken by Bluebeard."

"What's a Bluebeard?"

The woman sighed again and pushed her way into the house. "You are entirely tedious. I was led to believe that Scions at least had their wits about them, even if they were just Mortals." The woman looked around the disheveled house, her judgmental gaze deepening until she noticed the broken window. She looked more carefully at Tessa, puffy eyed and more than a little rumpled. "You look a fright, Scion—has something happened?"

"Well, I was attacked by something." Tessa said, trying to explain and rubbing her head, still confused by, well, everything.

Snow looked her up and down, still judging, "I should hope so."

"Something big and furry," Tessa reached her arms out showing how wide and tall it was before returning her hand to her head. She started rambling. "It was looking for something. Then it wanted to fight me. It had…a Norwegian accent?" Tessa collapsed onto the couch and looked up at the woman. "And it said something about goats."

"Ah," Snow said, and looked around the room, examining the books still on the shelves. She took her time but eventually pulled an old volume off a shelf and flipped through it. After a moment of this, she brought it over to Tessa and pointed a perfectly manicured finger at a black-and-white drawing in the book. It looked almost exactly like what Tessa had been fighting. Tessa snatched the book and sprang from her seat.

"Yes! That's it!" She then turned the book over. "What is this—" she stopped when she saw that the title of the book was *Fifty Famous Folktales*.

"The bridge Troll, from *Three Billy Goats Gruff*," Snow said, unimpressed, and then added under her breath, "Stupid Trolls just cannot shut up about goats. Gives them away, every time."

Tessa sat down and stared at her. Her head hurt.

"Wait. You're saying I just fought a troll from a Folktale? You expect me to believe that this thing, like, came to life and—"

"It didn't come to life, Scion. It was always alive. Stories are real. Everything in that book and every other book is alive," she said, gesturing to the shelves of books that lined the room. "They are and always have been alive, though they generally don't live in this dimension, which brings us back to Bluebeard."

Tessa stared at her dumbly and shook her head a little, as if her brain had come loose. "You can't expect me to believe that."

Snow shrugged. "I don't really care what you believe," she said sniffing and examining her nails for imperfections, of which there were none.

"Get out of my house."

"You can throw me out, Scion, but it won't get your minions rescued."

"Stop saying that! They're not minions! They're—wait—you're saying someone has actually, *literally* kidnapped them?"

Snow sighed dramatically, "Yes. Bluebeard. A big bad Story. Quite old, quite nasty.

Tessa swallowed her fear, but it tasted like acid. "And this person… thing…whatever…has Micah and Brand, because of me?"

"I can't think of any other reason Bluebeard would care about random minions."

Tessa stood up. She felt called to action. But then immediately sat back down again. She looked at Snow helplessly, "What do I do?"

Snow looked at her, a look of something resembling pity crossing her face briefly. "Well, you have all sorts of Scion skills, I'd say go get them back."

"Scion skills?" Tessa looked at her hands and thought about her fight with the Troll. That would certainly explain things, if it wasn't completely insane.

"What? You thought you fought off a Troll with your complete lack of charm?" She was dripping with sarcasm and then mumbled to herself, "They really should have sent someone more appropriate to do this."

"What is *this*?" Tessa asked.

"Listen, Scion, I'm happy to give you the full rundown, but you might want to rescue your minions before they're decapitated."

"For the last time, they're not—decapitated?!?"

"Yes, that's what he does. His M.O. if you will."

Tessa suddenly felt lightheaded. "I have no idea what to do. Can I call the police? Or is there someone else we can call for help? Someone else with *skills*...or whatever?"

Snow nodded, "Perhaps, if we knew anyone to call. There are Stories that would help The Scion I suppose, but *I* don't know them, certainly *you* don't. For now, I suggest picking up a weapon and heading over there to free them yourself. You're imbued with incredible power—you probably totally have a chance."

"You think?"

"Probably," Snow said shrugging.

Tessa sat quietly in the living room for two full minutes and then stood. "Okay."

"Okay, what?" Snow asked, watching Tessa move across the room and pick up a baseball bat.

"Okay to your plan."

"And that's your weapon?"

"It will have to be, I don't keep a stash of like, melee weapons on hand."

Snow seemed bored and made a move toward the door, "Well, you should get on that," she said, opening the door.

"Wait," Tessa said, pointing the bat at her. "Where do you think you're going?"

"Home," Snow said nonchalantly.

"Uh-uh. No way. You're coming. You're helping."

Snow shook her head, "I have no idea what you're talking about but the answer is a resounding no."

Tessa tried to reason with her, "Listen, I don't even know where they are, but you know, right?"

Snow nodded almost imperceptibly. "Yes, I tailed him after I saw them get grabbed outside."

"Good," Tessa said, holding the door open for Snow. "Then you can take me to them."

"How about I draw you a map?" Snow suggested brightly. Tessa scowled in response. Snow walked through the door grumbling like a spoiled child. "Fine. I'll take you there, but that's the extent of it."

"Yeah, we'll see," Tessa said, pulling the door closed behind her.

Tessa and Snow climbed into the Jaguar in Tessa's driveway and Snow took off through the damp and winding streets, taking hairpin turns with incredible speed. Tessa gripped the dash and tried not to complain in the hopes that Snow's speed would get them there in time to save anyone and everyone from decapitation.

"So, why *did* you follow his car?" Tessa asked, digging her fingers into the plush leather on a particularly sharp corner.

Snow pretended to ignore her.

"I mean, you didn't want to come help, you don't seem to care for me a bit, or them, why would you care that they were kidnapped?"

Snow sighed and then mumbled under her breath, "I suppose even I know it doesn't hurt to have The Scion owe you one."

Tessa almost smiled, but then scrunched up her eyebrows, "What's this word you keep using—Scion?"

"It's what you are." Snow said, her white hair trailing behind them like a streak of light.

Tessa groaned. "Elaborate, please. You can certainly talk and drive at the same time, right?"

Snow pushed her sunglasses back on her head and rolled her eyes. "Ick. I hate history. Okay, here goes. Story is another dimension where all Fictional characters from all Fictional worlds live. And The Scion is the only descendent of a Mortal and a Story getting it on."

Tessa eyed her like she was bonkers. "Lady, you have got to be kidding me."

"Do you want to hear about this or not?"

Tessa raised her hands in surrender before bracing herself for another turn. "Fine, fine. Continue."

"Okay, so some-thousand years ago or whatever a Mortal and a Story got it on—not as unusual as you'd think, by the way—however, in this case it produced a child, heretofore believed impossible and never having happened since blah, blah, blah. Thus, the offspring of that offspring has through the years been called The Scion. As the only creature that exists with both Mortal and Story blood, The Scion inherits a whole bunch of power on its 17th birthday —and—ta-dah!" she said, sarcastically gesturing in Tessa's general direction.

"And you expect me to believe all that?"

"I don't care what you believe, Scion, but quite plainly, the monsters under the bed are all real. All of them. And a whole lot of them hate you. So, you know, weigh your options or whatever."

"And you're supposed to be…The Snow Queen," Tessa said.

"I'm not *supposed* to be anything. I AM The Snow Queen."

"Never heard of you," Tessa said, just to piss her off.

Snow growled under her breath and then pulled to a stop outside a massive Victorian house not unlike Tessa's but far larger and more ornate, set back from the road and rather buried in a rural wooded lot. The nearest house was at least a mile away and it was getting dark. The whole set-up made Tessa nervous. She chewed her lip and looked at the house skeptically. "How did you just happen to see this go down by the way?"

Snow pursed her lips. "I was following you."

"Yes, but why?"

"The Story Court sent me. They wanted me to give you the drill, convince you to come to Story so they could give you the whole run down, begin the relationship on the right foot."

"They want to start on the right foot and they sent you?" Tessa asked.

"Yes, haha. Very funny," Snow said, thick with sarcasm, before reaching over Tessa to open the passenger door for her. "Okay, have fun!" she said cheerfully, as if dropping Tessa off for camp. Tessa wouldn't have been surprised if Snow actually tried to push her out of the car. Before she could do so, Tessa grabbed Snow's slender wrist mid-reach.

"You're coming."

"No way."

"Yup."

"I'm not a fighter," Snow said, taking back her arm and massaging her delicate wrist.

"Well, there's something we can agree on," Tessa said. "So fine, you can do what you're clearly best at. Go. Be pretty." Tessa said, waving her hand in the general direction that was Snow. Snow straightened her shoulders and looked blankly at the woods in front of them. Tessa snatched the keys from the ignition and got out.

Snow scrambled out as well and hissed at Tessa over the top of the car. "Okay. Done. See? Pretty. Now give me the keys!"

"Be pretty *at him*," Tessa said, nodding her head at the house.

"Eww. No." Snow crinkled up her nose in disgust.

"Yes. I need a distraction. I'll go in through the back, you keep him busy in the front."

"You really have language comprehension problems, Scion, I said no," Snow crossed her arms, faint hints of her shimmery sweater catching in the fading light.

"How about this," Tessa said, holding up the car keys, "Do it or I throw your keys as far as my new super strength will carry them into the woods."

Snow glared and stamped her impossibly tall heels into the dirt like a child. The temperature around Tessa dropped at least ten degrees. She raised her eyebrows at Snow in surprise. Snow's skin looked even harder and whiter, her eyes a crystalline blue, much brighter and sharper than before.

"Are you…are you doing that?" Tessa asked, flexing her hand as the cold bit at her skin and the temperature continued to drop around them.

Snow put her hands on her hips and harrumphed. Her eyes and skin softened slightly, and the temperature shot back up almost as quickly as it had dropped.

"Scion, you are already such a huge pain in my—"

"Yes, yes," Tessa said. "Don't worry, the feeling is mutual." Tessa pocketed the keys, shooed Snow away and took off into the woods, bat in hand. She waited a moment in the thick trees to see what the woman would do. Snow's shoulders fell into a little curl, but after a moment she straightened them and smiled broadly and began the hike up the winding drive, her heels periodically sinking into the dirt, her bright white hair and sweater like a beacon in the oncoming dark.

Snow climbed the front steps to the porch cursing under her breath all the way. When she reached the front door she rapped lightly, half hoping she had tailed them to the wrong house. If she was wrong she could go back home to Story and a long cool bath and forget all this Scion nonsense. Unfortunately by her second knock, the door swung open wide and Snow was faced with Bluebeard. She hadn't seen him in at least a hundred years. Unfortunately, he looked the same. Recognition sparked in his face immediately and his eyes widened in something between shock and fear. Snow spoke first.

"Don't worry, I'm not here on official Court business."

"Then they don't know I'm here?"

Snow sighed, "I don't know and I don't care, I just know that it's not what brings me here.

Bluebeard brightened ever so slightly. "This is a social call?"

"You wish," Snow said, pushing past him into the house. He stepped to the side, too late since she was already inside, but he tried to make up for it by bowing slightly. Snow rolled her eyes. She'd hated this guy the last time she'd met him and it seemed nothing had changed. When he looked up, Snow gave him a tight smile and looked around the grand house, filled end to end with antiques and fussy-looking furniture.

"Nice place," she said, turning on him. "I see you've been abusing your Story talents."

Bluebeard closed the door and stood with her in the large foyer. "Well…" he began.

Snow cut him off with a wave of her hand. "I don't really care. Get me a drink already," she said sighing. Bluebeard escorted her into the parlor and went to a bar cart in the corner while Snow sat back on a dark red velvet couch, crossing her long legs in front of her and inspecting the room if only to cure her boredom.

"So, if you're not here on Court business, then what?" Bluebeard asked, a creepy grin spreading across his face, "I don't suppose you're in the market for a husband."

"Gross," Snow said, frowning. Out the far window, at the back of the house, Snow saw a flash of Tessa running across the lawn. She slit her eyes dangerously and looked back to Bluebeard. "Get yourself a drink too. This is going to take a while."

X

Tessa looped around the back and was happy to find there was no fence, just more woods, endless woods. She arced around the house, trying to get a lay of the land before making her move.

Dropping through an unlatched basement window, Tessa landed with a soft thud on the concrete floor. The basement was piled high with paintings and furniture covered in white sheets. She hurried across the floor to the stairs near the center of the room. Tessa made her way up the stairs, listening for Snow's melodic yet cutting voice drifting through the house, demanding more ice, then her lilting false laugh, the occasional baritone of what Tessa assumed was Bluebeard. Tessa opened the basement door and found herself just under the main stair in the foyer.

She slipped up the stairs to the second level to find a slew of doors off of a long hallway. Tessa opened door after door to find only empty, overly furnished rooms. Finally, she reached the end of the hallway where a pair of doors stood opposite one another. Both were locked. Under the one on the right, Tessa could hear a distinctive shuffle that could totally be a couple kidnapped someones trying to escape. Tessa laid down on the wood floor and peeked under the wide gap at the bottom. She saw Micah, her hands and feet bound in thick rope. Next to her, similarly tied but knocked unconscious, was Brand and another man, perhaps mid-30s, dark hair, attractive in a stuffy young professor kind of way, his glasses broken and a trickle of blood running across his face. Tessa bit her lip.

"Micah," Tessa whispered under the door. Micah's head yanked up and she stopped struggling.

"Tessa?" she asked, shocked and confused, but clearly relieved.

"Stay back," Tessa whispered. "I'm coming in."

Micah scooted around a little behind the door and Tessa stood up. She sized up the door. She was pretty sure she could break it down if she still had whatever she'd had when fighting the Troll, but it would be loud. And then she'd have three tied-up hostages, two of them possibly unconscious, while Bluebeard came crashing up the stairs. But she didn't know how to pick a lock. She thought maybe she could just snap the doorknob off, but would that open the door or make it impossible to open without breaking it down? As she looked around considering her options, a key ring with at least a dozen large old-fashioned keys slid under the door right in front of her.

"Or I could go with the key," Tessa said to herself, picking them up and trying them in the lock one by one. On the sixth try, she got it and swung the door open to a smiling Micah, with Brand and the stranger just coming to.

"Ohmigod. What are you doing here?" Micah asked, blinking a tear or two from her eyes.

Tessa shook her head. "You wouldn't believe me if I told you," she said.

Brand struggled to sit up. "Does it have anything to do with the fact that we saw you fighting some kind of monster in your backyard and you seem like you're a superhero, that possibly IS made out of adamantium?"

Tessa shot him a look and then softened. "Maybe," she admitted.

The man spoke as Tessa worked on Micah's knots.

"Tessa. I am so sorry, getting taken hostage certainly was not how I wanted us to first meet."

"Dude, who are you?" Tessa asked as she fought with Micah's bonds.

"He's the freaking high school counselor," Brand said.

The man cut a look at Brand and then turned back to Tessa. "That's true, but much more importantly, I'm your Advocate, Benjamin Bishop. I'm supposed to help you with the—," he glanced at Micah and Brand and edited himself, "With—stuff—but we didn't know it was you—between all the boarding schools you were bouncing around in Europe and your dad kept listing you under his last name, instead of your mother's name—it wasn't until I saw your corrected name on the school register and the photocopy of your passport in your file this afternoon that I realized who you were, and that you were here. I came rushing over to your house, but—"

Tessa managed to free Micah's hands and started to work on Brand's while Micah began on her feet. "Mr. Bishop, I appreciate all that, but let's just deal with the present ordeal and figure out the rest later, okay?"

"Of course. You're right." He nodded before continuing, "I'm certain it's Bluebeard you're dealing with, he's rumored to have been living in Lore for a long time. Add that to the large number of young women that fit the profile disappearing over the last few years and…wait…is he still here in the house?"

"Yes, I've got someone distracting him." She looked at Brand and Micah, still trying to free their feet, as she began to work on Bishop's bonds. "Do they know what's going on?" she asked, nodding at Micah and Brand.

"I told them some, I felt I should given the circumstances, you know, kidnapped and bouncing around in the back of a van together. I'm not sure how much they believed, but whatever they saw at your house certainly put them in the mood for believing the unbelievable."

"The headless women in some of the rooms helped too," Micah piped in absently as she picked at the ropes.

"And also, you know, the beard," Brand chimed in. Tessa glanced at him, a questioning look on her face. "I mean, it's straight up blue," Brand said, shrugging his shoulders.

Tessa shook her head, nobody was supposed to learn this much stuff this fast. It couldn't be good for her brain. She tried to listen to Bishop explaining about Bluebeard while keeping one ear on Snow downstairs.

Snow was running out of things to say to Bluebeard and if he waxed poetic about one more useless antique tea set she was going stab him with a cup. She yawned as he pointed out the slight chipping on an otherwise flawless hand-painted set he'd acquired the previous weekend. He smiled at her as she stifled the yawn.

"I still don't understand what you're doing here, Snow. Not that I don't enjoy the company."

"Yes, well…that is something of a delicate matter," Snow said, walking back toward the couch. She made the mistake of glancing at the stairs. Understanding broke across his ugly face.

She saw it and opened her mouth to scream for The Scion but only got out the first half before he hit her across the face with a silver serving tray.

Tessa spun around as Snow let loose a scream loud enough to practically tear out all the windows in the house.

"SCIIIIIIOOOO—"

But it cut off abruptly, as if Snow had been silenced. Tessa looked into the hallway and heard someone coming up the stairs. Whoever it was, they sounded big. Tessa nodded at the three of them to help one another, and then kicked Micah the keys again before going into the hallway. Tessa gripped the bat with both hands and planted her feet some distance ahead of the door, fully prepared to take his head off if it came to it. Though she definitely hoped it wouldn't.

As he reached the top of the stairs, she drew in a breath. He was indeed big. Broad-shouldered and at least six foot four with a face that looked like it had already been hit with a bat today. His dark-blue, bushy beard looked like he had slept face-first in a basket of blueberries. Tessa drew in a breath.

"So then, that is a *literal* blue beard we're talking about," she said. A flash of rage swallowed up his face and he ran at her. There was no room to swing the bat in the narrow hallway, so Tessa thrust it in front of her and ran toward him as if it was a tiny battering ram and he, a castle gate. She swore that there was a hint of happiness in his eyes as she came at him. A second later, she understood why as he deflected her with seeming ease. She went crashing into the stairs that led to the next level.

Tessa nailed one of the steps with her chin and her jaw snapped shut with such force she was shocked her teeth didn't shatter. Rather than turning over to fight, she pushed herself up and ran up the stairs to the third level, hoping he would follow. He did but he was too fast, managing to grab her ankle just as she neared the top of the flight and yanking her back down a few steps. She came down on her jaw again, nearly shattering her teeth a second time. Tessa cursed under her breath and rolled onto her back just as he came at her. She was barely able to get her foot up in time to kick him in the gut, sending him flying down the stairs backwards. He landed with a crash but was back on his feet almost instantly. She groaned and scrambled up the last few stairs. She'd lost her bat on the second level and she looked around frantically for a new weapon.

At the other end of the hall, a pair of swords hung on the wall, all decorative and shining. Tessa tried to make a run for them but as she launched herself across the long hall, Bluebeard's hand came up the stairs. Unfortunately, the rest of his body followed. Tessa lurched to a halt and backed up a few paces, looking around desperately. Short of a table with a bright green vase on her left, there was nothing but drywall.

"I knew this was a good idea," he said, standing up straight and taking Tessa in, his face both amused and utterly unimpressed.

"What idea?" Tessa asked, unsure.

"Grabbing your little pals to flush you out. I mean, look at you. So green. Totally untrained. Word is spreading from Story to Story about you like wildfire."

"And the word is?" Tessa asked, gritting her teeth.

"Well, there are a few, but first and foremost that you're a girl, and thus The Last of the Scions. And if you're the last, then killing you will close the border to Story. And I like this world. I like it very much. If I can end you, I can close the dimension border and never have to worry about Story coming to drag me back, kicking and screaming."

Tessa blinked, she hadn't actually expected a villain-esque soliloquy.

Bluebeard smiled wider and added, "Someone also might have mentioned that you were like a stupid baby lamb, ready for slaughter," he said, shrugging. Tessa narrowed her eyes and while he was gloating, she flung her arm at the giant vase. It flew at him with shocking speed and hit him square in the face. The instant it connected, Tessa ran, launching herself over him. Her heels clipped the ceiling, but she cleared Bluebeard with ease and hit the hardwood a half-dozen feet behind him. Tessa tucked and rolled and stood up right in front of the wall-mounted swords. Tessa yanked one sword off the wall and as she did the other clattered to the floor. She grasped the sword with both hands and looked at Bluebeard as he turned around to face her. She felt good.

"Yeah, well, now stupid baby lamb has a sword, Beard-o," Tessa said, grinning.

Bluebeard growled at her and picked pieces of shiny green vase out of his face.

"That was 14th Century Ming, you brat."

"So sue me," Tessa said, shrugging. "But I don't think you're going to have the chance being all weaponless as you seem to be, what do you think of that?" But her witty repartee didn't seem to phase him, and she was instead rewarded only with another creepy wide-mouthed grin.

"I'm not worried," he said, reaching out his right hand and shouting, "La Colombe Noire!"

As soon as the words left his lips, there was a crackle of bluish-black light and a pinch of static. A massive double-headed battle axe that looked as much like a sharp, black bird as it did an axe appeared out of thin air and snapped into his outstretched hand. "You'll see I'm covered in any situation, Scion," he said, pointing the massive axe at her.

"Balls," Tessa said under her breath, as he came at her with the axe.

Tessa, having never used a sword before in her life, felt certain she was no match for Bluebeard's axe. The man looked like a freaking pro and a half. So instead of standing her ground, Tessa kicked down the door nearest to her and dove through it. She slammed it shut behind her just as he turned to follow her, but she'd broken the lock mechanism when she kicked it in, so she leaned against it to keep it shut. While her back was flush against the door, she felt the jolt of what must be the axe biting into the wood on the other side. She couldn't stay there long or she'd end up with the blade buried in her back. Tessa reached out in the dark and felt a chair, which she dragged over by its leg and wedged between the door and a big wardrobe nearby. Tessa could hear bits of wood splintering off into the hallway as she skittered back from the door. She stood blindly and groped around the room for a light switch in the dark. After a moment of panic, she found it and snapped it on.

The moment she did she wished she could take it back.

All around her hung the bodies of headless young women. At least a dozen women and girls hung from the ceiling like gruesome party decorations. "Oh my God," Tessa breathed, staggering backward. Bluebeard peered through the face-sized *Shining*-style hole he'd managed to chop into the door.

"Scion, meet my brides, er, former brides. Former brides, meet The Last Scion. I'm sure you'll all get along famously. Especially when I add your head to the pile. In fact, Scion, you can be the jewel of my collection."

Tessa plunged deeper into the room, away from the door and the bodies. She crashed into a window draped with a heavy, dark velvet curtain. Throwing the curtain back, Tessa yanked the window open, tearing it from the frame in her rush to escape. She heard the door to the room break. He would be through it in a moment. She slid out the window and edged herself around the gable toward the heavily steeped roof. In order to climb, she would have to lose the sword. She dropped it and clambered up the roof unsure if he would follow her or not (she guessed he probably would). At the top, she slid down the other side, catching her feet on the edge a moment before she went shooting off into oblivion. A matching gable met her on this side of the house and she wrenched open the window in front of her and climbed through, hoping more bodies didn't await her. In the light of the moon, she realized she had found the girls' missing heads. Tessa choked back something between a sob and a scream. She wanted to die. She wanted to just give up and go home. To forget all of this was happening.

To definitely keep her head.

But she thought of Micah and Brand, Bishop, and even Snow all trapped elsewhere in the house. She couldn't imagine a way in which she could live with herself if she actually escaped and left them behind.

She'd be better off headless.

Tessa inched the door open and peered into the hall. The sword that had fallen off the wall shined a few feet from her. Bluebeard was nowhere to be seen. Tessa slipped into the hallway, feeling both exposed and claustrophobically trapped. She picked up the fallen sword and crept down the hall. She made her way down to the second floor, but when she stepped onto the landing he came barreling at her from behind. They crashed together into the railing, and their weight snapped the wood with a sharp crack. To Tessa it was almost like they paused midair for a moment before they fell down to the ground floor, end over end. Tessa avoided landing directly on her head but still smacked the parquet floor with incredible force. Her vision spun as she looked for Bluebeard. He had landed similarly, and Tessa saw him lose his grip on the axe as it clattered across the floor toward her. Tessa reached for it, but as she did it disappeared right in front of her eyes. On her hands and knees, she stared at the place it used to be and heard him call out behind her.

"La Colombe Noire!"

She felt the same pop and crackle of energy as before and when she turned her head it was to see him standing over her, the axe magically in his hand again. A damn good trick. Tessa kicked him in the stomach from her low position, and he rocketed backward, smashing into a small table, sending all the things atop it crashing to the ground. He looked at them and grimaced.

"You're ruining all my things!"

Tessa scrambled away from him, catching a glimpse of Snow, nothing but a silvery-white unconscious streak on the thick, red carpet. Tessa's eyes searched madly for a replacement weapon. Her sword had been thrown deep into the parlor, her bat was still on the second floor, she was totally exposed. As Bluebeard swung the axe toward her, Bishop appeared from out of nowhere and jumped onto Bluebeard's back. He was half the size of Bluebeard, but he held on tightly as the giant man reared back and thrashed.

"Tessa, run!" Bishop shouted. Tessa scrambled into the parlor and grabbed the sword but as she did so she heard a horrible snap behind her that turned her blood to ice. When she whirled to face Bluebeard she saw Bishop on the ground at Bluebeard's feet, his neck turned grotesquely, his eyes wide open and fixed. Tessa blinked stupidly at the sight of him.

He was dead.

It had taken only an instant and he was dead.

It was so fast.

There wasn't even any blood.

This man Tessa barely knew had risked his life for her and now he was dead. So many thoughts and emotions swarmed Tessa that she didn't know where to put any of it. Bluebeard stared down at her, utterly unimpressed.

"Was that your Advocate, child? Tut, tut, what a shame. And what a truly terrible Scion you're turning out to be, last or otherwise." He slammed the axe down into the thick carpet narrowly missing one of Tessa's feet in the process.

Tessa half-ran half-crawled through the room, losing her sword in the process. Bluebeard's axe whizzed through the air so close behind her that she could feel the breeze it created. When she reached the dining room, Tessa dived under the giant wood table just as Bluebeard swung again and took a huge chunk out of the side. He shouted something Tessa didn't understand, but that sounded decidedly like cursing.

"TOVA! Tovaien ticcht!"

Tessa covered her face with her arms as he stood above her hacking the thick table into bits with his axe. When he broke through, she peered up to see him staring down at her, red-faced and breathing heavily. He looked completely insane and absolutely delighted with himself, the axe raised over his head, ready to deliver what could only be a killing stroke. Tessa could not believe she was going to be killed right now, here, in this stupid living room.

What a disappointment she must have been.

Tessa clenched her eyes shut, was this really how it all ended?

FIVE

Tessa opened her eyes as Bluebeard's axe came speeding toward her, no more thick, wood table left to shield her. If she was going to die right now, she was at least going to have her eyes open for it.

A blur of dark grey flew past Tessa's face and Bluebeard's blade landed just to the left of Tessa's head, deep in the carpet and shards of table. Tessa reached for the axe but just as she grasped the hilt it vanished under her fingers.

"Damn!" she cursed, glancing behind her to see a giant, grey wolf pacing in front of Bluebeard as the man struggled to get back up. The animal barely even fit in the parlor, its tail knocking into furniture as it paced predatorily about the room. It turned its massive head to Tessa as she extricated herself painfully from the wood and glass mess in the dining room and bared its teeth at her.

Bluebeard called out for his weapon again and though the wolf moved, it couldn't quite avoid the axe in the small space, and the axe clipped its furry shoulder. It howled and snapped at Bluebeard as he yanked the axe back, a little spray of blood coming with it. The wolf shuddered away, limping, favoring its damaged side. While Bluebeard was distracted by the massive creature, Tessa figured she'd best take her shot, and so she lowered her shoulder and ran at him. They went crashing into a glass coffee table, smashing it into painful bits as they landed, fortunately with Bluebeard underneath and taking the brunt of the impact. Even from beneath her, he tried to swing the axe but Tessa grabbed at it so that they were both holding it, wrestling for control. They rolled together out of the table and then, as Snow woke less than a foot away from them and drew back in shock, they worked their way to a standing position, neither releasing the axe.

Despite his size advantage, Tessa could feel in their struggle that she was stronger than he was. If only she could find a way to throw him off balance, she thought she might be able to gain the upper hand. And so when he pushed his size at her, leaning her back, she let him, and when he overcompensated, leaning too far forward, she turned her body slightly and pushed the head of the axe downward. Just when he had almost lost his balance, she drew upon all her strength and twisted back into him, thrusting powerfully with her right arm, the hand closest to the blade, and driving it with incredible speed up and through his neck with a satisfying sluishing sound.

And his head went sailing across the parlor.

Snow watched as Tessa angled the axe and then used the full force of her strength to send it through Bluebeard's neck. It was an incredibly complicated move requiring not just strength, but also an innate understanding of battle. The blade connected as if Tessa had been doing this all her life, not just a few hours. Snow blinked her eyes and clutched her own slender neck self-consciously, shuddering as Bluebeard's head landed with an impotent, bloody thud some dozen feet away on the red carpeting.

"Storykiller," Snow breathed, barely a whisper.

Tessa looked at her with sharp but weary eyes. "What did you say?" Tessa stood, spent and bloody in the middle of the parlor, the axe still in one hand, her face somehow both pale and flushed. Snow stared at Tessa, her hand still on her own neck, her eyes fixed and wide. "What did you say?" Tessa repeated.

Snow blinked and tried to regain her composure. "Storykiller," she said again, barely louder than the first time. "That's what they call you," she said, looking back at the Bluebeard head and blinking again, as if she hoped to erase what she had seen with her eyelids. "To your face they'll call you Scion, but behind your back, it's Storykiller. It's always been Storykiller," Snow looked at Tessa, "I've just…I've just never seen it." Snow continued holding Tessa's gaze for a moment and then looked away, as if wishing herself somewhere else.

Tessa closed her eyes and tilted her head back, letting out an exhausted sigh. She was bone-tired, not to mention more than a little terrified by both what she'd seen and what she'd done. She had just killed a man. And gotten another one killed. And yet both somehow seemed natural and normal and like something that sometimes just happened on Tuesdays. Tessa looked at her hands. Elaborate patterns of blood, both beautiful and deadly, laced across her skin almost as if she was wearing intricately woven, elbow-length, bright red gloves. She shook her head. What was wrong with her? How could she think for even a moment that it was beautiful? Despite the blood, she reached her hand out to help Snow up, but Snow recoiled back, rejecting her.

"How is that possible?" Tessa asked.

"What?" Snow asked, still disoriented and shaken.

"I'm guessing you've been around a long time, how can this be the first death you've ever seen?

Snow continued staring at Bluebeard's head. "I've never lived in the Mortal world before, so I've never seen a Mortal die. And Stories don't die."

Tessa pointed the axe at the dead body. "Clearly they do."

"No, I…" Snow stood up and smoothed her clothing, averting her eyes from both the body and the detached head. "They can't. Not by anyone but you. You're the only person in all of this world, or mine, that can actually kill a Story," she said. It was the most serious and non-snarky she'd been since Tessa had met her. Snow didn't strike Tessa as someone sincere, but she seemed genuine in this moment.

"That, that can't be true," Tessa stumbled over the words.

"I assure you it is. No mere Mortal has the power to kill a Story, and no Story can truly kill another Story."

"What do you mean 'truly'?"

"Just that we give it a try—with alarming regularity, in fact—but it never holds, not permanently. Everyone eventually comes back. It's like—think of your Mortal video games—even if we manage to kill each other, we eventually—*reset*, for lack of a better word. We don't have the power to erase one another the way a true death would."

"I…" Tessa started but she had no idea where to go. She tried again, "Wait, what do you mean by *erase*?"

"When a Story truly dies, it means their Mortal story dies too. You've not only killed Bluebeard, you've erased him. His Fiction no longer exists."

"Meaning what?"

"Killing him obliterates all record of him. He's a memory only you and Stories carry now. No Mortal will know, before, now, or ever again, of his Story. And perhaps worse than that, everyone else from his tale is now essentially a ghost. Trapped in a Story that no longer exists, they're like the walking dead, wandering without a sense of self or purpose. You have destroyed their home, what breathed them into existence. You've made them orphans. It's why we fear The Storykiller above all else—that we will become doomed shells attached to a Story you have destroyed."

Tessa sat down on a nearby chair, afraid if she didn't sit that she might faint. She laid the axe across her lap, and touched one bloody hand to her swimming head. She looked up at Snow with hawkish eyes. "You're lying."

Snow shook her head solemnly, "I'm really not, Scion."

"I, I didn't mean to do that."

Snow softened a bit, seeing how hard she was taking it, "You didn't really have a choice. What would you have done differently? He was going to kill you and your minions. And he killed your Advocate, the one who should have been your teacher. He left you no choice. Not to mention, I'm quite sure he was a serial killer of Mortals, not that I care about *that*," she added at the last moment.

Tessa lowered her head and spoke more to herself than Snow. "Yes. There were women upstairs, a lot of them. But I, I don't know. Maybe there was another way."

And at that moment Micah and Brand crashed into the room, Brand with Tessa's abandoned bat, Micah, strangely, with a pair of wooden drumsticks, their faces ready for battle, or something. But when they saw Tessa covered in blood, the headless body, blood soaked carpet, and ashen head they cringed. Brand's face had the look of someone who had just painfully swallowed a throat full of vomit, and Micah turned a sickly green. Tessa thought she might faint.

"I killed Bluebeard," Tessa said.

Micah and Brand looked at Tessa blankly and asked in unison, "Who?"

Tessa looked from Micah and Brand to Snow. Snow lifted her shoulders lightly as if resigned, a sad little shrug.

"See?" Snow said.

SIX

Tessa stared at Snow. "What do we do now?"

Snow looked at a clock up on the wall. "They'll be here any moment."

"Who?" Brand asked, still staring at the headless body.

As if to answer his question, there was a snap of electricity and a hum, the hair on Tessa's arms stood up, and a flash of bluish light illuminated the room. Tessa shielded her eyes against what best resembled a strike of blue lightning. When she could see again, there was another woman standing in the room with them—tall and beautiful, clad in luxurious dark brown leather from knee-high boots to a fitted motorcycle jacket. She wore thick leather gloves with steel fingertips that glinted in the light as she pushed a strand of hair from her face. A longbow made of rich brown wood was slung over her shoulder, and a quiver of arrows was strapped securely to her back. A mass of shiny golden-blonde hair, bound loosely in a thick braid, hung down her back. She was as impossibly beautiful as Snow, though different, her skin the color of a rosy peach, her eyes a much darker, stormier blue. Beside her stood a massive dog that Tessa at first assumed was the wolf that had saved her from Bluebeard's fatal stroke. But this was not a wolf and it was smaller, which wasn't saying much as its shoulder reached the woman's hips. The dog's fur was thick and deep black, its paws large and powerful. Its eyes glowed a steady orange-red that looked not unlike two tiny fires in its face. The woman and her dog stared at Bluebeard's body, then looked to Snow. Although Tessa could not read her expression, it made her shudder.

Brand spoke, perhaps on accident, from the corner of the room where he huddled with Micah. "Whoa."

The woman's eyes snapped to Brand and Micah, and her expression was now clear displeasure.

"Snow?" she asked, a warning tone in just that one word.

"Tal." Snow said, clipped, clearly not biting.

"Devlo. What a mess," Tal said flatly, the dog moving from her side to investigate Bluebeard's body.

"No kidding," Snow said, "I told The Court we should have waited for you to return. This isn't exactly my skill set."

"Clearly," Tal said, taking stock of the room. "You're in the Mortal world for half a day and we have a dead 300-year-old Story *and* mortal witnesses?"

"And a murdered Advocate," Snow added, nodding toward the foyer. Tal left the room and came back a moment later, the dog trotting at her side.

"Tova," Tal said in that same strange language that Tessa was sure she had never heard before. She watched Tal carefully. "Hecuba, search the house," Tal said, nodding to the dog who took off.

"And, of course, there's that," Snow said, gesturing disdainfully in Tessa's general direction.

"What?" Tessa asked, looking down at herself and then back at Snow.

The woman named Tal really looked at Tessa for the first time and let out a breath of shock, "Yae Simane."

Snow nodded, "I know. She's The Last."

Tal turned to Snow, "Does The Court know?"

"Not yet."

"We must get her there."

Tessa was fed up. "Stop talking about me like I'm not here!" she shouted. Neither Snow nor Tal paid her any mind. Tessa looked at Brand and Micah, "You guys didn't see a giant grey wolf anywhere did you?" They both shook their heads. Tessa returned her focus to Snow as she began talking about Brand and Micah again.

"What about her minions?" Snow asked, jutting her chin at Brand and Micah, who didn't seem to like being talked about either but were arguably even more freaked out than Tessa.

"Well, we can't take them to Story," Tal said, her tone suggesting it was out of the question.

"Yes, but then what do we do about them?" Snow said, her teeth gritted, "They have seen far too much."

Tessa had just about had it and so she yelled at the top of her lungs, "Knock it off!" When Tal and Snow finally looked at her, she added, "And nobody is going anywhere."

Tal looked at Tessa in a bored way. "Kid, you've killed a 300-year-old Story, your Advocate is dead, you've got two mortal witnesses, and you're The Last Tovaien Scion. There's no way you're not going to Story."

Tessa opened her mouth to protest again and Hecuba, who had rejoined the group, growled at her. Tal looked at Snow. "Leave the Mortals here. Maybe Morgana can whip something up to free them of these traumatic memories later on," she said, casting another glance at Micah and Brand. Micah spoke up this time.

"Um…that sounds a lot like brainwashing or something. I'd like to vote for no brainwashing."

Tal ignored her and turned to Snow, "Hecuba says the house is clear. I'm opening the doorway." Snow nodded almost imperceptibly and stepped back. Tal reached into her jacket pocket and pulled out a small blue pebble made of glass. It looked like an average marble any kid might have. She held it between two steel tipped fingers and then threw it into the air a dozen feet in front of her, shouting, "Yonep ge rupto!"

Tessa was starting to think they were making up these words. They *sounded* made up.

The pebble froze in midair (very unlike a kid's average marble) and then blue-white lightning snaked out of it, leaving behind a flickering blue doorway of light in the middle of the room. Snow stepped through the doorway and disappeared. Tal gestured to Tessa. "C'mon."

Tessa shook her head. "No freaking way."

Tal sighed slightly, like she had been here before. "Don't make me threaten to hurt your friends, okay?" Hecuba cast a growl at Micah and Brand, her eyes sparking even more brightly in her face.

"Fine, fine," Tessa said, raising her hands and realizing she still had the axe. She set it down, and it promptly disappeared. Tessa suddenly wished she wasn't covered in blood as she headed into whatever lay beyond that door. She stepped forward half a step and then looked at Micah and Brand. "I'm really sorry I got you guys into this. Really."

Brand shook his head. "What are you talking about? You saved our lives."

Tessa smiled weakly. "You guys are nice." She stepped forward and, after a glare at Tal, walked through the doorway. Tal followed, Hecuba on her heels. No sooner had the dog disappeared, then Brand stepped toward the doorway.

"We're going, right?"

Micah bit her lip, unsure.

"C'mon, Mike. If for no other reason than Tessa's the first friend we've made in, like, a million years, and she saved our lives, and she's in there alone."

Micah nodded and grabbed his arm. The doorway was already shrinking as they jumped through.

Tessa opened her eyes to find herself in a hallway that actually seemed more like a cave. The walls were intricately carved but dark and windowless and made completely of rock. The markings on the walls made no sense to her but somewhere deep inside something pricked at her, like a memory she had never actually experienced. The space was illuminated only by candles, and the effect was both eerie and magical at once, with shadows dancing across the walls.

Snow stood to the side, waiting anxiously. Tal and Hecuba appeared just behind Tessa. She was about to open her mouth and say something bitchy to Tal when Micah and Brand appeared as well.

Tal saw them and began to shout what could only be cuss words. "Tovaien kiaane! Neyersichita!"

Hecuba growled.

Tessa knew they shouldn't have followed her but she couldn't help but smile at them. She was still mad scared, but now just a fraction less. "Thanks, guys."

They shrugged their shoulders as if it was nothing, which made Tessa chide herself for writing them off as nice and adorable. They were both those things, but they were so much more. There was steel in them, and goodness, and incredible bravery to have followed her here, wherever *here* was.

Tal looked down and spoke directly to Hecuba. "I'm not sticking around for this." The dog snuffled in agreement and followed her into the darkness. Snow trailed after her, yelling something in the strange language Tessa couldn't make out.

A voice behind Tessa rang out, and she whirled around to see that they were not in fact in a hallway but rather at the end of one. Just behind them was an entrance to a grand open space. The room, like the hallway attached to it, was shaped from what still seemed to Tessa to be a massive cave, windowless and mysterious, and well, *cavernous*. But it also resembled the inside of a magnificent castle, with a ceiling soaring up high above her and decorations etched into the walls, patterns swirling deeply through the floor and ceiling, jewels set into those patterns so that everything sparkled.

The room was mostly bare, relying on the splendor of its jeweled walls and floor to do the work. Except candles. There were candles everywhere, like bullshit romantic, chick-movie style, just *layers* of candles. It must have taken, like, half the day just to light all of them. The only other thing in the room was a massive dais and on it, sitting in chairs that were more like thrones positioned behind a massive stone table, were four figures robed in hooded cloaks of such a dark purple that they appeared almost black in the candlelight. One chair on the end was empty. The man at the center squinted at Tessa.

Tessa remained in the shadows, anxious about what horrible thing would happen next and not terribly eager to give him a better look at her. The man stood and threw up his arms theatrically, his big robed sleeves falling down to somewhere just below his elbows, his gloved hands spread wide and dramatically above him.

"Battle. Step forward, for you are *The Scion!*" his voice boomed, echoing off the stonewalls. Tessa opened her mouth to speak but found she had no idea what to say. She stumbled forward, away from Brand and Micah, who stood dumbstruck, as if turned to stone rivaling their surroundings. Tessa peered at the man to see if she could make him out from under the cloak, but all she could see was golden-blonde hair peeking out from beneath his hood. Tessa took a few more steps into the light, closer to the dais, and Brandon and Micah followed her, keeping a slight distance, their mouths still hanging open.

The robed figure spoke again, throwing his arms open even wider, attempting even more grandeur than the first time (which was saying something).

"Yes, Battle. Welcome to The Court! We have been awaiting you—" he stopped midsentence and then threw back his hood and narrowed his eyes at Tessa as she came fully into the light. He squinted at her and then, his hands on his hips, and in a much less impressive, authoritative voice said, "Wait. She's…she's a girl." The three other robed figures leaned forward intently. He looked back at them, confused. "Why is The Scion a girl?!" he said to the others, almost as if he was offended. The rest of The Court threw their own hoods off and looked at her more closely, equally surprised.

Tessa walked closer to the dais, unsure, and Brand and Micah inched forward behind her. "Where are we?" Tessa asked.

The figures had been talking amongst themselves since the proclamation that Tessa was a girl, and Tessa had just decided to ignore it, annoying as it was. The man with the blonde hair, and Tessa could now see, an older man's once handsome visage, turned back to her. He recoiled slightly, and Tessa could tell he was looking at Brand and Micah.

"Oh great gods! Why does she have minions?!" he whined to the others. "Since when does The Scion come with minions?!"

Brand raised his hand tentatively in protest, "Um, we are definitely not minions." But then he chewed his lip and looked around unsure. "Okay, I am like fifty percent sure we're not minions." Tessa looked at him and he shrugged his shoulders. Micah just stared back, her eyes huge behind her glasses.

"Then what are you?" The head figure asked haughtily.

Brand shrugged. "I don't know, just along for the really weird ride?"

The man kept staring at them but muttered to the handsome, dark-skinned, dark-eyed man next to him, "Sounds like minions to me."

The handsome man nodded in agreement, "Mmmhmmm."

Snow came back into the room, now wearing a long white gown perched precariously low on her shoulders and made, so far as Tessa could tell, of actual diamonds. She walked toward the dais, her own dark purple cloak in hand, and sent an 'I told you so' glance at Tessa.

"See? Minions."

Tessa rolled her eyes. Snow ascended the dais, put on her own cloak to match the others, which seemed ridiculously formal, and sat in the only empty chair at the far end of the table. Fed up, Tessa stomped her foot like an angry child, forcing them to acknowledge her.

"Hey! Can you get it together up there!? What the hell is going on? Where are we?" The robed figures turned, and a few more whispers escaped before the blonde man shushed them.

"Okay. Yes. Sorry about that. A bit of confusion here. We weren't expecting you."

"Your people brought me here," Tessa said angrily.

"Well, yes. Yes, we did send for you, but it's your birthright that brought you. Traditionally on his 17th birthday, The Scion is activated, and when that happens, we bring him here—to the dimension of Story. It's just…usually you're a boy."

Tessa crossed her arms. "I'm *always* a girl."

"Yes, of course," he sniffed. "I mean, usually *The Scion* is a boy. Since you are, well, *not,* then that means you are something we have read about only in prophecy. Cryptic prophecy most of us stopped believing in a long time ago. You're something called 'The Last Scion'," he said, with heavy emphasis on the word 'last.'

Brand leaned forward to Tessa, "Oh yeah, *that's* not too ominous."

Tessa ignored him and tried to address the figures again. "And who are you?" she asked, getting angrier by the second. The man smiled broadly.

"I am Midas. I am the leader of The Court," he said. When Tessa remained unimpressed, he sniffed again, trying to hide his disappointment. Tessa nodded at the rest.

"And they are?"

"The rest of The Court—at the end is The Frog Prince, this is this is Aladdin, Morgana, and of course you have already met Snow." Tessa took them in. The Frog-man could only be described as just that, a Frog-Man. He stood and sat and gestured like a man, but he was simply a frog. Giant head and eyes, green skin, the whole package. The woman Midas called Morgana was stunning. Dark-eyed and dangerous-looking, with black hair that spilled over her shoulders and back like an overturned bottle of ink. Aladdin was painfully handsome, all enigmatic dark eyes and slicked back hair. Brand sucked in a breath behind her.

"What?" she whispered.

He sidled up to her. "They're dressed up as fictional characters," he breathed. "The Frog Prince, Morgan Le Fay, King Midas, Aladdin, Snow…I don't know…"

"Snow White?" Micah broke in.

"No, the look is wrong—The Snow Queen maybe?" Brand posited. Tessa nodded but kept quiet.

Midas laughed. "Silly Mortal minion, we're not "dressed up" as Fiction, we ARE Fiction. Though we prefer Stories. And that is where you are, in Story. It's where we live, where all Fictional characters live."

Tessa nodded. She wanted to laugh out loud and search the room for hidden cameras, but she'd also gotten superpowers, fought a Troll in her backyard, decapitated a guy named Bluebeard, seen an unbelievably giant dog, and an even more unbelievably giant wolf, felt a woman change the temperature in the air with her thoughts, and been teleported to another location via a shining blue doorway, so evidence was pretty piled up in favor of Fictional characters being real. She did worry that Brand and Micah's heads might explode, however.

Instead, Brand's eyes lit up. "Whoa. Like, Batman? Batman is real!?"

Midas sighed. "Yes. He's real. And frankly? He's kind of a dick."

From behind Midas, Aladdin shook his head in an emphatic "No" and then very clearly mouthed, "HE'S AWESOME."

Brand's face could only be described as elated.

The dark-haired woman, Morgana, came down from the dais. Tessa felt herself instinctively tensing up. The woman had a calculated expression on her face, as if she was approaching a baby deer that might be easily startled.

"Battle. We apologize for the frustration you must feel. Even for those that have been prepared, which you clearly have not, this can all come as a bit of a shock," she smiled beatifically.

"But what is *this*?" Tessa asked.

"*This* is your birthright," Morgana said. "The Scion has always been an important part of our world, bridging the gap between us, fighting to keep things balanced, policing the two worlds as is sometimes necessary. There is, as Midas said, a prophecy that the last of The Scions, who have all been male until now, would be female. So that means you're the much vaunted 'Last Scion' that some Stories have been waiting for—well, for a very long time."

"Because when I'm dead you guys won't be able to get back and forth or something, right?" Tessa asked. Morgana pursed her lips and Tessa pushed. "Because that's what Bluebeard said."

Behind her, Brand looked at Micah and whispered. "Who's Bluebeard?" Micah shrugged in response.

Morgana seemed to choose her words with care, "Yes, it is believed by most Stories that the death of The Last Scion will close the boundaries between our worlds permanently. Some Stories will want that very much and some will do anything to prevent it," Morgana paused and glanced at Snow, "But surely Snow has told you all of this."

Snow screwed up her mouth, "Well, about that."

Morgana's gaze hardened. "Yes?"

"I gave her the Cliff Notes. But we're actually here because Tal was summoned by a Story death. The Scion killed Bluebeard."

And then the shit hit the fan.

 SEVEN

"She did what?!?" Midas roared from the dais, incensed. For her part, Morgana stepped back half a step, as if Tessa was poison. "How dare you!?" Midas continued, all thunder and fury.

"How dare he try to kill *me*," Tessa said, surprised by the steel in her voice, the anger.

This shut everyone up for a minute.

Snow spoke up finally, though she clearly didn't want to. "In fairness to The Scion, he had kidnapped her minions and her Advocate. He did try to kill her, likely because he wanted the border closed, and he had been killing Mortals in some numbers. He also killed her Advocate before The Scion was able to defeat him."

The group took a long moment to consider this, and it gave Tessa time to think about how much trouble she might be in. What could they do to her? She didn't know the rules here, and she'd walked almost willingly into a totally uncontrollable situation, and she had to worry about Micah and Brand, too.

Somewhere inside her an ache for escape began.

"Still," Midas said weakly.

Morgana leaned against the dais and held her head as though she had a terrible headache all of a sudden.

"Still, what?" Tessa said. "Guy was a killer and also a complete douche bag. I didn't set out to kill him, but I wasn't about to let him kill me just because it's against rules I didn't even know existed."

Morgana stood back up. "Scion, we understand. It's just, he was an old Story, this doesn't happen everyday, the death of a Story. Snow has explained to you what this means?

Tessa nodded. "She has," and then opened her mouth to apologize, but felt a surge of anger over the whole situation and went on the offensive instead. "He didn't leave me much choice."

Morgana looked to Snow as if to confirm the situation. and Tessa registered an almost imperceptible nod from Snow. Wow, you really couldn't count on The Snow Queen to have your back. I mean, technically, she'd backed Tessa up, but *barely*. It made Tessa even angrier.

"Maybe if I had been the slightest bit prepared it could have been avoided." Tessa said flatly, not sure who to blame, but desperate to share blame she didn't understand.

"Well, if anyone is to blame for that, Scion, it's your own mother," Midas practically spit.

And with her mother thrown down into the mud with such disdain, Tessa fully lost it. "What did you say?" she asked through gritted teeth, practically rolling up her sleeves as she prepared to punch Midas into oblivion.

Morgana stepped in her path, forcing Tessa to pull up short. "Forgive him, Scion, he has no mother. He does not understand the impact of his words." Tessa looked at Morgana though her vision clouded with tears.

"What does he know about my mother—what is he talking about?"

Midas opened his mouth to speak again and Morgana hissed at him, "If you so much as open your mouth again I will permanently remove it!" Tessa could have sworn there was a flash of greenish-gold in her otherwise dark eyes. Morgana turned back to Tessa. "We apologize, Scion. Your mother should never even be mentioned."

"Then why—" Tessa began.

Aladdin stepped in. "Midas only meant to say that, for whatever reason, your parents did not tell you about this. Your mother surely knew, or suspected, and they have chosen to keep it from you. You have moved around much, have you not?"

Tessa nodded, her fists still clenched.

"So it was hard to find you. Even for your Advocate we must assume, since he did not find you until today."

Tessa's head swam with information and emotion. She just wanted to get away from these people.

"The past is the past, Scion," The Frog said. "What matters now is that you get to work and that you are trained and protected, so that you can defend yourself, preferably without using your gifts to kill Stories."

""Yeah, about that…" Tessa said, looking at her hands that seemed to almost hum with power.

"Standard superhero package, no need to thank us," Midas said, slumping in his seat like a spoiled child as Morgana threw another warning look his way.

"You people thought I was going to thank you?"

Morgana eyed her. "Well, no, but we didn't think you'd be so incensed, child. Besides, it's not like we actually gave it to you. Surely you felt the power come to you today when you turned 17?"

"If by 'felt' you mean puked up everything I've ever eaten, then yeah, sure, I *felt* that." Tessa continued to stare at her hands. "You realize that in the last six hours since I got these fancy superpowers two things have tried to kill me, I've gotten an innocent man killed, my friends have been kidnapped, my house has been ransacked, and I've killed someone, right? Why on earth would I thank you? Great power, great responsibility, yadda, yadda, yadda. I mean, I assume these superpowers come with some kind of expectation? That's what you've been going on about, right? You're not just going to send me on my way—this doesn't look like a place where I just get sent on my way with badass gift baskets." Tessa paused to look at the court. "What if I just say no?"

"Scion, it's best not to waste time denying something you cannot change," Morgana said, before adding, "Besides, when word gets out that The Last Scion has been called, things will only get more dangerous, I'm afraid."

Tessa eyed her, everyone, skeptically.

Aladdin spoke up. "Scion—"

"Don't call me that," Tessa snapped. "My name is Tessa."

"Apologies, Fair Tessa," Aladdin said, hands raised in surrender. "But there is no denying birthright. The powers, the destiny, all of that 'yadda yadda' you mentioned? We cannot do anything about it, regardless of how you feel about it or us. It comes to you regardless. You are the one."

"Balls," Tessa said under her breath and glanced at Brand and Micah standing there, stunned. Snow stood up and descended the dais, her glittering white dress flashing under the robe as she moved. Her purring voice was like clinking icicles, irritating clinking icicles.

"Scion. Listen to me. Everyone is handling you with kid gloves. You are no kid. Or if you were, you are one no longer. You're going to fight to save your world and ours, to keep the balance, there's no way around this, so just deal already."

Tessa clenched her fists and Morgana seized on her hesitation.

"And it's not just that, Scion. Something has been happening in Lore."

"What do you mean?"

"We don't know exactly," Aladdin said, "But we've had some very concerning reports coming in—some missing Mortals, some unaccounted for Stories."

"So they just live there, in Lore? Just running around pretending to be Mortal?" Tessa asked, trying to make all this new information fit in her head.

"They are not tied to Lore, they can go anywhere in the Mortal world, and many do. But many also stay in Lore because there is a dimensional rift there, and it's comforting to be close to home even when in another dimension," Aladdin explained.

"So what, they have, like, jobs and stuff?"

"Some of them, those that can pass or have magic to help them pass. Others have, let's call it family money. Stories, just like Mortals, come in all varieties, Scion," The Frog said.

Tessa lowered her head and closed her eyes. She took some deep breaths. There was so much to know.

And it was all freaking crazy.

Micah and Brand watched her closely and just as she opened her mouth to speak, Midas sighed again from his throne.

"I don't know why you are all even bothering with her. What can she do? She's just a girl. She's untrained, clearly irresponsible. The idea of her being able to help us at all is ridiculous. Let the child go. Really, what do we care if she gets eaten by lions, tigers, bears, or worse? We have adult problems, not bratty untrained Last Scion ones."

Tessa's fists clenched, her eyes narrowed in anger. The entire court was glaring at Midas when Tessa looked up at him, seething.

"Nobody ever wants to hear from the guy telling the truth," Midas said, gesturing dismissively at everyone. Tessa relaxed her hands.

"You know what? He's right. I don't want any part of this. I can't help you and I kind of don't want to. So—good luck!" She spun on her heel and headed for the hallway.

"Scion, wait!" Morgana called.

"What are you worried about, Morgana? It's not like she can leave anyway," Midas said, unconcerned.

Tessa looked back over her shoulder at him, her voice steely. "Wanna bet?" Tessa raised her arms in the air, looked toward the ceiling, and screamed, "Return me!" As she said it, there was a crackle of blue light and a snap of power and the doorway made of brilliant, glowing blue stood before her.

"Oh great gods," Morgana breathed.

"Tova," Snow whispered, stunned.

"She…she opened a door. How can she do that? Can a Scion open a door?" Aladdin asked, clearly shaken.

Morgana shook her head. "Not until now."

"Scion," Morgana pleaded, "Let's not be rash, there are many things still to discuss."

Tessa looked at Brand and Micah. "You coming non-minions?"

"Oh, hell yes," they said in unison. And the trio walked through the blue gateway, which swallowed them up, snapping closed behind them.

Gape mouthed, the Court stared at the empty space where, just moments before, the three teens had vanished. Morgana, closest to the closed gateway, turned to them, a helpless look on her face. Aladdin sat down, defeated.

Morgana spun on Midas. "You idiot!" she shouted and then unclasped her cloak and cast it aside on a chair, revealing a glittering red dress, too clingy and low-cut to be considered PG-13. She sat on a chair and leaned forward, massaging her temples. "Tova," she whispered, more to herself than anyone else.

"I don't know what all of you are so worried about," Midas groused.

Aladdin glared at him. "She has been The Scion for less than a day and she has killed a powerful 300-year-old Story. You do not think that is worthy of concern?"

Midas tried to shrug and looked to Snow for support. "Was it really that impressive?"

Snow looked at him. "To be honest, I have never seen anything like it in all my days."

"We didn't even have a chance to tell her about the war," Frog said.

"I doubt it will matter," Midas said dismissively.

Morgana rolled her eyes. "Only an absolute fool would think that The Last Scion is not going to play a part in this war. Things are going to come to a head much more quickly now."

Snow removed her own cloak and spoke to everyone but Midas, "We need someone from Story to be close to her."

Midas perked up, seizing on the idea, "Yes!"

Everyone ignored him.

"A spy?" Frog ventured.

Snow chose her words carefully. "An *emissary*."

Frog and Aladdin nodded in agreement.

Midas tried to join in. "Who can we use? A Story that's already in the Mortal world?" he ventured.

Morgana shook her head. "No, you know how twitchy some Stories get when they've been out there too long. We'll have to send someone ourselves, just to be sure."

"Agreed," Aladdin said, running a well-manicured hand through his dark hair. "Who should it be?"

Morgana looked up. "Snow."

Snow snapped to attention, her blue eyes flashing in anger. "Me?! What? Are you insane?!"

"She already knows you, it's half the battle," Morgana said.

Midas' hand shot up. "Seconded. All in favor?" Aladdin and Frog both raised their hands less enthusiastically. Midas surveyed the hands. "And the motion passes."

Snow turned on the lot of them and seethed, "No. No way am I going to LIVE in the Mortal world—you can't—you treacherous little imps—you traitorous fools!" and realizing the futility of her dramatic words she spun on Morgana. "You utter bitch."

Morgana eyed her coolly. "Regardless. It's done." She waved her hand and a crackling blue gateway similar to the one of moments ago opened next to Snow and she was sucked through it without another word.

The Court was silent for a long time, and then Frog cleared his throat.

"What about the mortal boy and girl?"

"Yes," Aladdin said. "Do you think they'll change?"

Midas sighed, annoyed with the level at which they were all ignoring and disrespecting him. "Of course they'll change. No Mortal has ever set foot in Story and not exhibited some side effects."

As much as she hated to admit it, Morgana knew he was right. "They'll change. Time will tell exactly what the change will be, but they'll change, that much is certain."

X

Tessa, Brand, and Micah lay prostrate on the floor of Bluebeard's home in an exhausted shape that looked part triangle and part circle. They had been lying there, face down on the plush carpet, breathing quietly and not saying anything for maybe three full minutes. Brand, as always, was the first to speak.

Without lifting his head and talking directly into the thick carpet, he said, "So, are we going to talk about this…or what?" Tessa and Micah turned their faces toward the center of the triangle. Brand did the same. Tessa sighed and pushed herself up to a kneeling position.

"What's there to say?" she asked, and then stood up.

"What's there to say?! Well, for starters, Fictional characters are real—including Batman—which I just have to mention again, because, well, it's awesome," he paused and then pointed at Tessa. "You're some kind of badass superhero and you can basically teleport. I mean, these are things that deserve to be discussed over pancakes."

Brand and Micah were kneeling now too, looking up at Tessa, waiting for her to say something. Just as Tessa was about to speak, there was a crackle and pop of blue energy and Snow came stumbling through a gateway. She was cussing and spitting in a rage, her gown even more inappropriate here than it had been there. Tessa crossed her arms defiantly.

"And just what are you doing here?" she asked, an unfriendly bite in her voice.

Snow spun around to see the trio staring at her and tried adjusting her totally unsuitable clothing. "It was decided that you needed an emissary."

"And you got the short straw?" Tessa hazarded.

"I volunteered," she said haughtily, straightening her wrinkled dress. "Honor and all that. I'm full of that honor crap." Snow had the look of a wild animal trapped in a suburban house. Tessa raised an eyebrow. Snow clearly didn't want to be here any more than Tessa wanted her here.

"Yeah. I vaguely remember The Snow Queen story, that's who you are, right? The *villain* of the freaking story. Yeah, you're just mad crazy with the honor," Tessa said rolling her eyes.

Tessa gazed at Snow for a moment and then left the room. Everyone waited for her to return, but after a few moments they heard the front door slam and ran after her.

"Tessa, wait!" Micah called. But by the time they got to the porch she was gone, the woods dark and teeming all around them.

"You think her powers include super speed?" Micah asked Brand, looking around, wondering where she could have disappeared to in so little time.

"Or flight," Brand said, looking up at the night sky and scanning it for some trace of her.

Snow sidled up behind Micah and Brand and cast a bored expression their way, "So, which one of you minions has a place for me to stay for the night?"

The two friends continued staring at the empty night sky and, in unison, said "Not it."

 EIGHT

Yesterday, Tessa had missed her first class since she'd also missed the bus. She was used to school and what passed for home being closer together, and she hadn't timed things right. Now that she knew Trig was her track one first class for the rest of the year she foresaw a whole lot of poor timing. Today, however, she'd actually gotten up early because she had decided to skip the bus so that she could also skip Brand and Micah.

Tessa had decided on the super-effective plan of pretending.

She was going to pretend yesterday hadn't happened at all. A full reset. It was all just a bad dream as far as she was concerned. Snow, Bluebeard, Story, and The Troll. Micah and Brand were the only real loss in the whole plan. But she figured they were way safer without her anywhere near their lives.

Well, and Bishop, of course. But Tessa wasn't sure how to live with herself for getting him killed, so if she could pretend it hadn't happened, then maybe she would stop feeling sick all the time.

So Tessa pretended really hard all morning. Pretended that she didn't smash her alarm clock to smithereens with her stupid super-powered hand, pretended that she didn't put a dent in the wall when she fell against it putting on her boot, pretended that she didn't break the handle off of the fridge when she opened it to get juice, pretended that the house wasn't still all messed up, and even pretended to ignore the book on the living room table, still open to the page with the Troll illustration. It was a lot to maintain, but Tessa was pretty good at pretending. She'd been pretending a lot in her life, she could do this.

But on the steps to the school, watching for her like two super nosy (but still relatively adorable) hawks, Tessa saw Micah and Brand and realized that they were going to make pretending nearly impossible. She steeled her shoulders and put on her bitchiest 'leave me alone' scowl in the hopes that it would scare away the only two people that, if not for her life being utterly jinxed, she would have been excited to see. She couldn't let them get any deeper into whatever this was than they already were. If she liked them, the best way to keep them safe was to get rid of them. Brand came at her full of enthusiasm and devotion. Micah seemed to see Tessa's expression and approached cautiously, her brow furrowed, her hands fidgeting inside the front pocket of an oversized blue hoodie.

"Where did you go?" Brand shouted out as he walked toward her across the lawn, and then made what could only be interpreted as the international symbol for Superman flying and made a face that said "yes?!" Tessa didn't even bother to shake her head, instead she let her eyes glaze over dumbly, a technique she had learned when bouncing rapidly from school to school, and moved right past them as if they were made of mist. "Hey," Brand said, half-wounded, half-pissed. It was the wounded part that bothered Tessa, but she tucked it inside and kept going.

Micah put a hand on Brand's arm as he moved to go after Tessa. "Brand. Leave it," she said, also sounding wounded but less so.

"Whattayoumeanleaveit?" he said, spinning on her. "We, like, went through stuff. Ran a freaking gauntlet together or something, and she's just going to what? Blow us off?"

"Yeah, I think that's exactly what she's going to do," Micah said, adjusting the messenger bag on her shoulder and heading for the entrance behind Tessa but at a pace that made it clear she wasn't trying to catch up with her. Brand stared after her, confused. He threw his hands up in the air and called after Micah.

"What am I supposed to do then? I've got the goddamn Snow Queen bunking on my couch!"

Micah turned back to him from the steps and gestured for him to follow her. Brand sighed, his shoulders dropping deeply, and joined her.

Tessa looked at her first classroom door and her stomach flip-flopped. "Jesus," she said to herself. "What kind of masochist can do Trig at eight a.m.?"

Tessa pulled open the door and surveyed the students while her new teacher, a Ms. Hatch, studied the piece of paper with her name on it. "Tessa?" she said, looking up from the schedule bleary-eyed.

"Yeah," Tessa said, taking the slip back from Hatch as she wrote something in a bright red book.

Tessa looked at the sea of faces staring back at her for the first time. She'd been through this a few times yesterday so it wasn't unexpected, though it wouldn't have shaken her anyway. She'd gotten used to new schools (although the last six had been all-girls schools, so the male faces looking back at her was an interesting change at least).

They looked the same as almost any other school at this time of morning.

Tired and bored.

Hatch handed Tessa a textbook and directed her to the only empty seat. Tessa plunked down, already dissatisfied with her schedule. She suspected it was her father's idea to make her do Trig first thing in the morning. Probably something about alertness divided by the exhaustion of a day times a coefficient of some kind or another. The teacher had begun talking and already it sounded like a boring hum of noises that Tessa could not force herself to care about given everything that was happening to her. The guy next to her leaned over and whispered out a "Hey."

Tessa didn't look up, just opened her textbook and her notebook and grunted a hey back at him. But then a big athletic hand was thrust into her view, and she pivoted to look at the boy speaking to her. Giant, flawless blue eyes blinked at her, and Tessa had to forcibly stop herself from getting a bit lost in them. When she finally got past the eyes she saw short dark hair, and perfect chiseled features, the kind of movie star good looks that would make other kids want to worship you in high school (while secretly wanting to kill you). In truth, he wasn't actually Tessa's type at all, conventionally handsome and disgustingly clean cut, too conservative. Then again, there was 'regular conventionally handsome' and the level of conventionally handsome that this guy had going on. This was like *Olympic* levels of conventionally handsome. The hand made a little gesture as if to alert her that it was still waiting for its handshake and Tessa slid her hand into his.

"Nash," he said, shaking her hand with just the right amount of pressure.

"Tessa Battle," she said, hooding her eyes with a practiced expression of boredom and releasing his big warm hand. So he was the most attractive person she'd ever seen up close. So what? She was a damn superhero or something.

"So you're new, huh?" he said, flicking his eyes back at the teacher briefly and then back to Tessa.

"What tipped you off?" Tessa shot back, getting her bearings back with every second that passed.

"And she comes back swinging," he said with a low whistle. "Well. Welcome to Lore."

"Back," she said.

"Excuse me?"

"Welcome *back* to Lore," Tessa corrected. "I lived here before. Until I was nine."

"Huh," he said, cocking his head, amused. "Then maybe you should show *me* around. I've only been here about three years which means you've got seniority on me."

Tessa arched her eyebrow and tried to focus on the blindingly boring Trig problem on the board. "And why is anyone showing anyone around?"

"It's the neighborly thing to do," he said, looking straight ahead. Tessa turned to look at him, his profile like that of a Greek god, his toned shoulders barely contained beneath the fabric of his t-shirt.

"You play sports?" she asked.

"Yeah—some—why?" he asked, not looking her way and instead throwing a winning smile at the teacher who was looking at them, annoyed.

"I just don't date athletes," Tessa said simply, swinging back around to face front and making sure to look incredibly interested in the board. Nash cocked an eyebrow.

"Who asked you out?"

"You were about to."

"Oh really?"

"Mmmmhmmm," Tessa said and then pointed her pencil at the blackboard and looked at him coyly. "You should pay attention," she said trying not to smile.

"And why don't you date athletes?"

"That hive mentality isn't good for boys your age," she chided.

"Is that so?" Nash said with a smirk. "Well, I don't play a lot of team sports. I prefer to be on my own—swimming, track, crew."

"*That's* a team sport," Tess said pointing her pencil in his direction when he mentioned crew. Nash leaned toward her, his smile deepening.

"I'll quit then."

Tessa turned to face his hypnotic eyes again and could feel the edges of her mouth drawing up into a smile despite how hard she fought it.

She had missed boys. Boys were good. So was being totally normal and not having to fight weird creatures on her lawn and decapitate serial killers. If she could get rid of those last bits maybe she could build some kind of not horrible life here.

Hatch glared at them both.

"Don't make me rearrange the seating chart, Battle. I hate doing that."

"Yes, Ma'am," Tessa said, nodding and digging into her book as Nash did the same next to her. The whole thing was definitely worth the reprimand though.

Tessa joined the crowd headed to second period, making sure not to look back at Handsome Nash as she left. She was very proud of herself. It had been exceptionally difficult to not look back.

Tessa's search for her next class was not going well, the halls were mostly empty when the numbers finally told her she was getting close. But as she turned a corner she saw Micah at a locker down the hallway and paused. She was about to turn around and go back the way she came when she saw a group of four boys walking toward Micah.

They had that look.

The look of trouble.

The look of mean.

Tessa narrowed her eyes and waited, watching, hoping she was wrong. As the group passed Micah, one elbowed hard into her back, causing her to drop everything she was holding.

"Watch out, double half-breed," he said. Tessa involuntary clenched her shoulders. Micah looked as if she wished she could disappear inside her locker. As Micah knelt to pick up her books, Tessa strode forward into the hall without even realizing she was doing it. As she passed the group they stared her down, like the douche bags and bullies that they were. Tessa ignored them, but when she reached the one that elbowed Micah, Tessa shot out her arm, smashing his head into a locker door. He left a little dent in it and slid to the floor in a slump. By the time his pals had turned around, he was out cold in a little pile. Micah looked up at Tessa wide-eyed.

"Hey!" one of the guys shouted, leaning over to examine his friend and looking accusingly at Tessa. A teacher's head popped out of a classroom.

"What's going on here?"

Tessa shrugged, "He must have tripped on something?"

The teacher looked at the group and pointed to one. "Go get the nurse. The rest of you, to your classes, now." Tessa turned and walked past Micah, trying her best not to catch her eyes. She was supposed to be ignoring her. It wasn't going so well.

She got better at avoiding Micah and Brand, but it wasn't easy. Lunch had been the trickiest, but she managed to escape them by leaving campus, which was against the rules for juniors it seemed, and returning late, after the final bell for fourth period had already rung. She also saw Nash twice more though she didn't think he saw her, or possibly she'd overestimated her appeal and he'd forgotten all about her already. Tessa barely noticed a thing through her last class, her thoughts darting around her brain like stray bullets. It was American History (she was almost sure) and Nash was there, sitting across the room from her—a painful but lucky distance—she probably didn't need even more drama than she already had on her plate. When the final bell rang, Tessa made a mad dash for the exit, hoping she could avoid everyone and get home without any more confrontations with Micah and Brand. She'd have to walk home (a long damn walk) to avoid them on the bus again.

But just when she thought she was clear of everyone, Brand stepped out from behind a tree and stood in her path, clearly not willing to leave until he'd been heard. He started before she could even protest.

"Listen. You need to make up your mind. You tell us off. You avoid us. Then you stand up for Mike—which is it?" he said more than asked, still more hurt than anything, though he was clearly aiming for angry. Micah was to their left, leaning against a tree, looking like someone had kicked her in the gut, and Tessa felt like she had.

"Brand—" Tessa began, looking around, worried about what new hell might be lurking and ready to tear everyone to shreds. Brand held up a hand signaling that he wasn't finished.

"I'm not done—" he said, taking in breath to continue. Tessa stopped him short anyway. She hated to do this to him, she already had an unheard of affection for both of them, whether it was because they were amazing, or because she'd never had friends before, or just because of the bizarre thing they'd been through together, but the only way to be sure to keep them alive was to keep them out of this nonsense she was caught up in, and the only way to do that was to break their damn hearts. Hard and fast.

"Yes," she said coldly. "You *are* done. You're done, and I don't want to hear from you again. Either of you," she said, cutting a mean look at Micah. "You're out of it, and I don't want to have this conversation again. Got it?" Tessa raised her eyebrows and stared Brand down. He crumpled into himself like a busted piñata.

"Tessa—" his voice came out soft and plaintive, and Tessa thought the sound of it would break her. Just when she almost caved on all of it, a horn honked and Tessa turned to see The Snow Queen standing next to her car in a bright white, backless mini-dress that was drawing stares from all the students still on campus.

Tessa couldn't believe she was relieved to see Snow. She must be even more desperate than she realized.

Tessa sat in the car with Snow in silence. She was grateful for her unexpected arrival as an excuse to escape Brand and Micah but that didn't mean she wanted to talk to her.

Also, sitting in a shiny convertible next to the damn Snow Queen made it pretty hard to pretend the woman didn't exist and that had been part of the pretending plan.

When they arrived at her house, Tessa put her hand on the door handle but stopped short of getting out.

"Why did you pick me up?" Tessa asked.

"I need a favor."

Of course she did.

"Alright, I suppose I do owe you from the other day. What do you want?"

"Send me back to Story."

Tessa couldn't help but laugh. "What?"

"Open the doorway, you did it before, do it again."

"Can't," Tessa said, shaking her head. "I tried to open it again, just to see if I could. It didn't work."

"Tova," Snow said quietly.

"Are you cussing?"

"Yes."

"In what freaking language?"

"We just call it Story. Since our original Fictions are all different origin languages we all learn Story so we can easily communicate," Snow said absently. "It's also all magical and crap and thus nearly impossible for Mortals to learn. An added perk."

"Kinda like the opposite of Esperanto, real inclusive of you guys," Tessa said meanly, but she didn't really care. "So, what happened to Bluebeard, like…his body?"

"Nothing. It is as you left it."

Tessa's shook her head a bit, surprised. "Won't that bring up questions?"

"When your minions look at him, they see a man named Rene Severin. It's the same for any Mortal. That is who he is now, just a dead body named Rene Severin."

Tessa felt tired.

The man Bluebeard was pretending to be in Lore still very much existed, although only as a body, and it was just Bluebeard and everything Fictional and related to him that had ceased to exist. Tessa put her head in her hands, "But how is that possible? I mean, the ripples it must cause to eliminate that Story. I'm no genius and even I can imagine that the ripples must be massive."

Snow shrugged. "It's magic."

Tessa glared at her and mimicked her shrug. "How can you just wave it away? I've changed the world in ways I can't even begin to understand, and you're just saying it's okay?"

"I didn't say it was okay, I said it was magic. It's hard to understand, it can be infuriating, but it is what it is," Snow said.

"That can't be all there is to it. What about somewhere, someone, who has, for whatever stupid reason, built their life around this Story—what happens to them now?"

"Their lives will change. They won't know any better, but things will shift until it all works again. Most of it will be subtle, like you said—ripples. It's instantaneous."

Tessa shook her head again. "It doesn't make sense!"

Snow nodded wearily. "Again, I didn't say it makes sense, I said it was magic."

Tessa pounded her hand on the dashboard too hard. "Argh! I don't want to believe that's possible—that everything can be so easily undone."

"Well then, how do you explain any of this, Scion? Somewhere someone puts pen to paper and whole worlds are born. Worlds that change lives—both Mortal *and* Story—what can describe that *except* magic. Our whole lives are magic."

The words were poetic and even beautiful, but they felt to Tessa like a slap across the face. Until now, Tessa had been just rolling with the insane punches. How could she not? Evidence supporting all the weirdness had been massive. But now as Tessa really thought about it, she felt like her brain would explode. Every Story she'd ever read and the millions she hadn't, millions she would never even get to, were all real. Unless she destroyed them first, of course.

Tessa sat silently for a moment. "I gotta go. Where can I find you, if I have to?" She paused while opening the car door.

Snow screwed up her mouth as if she didn't want to say but then relaxed. "I'm in a penthouse downtown."

"Can you be a bit more specific?"

Snow cast a skeptical glance at Tessa. "It should be obvious when you look."

Tessa sighed, some kind of test or something. She was all ready to be annoyed but then gave up, She didn't want to have to call on her anyway. She got out of the car but just stared at her house blankly. "I've got to get them away from me, don't I?"

"Who?"

"Micah and Brand. They'll die just like Bishop, won't they?"

"Who can know? It's definitely not the safest life for them."

Her sentence sounded unfinished. Tessa prodded her, "What?"

"Nothing."

"That doesn't sound like nothing. Spit it out, Snow."

"They're going to change," Snow said simply.

"Change?"

"They've been to Story. Mortals are not supposed to go to Story. It will infect them. Change them. Nobody can know what they will get, or when, but it will happen, that much is certain."

If Snow was hoping to drop the hammer that would break Tessa, that had done it. Tessa's vision swam with tears. What had she done?

"Your minions acted loyally, as minions should. They were noble, even, to follow you into the unknown. And this is what nobility gets you, Scion. You should remember it."

Tessa wished for a moment that Snow's "good advice" could at least be comforting. She closed the car door without saying goodbye.

NINE

Tessa tossed for hours worrying about Micah and Brand, how she was going to tell them, what was going to happen to them, how it was almost entirely her fault. Around three a.m., with sleep still eluding her, she heard something in the house, again. Her first thought was naturally *'Troll!'* but this sound was too quiet for the Troll. This was a sound she could not have heard without superpowers.

This was something different.

Something scarier.

Tessa's heart fluttered in her chest as she reached for the bat by her bedside. Her hand shook, and she clenched it to stop the tremor. Was her life always going to be scary now? She worried it would. Would she actually become brave at some point? It seemed like that should have been part of the "standard superhero package." It was kind of a glaring oversight that it had been left out. Tessa looked doubtfully at the bat. It seemed she really was going to have to invest in a weapons cache of some kind. She took a deep breath. *'Show no fear'* she said resolutely inside her head while squeezing the bat in her hands. Tessa inched into the hallway and then down the stairs, avoiding the always-creaky eighth and third steps.

From the foyer she could see a tall man standing in the shadows of her living room. He seemed to be examining the pictures that sat on the mantle above the fireplace. He was wearing dark jeans and a black t-shirt that strained against broad well-muscled shoulders. As he moved into some moonlight drifting through the window, Tessa could see that he was, in fact, gorgeous, with dark hair that had recently been shaved very close. He had the strong jaw line of superheroes and the general bone structure of supermodels. Tessa had to remind herself that this superhero/model person had broken into her house. She cleared her throat loudly, hoping to startle him, but he just turned his head slightly, acknowledging her presence but otherwise not moving. There was no surprise in him, as if he'd known she was there all along. This unnerved her further, but she was determined not to let him know that.

"Hello, Scion," he said, his voice rough and dark.

Tessa sighed deeply. "I guess I should be pissed, but since you're the more attractive thing to break into my house in the last 24 hours, and you're not running around breaking shit, I'll just thank you for apparently not coming through one of my windows and ask you to get the hell out." Tessa raised the bat and rested it on her shoulder, one hip cocked to the side. The stranger chuckled.

"I'd heard you were funny," he said, still not facing her.

"Yeah, there are a lot of rumors going around about me, it seems. I have to say, I like that one better," Tessa said. The stranger turned around, one of the pictures still in his hand. It was a picture of Tessa and her mother, taken not long before she'd left, when Tessa was eight. "Your hair is different," the stranger said without looking up at her, his eyes fixed on the picture alone. Tessa blinked. She wasn't sure what to make of this guy.

"I was eight. A lot is different," she said, trying to be bored, trying to be calm, trying very much to *not* notice how well-shaped he was. Dude was clearly Fiction, only the imagination could make someone this brutally hot.

"True. We don't have that you know. I mean, I was never eight. I was always *this*, or some form of this. Children are a funny thing to me—how they turn into something else—it's like magic." His voice was hypnotic. He spoke with a strange, almost poetic cadence and an accent that Tessa thought was vaguely British, but British by way of something she couldn't quite place.

She felt oddly drowsy.

"Get out," she said again, trying to get her bearings, trying to shake off the rhythm of his voice. He took a step closer to her, and Tessa raised the bat off her shoulder and pointed it at him. "Yo," she said, as if that one word alone was a whole sentence full of warning. He put up his hands in protest, one still holding the picture frame, and a wide, gleaming white smile broke out across his face.

"No need for that, Hardcore. I'm not here to harm you."

"Oh, yeah. I totally believe that. You broke into my house in the middle of the night so we could, what? Have tea?" Tessa said, the bat still raised. He ticked his head to the side like he was thinking about it.

"Sort of, yes," he said.

Tessa blinked at him confused. "Huh?"

"Well, I am here to tell you a tale of sorts, and no, I certainly wouldn't turn down tea," he said, his grin becoming a gentle tease. Tessa shook her head but kept the bat leveled at him. Nothing about this was going the way she expected.

"What? I mean, no. No tea for you. Tell me what it is you want and get out."

The stranger sighed a bit and his smile dimmed slightly. He put the picture frame down on the coffee table. "I'll come back," he said. "You're clearly not in the right frame of mind."

"You're the one who got me up at three a.m., which, while we're on the subject of time, is not an appropriate time for social calls."

"Depends on who you are, I suppose."

"What does that even—ohmigod—are you some kind of vampire?"

The stranger's controlled expression broke for just a moment, and he looked horrified. "Gods, no," he spat, disgusted, before his face slid back into effortless stoicism. Tessa breathed a sigh of relief before looking at him confusedly.

"'Gods, no' why? What's wrong with vampires?"

"Bunch of dramatic fops, fawning all over themselves and acting like idiots," he said, his mouth twisting but less dramatically this time. "Not really their fault, I suppose, so many of them are written as sexy little emo-fantasy boys, but still."

"Okay, whatever you say. Vampires are the worst. I'm sure you're something awesome," she said, half-joking, half-fishing for answers. He turned smoothly.

"I am indeed," he said, his rocky voice with that same strange cadence Tessa was finding so hypnotic. She shook her head in the hopes of perhaps literally shaking the stranger out of her head.

"Listen, what is it that was so damned important that it couldn't wait until a more rational hour?"

"I thought you might want help finding your new Advocate," he said simply. The words shocked her and Bishop's vacant-eyed face immediately flashed unbidden in her head. The bat wavered and then she let it drop, almost unconsciously. He watched her with a curious expression, as if he was surprised to see the pain that crossed her face. As he saw it, his smile fell away and his teasing manner became serious. He tilted his head to the side as if examining every fiber of her.

"Get out," Tessa said, unable to hide a tremor in her voice. The stranger moved closer to her, dangerously close if he was something dangerous, which Tessa had to say, she guessed he probably was.

"I'm offering you my help," he said softly. Tessa racked her brain. She *did* need help, so much help she didn't know where to start. But she doubted she could trust him. Was he a better or worse bet than Snow? Snow was clearly in league with The Court, and Tessa didn't know where The Court really stood, or if they even stood together. She had no idea how to judge it, her gut was so churned up she doubted it knew which way was up, let alone how to lead her to a good decision. She didn't want a new Advocate, she had just been responsible for the death of her first. She didn't want to get anyone else killed. But it was obvious she needed help.

"I don't want a new Advocate," she said, straightening her shoulders and looking him in the eyes as coolly as she could manage. "But you're a Story, you seem like the kind of guy who's got mad connections. I need someone to help train me, educate me about some of this Story crap. Can you get me someone to do that?"

He moved so close to her that parts of them were actually touching. Tessa tried not to step back, but failed. "What about me, Hardcore?"

Tessa took an additional step back. "I don't fancy training at three a.m. Besides, I'm looking for a hero Story and you strike me as decidedly un-hero-y."

He stepped close again, and it was almost like they were dancing for a moment. "The Advocate can do all those things," he said. The mention of the A-word again sent shivers of guilt running through her.

"I said no."

"Scion—"

"Get out," Tessa said, stepping back from him several feet and raising her bat aggressively between them. *'Get out'* was in danger of becoming Tessa's catch phrase.

"Scion, be reasonable—" he began again but Tessa kept the bat raised and pointed it at him.

"Did I freaking stutter?" she asked. The stranger held up his hands again in a defeated gesture.

"As you wish, Scion," he said and moved toward her so fluidly it looked almost like liquid. As he passed her, headed for the front door, Tessa felt a strange flutter in her, some kind of ancient warning system. It was hard to describe, a slight chill of something decidedly dark running through everything she was for just a moment. She went to the door to see where he would go, but when she got there, he was gone. Swallowed up into the night. Tessa breathed deeply.

"Oh yeah, that's not too creepy." She closed the door, locked it, for all the good it seemed to do, and went back upstairs to try to catch a few hours of sleep before something else decided to break into her house.

She didn't sleep at all.

Even though nothing else burst into her house. Instead she lay there, exhausted but wide-eyed, until the sun came up. When it did, she sprang into action and was ready in record time. On her way out the front door, she grabbed her largest duffle bag and flung it over her shoulder. In half an hour she was downtown and trying to determine which building The Snow Queen would want to live in.

It was easy. Though Lore had a surprisingly large and thriving downtown for its size, there was only one building that looked like a bright glassy icicle shooting into the sky. Certainly the only building a "Snow Queen" would deem fit to live in. On the top floor there were two penthouses on either side, one called "A" and one called "B". Tessa went for the more obvious "A." As she drew closer, she felt a decided chill from behind the door. Bingo.

Tessa knocked on Snow's door softly at first but began pounding after three minutes of silence on the other end. Finally, she heard some movement inside and upped her pounding in an effort to get Snow to hurry. Snow flung the door open, clearly irritated. A wave of cold air hit Tessa as she did so.

"Scion. What a damned surprise," Snow said, leaning on the door yet not opening it wider to let Tessa in. Her eyes had looked hard like pebbles when she opened the door but they softened slightly and the temperature raised a few degrees at the sight of Tessa. Clearly she didn't consider Tessa much of a threat. Tessa pushed past her into the apartment. Snow groaned. "Please, by all means, why don't you shove your way in?"

The room was still unreasonably cold, cold enough that Tessa was glad she had her jacket. As she took in her surroundings, she couldn't decide whether to burst out laughing or be impressed. The condo was one of two loft-style penthouses on the floor and thus had a sweeping 180-degree view that wound from the distant woods on the east end beyond the city clear down to the ocean on the west.

Tessa stood at the floor-to-ceiling windows and marveled at the city. When she was a child, Lore had seemed magical to her, and now she guessed that wasn't just a convenient word. It wasn't just coincidence that the city had everything. It was almost like a fictional paradise. To the northeast of the city were woods as thick and wild as the imagination could conceive, while to the far west the city trailed off into a stunning rocky coastline, like something out of a picture book—epic waves falling against perfect shores. Between the two— ocean and mountainous woods—was a city that made more sense now—a downtown too big for the city's actual size, too many parks, too many cemeteries, too much of everything, really, and all of it a bit unreasonably beautiful. Tessa 'tched to herself. She would never be able to look at Lore with the same casual approving eye she once had.

Tessa turned from the window to examine Snow's apartment. The rooms themselves looked more like movie sets than any place a real person lived, which was fitting she supposed. The floors were a gleaming white, perhaps some kind of thick lacquer on top of wood, and everything else was white or faint grey with occasional pops of either a pale or electric blue. The kitchen was all gleaming stainless steel and white marble, and marble statues littered the wide-open spaces, figures mostly, a few of which Tessa recognized, and all looking like beauty frozen in time. Tessa figured that was part of the appeal. Huge pieces of pale art hung on the walls. Snow stood next to a giant painting that was mostly white and almost blended into it with her pale skin, hair, and long, white silk robe. She looked effortlessly beautiful despite the hour. "To what do I owe the extremely early honor, Scion?"

Tessa looked away from her and took in the view again. "I need your help," Tessa said, crossing her arms.

"I'm unsurprised," Snow said, bored. "With what *exactly*."

"I need to get something out of the school, and I need you to take it from me and keep it here for a little while."

Snow raised one eyebrow suspiciously, "Sounds deceptively simple. Is that all?"

Tessa nodded. "Yes, but we need to go now."

"Yes, yes, of course it's now. Everything is always now with you, Scion," Snow said, walking to the back bedroom. Tessa sat down on the white angled couch. She figured someone like Snow would take just this side of forever to get ready, but nearly as soon as Tessa sat down, Snow breezed out of the room again. Her hair was piled elegantly on her head, and she was clad in a plunging, bright white sweater dress that belted at her waist and hugged her slender curves dramatically. She wore a pair of amazing grey boots that came up above her knee, artfully covered with straps and buckles. She looked like a freaking supermodel. Again. A jerk, but still a supermodel. Damn.

"Um…okay," Tessa said, looking her up and down then self-consciously running a hand through her own hair which she had barely even bothered to comb. Snow grabbed some keys, sunglasses, and a soft grey bag (that must have cost at least a thousand dollars) off a table by the front door and nodded at Tessa impatiently.

"Coming, Scion?" she called. Tessa scrambled to her feet, grabbing her giant empty duffle in the process, and followed Snow out into the hall and down into the underground garage. Snow turned the key and the engine roared to life.

"How do you manage it? You've been here barely two days and you have a car, a completely outfitted penthouse, a slew of gorgeous clothes, who knows what else?"

Snow rolled her eyes. "You know the part of my name you keep leaving out?"

"Huh?"

"QUEEN. I'm The Snow QUEEN, Scion. You think I got that way by not knowing how to get things done? Please," she said, peeling out of the garage at a bracing clip.

"Someone was in my house last night."

"Mortal or Story?" Snow asked, as she took a tight turn going at least forty.

"Definitely Story," Tessa said, grimacing at the speed.

"Who was it?"

"I'm not sure. I didn't get a name...didn't even ask, come to think of it. Although, that's hardly my fault since it was three am. I figure I'm lucky I was conscious and wearing clothes."

"Well, describe them, perhaps we can narrow it down. Male or female, or something else perhaps?"

"Male, definitely male. Devastatingly handsomely male."

"That doesn't narrow it down much."

"Yeah, are you all like that?"

"Like what?"

"In a word? HOT."

"I suppose. You're unlikely to find a lot of wallflowers. Very few plain janes. Most are written as 'the most beautiful' or, of course, the reverse. Extremes are popular in Fiction. Some of your more modern tales are deliberately not that way perhaps, but you're less likely to run into them."

"Why's that?"

"New Fiction tends to play itself out for a hundred years or so before it gets bored and starts pushing on its boundaries, discovers what it truly is, how it can cross into other worlds. Since they each live in their own perfectly constructed worlds, some Stories can go centuries before they even realize they can step outside those—pages—for lack of a better word."

"Interesting," Tessa said, and then flinched as they careened past a busload of elementary school children while going a cool seventy.

"I suppose. So what else? I'll need more details than 'devastatingly handsome'."

"Oh, right. Um, tall, at least six foot three, maybe four. Dark hair very short, shaved down in fact. Broad shouldered, moved like…liquid. Had a dark voice, almost a British accent, sort of. It was hard to tell his eye color but I think they were dark grey. Big strong hands, lots of muscle, wearing jeans and a black t-shirt," Tessa detailed, trying to conjure up the visual from memory.

"Sorry, doesn't ring a bell."

"Seriously?"

"Scion, you just described half the fantasy men of Fiction. I mean you could have just said 'tall, dark, and handsome' and I'd have about as much to go on. The accent is your best clue, Stories frequently have the accent of their original story, although you said it didn't sound like true British so that could mean it's not his original language. It could be a blend or something he picked up here, depending on how long he's been in the Mortal world." Snow shifted into a lower gear and jammed her foot down on the accelerator. Tessa winced at their speed as a 25 mph sign whizzed past them. "What did he want?"

"I'm not sure. He *said* he was there to help. He mentioned me needing a new Advocate. Is that something I need?"

"It certainly would make things easier. And perhaps you'd annoy *me* less."

"Very funny." Tessa sat in silence for a moment.

"Did he provide any actual help?" Snow asked, pushing a strand of white hair from her face.

"No. I threw him out." Tessa paused. "Should I have let him help?"

"I have no idea, Scion," Snow said, and it sounded both honest and as if she didn't much care one way or another. Tessa frowned and looked at Snow.

"Is there another Advocate? I mean, can I just go to The Advocate store and get a new one?" she asked, and then bit her lip. Bishop hadn't even been dead for two days and here she was trying to replace him. She felt like a complete jerk.

"I don't know much," Snow said. "There used to be loads of Advocates, a handful of families that knew about the Story dimension and The Scion, that trained and studied and helped new Scions, that passed information down to their children, almost like a calling. Like any kind of tradition, I guess, with parents wanting kids to grow up and be doctors or lawyers, but these families wanted them to be Advocates. A lot of honor in it, I suppose.

"Knowing secrets that nobody else does, knowing magic is real, all that crap. I don't know how they decided who was next amongst the handful of families involved, who should be called, if there was anything prophetic about it or if they just drew straws. We didn't have a lot of direct contact with them. The relationship between Story and The Advocate has always been a bit *adversarial*.

When Scions stopped being called, we stayed in touch with some Advocate families for a while.

"But a hundred-and-fifty years is a long time for Mortals and most of us in Story honestly believed it was over. That 'The Last Scion' prophecy was hogwash and that you'd all died out." Snow cast a glance at Tessa who was gripping the dash in silent protest of their bracing speed. "Obviously, that's turned out not to be the case."

"Bishop seemed to know a lot, like he had training or something," Tessa said, gritting her teeth.

"Could be," Snow said, disinterested. Tessa scrunched down in her seat. Her stomach hurt. Not from the crazy driving which she was actually getting used to but from a feeling of dread in her gut. She didn't know if it was guilt tied to Bishop's death or something else, but whatever it was, it was horrible.

The car screeched to a halt in the barren school parking lot. "Not here," Tessa said, looking around. "In the back, where the faculty parking is," she said, pointing to the side of the building. Snow drove them around to the back and parked in a space up front marked with yellow lines. Tessa almost said something and then figured it was pointless. She *was* The Snow Queen, surely she could get out of something as mundane as parking tickets. Snow looked at Tessa and raised her fingers on the wheel expectantly.

"What now?"

"I'm going into the school. I want you to go stand by those windows," Tessa pointed to a bank of windows perhaps fifty yards away under a large tree. "In about five minutes I'm going to drop this bag out that window, and I want you to take it to your apartment for safe keeping."

"Ugh," Snow rolled her eyes. "It's going to be heavy, isn't it?"

"Yes. Yes, the bag will be heavy," Tessa said, annoyed. Snow motioned around the car dramatically.

"You know Scion, has it occurred to you that I don't actually have any minions here? This is minions work. Why don't you get yours to—"

"No. We're leaving them out of this. Besides, neither of them have cars, or at least I can't imagine they do," Tessa said opening the door.

"Fine, Scion, but if I break a nail—"

"—If you break a nail, what? You'll just have to magic it back together?"

"Well, *yes*," Snow said, pouting her lip out.

Tessa rolled her eyes. "Oh, the horror!" she said, her face wrenched in mock terror. "Get over it," she added, yanking the duffel out and slamming the door. Tessa leaned down through the window. "And pick me up at 2:55 this afternoon out front. I need your help with something else." Snow scowled and then did a half-decent impression of what Tessa thought a real minion probably did sound like.

"Yesssss my lieeeegeeeee."

Tessa rolled her eyes again and ran toward the school. Snow sat in her car for five full minutes without moving. She thought about leaving for every second of those five minutes and then sighed, opened her door in a huff, and hiked through the damp grass over to the windows Tessa had indicated.

Tessa had timed the visit just right, likely thanks to Snow's insane driving. As it was, it was late enough that the doors were open and early enough that there were only a few crazy over-achieving souls present. Tessa ran down the hall to the administrative office and, after a quick peek assuring her it was still quiet and dark, she walked through the open space, past the massive front desk, and to a small cluster of offices to search for Bishop's office. It was the first one, with his name on a plaque beside the door and two chairs, Tessa assumed for misbehaving students, in the hallway beside it.

Tessa pushed on the handle but the door was locked. She then pushed harder, a whole lot harder, and it snapped open. Tessa edged the door open and strode inside. It felt wrong to be there, but ever since The Stranger had appeared Tessa hadn't been able to shake the idea that there might be something here that could help her, even if she wasn't ready or willing to have a new Advocate. Looking at the small office, she discovered she had been really, really right. So right that she should have brought another bag, or five. The whole wall was bookshelves and they were filled beyond capacity, mostly with books that looked like they had nothing to do with being a high school counselor and everything to do with Scions and Stories.

Tessa flung the massive duffel onto the desk and opened the mouth widely. She surveyed the wall of books and tried to decide what to take, where to start. She began yanking the largest books off the shelves, as well as the ones that looked the oldest and most worn. In moments, the bag was filled to bursting. She zipped it up just as she heard people in the hallway. Tessa had intended to toss the bag out the window by the front desk, but Bishop's office had a window and so she used that instead, hoping Snow wouldn't be thrown by the small change, if she was even still out there. Tessa opened the window and tossed the bag, with all the gentleness she could muster, onto the damp grass below. Tessa thought of going through the window herself, but there was no time as the voices were now upon her. Instead, Tessa let the window fall shut behind her and reached for another book on the now somewhat ransacked shelves. She looked up as she heard a key in the lock.

"That's strange, his office isn't locked—"

Tessa tried not to look guilty as the woman who had given Tessa her class schedule on her first day pushed the door open and snapped on the light before clutching at her chest in surprise to see Tessa standing there. Tessa tried hard to remember her name…Amy or maybe Angela, something like that. Damn. She wasn't sure.

"Sorry," Tessa said, one hand raised in what she hoped was a calm, *'let me explain'* kind of way. Behind the startled blonde administrator were two people that were in no way schoolteachers or administrators. A black woman, about five foot eight with close-cropped hair stood directly behind the administrator. She was fit and maybe thirty years old, wearing a white t-shirt, jeans, flat boots, and a brown leather jacket. She was striking, with large dark eyes that seemed like they didn't miss anything. Tessa immediately felt anxious under her gaze. The man next to her was slightly taller and perhaps half a dozen years older, white, with short, dark-brown hair. He was ruggedly handsome and wearing similar clothes to the woman, but his t-shirt was black as were his boots and leather jacket.

They both had shiny Detective badges dangling from their necks on chains.

Crap! Tessa thought inside her head so loud that she was sure everyone in the room could hear it.

"Miss…" the administrator trailed off as if searching for Tessa's name the same way Tessa had searched for hers a moment ago. Tessa quickly volunteered her last name.

"Battle."

"Yes," the blonde woman said looking at her and then back to the Detectives, "Miss Battle, whatever are you doing in Mr. Bishop's office unattended? How did you even get in here? It should have been locked," she looked around, a bit thrown.

Tessa shook her head and shrugged her shoulders. "It was open."

The administrator squinted her eyes at Tessa waiting for her to answer the other questions.

Tessa looked at the book in her hands.

"Oh. Uh. My book, I came back to get my book, which I left here, yesterday," she said, hoping the lie sounded remotely plausible. "So um, I have it now and so I'll just be going then," Tessa said, and made a slight movement toward the three of them. The administrator moved a bit as if to let Tessa through but the detectives didn't move at all. The man looked at the administrator and smiled charmingly.

"Angela. Thanks so much for your help, we can take it from here." Angela fairly melted into herself, nodded, said something even Tessa's superhearing couldn't pick out and excused herself. The whole time the other detective stared at Tessa, who had begun to sweat.

"Um, is there a problem?" Tessa asked, knowing full well there was a very serious problem.

"Miss Battle," the female detective began, "I'm Detective Wade, this is Detective Ripley. We're investigating the death of Mr. Bishop." Tessa was a practiced liar, but she found something especially repellant in lying about Bishop, pretending she didn't know and faking concern when she felt quite real guilt and sadness.

"I…I'm sorry," Tessa began, "I didn't know." Tessa tucked her head and clutched the book to her chest.

"How could you have?" Detective Wade said, looking at Tessa even more intently than before. Wade finally broke the stare and turned to Detective Ripley, who was examining the ransacked shelves.

"Looks like everyone took a book, Miss Battle," he said, his words careful but somehow not as accusatory as they seemed. Tessa glanced at the shelves.

"I wouldn't know. I only took this one. Mine."

Detective Wade reached out her hand. "May I see it?" Tessa hesitated, she didn't even know which one she had taken. Could be something horribly implicating, or totally innocuous.

"Of course," she said, extending it to the detective, her heart hammering in her chest so loudly it was making it hard for her to hear herself speak. As she did so, she saw that it was emblazoned with elaborate gold foil script that said only *Fairy Tales*. Detective Wade raised an eyebrow at the title while Detective Ripley shot her a look Tessa couldn't quite understand.

"Fairy Tales?" Detective Wade asked.

"It's—a family heirloom."

"And so why did Bishop have it?" Ripley cut in smoothly.

"He asked to see it," Tessa said, wishing she had something to do with her hands and so she thrust them in her jacket pockets. Wade flipped through the book casually.

"Where were you last night between the hours of eight and ten p.m., Miss Battle?" Wade asked, without looking up. Tessa noticed that now while Wade ignored her, Ripley was clearly studying her.

"Home," she said flatly. Ripley opened his mouth to speak. "Yes, alone. No, nobody can verify it," Tessa continued, growing weary of the charade.

"Well, aren't we a little Miss Junior Detective," Wade said, looking up from the book and smiling. Tessa returned the smile, growing bold, perhaps foolishly.

"No. Just seen enough *Law & Order* episodes to last me a lifetime." She caught Ripley smiling despite himself.

"Your parents can't verify this?" Ripley asked.

"My dad is in San Francisco for work. My mom isn't in the picture."

Wade looked at something in the front of the book she had taken from Tessa and then snapped it shut. "Here," she said, handing the book back to Tessa. "Don't leave the county, Miss Battle," she added, as if that was a way of saying goodbye. Tessa rolled her eyes.

"I'm seventeen, where do you think I'm going? Cross-country murder spree?" Tessa took the book back and was outside the busted door before either of them could answer her. Standing just around the corner, catching her breath and trying to not sweat through her jacket, she overheard Ripley speaking.

"Why'd you give it back to her?"

"Had her name in it," Wade said matter-of-factly.

Tessa blinked and threw open the book. Sure enough, inside, written in faded but otherwise elaborate, elegant, and absolutely perfect calligraphy were the words *"Property of The Battle Family."* Tessa's head rocked back in surprise, her mouth open.

"Holy crap."

ELEVEN

Standing next to Tessa's locker were Brand and Micah, who surely deserved to win prizes in the 'never giving up' category if nothing else. Tessa almost went the other direction, but she needed to get in that locker, as much to hide the massive tome in her hands as to get the book she should have taken home for first period, but hadn't.

She still had to get rid of them though. Things were even worse than yesterday if that was possible. She could now add prime murder suspect to her list of massive problems. Man, she had to be the worst Scion in the history of Scions. She was just absolutely unwilling to get two of the only people she'd ever liked killed because she was crappy at being some kind of destiny-superhero-chosen-one-type-person, even if that meant her only "friend" was the goddamn Snow Queen.

But this "infection" Snow had mentioned was a new wrinkle. Tessa had no idea if it was better to tell them now or not, but she was leaning toward not. At least until she had more information. So, for now, Tessa hooded her eyes into a practiced look of boredom and cruised up onto her locker as if she had not a care in the world. Naturally, Brand dived in first.

"Tessa, c'mon. You have to talk to us. Are you alright? Has anything else…*insane* happened?" The words came out so fast they started to merge before he finished one question and started another.

"Brand," Micah said calmly, putting a hand on his arm and locking eyes with him briefly. "Stop."

Tessa yanked the locker open and jammed the *Fairy Tales* book inside, exchanging it for her book and a spiral notebook which had exactly zero pages of completed homework inside.

"Tessa," Micah began. Tessa raised up a hand but Micah rolled right over her. "No. Yesterday *you* talked. Today you listen. We're not your pets and you need to stop treating us like we are. You may be a superhero, but that doesn't make you better than us and you need to stop acting like you are. Our lives are clearly in jeopardy because we know you. Now, we're reasonably okay with that because we like you when you're not being a raging hell-bitch, but you can't keep trying to shut us out. It's obviously dangerous for us no matter what at this point, since, you know, we were kidnapped and almost killed just for meeting you. So you need to just accept it. We're in this, if only because the best way to keep from getting dead is to arm ourselves with as much knowledge as possible. You have until lunch to get over this whole idea of stonewalling us into going away, okay?" And with that, shy Micah Chen turned on her heel and walked away, her hands jammed into the front of yet another faded hoodie. Tessa stared after her, shocked and more than a little impressed. Brand did the same.

A moment later, he snapped out of it, looked at Tessa, and added, "Yeah. What she said!" But as he walked away, he turned a corner and a giant grin broke across his face. "We'll see you at lunch!"

Tessa smiled. They'd made it impossible to get rid of them.

She couldn't believe how thankful she felt for it.

She hoped it didn't get them killed.

In class Tessa saw Nash walk by in the hallway and he threw up a little wave that caused her stomach to flip-flop. Life had become very strange, very suddenly. She wished there was a way to keep parts of it—some actual friends, flirting with boys, knowing a person with a perfectly restored 1969 silver Jaguar—and ditch the rest. All the destiny, horror, murder, guilt, and fear. Not to mention the feeling in all of it that she was now, and for the rest of her life, short though it may turn out to be, an outcast that would never again fit in.

Tessa had felt like an outcast for about as long as she could remember. She had embraced it at some point, learned to use it to her advantage. Because once you already feel like you can't fit in then it feels better if you try to own it, if you try to pretend it's your decision. The way she chose to look was a nice comfortable cover to trick people into thinking that she didn't fit in on purpose. That she'd made the decision herself. And most of the time, she felt okay about it, and at some point, the pretend became true. But now. Now that she knew there was no way to go back, that no matter what she did, she would never be able to belong or fit in, that she was a true outcast, forever, well, an ocean of fear and sadness had settled on her and she didn't know if it would ever go away, worse, she feared it might swallow her whole.

Micah watched Greyson utterly destroy a violin solo, effortlessly moving from dark to delicate and then back again. A year ago, Micah would have seethed with jealousy from her second chair, but ever since she'd fallen in love with the drums, she didn't care whose chair was in front of hers when it came to violin. Her lack of caring bothered her teacher immensely, almost as much as it bothered her parents, but Micah was beyond caring about either. Keeping her love of the drums a secret from her teacher had been difficult; it had been surprisingly less difficult to keep it from her absentee parents. She was still a great violinist which kept them off her back in general, though the looks from both as she fell from first chair to second could have been printed in the dictionary under "disappointment."

Micah had known without asking that "badass drummer" didn't fit into the whole "Asian Musical Prodigy" thing her parents were so fond of, so drums had become her own little happy but very secret rebellion. She had hated the Asian cliché aspect of the musical prodigy thing anyway. In fact, she liked to pretend to Brand that her hatred of the cliché was why she didn't get better grades. *"Gotta break stereotypes, Brand."* She liked to say when her report cards came back filled with B's and C's. But if the cliché was part of what made her so good at playing the drums then she was grateful for it, even if she'd never admit it out loud. Her secret rebellion meant she kept her drums at Brand's house and she wore even bigger clothes than usual—almost exclusively hoodies and cargos—so she could keep her sticks with her at all times. Was a secret rebellion even a rebellion? She wasn't sure. She didn't care.

She'd found the drums and that was all that mattered.

Watching Greyson be brilliant on the violin did nothing but inspire her with respect. It also made her think how much she'd like to be in a band with him. Her raw powerful drumming paired with his sweetly smooth violin. She could totally hear it. It sounded like bliss.

The bell rang, shattering the moment. Greyson stopped and smiled, lowering his instrument and bow. Their teacher beamed and then clapped, as did a few others before putting their instruments away. Greyson looked at Micah, pleased with himself, but hoping for her approval.

"Amazing, Grey," she said, smiling and truly happy for him. The way he looked at the violin was how she looked at the drums and that made her feel united with him even as they were pitted against one another.

"Thanks, Micah," he said. "I'm really happy with it."

"You should be," Micah said nodding. "You've really mastered that piece."

Grey ducked his head shyly and gathered his things together. "You going to lunch?"

"Yeah, meeting Brand, you wanna come with?"

"Maybe for a minute."

In the cafeteria, they stood in line and Greyson feigned interest in the macaroni and cheese rather than in Ian Powell, a few students ahead of them in line. Micah bumped him with her elbow.

"Obvious," Micah said, covering it with a cough that was also a laugh, staring at Greyson over her glasses.

"What?" he asked innocently and then rolled his eyes. "Fine. I have a crush."

"No kidding," Micah said, paying for her lunch and looking for Brand. She spotted him in the courtyard as Brand gestured from a reasonably quiet table where he sat with a sulking Tessa. Micah nudged Grey, and they weaved their way over.

𝕏

Tessa looked up, her face stormy and confused, but when she saw Micah wasn't alone she pushed it away and smiled a smile anyone would have believed genuine. The boy with Micah smiled back, all charm.

"Hey," he said, nodding and putting down his tray.

"Hey," Tessa echoed. Micah nodded at Grey and then nodded at Tessa as she sat down.

"Tessa, Greyson. Greyson, Tessa."

"Hey," they said in unison again and then smiled. Tessa reached across the table to shake his hand. He joined her and then Brand piped in and reached out a fist, which Greyson bumped.

"Long time no see, man. Where you been?"

"Oh, um, traveling a bit, I guess," Grey said, shrugging, and then he cast an expectant look at Micah. "So, you think I got a shot?" Tessa and Brand exchanged puzzled glances. Micah put down her fork.

"What's all this?" Brand asked, gesturing between the two of them, half a sandwich crammed in his mouth.

"Grey has a thing for Ian Powell," Micah said as she fluttered her eyes dramatically. Grey smacked her on the arm.

"Don't make fun."

"Oh, we will indeed make fun," Brand said, inhaling the other half of his sandwich.

"Ian?" Tessa asked. Micah scanned the windows into the cafeteria. She saw him at a table with a few friends and pointed him out to Tessa.

"There. Shaved head, dark eyes, flawless skin, blue t-shirt, lean build, *exceptional* hands," Micah recited. Tessa followed her gaze, and Brand cut Micah a look and threw a chip at her.

"Exceptional hands? Are you sure *you're* not crushing on him?"

Micah sniffed with a superior air. "I say it with the eyes of a musician, not the eyes of a lusty teenage girl."

Grey laughed, everyone laughed.

"So go over," Tessa urged. Grey spun on her, rather horrified.

"Oh. Oh no. No way."

"Why not?" Brand asked licking his salty fingers.

"He doesn't even know I exist."

"And he won't if you keep this up," Micah said.

"I'm planning my move," Grey said, not entirely convincingly.

"Dude. You have *no* moves," Brand said more convincingly.

"I do so have moves. They're just old, and slow, and…totally untested," he said, generating a chuckle from the table. Tessa watched Ian move across the lunchroom. Micah was right, he had beautiful hands.

"You'd best hurry. Handsome like that doesn't stay single long," she said and took a sip of bottled water. Just as she did so, Nash walked by the table, casually bumping fists with Grey wordlessly and then smiling at Tessa.

"Hey, Tessa," he said, without stopping. Tessa's face flushed and then bulged as she choked on her mouthful of water. She turned just in time to *almost* avoid hitting Grey in the face with the spray she coughed up. Brand burst into laughter. Grey patted himself dry with a napkin while Micah chuckled, watching Nash walk away. Tessa buried her head in her hands.

"I'm so sorry," she said to Grey, still hiding her face.

Grey laughed good-naturedly, wiping some water off his cheek. "The sound of Nash saying one's name is more than enough reason to lose control of bodily functions."

"Gross," Brand said.

Grey nodded, "Yeah, that sentence went wrong."

"How do you know Nash?" Micah breathed at Tessa, more than a little awe in her tone.

"I don't. I mean, he's in my Trig class and American History," Tessa fumbled, still avoiding their eyes. Micah let out a long low whistle and Grey nodded appreciatively.

"Lucky, lucky girl," Micah said.

"He not only knows her name but is using it all casual-like. Takes most of us lesser beings ages to get a casual hello like that from Nash. And I should know. I row crew with him and it took me a month to get a casual name drop," Grey said while Tessa turned a shade of red just shy of her bright hair.

"You guys are making a big deal out of nothing," she said, waving them off. A bell rang somewhere in the distance, and Grey sprang up, pulling his mostly untouched tray of food with him.

"Damn. I've got to get across the quad," he said, already heading away from the table. "Later." Everyone offered half waves, and Tessa started to get up too.

Micah yanked her back down. "That wasn't our bell," she said, looking at her watch. "We've still got ten more minutes. So. You're here. I assume that means you're done pushing us away?"

Tessa sighed heavily, "Micah, I'm not going to accept this idea of you two getting involved in all of this, I'm just not, but I can't deny that you may be in trouble." Micah and Brand listened and chewed their food. Tessa cast her eyes down, embarrassed. "Yesterday Snow said something about, well, that Mortals can't go to Story without changing."

Brand sputtered to life. "CHANGING?!" Micah and Tessa hissed at him and looked around to see if the other tables had noticed. They had, but they seemed to lose interest fast. "Are we talking superpowers? Or something like, oh, I don't know, ending up with a FROG'S HEAD!?!?"

Tessa shrugged helplessly. "I don't know. She used the word…infected."

"INFECTED!?!" he shouted, and at this everyone left in the courtyard turned to stare at their table, looks of horror and more than a few expressions of absolute delight on their faces.

"Hush!" Micah whisper screamed.

"Mike, she just said infected!" he yelled again, heedless of her pleas to lower his voice.

"I heard her. Stop screaming, you're freaking me out. Tessa, who can we ask, what can we do?"

"I can ask Snow more questions, I guess?"

"Oh yes, let's ask the evil freaking Snow Queen!" Brand shouted. Micah shot him another look.

"Do you think she'll know, or that she'll even be willing to help?" Micah asked.

"I don't know, Micah. I mean, we obviously can't trust her but she's been pretty helpful in general. She's picking me up from school today so I'll ask her then."

"*We'll,*" Brand cut in, decidedly calmer, "*We'll* ask her then." Tessa dropped her gaze.

"Okay, meet me in the back parking lot after school and we'll ask her together." Tessa stood and reached for her tray. Micah looked up at her. Tessa looked down at her two new friends, the only ones she'd really ever had, and wished she'd never met them, wished she'd never gotten them involved in any of this. "You guys, I'm sorry. I, I wish I could take it all back."

"But you can't Tessa. And it's not your fault. We made our own choices. Let's just figure out what it means, okay?" Micah cut the comment with a light smile that was full of forgiveness and friendship, despite everything. Tessa smiled back and hoped hers looked the same but knew it was likely full of guilt and sadness. Tessa turned to go, but as she did, her tray was smacked violently upward, and the remaining food barely missed covering her. Tessa looked up to find the bully from the hallway, plus three more, standing in front of her. Tessa couldn't help but smile. She'd had her fair share of tussles with bullies, but bullies were gonna be WAY easier to handle now. Brand tugged on her jacket sleeve.

"Um…ixnay on the uperpowersay," he said, glancing around and indicating the straggling witnesses. Tessa blew out a breath, he wasn't wrong. Tessa smiled at the bully and his mini cadre of evil.

"Back for more?" Tessa asked.

"Oh yes, please hit me again when I'm not looking," he said, his words drenched in sarcasm. Micah tried to stand up and the lone girl of the group laid a hand on her shoulder and pushed her down, hard. Tessa wanted this over fast, or she wasn't going to be able to stop Micah and Brand from getting pummeled and an even bigger scene. The courtyard was mostly empty now, only a few audience members. Tessa mentally restrained herself as much as humanly possible, made a fist, and threw a punch straight at the bully's face. He couldn't possibly miss it coming at him this time. He went rocketing backwards at least ten feet and collided violently with a trashcan, falling to the ground like a mean sack of potatoes. His toadies stood around, mostly shocked and unsure. Tessa looked pointedly at the others.

"Anyone else?" she looked from face to face, which either stared blankly back at her, or cast their eyes to the ground. "I thought not," Tessa said, and then added. "You bother me or my friends again, and that is so the tiniest sliver of the beating I'm going to dish out." Tessa motioned to Brand and Micah to follow her.

Brand smiled proudly. "I could soooo get used to this," and then after a pause added, "Well, without the whole infection thing, of course."

At 2:55 pm Tessa walked outside the building to find Micah and Brand anxiously waiting for her, Micah leaning against the building, banging some drumsticks on the bricks, and Brand pacing a little brown patch into the grass. He may or may not have been talking to himself. Snow was, naturally, nowhere to be seen. When Brand saw Tessa, he stopped and his shoulders slumped.

"She's not here," he said, dejected.

Tessa looked around the emptying parking lot. "Let's give her a minute. She strikes me as someone that enjoys making others wait." The three friends sat on the metal railing, their feet dangling, and waited as the school grounds and parking lot emptied. Nash strolled out about ten minutes later and stopped when he saw Tessa.

"Hey, Tessa. You need a ride somewhere?"

Tessa tried not to blush, and managed to shake her head. "No, we're waiting for someone, thanks."

Nash looked from Tessa to Micah and Brand and then back to Tessa, "Oh, sorry, I didn't realize you were all waiting together—" he nodded at Brand and Micah. "Hey, Micah, Brand." They nodded back at him, transfixed. Tessa smiled at their stunned silence. Nash smiled at Tessa again. "See you tomorrow." Tessa gave him a half wave as he disappeared across the parking lot. Brand and Micah looked at one another.

"He knew our names," Brand said, his smile huge in his face.

Micah mirrored him. "Did you know he knew our names?"

"No way." Brand shook his head. "Today is looking up, infection or no." Micah nodded in agreement and Tessa chuckled at both of them amazed at their ability to stay positive. She should take lessons from them.

Five minutes later, Snow's silver Jaguar screeched into the parking lot and came to a halt in front of them. Brand jumped off the railing and Tessa put a hand up. "Wait, okay?"

Brand hesitated briefly before obeying. Snow climbed out of the car and looked at Tessa over the roof.

"You're late, Snow," Tessa said, trying to keep things light-ish.

"Apologies, Scion. But the responsibilities of an emissary are many."

"Such as?" Tessa asked, eyebrow cocked, her arms folded across her chest.

"Specifically? Someone woke me up far too early, so I had to catch up on my beauty sleep. Despite what you may think, *this*," and she paused to gesture toward her general self, "Does not come easily."

Tessa groaned a little. "Okay. Well, thanks for showing up at all then, I *guess*. But before we go, I have to ask you something." Snow cast her bored eyes at Tessa who gestured to her friends standing behind her. "What's going to happen to Micah and Brand? They deserve to know."

Snow sharpened her eyes at Tessa. "I don't know what that change will be, Scion. Nobody does." At this, Micah and Brand could hold back no longer and rushed to the car. Snow rolled her eyes, irritated. "Oh joy. More minion contact."

Brand brushed off the insult. "How can you not know?"

Snow smiled at Brand. "As I understand it, and please keep in mind, I have never actually seen it, the change is based on the individual," she said. "Something in the person that visits—maybe a latent talent or skill, a passion, or perhaps some aspect of their heritage—Story can latch onto it and can *embellish* it, for lack of a better word."

"And it's permanent?" Tessa asked.

"Yes," Snow said definitively. "It's like a little bit of Story getting wedged into you, only there's no way to un-wedge it."

"When will it happen?" Micah asked, pained.

"No way to know," Snow shrugged. "Could be tomorrow, could be in a year. Could have already happened. Sometimes it just comes, sometimes something triggers it, like an evolutionary leap."

"Great, we're gonna end up mutants, probably useless ones," Brand mumbled.

Tessa looked at her friends, "Guys I…"

Brand hung his head in despair. Snow studied him for a long moment and her eyes flashed briefly with something she'd long ago forgotten. She smiled at him in a new way. "Cheer up, my dove. Maybe it will be something delightful."

Brand looked up at Micah and Tessa and mouthed *'My dove?'*

Tessa looked at Snow suspiciously. "What happened to 'minions'?"

Snow scrunched her pointer finger up and down playfully at Brand like she was waving to him with just her finger. "I've decided I like that one. He smells innocent."

Brand's eyes widened, horrified. "What? No. No way. I DO NOT." Micah and Tessa both stifled a laugh. And just as they did, Greyson walked out of the building behind them.

"Whoa. Amazing car, who—" he stopped midsentence as he saw Snow, "—oh shit," he said, his mouth dropping open in shock.

"Hello, Romeo," Snow said coolly, a devious smile taking over her beautiful face.

TWELVE

"What?!" Tessa said, looking from Snow to Grey confused, "Not—you're not—you mean—?"

"Spit it out, Scion," Snow said, a smile somehow both devious and bored on her face.

"Scion?" Grey repeated, dumfounded, looking at Snow as Micah and Brand stood, watching the back and forth like a tennis match, their mouths hanging open. "But, The Scion—"

"Is a boy," Snow said, finishing for him. "Unless it's 'The Last'," she said making air quotes around 'the' and 'last.' "In which case, it's *this*," she said, pointing disdainfully at Tessa.

"But that means—"

"End of days if you want to go home, Romeo."

"But I don't want to go back."

"Well, then, HAPPY DAY, maybe you'll get stuck here," she said gesturing around her with false gaiety.

"But only if she dies, right?"

"HEY! *She* is right here," Tessa said, annoyed. "And she is very much alive and plans on staying that way!"

Grey ducked his head apologetically but said nothing.

Tessa began again, "Let's get back to the topic at hand. You are Romeo. Like *Romeo and Juliet*, Romeo. That one. The big one. *The* Romeo."

"Yes," Grey cut Snow a look. "And thanks, by the way, for outing me, Snow. Very classy."

Snow shrugged as if she couldn't care less. Brand jumped in, "No offense Grey, but I thought Romeo was white?"

Grey nodded, "Yes and no. The rules on something like that are a little flexible. There are different version of me throughout the years, not all of them traditionally white or European. My story is an obvious one for the exploration of race issues, which has happened a lot in more modern times. Those variations give me a flexibility about how I appear. Here in the Mortal world, my appearance is even more versatile, and this is what feels right to me." Brand nodded but looked as flummoxed as Tessa felt. She looked between Snow and Romeo.

"But if you don't always look the same then how did she recognize you?"

"He still looks like Romeo," Snow said flatly, "You can't hide something that fundamental with the spell he got. Certainly not from another Story."

Tessa shook her head, even more confused. "They really should make a handbook with all these goddamn rules," she said. Micah and Brand nodded soundlessly in agreement. Tessa looked back to Greyson. "What are you doing here? At Lore High?"

"I, I had to get out. Made a deal, paid for a favor. Got myself jaunted here and hidden away, well, until now," he said motioning at Snow.

"Why did you leave? I mean, you're *Romeo*, man! That has got to be a good deal, well, until the end," Brand said, still trying to wrap his brain around it.

"Oh." Micah said and then closed her mouth.

"Oh." Tessa said, catching on.

"Yeah," Grey said twisting up his mouth.

"Oh what?!" Brand demanded, looking between the three of them. "What am I missing?"

"He's gay," Micah said.

"Oh," Brand said, and then a moment later, "OH."

"Yeah," Grey repeated. "Juliet is great, she's amazing, I love her, I just don't *love* her, or at least I don't think I do. The more I'm here the more sure I am. I had to get out and find out for myself. It's felt wrong for ages. But I didn't know why," he said, stuffing his hands in his pockets. Micah turned to Snow.

"And you two know each other?"

"Romeo knows everybody, don't you, darling," she purred. Grey looked at her flatly.

"No. No, I don't know everybody. But I know Snow," Grey's lip curled into a cartoonish half-sneer. Tessa, Brand, and Micah stood there expectantly.

"Annnnnd?" Tessa asked, prompting him to get on with it. Grey sighed heavily, defeated, and the gesture seemed refreshingly honest to Tessa.

"I know Snow because Father Laurence sent me to her to help get me to the Mortal world. To Lore."

"—Cause plans made by that dude always go so well," Brand muttered.

Grey nodded his head in acquiescence before he continued. "Anyway, she hooked me up with Fairy Godmother, and the rest is history…or something," he finished. Tessa looked between Grey and Snow.

"Do you owe her anything? Payment, favors—anything? Are you all paid up, or whatever, for her connecting you to—and I can't believe I'm saying this out loud—Fairy Godmother?"

Grey cast a hard glance at Snow. "We're all paid up." The steel in his voice made Tessa never want to know what Snow's price had been.

"Good. Second order of business. Do you have any intention of killing me in order to close the dimension border?"

"What?! Of course not. I'm no killer. I mean, except, like…myself."

The group stood around awkwardly, caught between the weirdness and the discomfort of the statement. Tessa broke the silence.

"Good. Then you can live and we can all be friends," she said, turning to get into Snow's car.

"Wait!" Grey cried and put his hand on the door. "I mean, you can't just walk away, I have so many questions, I haven't seen a Story in more than a year, and you're The Scion, and—" Tessa got in the car and pulled the door shut. She looked back up at him through the window.

"Do you have a car?"

"Yeah," Grey said, nodding to a big beat-up jeep at the end of the parking lot.

"Okay, meet us at Grand and Fairfax downtown. Bring Micah and Brand with you, I can't fit them in here." No sooner had she finished the sentence, then Snow gunned the engine and the car leapt away from them at an alarming speed. Micah, Brand, and Grey stood in the exhaust, dumbfounded, watching the streak of silver exit the parking lot.

"Wow. She's very—take charge, isn't she?"

"We call it bossy," Brand said, pulling on the strap of Grey's backpack. "C'mon, man." The trio headed for Grey's car in silence. Nobody knew what to say. Everything had been turned on its ear. Nothing fit or made sense anymore and yet, in other ways, nothing had changed at all. It was disturbing. And exciting. And strange. And scary. And nobody knew what might happen next.

There were four things on the corners of Grand and Fairfax downtown. One was a Starbucks, naturally. One was the entry to a large residential condo building. One was a rival coffee shop that didn't look like it was going to last long, despite being completely adorable. And one was a weapons store called BLADE. All caps, BLADE.

Nobody in the jeep was surprised to see Snow's gleaming car parked in front of BLADE. Micah, Brand, and Grey climbed out of the jeep and walked into the store. A sign hung in the window: *Proprietor: Sammy Dee Profit.*

The trio plunged into the dark store where they watched, mouths agape, as Tessa swung a massive broadsword about the room, narrowly avoiding a variety of objects. A slender middle-aged woman in a superhero t-shirt and jeans, who could only be Sammy Dee, proprietor at large, winced as Tessa barely missed slicing the helmeted head off some antique knight's battle armor. Tessa put the sword down on the counter that Snow was leaning against, clearly bored out of her mind.

"I'll take it, Sammy, er, rather, she will," Tessa said, thumbing her finger at Snow, who nodded. Sammy, clearly having seen far weirder things in her life than a teenager with a broadsword, smiled easily. Tessa turned to face her friends and gestured widely to the store. "What do you guys want? Snow's buying."

Micah looked around, wide-eyed. "How does something like this exist? I mean, Lore's a decent-size city but enough to warrant a shop like this, and called BLADE no less?"

Romeo smiled at her. "Your thinking is backwards. This shop surely exists because this is Lore, regardless of the size. I'd bet now that you know Tessa, and know about Story, you're going to notice a whole lot more weirdness. The kind of weirdness that justifies a shop like this."

Micah nodded and then looked at Sammy. "Got anything a little less intense than a broadsword?"

"Smaller blades are in the back, on the left. That includes hatchets and daggers," she said, gesturing absently as Tessa's pile of potential weapons purchases grew ever larger. Micah nodded and she and Brand headed to the back of the store.

Grey moved to follow Tessa. "Tessa, can we talk?"

Tessa picked up a long cruel looking sword with spikes on one side. "Yeah, but talk and browse. I've got a weapons cache to build. Some new thing breaks into my house every damn night and all I've got is a baseball bat. It's a good bat, but I need an upgrade. Besides, my dad will kill me if I break that bat."

"Sure," Grey said, running his fingers across some of weapons on a rack absently. "So, are you going to tell anyone where I am? Who I am?"

Tessa looked up at him, surprised. "Of course not. Although, I obviously can't say what 'Her Worship Of The White' will do," Tessa said, nodding her head in Snow's direction. "Not really in control of her at all. She seems to help me, at great aggravation to herself, but I have no idea what her endgame is," Tessa said, pointing a rifle at Snow and staring at her through the scope and then putting the gun down abruptly.

"Great," Grey said, following Tessa's gaze and watching Snow check her flawless reflection in the shiny blade of an axe on the wall. "So what you're saying is, I'm screwed."

"Probably," Tessa said and then added, "Who exactly is looking for you?"

"If I had to guess? Everyone. It doesn't sit well when the title character, or half of them, up and abandon their Story without a word. Juliet in particular is sure to be pissed. And as you know—" he paused and looked at Tessa. "You do know my Story, right?" Tessa shrugged.

"I saw the movie."

"Which one?" Grey asked, one eyebrow cocked and then waved his hand. "Never mind. Anyway, our families are always at war, or on the brink of one. My leaving can't have been good. I'm sure even if Juliet gets it, even if she doesn't despise me, her family has certainly not taken it well. A slight against their daughter, a slight against them, any excuse to rekindle the fires of war, which have never gone out, quite frankly."

"Gosh, I can't image why you would ever want to leave," Tessa said.

"But that's not even it," Grey said, taking down a sword, thin and tapered, with a decorative hilt, elegant compared to the brutish broadsword Tessa had been swinging.

"Nice," Tessa commented regarding the sword while she took down both a modern and an ancient looking crossbow to compare them. Grey swung the sword a few times expertly, as if it was second nature, which Tessa supposed it must have been. "What were you saying?" Tessa asked as she loaded the crossbow with a sturdy bolt. Grey turned to her quite seriously.

"I was saying I didn't leave because of the warring. I left because I was dying there. So much expectation and I never felt like it fit. I felt jammed into some mold that wasn't me, maybe it never was. I was drowning. And I don't think it *has* to be that way. I want to forge my own way, be my own man, whatever that means," Grey said, staring at the sword. Tessa had stopped fussing with the crossbow and was watching him.

"I get it," she said. He looked at her, his face full of emotion. "I get it," she said again and turned away from him. She plunked both of the crossbows on the counter next to the broadsword, then a brutal looking dagger, a shorter, less aggressive-looking dagger, a handful of Chinese throwing stars, a small axe, and an armload of bolts and arrows for the crossbows. "Brand, Micah! Pick and get up here!" Tessa shouted. She turned back to Grey. "You have nothing to fear from me, okay? And I'll do whatever I can to control Her Worship," Tessa said. Grey smiled, grateful. "And throw that sword on the pile," she said, nodding at his sword. There was a scrabble and a shout at the other end of the store. Tessa and Grey looked on, interest piqued. Brand and Micah eventually emerged, Brand empty handed and Micah with a badass hatchet. Brand looked around at a loss.

Sammy nodded at a pretty sword on the wall, "Try the Katana, kid."

Brand looked up at it and pulled it down, he broke into a big smile and brought it to the counter. Sammy Dee smiled at Brand's reaction, clearly pleased that she had helped Brand find his weapon, like a gifted matchmaker of violence.

"Ring her up," Tessa said, pointing to Snow, who stood up and walked over to Sammy Dee to do whatever thing it was she did that seemed to get her whatever it was she wanted.

Loading the weapons into Snow's trunk, minus the three items Micah, Brand, and Greyson had picked out, Snow, who had been eerily silent during the whole "weapons adventure," eyed Tessa. "Do you even know how to use any of that stuff?"

Tessa shrugged her shoulders and closed the trunk. "Not really." She paused and walked to the passenger door, "But I did pretty well with that awesome axe."

Snow nodded at her across the top of the car. "Perhaps we should get you a trainer."

Tessa said nothing. She wasn't sure if she should confide in Snow that she'd already sort of asked the mysterious nighttime Stranger to get her one.

"I'll reach out to The Court, perhaps they can put me in touch with an appropriate Story living in the Mortal world," she said. Tessa shook her head. "I don't want anything from them."

Snow glowered at her. "That's an interesting change of tune. You've been using my help quite freely, now you suddenly don't trust me?"

Tessa looked at Snow sideways. "What on earth gave you the impression that I trusted you?" Tessa opened the door and slid into the car. It was true that she had been leaning heavily on Snow the last few days for information, to get her things, and to get her from point A to point B, but it didn't mean she trusted her. Quite the opposite, in fact. Part of the reason she was staying so close to her was to keep an eye on her. And while she couldn't help but feel grateful that Snow had warned her about Bluebeard, and that intervention had probably saved Brand and Micah's lives, there was a difference between using Snow and trusting her. No, Tessa didn't trust anything about Snow, and it was hard to imagine that changing.

Snow got in the car and gunned the engine. They took off in silence. But Tessa couldn't help but notice a deadly chill in the air, despite the bright sun outside, as they rocketed down the street.

THIRTEEN

After one night of peace, Tessa woke up in the early still dark hours of Saturday morning to something breaking into her house, *again*. This time, she was more prepared.

Broadsword in hand, she went to investigate.

She found a giant jungle cat the size of a couch lying on the middle of her living room floor. It purred angrily at Tessa (if such a thing was possible) as her bare foot hit the foyer floor. Tessa recoiled in fear before catching herself and slowing her breathing. "Show no fear," she reminded herself quietly, hoping the thing didn't understand English. The tiger watched her closely, unmoving. Tessa racked her brain for fictional jungle cats and could only think of the *Jungle Book*.

"Nice Shere Kahn kitty," Tessa said, approaching the cat, her sword at her side but lowered, as if in the hopes that the cat just wanted some nice milk. All the milk in the world and brought to it in the form of big meaty cows, but milk just the same. The cat roared and Tessa froze. The Tiger began to rise, and Tessa thought about just running full tilt for the front door, but partway through the motion of standing, the animal began to change shape. No sooner did she recognize what was happening than it had become a bird. A dark black crow. Could Shere Kahn shape-shift? She certainly didn't remember that from the story. The crow flew up and perched on the mantelpiece for just a moment and then flew right at her head. Tessa threw her arms up to protect her face and felt the bird snatch a piece of hair from her head. Tessa yelped and spun around to shoo the bird away, only to find that it had disappeared. Or perhaps it shifted into a mosquito, Tessa thought, rubbing her head. Tessa climbed back up the stairs, dragging the broadsword behind her, bone-tired but anxious. Not three minutes later, her cell phone buzzed on her nightstand. Tessa answered it on the second ring and quickly pulled it away from her ear as Micah and Brand screamed simultaneously something nearly unintelligible about a crow and hair.

"One at a time," Tessa shouted over the din and then added, "Wait, are you guys having a sleepover?"

Micah piped in. "We live next door to each other, have since we were five, our bedroom windows face each other."

"It's like an old time-y sitcom over there," Tessa said, trying to picture Micah and Brand talking to each other from their respective windows with tin cans and string over a small patch of grass.

"Haha," Brand said sarcastically. "Can we get to the 'what the hell' just happened part of this conversation?"

"Yeah, okay. Same thing happened to me. Did your crow start out as Shere Kahn?"

"Shere Kahn the tiger from freaking *Jungle Book*?!" Brand asked, his voice pitched high.

"I'm guessing that's a no," Tessa mused.

"No," Micah confirmed. "Just a crow. Yours was a tiger?"

"First a tiger, and then it shifted into a crow, took some hair, then disappeared."

"Yeah, minus the tiger—and thank God for that—we had the same," Micah said. "So what does it mean?"

"I don't—" Tessa began.

"Magic," Brand said, cutting her off.

"Magic?" Micah echoed.

"They use hair in magic all the time, it's like a standard ingredient, I see it all the time in magic stories," Brand said, his voice sounding not remotely pleased with himself for knowing it.

"Damn," Tessa breathed into the phone. "That can't be good."

"I'd say that's an understatement," Brand said. Everyone was quiet.

"Anyone have any ideas?" Tessa asked finally, and the line was so quiet you could hear your own heartbeat.

"Maybe we should try to get some sleep, talk tomorrow?" Micah offered.

"Yeah," Tessa said, glancing at the clock. She had to get some sleep, she hadn't slept a full night through since she'd gotten here. "Why don't you two come over here tomorrow. Maybe noon?"

"Okay," Micah and Brand said together.

When they hung up, Tessa remained sitting and listened to the sounds in her house. Nothing was ever quiet anymore, her "superhero package" had taken care of that. Life was loud now and, she guessed, forever. Tessa tried to identify each of the sounds bouncing through her house: wind against the front door, rain drops hitting the plastic sheeting over the dining room window, the tick of a clock in her father's room, a creaking spring in her bed when she breathed too deeply.

The sounds were all mundane and Tessa breathed a sigh of relief. She was alone.

She laid back down and pressed her eyes closed tightly. She could hear her eyes swivel in their sockets. Gross.

Micah and Brand stood on Tessa's front porch ringing the bell for a full five minutes before they got worried and snuck into the back yard, which was still somewhat torn up. They climbed into the house through the broken dining room window. Creeping into the sunlit kitchen, Brand whispered, "Maybe this was a bad idea, she did just buy a whole mess of weapons." And before Micah could agree, Tessa jumped out at them with a raised dagger.

"AHHHHHH!" they screamed together. Tessa blinked at them sleepily and lowered the dagger.

"Oh. Hey," Tessa said, her shoulders slumping, while Micah and Brand clutched at their chests and tried to hold off heart attacks. Brand fell into a nearby kitchen chair.

"We ring the doorbell for five minutes, and you can't hear it, but you sense us climbing in the window?!" he asked, incredulous. Tessa shrugged.

"Guess I'm not used to hearing the doorbell but getting super-used to hearing the sounds of a break-in."

Brand gestured at her appearance. "Sleep in much?"

Tessa put a hand through her mussed hair and pulled absently at her tank top with the other one. "Hey. Judge much? I haven't gotten a lot of sleep. Trying to catch up before the next thing that tries to kill me shows up," Tessa said. Micah opened the fridge.

"I'm starving. Do you have any food?"

"Not much," Tessa said, "There's juice." Micah rooted around inside while Brand continued to stare at Tessa. She pulled self-consciously at her clothes again, wondering what she was missing, fearful it was something crazy-embarrassing.

"What?!" Tessa snapped.

"You do know you have itty bitty chickies on your pajama bottoms?"

Tessa glared back at him. "Yes," she said and there was an edge to her voice, a *'don't you dare even go there'* edge. Brand put his hands up in defeat.

"I was just going to say that I like that you've paired it with a skull and crossbones tank top. Nice juxtaposition." Tessa looked down. She hadn't even noticed. She smiled and laughed a little.

"Make yourselves at home, I'm going to get dressed, maybe brush my teeth, a few other luxuries. Back in a second." Tessa disappeared, and Micah and Brand took her at her word, but in different ways. Micah began pulling things out of the fridge and cupboards and cooking something legitimate for them to eat while Brand walked around the house exploring.

Tessa came down some ten minutes later to find the kitchen smelling sublime and Brand and Micah talking about her. She felt guilty but eavesdropped anyway. It was hard not to with super-hearing.

"Find anything interesting?" Micah asked, more than a little teasing, as Brand re-entered the kitchen having made a full circle of the bottom floor of the house.

"It's kinda like a museum," he said, still touching and examining things in the kitchen. "Like nobody lives here. Like it belongs in another time or place, one slavishly devoted to something that maybe doesn't even exist anymore."

"Well, that's a four-dollar answer," Micah said taking three plates out of the cupboard.

"There are some great books in the den though, awesome collection, even some I haven't read." Brand said.

"There are books you haven't read?" Micah asked in mock horror.

"Har-har," Brandon shot back. "Found a picture of Tessa's mom too, total knockout."

Tessa cleared her throat and walked into the kitchen. "That smells amazing, Micah. I can't believe that was in my kitchen all along," she said, looking shocked at the three steaming plates of food.

"Yup, it wasn't as grim as it seemed," she said, taking the plates to the table as Tessa and Brand pulled out chairs for themselves. Micah brought juice to go with the eggs and toast and sliced fruit and then sat down herself. The friends ate in silence for six straight minutes until Brand downed his juice, wiped his mouth, and started talking at a Brand-like clip.

"So what are we going to do about this witch situation, or magic situation, or whatever?"

Tessa shrugged her shoulders hopelessly. "God. I have no idea. Did you come up with anything? Either of you?"

Brand and Micah shook their heads.

"Maybe the books I stole will help?" Tessa suggested.

"What books?" Brand asked.

"A bunch of research books from Bishop's office."

"Great!" Brand exclaimed and then looked around. "Where are they?"

"Snow has them at her place."

Micah and Brand groaned.

"I'll just tell her to bring them over," Tessa said, pretending to herself and everyone else that it would be just that simple while Micah and Brand exchanged skeptical looks. The doorbell rang, and Tessa looked at her two friends. "Maybe that's her?" Brand and Micah continued to look skeptical. "Pretty much everyone else I know is already here," Tessa said throwing up her hands. "And the ones I don't know tend not to use the doorbell." The three friends walked into the living room and Tessa opened the door, expecting to see Snow before her.

Instead, it was a lean figure in torn well-worn jeans and a black motorcycle jacket over a hooded sweatshirt. His back was to Tessa and the hood was up, but when he turned around, she nearly fell backward through her front door.

FOURTEEN

"Holy hell in a goddamn hand basket," Tessa said under her breath, as the striking stranger peered back at her from under the green hood. His eyes were a clear green that pierced clean through her, and he had a sexy scruff of facial hair, like he had just rolled out of a sexy bed and thrown on some sexy clothes. He smiled at her and pushed off the hood to reveal short dark hair, a mohawk that was growing out, just the right kind of messy, and a face that probably made people do whatever it wanted. Tessa could make out the edges of a dark tattoo crawling up his neck and part of one on his hand, creeping out from underneath his jacket sleeve. Some silver piercings and chipped black nail polish completed the requisite bad boy/punk rock/anarchy thing that Tessa couldn't even begin to pretend wasn't right up her alley. She felt something inside her draw her forward dramatically, while from behind her, Micah made a sound that resembled a "woof" more than anything else.

"Scion," he said, never breaking Tessa's gaze. Tessa felt quite literally spellbound and only a too-sudden kick to the back of her leg from Micah shook her out of it.

"Um. Yeah? I mean, yes, yes. Tessa," she added, dropping her head and blushing. He politely ignored her awkwardness.

"I'm Robin," he said, his already bright smile somehow becoming more so, and his outstretched hand looking like maybe the most delectable thing Tessa had ever seen.

"Robin?" Tessa trailed off, trying to pose it as a question and outstretched her own hand.

Just as they touched, he said, "Robin Hood."

And Tessa could swear that a little spark of sexy electricity shot through her.

Tessa chuckled. "Of course. I mean, who else would you be?"

He smiled again and they broke off the handshake, though Tessa felt like a little bit of her died when they released one another and she all but swooned. She blinked and shook her head a little as if it could wake her from the sexy trance. Who was she? She didn't swoon. She'd never swooned. She just wasn't a swoon-er. Who was this guy that he'd turned her into a swooning kind of girl in under ten seconds. Well, he *was* Robin Hood, perhaps it was as simple as that.

"Um. Come in," she said, stepping to the side to let him into the foyer. He ducked inside, his movement silken and controlled. Tessa remembered her friends standing not three feet away. "Um...Robin, this is Micah and this is

Brand, my friends," she said, standing just behind him and making 'can you believe this?!' faces at Micah. Robin shook both their hands, and Tessa ushered him into the living room. Brand and Micah hung back, and Brand hissed at her under his breath.

"I don't get what the big deal is, he's not all that, I mean, handsome and athletic, sure, but otherwise like Joe Average, even. He's not even that tall!"

Micah stared hungrily after Robin as Tessa offered him a drink less than a dozen feet away. "Again, I say WOOF," she murmured, mostly ignoring Brand, who sighed and shoved his hands in his pockets with a scowl. Micah and Brand joined Tessa and Robin in the living room on the silly overly formal couches that none of them looked comfortable sitting on.

"So, what can I do for you?" Tessa asked, hoping that indeed there was something she could do.

"I hope it's what I can do for you," he said, "I was sent to train you—weapons, hand to hand combat, battle strategy."

Tessa couldn't help but feel pleased, but she raised an eyebrow wondering if it was Snow or the handsome stranger who had sent him, or maybe someone else entirely.

"Well, that's incredibly generous of you," Tessa said, feeling weirdly girlish and blush-y. "But can you tell me who sent you?"

"Mmm. No. The message was passed to me from Tuck, but we don't know the origin point." He paused. "And we did check. I wanted to know too."

They both nodded together, as if sharing some secret. Micah and Brand stared at them. "Um. Anyone want to clue us in?" Micah asked.

They began to speak at the same time. "Knowing who—"

They both stopped and laughed a little. "You go ahead," Robin said.

Tessa smiled and pushed some hair from her face nervously. "Knowing who sent him could help us know who's really trying to help, or who might be trying to hurt—" Tessa looked back at Robin. "Of course, if your intentions are pure, then it doesn't really matter where you came from, or what the sender's intentions were."

"I agree. That's why I came anyway," he said, smiling back. "And they are—pure."

Now Tessa blushed for sure. "Well, thank you. I'm grateful to have you."

Robin smiled back at her, and Tessa sprang up out of her seat, worried she would next catch herself nearly swooning, again. She was almost thankful when the doorbell rang.

This time, it *was* Snow. When Tessa opened the door, Snow ungracefully (and it was the first ungraceful thing Tessa had seen Snow do and thus she made a mental note of it) pushed the giant bag of books into Tessa's house. But even ungracefully pushing a bag across a threshold, she was dressed in an all-white leather catsuit and knee-high leather boots. Her hair was loose behind her, and she had big silver hoops in her ears and several very sculptural silver rings on her fingers. The clothes this woman had. Tessa wanted to hate her for wearing a white leather catsuit, but it was impossible. She rocked it like, well, like a freaking rock star. Snow straightened up and kicked at the bag angrily.

"Ugh. That's the last minion-like task I do for you, Scion," she said, putting her hands on her slender hips. She caught sight of Brand and Micah. "Oh, hello minions," she said, waving her hand at them dismissively.

"You have just GOT to stop calling us that," Micah moaned. Snow was about to reply when she noticed Robin standing next to them.

"Robin Hood," Snow said. It was a bit breathless, and something about it made things inside Tessa clench uncontrollably.

"Snow," Robin repeated, and there was a decided chill in the air that did not come from Snow.

Snow looked at Tessa. "I suppose this is your idea of an appropriate trainer?"

"Well, it's someone's idea and it seems like a damn good one," Tessa grinned.

"Oh yes. Robin Hood. Anarchy and theft. The absolute best role model for a super-powered teenager," Snow said, rolling her eyes.

"Where you see anarchy and theft, I see passion and principles," Tessa shot back without even thinking. Snow stiffened.

"Fine. At least he can teach you how to use a sword and a bow. But I think we should keep looking," Snow said, crossing her arms and shooting a look of icy daggers at Robin across the room.

"Qeen re mec ghen bewien, Nueve? Triulien ba feenek ai gre yain sael ge reastk hew ge pennacae?" Robin said, hurling the words across the room violently. This was by far the most of the Story language Tessa had heard and it still sounded unlike anything she had ever heard. It was both lyrical and harsh at the same time, strange to her ear. She guessed that made sense since Snow had admitted that the Story people had created it and created it specifically so that Mortals would have trouble understanding or learning it.

"Mec ghoun venuii mec prishaa crimaane. Mal ba novel loush el mec!" Snow shouted. It was easy to feel the brutality of their words without understanding a thing.

Tessa was about to shout at them both to speak English when Brand looked at Robin and asked, "What does that mean, *tears of the innocent*?" Robin and Snow both looked at Brand, mouths agape.

"You understood what I said?" Robin asked. Brand nodded and shrugged.

"Yeah, something about Snow *'getting rich off of the tears of the innocent'*," he said matter-of-factly. Snow smiled deviously at Brand.

"Well, my dove, I think we've just discovered your change," she said.

FIFTEEN

Robin and Tessa hiked to Northside Park not far from Tessa's house. Northside was the biggest park in Lore, a massive green space that was largely wild once you got a quarter mile in, and eventually turned straight-up wild in the form of legitimate woods if you went east long enough.

When they left the house, Brand had been reading Tessa's father's old French books like he'd been born in Provence. Apparently the whole understanding the Story language thing didn't stop with Story; he understood all the languages. Even dead ones, like Latin. He was giggling like a mad scientist (in Russian) when they left, though he'd pouted when nobody else had been invited along for the training session. Tessa was pretty sure he'd cursed at her in Chinese. Chinese cursing be damned, Tessa had felt a huge wave of relief that Brand had exhibited his change and it seemed so far to be something positive and decidedly non-threatening. Snow, Tessa noticed, seemed both pleased and vexed. Snow put up a good front of not giving a crap about anything, but she was definitely more than surface. And despite all her complaining, Tessa could see her puzzling things out. It was a concern. While deep in her thoughts, Robin had pulled ahead of her and so Tessa ran a few steps to catch up.

"So, I had been thinking more along the lines of—do some push-ups, a little weapons training, maybe a dreaded rope climb—you sure this instant field test is the way to go?" Tessa asked a little breathlessly. Robin cast his eyes over to her, seductively, Tessa thought (or perhaps hoped).

"This is the best way for me to see what you know, what you don't know, and what you desperately need to know. It's like a dozen…sessions all at once."

"You paused there, what were you going to say?" Tessa asked, swinging her broadsword a bit, like a kid that probably shouldn't have access to a broadsword. Robin hesitated before answering her.

"I almost said dates."

Tessa stopped mid-broadsword-swing and almost dropped the damn thing. "Dates?" The word rolled around in her mouth like tasty treats. Robin shrugged and laughed.

"Sorry," he said, a little embarrassed.

"Sorry? Don't be sorry. I'd happily upgrade this to a date," Tessa said, and then slapped her hand across her mouth, horrified she'd said it aloud. Robin smiled, his eyes glinting. "Oh hell," Tessa said. "That was supposed to be said only inside my head." She tilted her head back and wished herself into a passing bank of gloomy clouds.

"Now I'm not sorry about it at all," he said, his smile turning a bit more serious, a bit more dangerous, but in a horribly exciting way that made Tessa quiver down into her damn boots. He moved closer to her and pushed a stray stand of hair from her face. "I like your hair," he said, staring at the red strands, bright even in the dimming light.

"I like your...all of it," Tessa said, unable to settle on one feature in particular. Robin laughed again and she wished she'd said smile. Smile was definitely the way to go. Or laugh. Or eyes. Or yeah, everything. She had been right the first time. He was close now, close enough that the leather of his jacket brushed against hers. He stared into her eyes, and Tessa sort of forgot where she was. She blinked and turned away, trying to jolt herself out of the intensity of the gaze and started walking again.

"Can I ask you something?" Tessa asked.

"It's what I'm here for."

"With Bluebeard—"

Robin cut her off, "—I heard about that. Don't let them make you feel you did wrong. Like any Story, it shakes me to hear when one is killed, but that was one very bad man, by both Mortal and Story standards. I'm sure he gave you no choice."

Tessa took a deep breath. "Thanks. Thanks for saying that."

"I should have said something sooner."

"There's something that's been bugging me about that night. I mean, there are a lot of things, but—"

"What?"

"Why did Bluebeard give Micah the keys to her own room? When I was upstairs, when I was going to break down the door, Micah pushed the keys out to me. She said he gave them to her. Why would he do that?"

"It was part of his Fiction," Robin said. "In his Story, Bluebeard gives his new bride the keys to all the rooms in the house, telling her she may enter them all, save one. When she, of course, enters the one forbidden room, she discovers his headless former wives."

Tessa looked at him blankly.

"It's like—a *compulsion*. He wouldn't have wanted to give her the keys, or it might not have even occurred to him, but he felt compelled to do it regardless. It's hard to fight our Fiction. Some of us are better at it than others. Given what I heard you found in his home, I'd wager Bluebeard wasn't good at it or didn't care to fight it. When our Stories have different iterations and interpretations over time, it can sometimes loosen those bonds a bit, give us room to breathe. On the other hand, the same Story told without much variation can sometimes strengthen the Story, make it even harder to fight what shaped us. In Bluebeard's case, that element of his Story is...was vital. Whatever adaptations, the test of the key, or at least what it represents, always appeared. That likely made it a very hard pattern to break. Still, some Stories don't even want to fight it. Given what I know of Bluebeard, I wouldn't be surprised if he was happy to revel in his Fiction, no matter how grotesque."

Tessa sighed wearily. "It's complicated."

"Yes. And that is a word I suspect you're going to get sick of very quickly."

There was a long pause between them, Tessa's mind racing about everything she knew, or thought she knew, about Robin's stories. What part of his Fiction would he have to fight, or not fight? It made her feel anxious, and so she tried to change gears.

"So. You and Snow, not such great pals, huh?"

Robin shrugged. "She's a Queen. A bad one. And I don't handle authority well under the best of circumstances."

"Like *how* not well?"

"Like don't leave us alone in a room too long. It'll end badly."

"Well, that depends on whether I actually like Snow, which, you know, I *don't*. So, it *could* end awesomely." Tessa said, shrugging.

Robin smiled. "Well, we'll keep that in our pocket for later then." Tessa smiled too and then tried not to trip over her boots while admiring him.

"We're here," he said looking up.

"Mmmm?" Tessa mused, still staring.

"The park. You ready?" There was a challenge in his question, and in his smile. Something surged in Tessa, more than just silly hormones, and she wanted to take on whatever challenge he laid out for her. Take it on and crush it. Surpass all expectations.

Be an utter badass.

"Yeah," she said. And then turned away from him until she was facing the park entrance. "But, I mean, what are we even going to find in here—it's just a park."

Robin looked at her, not unkindly, but with an expression that said she should know better. "The first thing you should learn Tessa is that nothing is going to be just as it seems anymore. There's always something, and it's usually something dangerous." Robin pulled a sword out from a scabbard strapped to his back, and they both faced the park entrance in silence for a moment. It was getting toward dusk, that magical twilight-y time where it's extra hard to see. Not exactly ideal conditions for her first training session. They plunged headlong into the park with their swords drawn, running, and as they did it, Tessa realized they were hunting.

X

Back at the house, Brand had run out of new languages to try reading and had begun watching some kind of Spanish soap opera on cable, laughing frequently and far too loudly.

"This show is hysterical!" he called to Micah, who was in the kitchen cleaning up the dishes from earlier. Snow watched her, which was irritating the crap out of her. Micah finally spun around on Snow.

"If you're going to just stand there watching me, you could at least help."

Snow shook her head, her smile widening. "I like to watch you. It reminds me of home."

Micah rolled her eyes. "Let me guess, your minions?"

"Silly girl, my servants. You don't let minions in the kitchen. Ridiculous."

Micah growled a little and dropped a plate, which broke into two neat pieces.

"And THAT is why," Snow said, pointing at Micah's broken dish. Micah breathed deeply and tried not to throw the next plate at Snow's head. She had seriously considered shoving a drumstick up her nose. More than once. Maybe today was the day.

"Are you worried, minion?" Snow called from her dishes-free perch on a stool at the kitchen island.

"I'm not going to talk to you if you call me that," Micah said, not turning around.

"I'm sorry, are you worried little Asian minion?" Snow asked and Micah turned around so suddenly that she flung soapy water all over Snow as she did it. Micah burst into a fit of laughter at the sight of Snow, drenched and foamy.

"You did that on purpose," Snow seethed, her eyes shining brightly. The temperature in the room dropped at least ten degrees in an instant. Micah's eyes widened. She hadn't ever actually seen, or *felt*, Snow use her powers.

"Are you, are you using your powers on me?!" Micah demanded. Snow didn't answer but it was clear from her appearance, her blue eyes harder and sharper than usual, her face fixed into a stony expression and her skin taking on an almost glassy quality, that she was. Micah whipped out one of her drumsticks from her deep sweatshirt pocket and pointed it at The Snow Queen. "Stop it right now, Snow. If you lay so much as a snowflake on me, when Tessa gets home I don't think there's a thing on earth that will stop her from killing your white ass." Neither of them moved for a moment and then the room warmed, inch-by-inch, or degree-by-degree rather. Micah lowered her 'drumstick as weapon.'

"Overreact much? It was just water, *and* it was an accident," she added, turning back to the sink. There was a long silence, and then Snow spoke as if nothing had happened.

"You didn't answer me. Are you afraid?"

"Of what?" Micah asked, knowing full well Snow was talking about her 'eventual change.' She had to admit, now that Brand had experienced his change, it was more on her mind than ever.

"Of your change. Your infection. Your mutation."

"Okay!" Micah said not turning around. "Enough of THOSE words, change is fine. And the answer is no. I'm not nervous."

"Liar," Snow said, with no malice. Micah ignored her, but in truth, her mind had been racing ever since Brand had changed. What would hers be? Would it be benign and even beneficial as Brand's seemed to be? Was his as simple as it seemed? Would hers be a reflection of what she loved the way Brand's had been? Stories were his first and last love, well, except for Trisha Madsen, but since she had never given him the time of day, stories were the only thing that he loved that sorta loved him back. And so when he ended up with the ability to speak any language, on some level, Micah hadn't really been surprised. It made a ton of sense actually. Would hers be like that? Would it be something about music? Surely that was what *she* loved more than anything. Somewhere deep inside, she was hoping very hard that it would be something just like what Brand got. Something that not only didn't ruin her life but actually made her better. Something that related to what she loved most and enhanced her. Her best friends were now a badass, chosen one superhero and some kind of language savant—was it wrong of her to want something cool? Something that would make her extraordinary? What if instead she just got a frog head?

"Maybe I am a liar, but at least I'm not trapped here with people that despise me," she said, grinning into the window where she could see Snow's constantly superior expression reflecting back at her.

Robin and Tessa had been running around the park for nearly an hour with not a thing of interest to report. They'd come across two couples making out, six joggers, and another dozen people walking dogs, but it was all incredibly normal.

Certainly nothing that called for a broadsword.

But not long after Tessa had started to think that they would have been better off in the backyard with a rope climb, a single, faint but still blood-curdling scream sent them running north. A second scream a moment later sent them up a narrow running path surrounded by dense trees. And a few minutes later, Tessa collided with a panicked woman on the path. The woman bounced off Tessa and fell back on her butt roughly. Tessa reached down to help her up as the woman looked frantically behind her on the path, her eyes crazed, twigs in her hair.

"Are you okay?" Tessa asked. Robin came up behind Tessa but stayed back so as not to startle the woman further. The woman nodded blankly at Tessa, and Tessa took the opportunity to look her up and down. She didn't see any cuts or anything serious. The woman seemed more frightened than anything else. She tried to speak but couldn't catch her breath. Tessa nodded at her. "Just go, get home."

The woman nodded again and ran full tilt down the path as if she could not get home fast enough. Tessa looked at Robin and shrugged. "What do you think?" she asked. And just as she finished the sentence something lumbered out of the trees toward her, all gaping jaws and decomposed flesh. As it tackled her, Tessa's only thought was, 'Holy crap, Zombies are real.'

SIXTEEN

The zombie hit Tessa with a force that threw them both backwards, but Tessa was able to use the momentum to her advantage, and as she rolled back, she flipped the thing over her head with her legs to send it crashing into the bushes behind her. Tessa scrambled to her feet and looked for her sword. Robin jumped forward as the thing climbed to its feet again. Tessa looked at him.

"Zombies?! Seriously? ZOMBIES?!" Tessa shouted more at the world than at Robin. Robin gave a half shrug and waited as the thing stumbled through the trees toward them. It seemed to be caught on some brush. Tessa found her sword, picked it up, and then covered her mouth with the crook of her arm. Good Lord, the smell. There was no way to describe it as anything other than what it was, walking death. Tessa raised her sword at the zombie and looked at Robin, "So does the Fiction hold?"

"How do you mean?" Robin asked, watching the thing as it struggled against the tangled bushes that held it back.

"I go for the head? Cut it off, or destroy the brain or whatever?"

"Probably," Robin said with another slight shrug.

"Probably?!" she said in a hissing whisper. "What do you mean probably?! I thought you were supposed to know about this stuff!"

"That's definitely what you should do," he said, still watching. "But keep in mind, if these are *Story* zombies, I'm not going to be able to kill them. I can slow them down, but you'll be the only one that can kill them permanently." Tessa shot a glance at him.

"Oh you've got to be f'ing kidding me," Tessa said to herself. And then, seconds before the thing freed itself from the branches, asked, "You think they're fast ones, or slow ones?" and as she said it the thing tore free and ran at her full speed. "Shit! Fast ones!" she shouted and raised the sword, hoping to swing it at its neck and decapitate it. But just as she did something hit her from the side, tackling her from the bushes. She launched it off her body a literal second before it chomped down on her wrist. Luckily, it crashed into the other one, and they both went down like bowling pins. Tessa looked for Robin to see why he hadn't stepped in, only to see him in a similar situation, with two zombies trying to eat him alive. She ran at the clump of them, knocking one of them down as Robin elbowed the other one off of him. "C'mon," Tessa shouted. "We have to get clear of these trees, who knows how many are in there!" Robin followed her as she ran down the path toward the clearing some

150 yards away, the zombies crashing awkwardly but way too quickly through the tight path behind them.

At the clearing, Tessa and Robin got a reasonable distance from one another and stood back to back. Seven of the undead creatures came charging out of the woods toward them.

"Ohmigod," Tessa breathed.

"Stay calm," Robin said. "Quick clean strokes, don't waste any of your movements. Don't let them in too close. Don't be afraid to move. They're fast, but you're faster. And no matter how fast they are, they're dumb. They're always dumb."

"Tell that to Romero," Tessa breathed. "And if they bite us?" Tessa asked, shuddering at the question.

"Don't get bit," he said, refusing her question.

"But if I do?"

"You'll turn," he said and then, as if to reassure her, "I won't let that happen."

But it was cold comfort. Not that Tessa doubted him or his heroic streak a mile wide, but they weren't even sure he could kill them. Tessa took a deep breath. She was going to kill them so damn hard. She wasn't about to be a zombie after less than a week of being The Scion. "Zombie-Scion" just didn't have a good ring to it. Robin was beside her as the first one closed in on Tessa, alone, the other six a short distance behind it.

"That one's yours," he said. Tessa took half a dozen steps toward it and lifted her sword. As it got in range, she swung the sword toward its neck.

And missed the neck entirely.

The sword went deep into the thing's head with a thunk. It dropped to the ground, pulling Tessa's sword with it, still stuck in its skull.

"That'll work," Robin said appreciatively, stepping in front of Tessa to intercept the next one. "Get your blade out."

"I was aiming for the neck," Tessa muttered, as she put her boot on the thing's face so she could get leverage to remove her sword from its brain. The sword made a disgusting sluishing sound as it came out, and she had to resist throwing up on the zombie corpse. The smell was so potent it felt solid.

"Fortunately, you've got enough strength that it worked anyway," Robin said and swung his sword at the next one, going cleanly through the neck, the head sailing off onto the grass. "Good news," he said, as the thing lay double dead before him. "They're Mortal." Tessa's stomach did a flip-flop. She knew that was supposed to be good news, but it made everything a little more horrifying. The next five were all together and looked as though they were going to hit them basically at once. Tessa stepped up next to Robin, her sword raised as his was. She looked at him and swore she saw a little flash of excitement in his eyes. 'Action-junkie,' she thought, and then felt a surge inside her and wondered if she was one too. Her heart hammered in her chest, and she locked eyes with the one coming right at her. It had been a man once. Maybe mid-30's, kind of handsome in a young dad kind of way. Except he was missing a good section of his torso and part of his face was scraped off. Also, he was all grey-ish brown and decomposing. But that wasn't his fault. Tessa wondered what had killed him. Car accident, maybe.

Tessa raised her sword at the walking dead dad and swung it with less power but more aim than the first time. The sword passed through the thing's neck like it was warm butter, which made Tessa gag again. Out of the corner of her eye, Tessa could see Robin's sword arcing gracefully through the air, glinting in the moonlight. The second of Tessa's zombies came at her but she didn't have time to get rid of it before the other was going to chomp on her, so she kicked it in the chest and it stumbled backward. Tessa sent her sword through the third zombie's middle, and it gurgled and continued coming at her as if she had just shaken its hand. She levered her strength upward, and the sword yanked up through the thing's torso, then neck, and clean through the head, until the top half of it was in two neat pieces and the thing collapsed. Tessa swallowed the bile in her throat and as the last one came at her she arced her sword up, swinging it with incredible speed through the creature's neck. It fell to the ground impotently at her feet.

Robin was staring at her.

"Beautiful," he said, and Tessa blushed and then thought how bizarre it was to blush considering the circumstances and covered her mouth with her sleeve again. She looked around at the mess.

"Do you think that's all of them?" Tessa asked, looking at the tree line and listening intently. With all their moaning and crashing through trees, the zombies hadn't exactly been subtle. The woods were silent.

"I hope so. They made enough noise that I'd think it would have drawn out others—"

Tessa cut him off, finishing his thought, "—But if not, we're going to have a zombie apocalypse on our hands.

Robin nodded. "Yes."

"Balls," Tessa said, to herself more than Robin, and then, after a long pause, "So what now?"

"I think we should burn them," Robin said. "I don't want anything eating them, just in case." Tessa shuddered at both ideas, but she helped Robin drag them into a pile and then lit it on fire. They gazed into the blaze, covering their noses periodically to hide from the smell, which was a particular brand of horrifying, reanimated dead, now sizzling.

"So, you were able to kill them, which means that they're Mortal?"

"Yes, they're not Stories," Robin said, crouching down and looking into the fire.

"So, what does that mean?"

"I don't know, could be a lot of things."

"Well, that narrows it down," Tessa said, sulking.

"Sorry," Robin said, as if embarrassed. "I'm not much of a detective, not a book guy, just a fighter, a hunter, maybe I'm not much use to you—"

"Oh no," Tessa broke in, "I didn't mean that, I, you were great." He looked at her, his eyes kind. Tessa tried to start again, "I—" Everything had gone wrong, and Tessa didn't know how to get it back. She scratched her head absentmindedly as she racked her brain for how she could remove her foot from her mouth, but instead something else came to her. "Magic," she said suddenly. Robin looked up at her, puzzled. "Could it be magic?" Tessa asked.

"Sure," Robin shrugged. "That's one of a bunch of options, I suppose. Why?"

"Because last night something broke into my house and took some of my hair, and Brand said—"

"What?!" he cut her off, and stood up.

"Yeah," Tessa said, scratching the sore spot where the crow had snatched her hair from her head. Robin moved closer to her and touched her forearm, looking all around them, clearly spooked. Tessa tried to ignore the shudder of electricity that ran through her at his touch.

"Why didn't you tell me?" he demanded, his face full of concern but his voice severe.

"I didn't think it was important, *is* it important?" By way of answering, Robin took her by the elbow and led her toward the park exit, toward home.

"We have to get you home."

"Why?"

"That's black magic. Tessa, someone's trying to curse you." Robin said, looking around them, scouring the tree line.

"What about the fire?" Tessa asked, gesturing back to the blaze, still going strong.

"Let it burn."

When Robin and Tessa burst through the front door, Snow seemed to be arguing with Brand and Micah about the very same black magic.

"Unbelievable! Here you are doing dishes and watching foreign soap operas when someone is working to level a curse on you! No wonder you're minions! You're IDIOTS!" Snow said, her voice nearly at glass-shattering level. Micah and Brand sat on the couch transfixed, having clearly moved past annoyance with Snow to sheer horror, their eyes like teacups in their faces.

When Tessa and Robin arrived they turned to Tessa in unison, their faces white as sheets. Snow turned and gestured toward the door theatrically, "It's about damn time, Scion! Tova! Why didn't you tell me about the hair!" Tessa looked at her blankly.

"I…" she raised her hands and then dropped them. "There's been a lot going on?" she offered weakly. Snow threw up her arms in frustration.

"Neyersichita!" she yelled at the ceiling.

Tessa looked from Snow to Robin. "So, what do we do?" At that, the room went deadly silent. "Well?" Tessa urged.

"I don't know," Snow said, pacing and seeming legitimately worried. She turned to Tessa. "Yours was a Tiger that shifted into a crow and then disappeared?" she said, more than asked. Tessa nodded. Snow tapped her bottom lip with a slender finger.

"I take it the tiger was *not* Shere Kahn," Tessa said. Snow gave her a pathetic look that had *'you're a moron'* written all over it and returned to pacing. "So? How many Fictional witches can there even be? We'll just narrow it down."

At this, both Snow and Brand looked at her like she was a moron. Snow began ticking Story witches off on her fingers.

"Well, let's see, Scion, there's Le Fay, Baba Yaga, Nimue, Harkness, Karaba, Nessarose, Bavmorda, Enchantress, Galadriel, Black Forest, Maximoff, Kiki, The Mayfairs, Lin, Maleficent, Mombi, Willow, Amy, Yubaba, Blackwood, The Three Sisters, Cassandra, Endor, Sendo, Dalma, Taranee, Zatara, Traci Thirteen, Nico, Circe, Medea, The White Witch, Nutter, Pekkala, The Queen, Sycorax, all the damn Potters—"

"Ohmigodharrypotter," Micah breathed.

"Okay, okay, I get it. Lotta witches," Tessa said, defeated.

"I should go," Robin said, and Tessa's head snapped toward him.

"What?! Why?"

"I want to make sure the bodies are destroyed, and then I should put the word out to a few Stories I know that might be motivated to help us, see if anyone knows anything," Robin sheathed his sword, pulled his hood up, and looked at Tessa for just a moment before leaving.

"Okay," she said, watching him head down the front walk. Things already felt lonely and less safe and warm (and sexy) without him. She turned toward her friends and Snow.

"Bodies?" They all asked at once. Tessa shrugged.

"Zombies."

The three furrowed their brows and said, "Ohhhhhhh."

Tessa nodded. Brand looked at his feet, his head in his hands.

"Man, zombies are real. I can't decide whether to be horrified or giddy," he said, as if in real conflict on the issue.

Tessa picked up the massive duffel bag of books Snow had brought over and took it into the dining room. Brand, Micah, and Snow followed her and, without a word, the four of them each pulled a book from the bag and sat down in a chair to begin reading.

An hour and many volumes later, the quartet, grouchy and bickering, the pile of discarded books massive between them, collectively jumped as the doorbell rang again. Tessa raced for it, hoping to find Robin. Answers or no, she already felt better when he was around. Brand and Micah gathered a bit behind her in the living room. Tessa threw open the door, her face alight with anticipation, only to find the three a.m. stranger standing on her porch, even though it was only ten p.m.

"Oh," Tessa said, her face falling.

"Well, that's not 'happy to see me'," he intoned. "I thought a non-three a.m. visit was the current request by—" he stopped mid-sentence and leaned to the side to take in the view of Brand and Micah in the living room. Tessa followed his gaze. "Annnnd this is why I prefer three a.m.," he said under his breath.

Tessa turned back to him. "I suppose you want to come in?"

The stranger seemed to consider it, weighing some options Tessa wasn't privy to, and then stepped inside.

"Jesus H.," Brand mumbled. "Is this place a parade of damn supermodels or what?" Micah stifled a laugh and tried not to stare. Taller and broader than Robin, he was attractive in an entirely different way. Snow had said 'tall, dark, and handsome' described many of the men in Fiction, and Tessa was struck by how that was technically true both of the stranger and Robin, and yet they could not have appeared more different, could not have stirred different emotions in her.

Just as Tessa was about to finally ask the stranger's name so that she could introduce him to her friends, Snow stepped into the room and drew back with a cartoonish villainous hiss. "Anivaine Fucol," she said, and the words sounded like some kind of ancient evil far worse than Snow herself. The temperature in the room fell rapidly.

The stranger's face registered nothing, his voice was that same sound like water breaking over stones, smooth and magical, "Snow. It's been an age."

"Not enough of one," she said, her voice more like icebergs breaking apart.

"I thought I smelled you before," he mused. "All icicles and bitchiness. You haven't changed a bit."

"Nor you," she said, and everyone shivered as the temperature continued to drop, now perhaps twenty degrees below where it belonged.

"Snow," Tessa cautioned. Snow looked at Tessa, her eyes like steel balls in her hardened face. "The temperature?" Tessa asked, a gentle reminder that the rest of them were going to freeze to death. Snow seemed to unclench and the room softened, everything softened, including her features.

"Yes, of course," she said, a thin, forced smile spreading across her face.

"So, who are you?" Tessa finally asked the stranger, folding her arms across her chest.

"Don't you know, Scion?" Snow snarled. "This is Fenris, but you'd know him best as The Big Bad Wolf."

SEVENTEEN

"What the hell?" Tessa said, backing up from the stranger (now, officially, The Big Bad Wolf) a few feet and putting herself between him and her friends.

"Mmmmm," Fenris mused. "Yes, I am what Snow says, though I prefer to be called Fenris. The Big Bad Wolf is so…" he trailed off.

"Accurate?" Snow supplied, almost chipper.

"Cumbersome," he finished, smiling at her with a look that Tessa now felt was less 'sexy' and more 'devour-y,' although perhaps, given who he was, they were a bit the same. Tessa was about to launch into an accusatory, judgmental tirade when she remembered the giant wolf that had saved her from Bluebeard.

"Wait," she said, one finger raised, her eyes thoughtful, curious. Fenris looked at her, his interest piqued, and now that she knew who he was, Tessa could not help but think 'hungry'. "It was you," she said. He smiled at her. Something about it made her shiver, and she looked away.

"What was you?" Micah asked, and Brand raised his hand and shook his head as if to signal that he too was lost.

"At Bluebeard's, the wolf that saved me," she paused again, now sure of herself. "It was you."

"Guilty, Red," he said, and it sounded like he was used to saying the word, both words actually.

"Why?" Tessa asked, her face a storm of conflicting emotions. But before he could answer, Snow broke in.

"Why indeed, Scion. If he did it, you can guess that it's for his own selfish reasons," Snow snarled. Tessa didn't really want to be best pals with The Big Bad Wolf, but she had to admit that the effect he was having on Snow was almost worth it.

Brand cast his eyes at Snow. "And your motives are pure as the driven snow, *Snow*?"

Snow turned on him. "What do you people want?!" she rather screeched. "I'm here trying to help you for just *days* now," she complained, emphasizing 'days' as if it meant 'eternity.'

Tessa crossed her arms again and rolled her eyes. "Oh yes, DAYS, such a test of loyalty, whole *days* devoted to us." Snow stalked out of the room. Tessa sighed, knowing she may have to apologize which was an abhorrent idea. But it would come later. For now, there was The Big Bad Wolf in her living room, *again.* "But she's not wrong. Your reputation has obviously preceded you here. What's the game?"

"No game, Scion. I come to help. I offered you help in finding your new Advocate. I offer it again, at a more reasonable hour, per your rather grouchy," he paused and looked her up and down as if she was on a very specific menu, "but rather adorable, baby-chickie pajama-bottomed request several nights ago." A pinch of pain flashed in Tessa as she thought of Bishop.

"I told you, I don't need—" her voice caught on the word Advocate and she substituted instead, "One."

Fenris walked further into the room and returned to the photos on the mantle he had examined last time. He picked up the same one from before, of Tessa at eight.

"I thought things might have changed, considering the curse," he said casually. Tessa, Brand, and Micah looked at him, wide-eyed.

"How did you know about that?" Micah asked.

"What big ears you have," Brand whispered to her.

"Indeed I do, kid, indeed I do," he said, putting down the picture frame and turning to face them. Tessa thought she could hear Brand gulp and Micah's heart begin to pound harder as if they were cartoon characters.

"You think The Advocate can help us if we've been cursed?"

"No better person around for such a thing," Fenris said, and as he did, the door swung open and Robin came in.

"I can think of one better person," Robin said, pushing back his hood. Fenris narrowed his eyes at Robin but Tessa couldn't quite read his expression. Truth be told, she hadn't been able to read any of his expressions. They were such a strange mix of things that felt foreign to Tessa. Tessa looked between them, and though both Robin and Fenris standing there in the same room shamed the words handsome, sexy, hott (double t) and a slew of others besides, they could not be more different. Where Fenris was broad and muscled, tall and imposing, full of practiced calm, Robin was more slight, lean but strong, agile, and full of barely contained energy. Robin made her feel safe and protected, but also excited, glowing and almost *embarrassingly* warm all over. By contrast, Fenris, no matter how attractive, rankled something deep and sour within her, causing the hair on the back of her neck to stand up and goose bumps to break out across her skin. "Didn't expect to find me here, did you, Wolf?" Robin said, shutting the door.

"Quite the contrary," Fenris purred. "I'm the one that sent you here." The admission stunned everyone in the room, but Robin most of all.

"I don't believe you," Robin said, low and quiet and with barely concealed rage.

"What a surprise, anarchist," Fenris said, his eyes strangely playful. Robin made a move for his sword, and Tessa reached out to stop him.

"Whoa! None of that," Tessa tried to catch Robin's eye, and after a moment, she did. He seemed breathless and almost out of control but became steadier when they locked eyes. "That's not helping me," she said, and he nodded and let go of the sword. Tessa turned back to the rest of the room. Fenris and Robin were in some kind of bizarre Mexican standoff, Robin in the foyer, Fenris in the living room, leaning against a door-jamb. Brand and Micah stood close together in the living room between the two, confused as all get out, scared, and more than a little curious. Snow had rejoined the group, begrudgingly, and stood in the doorway between the living room and the kitchen, her eyes trained on Fenris. Tessa raised her hands in an 'everybody calm the hell down' gesture.

"Robin. What did you find?"

"The Troll," he said. Tessa snapped around, and Fenris raised an eyebrow, intrigued.

"Troll? The Troll was in my house five days ago! Did you know?" Tessa trailed off.

"He rambled something about The Scion, along with the required bit about goats. I figured there must be something there. I left him bound in the woods."

"You think he might know something about what broke in and stole our hair?"

Robin shrugged. "I think anything that's already attacked you once is worth questioning."

Tessa nodded vigorously. "I agree. Let's go get him." Tessa felt almost giddy at the idea of actual progress being made, mysteries revealed, *something* making sense. She caught Fenris's eye and paused, "You disagree?"

"No, it's a good plan, you should do it. I just also think you should find your Advocate as soon as possible."

"You're coming," Tessa said, which surprised him. He raised an eyebrow at her.

"Am I now?"

Tessa could feel Robin protesting inside, ready to burst forth with something. She put up a hand to stay him. "Yes. Until we know what your game is, you're staying around. For the same reason I keep Snow close, or did you think it was for her magnificent personality?"

A blast of cold air hit the room, and Snow spun on her heel and returned to the dining room, mumbling something that sounded a lot like *'bitch.'* Fenris ticked his head to the side, which Tessa had seen him do before, as if he was trying to puzzle something out.

"Do you think you can make me stay, Hardcore?" he challenged.

"No. But I think you want something. And if you don't stay, I'm going to make whatever that is as difficult as possible. You hang around and I'll see what we can do about getting you whatever it is you want," she said. Robin blew out a frustrated breath.

"Deal," Fenris said, smiling a too-charming smile and then all but sticking his tongue out at Robin. Tessa turned to Robin.

"So where is this Troll?"

"In the park, not far from where we encountered the zombies."

Fenris's head kicked up. "Zombies?"

Tessa turned to him. "Yes?" she prompted.

"Mmmm," he said. "Nothing yet," and lowered his head again.

"Okay, so the four of us will—" Tessa started but Brand cut her off.

"Four?"

"Robin, Fenris, Snow, and me," Tessa said, looking at her friends, whose faces fell.

"No way. We're coming," Brand said, and Micah nodded emphatically next to him.

"I need you guys here."

"Why?" Brand asked. "So we'll be all nice and out of the way?"

"Tess, this thing has our hair too. We're marked. You have to let us help."

"And I am," Tessa said. "I need you guys here figuring this out, doing research. We can't put all our eggs in one basket. Look for wielders of black magic in Fiction, specific spells that use a victim's hair. Cross reference whatever you find with The Troll from *The Three Billy Goats Gruff* story. Maybe we can find something connected to him with Magic."

Brand and Micah nodded, disappointed but resigned. "But, the books, I mean—they're just Stories, Tessa—they're not going to cross reference, right?" Brand asked.

Fenris raised his head again. "What do you have? Show me." Tessa walked past him into the kitchen, and everyone followed her to the dining room and the pile of books. Fenris's eyes searched the piles of books on the table and then he went digging into the bag, pulling out handfuls of large volumes. Finally, he found one he was looking for.

"Here," he said, holding it out to Tessa.

"What is it?" she asked, creaking open the old leather binding. The inside was completely handwritten.

"It's an Advocate journal," Fenris said. Tessa's blood went cold and she put it down as if it was poison. He held out another volume, and Micah took it. "Here's another. There are certainly more, but the journals will be more helpful as they discuss Fiction outside of their original context, how they have behaved once they reached beyond their Stories, and in particular, their behavior in the Mortal world. It should also include known associations, things like that."

Tessa narrowed her eyes at him. "How do you know so much about Advocates?"

"I've been around," he said, not looking at her but rummaging through the rest of the bag.

Tessa left it alone. For now.

"Okay," Tessa said, looking at Brand and Micah. "This is great. Can you guys do this?" They looked at one another and then back to Tessa.

"Okay," they said together.

Tessa looked at the rest of the group. "We leave in five minutes," she said, walking out of the room. Snow opened her mouth to protest. "You're coming," Tessa said, without even pausing. Snow closed her mouth and pouted. Tessa left everyone and went upstairs to change. Halfway through, she heard a light knock on her door, and after getting her shirt on, she opened it to see Robin standing there. Her heart skipped at least one beat. "Hey," she said.

"Hey," he said and then stepped inside her room as she moved to the side. "I don't know about this, Tessa. They're villains. Fenris especially is dangerous, we'll be out there with them alone—they could betray us at any moment."

"They could," Tessa said, hunting around for a sweatshirt in her pile of clothes still abandoned in suitcases she'd never had a chance to unpack. "But we don't have much choice. They're powerful, and I need them. For now, at least. I can't let anything happen to Micah and Brand. Whatever this curse is, I have to stop it before something horrible happens to them. I need manpower…er…Storypower. Besides, they both have things they want, and for whatever reason, so far at least, that doesn't seem to include me being dead."

Robin shook his head, "Tessa, I know you're new to this, but you can't trust them."

Tessa smiled and moved closer to Robin. "And I can trust you? I barely know you. I've known you about—" she looked at her watch. "—nine hours." She couldn't help but lean closer to him. He breathed her in and touched her cheek, in a surprisingly intimate gesture.

"I know, but it's different with me."

"How so?" Tessa asked, searching his face. She did trust him, but she didn't know why. He *was* barely more than a stranger.

"I'm a hero," he said.

Tessa laughed, "And so humble!"

"I don't mean it as a compliment to myself. It's a fact. It's in my DNA. It's what I was written to be. The hero, the good guy, the one who does the right thing, whether unpopular or not. It's in my design the same way being the bad guy is built into them. Deception and conquering, killing and lying, betrayal and horror, it's all they know on some level, and it's destiny, pure and simple," he said.

Tessa shook her head. "No, I don't believe that," she said, backing away from him and looking at the sweatshirt in her hands. "Destiny doesn't define everything. They can choose. You said yourself that they can fight their Fiction."

Robin shook his head and reached out, turning her toward him again. "Tessa, you don't understand, it's just not that simple. Fighting your Fiction…it's extremely complicated, and that's even if they WANT to. I doubt Snow or Fenris even care to," he said. As he stared into her eyes, Tessa could see that he believed it whole-heartedly. She pulled away again, bristling, annoyed for reasons she didn't fully understand.

"We don't know that," she said, stepping into the hall, stepping back from the moment they had shared.

In the living room, Tessa took a vase and a stack of books off of an old trunk and opened it up to reveal some of the weapons she had picked out yesterday. Robin politely declined.

"I'm good."

Tessa looked to Snow, who shook her head lightly. She looked at Fenris ,who smiled widely, his teeth glinting.

"I've no need of weapons, luv." Tessa saw Robin roll his eyes, and she reached for the broadsword.

"Okay then, I guess that's it. Everyone ready?" There was a general grumble of agreement from the group, and the quartet headed out.

The walk to the park was a strange, silent one with Robin and Tessa next to one another in front, Tessa with her sword, Robin with a longbow and sheath of arrows, Fenris off to the side, and Snow bringing up the rear, grumbling all the way in her four-inch wedge heel boots.

When they reached the park, Robin led them straight east and then, after ten minutes, veering north. Robin motioned them forward and they moved from the heavily wooded area into a clearing. "He's not far into the woods, just beyond this clearing," Robin said, turning to Tessa. As he did so, Fenris, on the far right of the group, growled and stopped.

It was a sound that paralyzed them all.

"What is it?" Tessa whispered. She saw nothing, sensed *almost* nothing. Fenris just pointed. In the dark near the tree line, over a ridge and housed in a totally creepy mist that had rolled in, Tessa saw a huge black dog. Snow, just in front of Tessa, squinted at the animal. "Is that…is that Hecuba?" Tessa asked, unsure whether she was hoping the answer was yes or no. Snow squinted harder.

"No." she said, and Tessa could tell from her tone that Snow had hoped it was.

"And it's not you," Tessa said lightly, looking at Fenris, who looked back at her and shook his head, his playful smile absent. The group looked again at the hulking animal. It was massive and oddly shaped, and Tessa was almost certain she could hear it growling, low and brutal, even at this distance. Snow sucked in a breath.

"There's more of them," she said. Tessa was about to object since she saw nothing but then noticed a rustle in the trees. Almost as if shedding camouflage, two more shapes emerged, then six, then twelve, then fifteen, then, well, Tessa couldn't easily count them anymore.

"Oh my God," Tessa said. "I hope these aren't Stories."

Fenris glanced at Snow. "Can you take them all?" he asked. Tessa looked at Snow, shocked. What was she going to do, scowl at them and offer pointed criticism? She'd mostly just brought Snow to keep an eye on her, it hadn't occurred to her she'd be an actual asset.

"No," Snow said solemnly, and turned her head to look back at Fenris. "It's too many, especially if they run at us. Which they are going to do."

Fenris nodded in agreement.

Tessa suddenly felt like a very unnecessary third wheel.

"I've seen you take that many," Robin said.

"Not in this climate," Snow said, her tone definitive.

"How many *can* you take?" Fenris asked.

Snow grimaced, "Depends how fast they are, how strong. Maybe a dozen, perhaps 15 if we're lucky." The temperature around them dropped rapidly, and there was a cold, almost electric snap in the air. Tessa noticed that Snow's hands and eyes were faintly glowing with a pale bluish-white light.

"That's not enough," Robin said. "It will leave too many to deal with at once."

"So what's plan B?" Tessa asked, and as she finished, she heard a rumbling growl on her right. She turned to see Fenris, partially shifted into a wolf. His handsome features morphing into something else, his clothes tearing as his shape shifted underneath. She couldn't tell if he was losing control or just suiting up for battle. "Fenris?"

"They're going to attack," he said, his voice so guttural and inhuman that it was almost unintelligible. "Now," he said, and it was something between a bark and a barely contained shout. As he said it, the entire pack lurched forward as if they were one animal. They weren't graceful and fluid like real dogs, but they were unnaturally huge, powerful and fast.

Very, very fast.

EIGHTEEN

"Another one," Brand said, looking up at Micah, who put down the journal she was poring over and picked up a pen. "Baba Yaga," he said. Micah scrunched up her nose.

"I'm just gonna spell that phonetically."

"How many is that?" Brand asked, trying to read her scrawling notes upside down.

"Nine," Micah said, sounding defeated.

"So it's been an hour and already, we've found nine magic wielders that have had 'adventures' in the Mortal world. I feel like we could do this for the rest of our lives and not figure this out," Brand sighed.

"Maybe we should stop and research these nine a little more. See if there's any connection to The Troll, or to zombies," Micah said, rubbing her chin with the pen.

"You know they're not even *really* that attractive," Brand said, looking with renewed interest at the journal pages in front of him.

"Huh?" Micah asked, looking up. "Who?"

"Who?! *Who!?!* The parade of supermodel-meets-rock-star-meets-professional-athletes that have been in this house all damn day!" he said, throwing up his hands. Micah smiled.

"I thought you said they weren't that attractive?"

Brand blew out a puff of air. "I was lying." He fiddled with the corners of the journal pages. "I thought this whole language thing was pretty cool, but now—"

"Now you wish you were a supermodel-meets-rock-star-meets-professional-athlete?"

"Yeah, of course. I mean, how can a guy have healthy self-esteem hanging out with these dudes?" he opined, drawing obsessive circles on the notebook in front of him.

"You sure that's it? It's not jealousy of the competition?"

Brand blinked at her blankly. "Competition for what?"

"You don't have a thing for Tessa?"

Brand blew out another puff of air, "Pshaw. No."

"How can you not? She's awesome, and she's, like, a legit superhero. And I hate to break it to you, but you, my friend, have a thing for superheroes."

"You know I prefer blondes, Mike."

"Oh yes," Micah said, rolling her eyes. 'The Trisha Madsen factor, how dare I forget."

"Please, I am so over her."

"Right, right," Micah nodded, looking back at her list of names.

"Whatever. I'm beginning to think *you* might have a crush on Tessa, though," he said, winking.

"Nah, but I figure if I stick around long enough I'm sure to get some of her hot Fictional leftovers," Micah said, adjusting her glasses demurely.

"Smart," Brand said, tapping a finger against his temple. "Smart. Also? Classy."

"I think so," Micah said, grinning.

"You got your eye on anyone particular?"

"Keeping my options open," Micah nodded. Brand laughed and then called out the name Mombi, which Micah added to the list of witches.

Snow glowed much more brightly, and the temperature around them dropped another twenty degrees as the pack of strange giant dogs ran at them. A shot of bluish-white lightning snaked out of Snow's outstretched arm and through the pack of dogs. Ten of the dogs stopped in their tracks some hundred feet away, apparently frozen solid. Another four didn't freeze to blocks of ice but slowed, and then fell over unceremoniously. Tessa smiled happily until she noticed Snow wavering unsteadily beside her. She reached out to catch Snow just before she passed out.

"Dammit," Tessa said, and looked up to see Fenris, fully a wolf—giant, and grey, and snarling—run at the line of dogs. Even if he could take on three or four at once, that still left nearly a dozen for Robin and Tessa. Tessa shook Snow who was still swooning in her arms. "SNOW!" Tessa shouted, and Snow's eyes flickered open. In fairness, the second Snow stopped swooning, she got her bearings and crouched down into a reasonably impressive fighting stance so that Tessa could draw her sword rather than hold her up. Tessa was seeing Snow and all her gorgeous clothes and perfect manicures in a whole different light. She seemed like a battle-tested warrior and had Tessa had time to be impressed, she would have been. But though Fenris had managed to intercept and engage four of the dogs, the rest were barreling toward Robin, Tessa, and Snow. Tessa watched as Robin lodged an arrow in the pack leader's chest, but it kept coming. Two more arrows in rapid-fire succession landing in its neck finally brought it down.

"The neck," Robin said to Tessa before breaking away from her and Snow to draw some of the dogs off. As he moved, he fired and reloaded, making every shot, but there were just too many.

"You have any more left in you?" Tessa asked Snow.

"No," she said. "Not yet. I need a minute." Tessa looked at the handful of dogs barreling down on them. "Maybe two," Snow said, her hands flickering light briefly and then fading as if she was out of juice.

"You'll have it," Tessa said, swallowing a lump of fear, drawing her sword, and stepping in front of Snow. The first dog reached Tessa and jumped at her, colliding painfully with Tessa's chest. Tessa and the dog rolled together down a slight slope and away from Snow. As they fell, Tessa couldn't tell where the dog ended and where she began. It was disturbing. When they stopped, they were thrown apart, but the dog was on its feet instantly and it circled Tessa, looking for an opening. Up close, she still couldn't tell what was wrong with it, but it looked almost like it was part-wolf. It jumped at Tessa, and she got her blade up just in time to skewer it. It howled but didn't get back up when Tessa removed her sword.

Tessa climbed back up the small incline to find Robin partway up a tree and shooting his arrows with blinding speed. He took out a creature mere inches from Snow. Another made its way toward the still fallen Snow, who was sending small snaps of blue light at it in an attempt to keep it at bay. But she was weak and the cold light she produced seemed to be wavering; the dog advanced steadily toward her. Tessa ran at the dog and tackled it a moment before it collided with Snow, her hand raised, the light flickering in her hand, spent.

The dog scrambled out from under Tessa, and as she raised her sword, she heard Snow shout her name. She felt a pair of massive teeth dig into her shoulder. Tessa let out a cry and reared backward, tossing the dog off of her. It landed, doing a fine impression of a cat, and rushed her. Tessa balled up her fist and threw it at the dog. She connected and the animal fell backwards, dead or just stunned, Tessa couldn't tell. The first dog was already coming back at her, and Tessa looked frantically for the sword she'd dropped. It was just out of reach, so as the dog lunged at her, Tessa threw up her arm to keep it from eating off her face in a giant chomp. The dog sunk its teeth into her forearm, and Tessa let out another cry, this one deeper and throatier. She could hear Snow cussing in the background, even under all the snarling.

The thing was powerfully built, and as Tessa thought it, she realized it was true. The dog was *built*. That's why it was so odd-looking, it was part-dog, part-wolf. Stitched together into some kind of horrifying Franken-Dog. The animal pushed into her, and Tessa winced as its jaws barely missed her again. Snow yelled something at her over the din of growls and barks, snarls and snaps.

"What?!?" Tessa shouted back. "I'm a little busy here!"

"The axe!" Snow shouted, "Call the axe!" The animal released Tessa's forearm and made another play for her face. Tessa moved just enough to avoid losing an eye to its snapping jaws. She had no idea what Snow was talking about but then remembered Bluebeard and his magical axe. She didn't know why Snow thought she could call it, but it was certainly worth a try.

Anything was worth a try at this point.

Tessa racked her brain for the words he'd used, and as the animal reared back, ready to push into her for a deadly final strike, she raised her free hand and called out "LA COLOMBE NOIRE!" The same blackish blue light crackled, and the axe snapped into her hand as if it was made for her, as if it had been simply waiting for her to call upon it. Tessa swung the axe down toward the animal and it landed with a thunk in the creature's neck. Tessa lost her grip on the axe as she pushed the heavy, now limp animal away from her and clawed her way to her feet. A moment after Tessa released the axe it disappeared again. Maybe a dozen feet away, the Franken-Dog Tessa had kicked came to and made a run for her. Tessa shouted for the axe again, "LA COLOMBE NOIRE!" and, like clockwork, it snapped into her hand. The animal jumped at Tessa and she swung the axe as it did, decapitating it mid-air so it fell into two neat pieces at her feet.

Tessa gagged.

She turned back to make sure Snow hadn't been torn to shreds and blinked at the sight of her, curled into a ball and covered in a spidery web of protective ice. Lady was a survivor, that was for sure. Tessa rubbed a bloody hand on her jeans, and in the distance she saw Fenris, more than twice the size of the largest of the Franken-Dogs, leaping at the leader, all grace and horrifying power. His jaws bent around the neck of the dog, and it let out a cry. Tessa winced as a horrible snap left Fenris standing above the animal, panting, his eyes fierce and completely inhuman, even at this distance.

He stared at Tessa.

Dead creatures littered the ground all around him.

They locked eyes.

Tessa couldn't tell what he was thinking, but she couldn't tell that when he looked human either. She wondered if he was thinking anything at all in that form, or was he mostly animal now? Tessa broke the gaze first, overcome by the intensity of it, and would only later remember that you're never supposed to look away first from an animal.

Two smaller dogs approached him, cautious and distracting, enough so that he didn't notice the third, larger animal coming behind him. Tessa looked at the axe in her hand and threw it end over end as hard as she could at the third animal. It hit with a deadly thunk. Fenris turned just in time to see the axe disappear from the animal's lifeless body.

To her left, Tessa saw Robin, down from his tree, his bow on the ground, apparently out of arrows, and using his dagger to fight with the remaining animals. Tessa called the axe to her again and ran toward him, snatching an arrow out of a fallen dog as she did. When she was still too far away to help, she saw a dog overpower him and take a chunk out of his shoulder. He howled and fell backwards.

"ROBIN!" Tessa shouted, and threw the axe. But she missed this time, and with nothing to hit, the axe just eventually disappeared in mid-air. The animal had been forced to pull back however, and Tessa slid between Robin and the remaining dog, as it circled back toward them. "Are you all right?" Tessa asked, worried by the blood pouring from his shoulder. He nodded but said nothing, thrusting the bow into her hands. Tessa could feel the animal coming back faster now. She tried to nock the arrow, but the string slid on her fingers, slippery with blood. Tessa sensed the dog was almost upon them and could see the truth of it reflected back in Robin's eyes and the breathless way he said her name.

"Screw this," Tessa said, giving up on the bow and gripping the arrow in her fist. As the dog leapt at them, Tessa turned, raised the arrow, and stabbed it in the neck. It fell dead at her feet, like a massive, molting rug.

"Well, that's one way to do it," Robin said, dropping his head back to the ground, relieved.

They all stayed where they were for perhaps a full minute, breathing heavily and clutching their sides, saying nothing, Tessa held her arm, which was bleeding badly, and looked out across the clearing now filled with unreal creature carcasses.

But the peace didn't last long.

Tessa noticed that Fenris hadn't shifted back out of his giant wolf shape and, in fact, suddenly tensed up and turned to look back at the woods. At the tree line in the distance, another half dozen Franken-dogs stood, staring at them, growling and breathing hard. They seemed mere moments from attacking. How many of these damn things were there? It felt like they'd already killed an army.

"Oh God," Tessa breathed. Fenris, far closer to the woods than the rest of them, looked back at Tessa, and spoke, his words almost impossible to understand.

"Run," was all she could make out before he was overcome by an unreal howl. Tessa looked to Robin, who nodded in agreement. She helped him up and they hobbled over to Snow's ice cocoon, which was melting rapidly. Tessa shattered it with one sharp blow from the hilt of her sword and they helped her up.

She wasn't much more than a rag doll. They began running, Snow barely conscious between them. Tessa looked back once to see Fenris running at the line of creatures and heard that horrible yelping that indicates a dog is injured, a sound Tessa had heard more tonight than she wanted to hear in a lifetime. She couldn't tell if it was Fenris or the creatures that made the sound. A few minutes into their escape, she heard Robin cuss.

"What?" she asked, looking at him across Snow as they ran.

"A couple got past him," he said, casting his eyes somewhere behind them. Tessa turned her head and, sure enough, at least two were following them. "We should split up," he said. Tessa looked at Snow.

"We can't leave her alone, her power hasn't returned, she's too weak."

"Stay with her, go toward the main entrance, get home. I'll try to draw them off," he said.

"No," Tessa said, "You do that, I'll take them."

"No," Robin said, standing firm. "You're stronger. It's easier for you to carry her and still move fast." Tessa nodded in hesitant agreement. Robin put his hand on her cheek, and the intimacy of it shocked her. She thought for a moment he was going to kiss her, and she had to admit that she wanted it, however inappropriate the timing.

Instead, she handed him her sword.

"Take it, you're nearly out of arrows, and I can't carry her very well with it anyway," she said. "I can call the axe if anything goes wrong."

He nodded. "I'll meet you at the house, I promise," he said, and then without waiting for a response, ran at the dogs, the sword drawn and shining in the pale light. Tessa and Snow turned and continued running for the exit, Snow leaning heavily on Tessa, Tessa trying not to hear the sounds of battle behind them. When they got to the entrance, Tessa looked back into the depths of the shadowed park and saw and heard nothing. It was as quiet as a tomb.

"Scion. We have to get inside," Snow said. Tessa put her head down, resigned, and they continued toward the house.

By the time they made it to Tessa's house, Snow was in and out of consciousness and Tessa had carried her most of the way. Tessa herself had lost a lot of blood, and her vision was swimming.

They made quite a pathetic pair.

Tessa kicked the front door in with the remainder of her strength and staggered through the door, nearly dropping Snow in the process. Micah and Brand came running and took Snow from Tessa, helping her into the kitchen. Snow half fell into a chair, and Tessa stumbled behind them toward the sink. Micah rushed to her aid while Brand hung back, looking at the front door, as if waiting for everyone else to arrive.

"Where are Robin and Fenris?" he asked. Snow shook her head at Brand, all the fire and bitchiness yanked right out of her.

"We had to split up," Tessa said. Micah stripped off Tessa's sweatshirt to get a look at her wounds.

"Did something bite you?" she exclaimed, "What bit you, Tessa?"

Brand looked on horrified. "Was it zombies?!" he asked, his voice pitching widly. Snow and Tessa both shook their heads, and Brand blew out an audible sigh of relief. Micah pulled two dishtowels off a rack and pressed one against Tessa's forearm and one against her shoulder. They both winced as she did so.

"Sorry," Micah breathed. Tessa nodded.

"We were attacked by these, I don't know—Franken-Dogs—parts of dogs all stitched together. Big, fast, mean, and pretty much the crap nightmares are made of. There were so many. We got separated," Tessa said, glancing at Snow who looked like she was ready to pass out. Brand stared at Tessa's gushing wounds.

"We have to get you to a hospital," he said.

Snow shook her head. "The Scion will be fine if you can slow the bleeding."

Brand and Micah looked at her, her eyes fluttering, her face flushed, and she continued. "Superfast healing comes with the superhero package, just slow the bleeding and she'll be fine. I promise."

"Oh yes, a promise from you—" Brand began but Tessa cut him off.

"Give her a break," Tessa said wearily. "She did good." Micah and Brand looked at Tessa, perhaps to check to see if she was delusional.

"She doesn't have a scratch on her Tessa, she's covered in *your* blood," Micah said to Tessa, a bite in her voice. Tessa tilted her head back and pressed on her wound.

"Trust me. In fact, Snow—" she looked at her, beautiful despite being wounded and nearly unconscious, in the kitchen chair. "What do you need, what can we do?"

Snow blinked at Tessa dreamily. "Have your minions draw me a cold bath, Scion." She blinked again, her eyes fluttering. "You should see me in the winter. I am magnificent in the win—" And then before she could finish the sentence, she slumped out of her chair and onto the floor, passed out, somehow still looking elegant.

"Pfft," Brand said waving a dismissive hand at her theatrics. But Tessa pressed him.

"No, something's wrong with her," she insisted, even as her vision swam. Brand crossed to Snow and touched her cheek. He drew back in shock. "What?" Tessa asked, "Cold?"

"No, she's burning up," Brand said, holding his hand as if he'd been burned.

"Well, that can't be good," Tessa said, before she too passed out, everything going black.

NINETEEN

When Tessa woke up, she was on the couch in the living room, a blanket laid over her. She had a brutal headache, but she felt strong again, unlike how she had in the moments before she passed out. Tessa raised her arm and found it well bandaged. She touched her shoulder and neck and found the same. Though both injuries throbbed lightly, they were a dream compared to the pain she remembered before passing out. Snow must have been right about her healing ability. Asleep in a chair across from her was Brand. Tessa didn't see Snow or Micah but there were lights on upstairs, so she threw back the blanket and followed the light. The light in the master bathroom, accessed only through her father's bedroom, was on. When she got there, she found Micah hovering over Snow, still unconscious, but naked and submerged to her neck in the big bathtub. Micah jumped at the sight of Tessa and then breathed a sigh of relief.

"Thank God you're okay," she said, and went to hug her, careful of her bandages. When they broke apart, Micah cast a worried look at Snow in the bath. "I don't think it's working," she said, her brow knitting in concern. Tessa reached down and felt Snow's cheek. It was dangerously warm. Tessa touched the water, which was cold but could be colder.

"Let's try this," she said, and unstopped the tub, turning the cold water on to let it run. She looked around the room. "Hold on," she said. When she came back five minutes later, she was balancing two pair of socks, two sweatshirts, a blanket, and two big bowls of ice. Micah raised an eyebrow at her in confusion as Tessa closed the door behind her and put towels at the base of the door to stop any air from escaping. "I turned on the upstairs air conditioner and shut the vents in the other rooms," she explained, handing Micah a sweatshirt and a pair of socks. "It's about to get very cold in here." Tessa dumped the ice into the cold running water and pulled on her own socks and sweatshirt. Then she sat next to Micah, both of them huddled under the blanket, on the cool tile floor and watched Snow for signs of life.

"By the way," Micah said, "I'm pretty sure Brand's going to wake up in love with her."

Tessa smiled and cocked her head. "Why's that?"

"Turns out it's harder than it looks to get an unconscious woman out of a skin tight leather catsuit. I needed help," she said. Tessa tried to keep a straight face and then burst out laughing. Micah tried to resist but failed, joining her. "I thought his eyes were going to fall out of his damn face," she said between peels of laughter. After a few minutes, they caught their breath and resumed stoically watching Snow.

"Nothing on Robin and Fenris?" Tessa asked. She had avoided the question as long as she dared.

"No," Micah said. "Not yet." She reached out for Tessa's cold hand and held it. After perhaps ten minutes, and with both Tessa and Micah's teeth chattering thanks to the icy conditions they had created, Snow finally let out a soft moan. Tessa and Micah shot up as if one. Tessa reached out to feel Snow's forehead, which was cool, bordering on cold. She looked back at Micah and smiled optimistically.

"I think she's out of the woods."

Snow slitted open just one of her eyes. "I'm never going back to the woods again, Scion. Not least in this godforsaken climate."

Tessa smiled. The bitch was back. And it was good.

Tessa left out some fluffy towels for Snow as well as clothes that would be at least three sizes too large and also be nothing she would want to be caught dead in (which Tessa had to admit was half the fun). Micah searched the house for more ingredients to make an actual meal since it was well past time that any restaurant in Lore would deliver food, while Tessa woke up Brand to see what they'd found in their witch research. Brand showed her their list of witches, now totaling twelve, and Tessa sighed at the futility of the effort. They hadn't found any connections to the Troll; the research was far too broad. How on earth would they find what all of this meant? But just as she was lamenting it, Brand turned everything around.

"Well, I mean, I guess maybe it's too obvious, but aren't we talking about something very specific now?" Tessa looked at him blankly. "I mean, 'Franken-Dogs', that's what you called them. Is there a reason we think we're not dealing with Dr. Frankenstein?" Tessa looked at him stupidly for a moment and then jumped onto him with a full body hug.

"Ohmigodyou'reagenius!" she shouted. Tessa released Brand and he sat back up, dazed. Superpowered full body hugs were no bullshit. "I can't believe I didn't realize it. Of course! Dr. Frankenstein!" Tessa shouted. Brand shrugged nonchalantly but was clearly pleased with himself. As Tessa got up to tell Micah, the front door sailed open and Robin walked in. Tessa's heart leapt and she threw herself into his exhausted arms, not caring about anything except that he'd come back, and in one piece, mostly. He hugged her back, one hand on the back of her head, drifting into her hair, his face buried in her shoulder, as hers was in his. It was the kind of hug people write cheesy movies about. Full of promise and genuine affection, things to come, other things better left unsaid. Robin stroked Tessa's hair and breathed her in.

Things happened so fast.

As they separated, Snow came down the stairs, somehow looking herself despite the Halloween costume that were Tessa's shorts and Oxford sweatshirt, both of which she was swimming in.

"Snow," Robin said, nodding his head at her in acknowledgement.

"Robin," Snow said, doing the same.

"Wow, you guys really bonded on that death-defying mission," Micah said from the kitchen doorway, rolling her eyes.

Tessa looked between Robin and Snow. "Baby steps Mike, baby steps."

Snow cast her eyes at Brand and Micah. "Thank you, minions, for reviving me. I…I owe you," she said. Tessa could see the sentence was painful for her. Micah smiled and waved a spatula in a gesture implying it meant nothing, and Brand looked at his shoes and seemed to wish himself into the hardwood.

"No, uh…no, uh problem," he said. The group moved into the kitchen to tend to Robin's wounds, and Micah shooed them over to the kitchen table away from the food, which was pancakes and which smelled amazing. Snow sat in a chair at the table. Brand perched nervously on a stool as far away from Snow as possible. Tessa pored over the first aid kit for things to patch up Robin's injuries, which were many, but none as significant as Tessa's had been.

"Any sign of Fenris?" Tessa asked, as she wrapped Robin's hand in thin white gauze.

He shook his head. "Are you okay?" he asked her as if she was the only person in the room. Tessa nodded.

"I'm fine."

"Yes, yes, we're all fine here. Thanks for caring," Snow said waving her hand around, annoyed. Robin bit his tongue, likely remembering how useful Snow had been mere hours ago.

"We have an idea about who might be behind all this," Tessa said, and looked to Brand.

"Dr. Frankenstein," Brand supplied. Robin sat back in his chair, chewing on the idea.

"Makes sense," Robin mused.

"But it doesn't fit with magic," Snow said, pressing her lips together in thought. "Dr. Frankenstein is science, not magic. Magic and science are, of course, more related than most realize, but not The Doctor. Magic feels *wrong* for him. Perhaps the two events are unrelated?"

Tessa chewed on her lip. "It's possible." She looked dejectedly at her friends, lost and tired, hurt and confused. Robin spoke up.

"Can I have pancakes?"

The absurdity of their lives must have hit each one of them in that moment because they burst into laughter. Even Snow smiled, sort of. Micah began doling out plates of the fluffy, golden-brown discs and started another batch. They ate in blissful silence for whole minutes before something crashed powerfully against the front door.

Tessa reached out her hand for the magic axe. "La Colombe Noire!" she shouted, and the now familiar crackle and pop of energy flashed, followed by the axe snapping powerfully into her hand. Micah and Brand gasped at the sight and the group, following behind Tessa, moved toward the doorway. As they turned the corner, the door fell open and a massive Franken-Dog was quite literally thrown through the doorway. Micah and Brand both shouted out in relative terror, but it didn't move. A moment later, Fenris, injured and completely naked, stumbled through the doorway. Tessa dropped the axe and ran to him. She got under his shoulder just before he lost his footing. He looked up at her, his eyes still piercing but strangely unguarded for the first time. They took her by surprise.

"I have an idea," he said, and then collapsed, the full weight of him surprising her. As he lost consciousness, he shifted and Tessa found herself trying to hold up a ten-foot unconscious wolf in her foyer.

 TWENTY

Robin ran to Tessa and helped lift Fenris. Together they half-carried, half-dragged the unconscious wolf to the couch. Realizing there was no way he would fit, Micah and Brand moved some chairs away and they laid him on the floor. He was leaking blood all over the hardwood, but it was impossible to see where his injuries were beneath his thick grey fur.

"He's HUGE," Micah said, staring at Fenris and then looking from face to face in the room, hoping for some acknowledgement of the very obvious fact. Tessa looked up at Snow and Robin.

"Why did he shift?"

"It's his natural state," Snow said. "He can't maintain a human form without exerting his will, at least not naturally," she added. Robin nodded in agreement.

"We can't fix his wounds like this, I can't see anything!" Tessa said, holding a hand against an area that was bleeding badly and pulling at the dense fur helplessly.

"We could completely shave him," Snow offered brightly, already chuckling at the idea of an embarrassingly hair-free wolf version of Fenris. Tessa and Robin both shot her looks that said 'shut up' and she grumbled something about how she was only joking. Micah went to the kitchen and brought back the first aid kit, which was getting slimmer by the moment. Tessa nodded at her to set it down but then saw what she had in her hand.

"That could work," she said, nodding at Micah.

"What?" Robin asked.

"It's smelling salts. It could wake him up, so we could work on him," Micah said, showing him the bottle.

Snow shook her head, "But he'll be disoriented and still a wolf. He could kill us all."

"Why would he do that?" Tessa demanded. "He saved our lives out there. I doubt he did it just so he could tear us to pieces in the living room a few hours later."

Robin shook his head. "That's not what she means. She means that he won't be in control. He's less in control of his actions in his wolf state, and that, added to the disorientation and pain—it could go badly." Tessa rubbed her forehead with a bloody hand.

"We have to try it. We can't just leave him like this."

Robin thought for a moment and looked at Fenris's giant, exceedingly dangerous form and then nodded in agreement. Snow sighed. Tessa repositioned herself so that she could pin down his neck and front legs. She nodded her head at Robin and Snow. "You two hold down his back legs. Brand?" Brand stepped forward. "Uncap the salts and hold it over him and then get out of here." Brand nodded and took the bottle from Micah, who stepped back toward the kitchen. "On three," Tessa said, meeting everyone's eyes and waiting for their nods of understanding. "One...Two...Three," Tessa said. As soon as Brand uncapped the bottle near his head, the wolf sprang to life and threw the entire group off of him with one powerful convulsion. Brand was halfway to the kitchen, and Robin and Snow skittered back toward the door as well, but Tessa found herself face to face with the giant animal.

"I know you're in there," she whispered, her face mere inches from his, a snarl curling his black mouth. "Fenris," she said more firmly when he didn't shift but didn't attack either. "You need to shift so that we can fix you."

Something akin to understanding flickered in the wolf's eyes, and then he shifted, becoming human (and still very naked). Tessa pulled a blanket from the sofa over his shoulders and helped him into the kitchen, or as she had now come to think of it, 'Triage 1.'

Micah brought some dishtowels over to flesh out the pillaged first aid kit, and Brand brought some water in a bowl. Everyone stood in the kitchen staring. Fenris stared back at them, seeming inhuman and empty, stiff and barely in control of himself. Tessa turned away from him to the group. "Guys. Can you give me a minute?" Micah, Brand, and Snow shook their heads as if being woken from a dream. All three nodded, leaving the kitchen for the dining room and the pile of unread books there. Robin hesitated.

"No," he said, his arms crossed, his eyes some mixture of protection, suspicion, and jealousy that Tessa both loved and hated. Fenris started to shift and groaned as he fought the urge to return to wolf form. Tessa looked imploringly at Robin.

"Please, Robin," she said. His mouth twitched, and then he turned to join the others. Tessa watched him go for a moment, and when he was out of sight, she turned back to Fenris. She didn't meet his eyes, as she wasn't sure what she would find there and wasn't sure she wanted to know, regardless. The shoulder wound was the worst of it, something that looked born of both claws and teeth, so Tessa stood up and cleaned the gash. He winced and tensed up, and twice started to shift before regaining control. It was terrifying to watch. Both to see his features move, almost like water, shifting from something so stunningly beautiful to something both beautiful and terrifying. From a man that most women would delight to dream about into a wolf, a monster, that would haunt your worst nightmares. Watching him struggle to maintain control raised all sorts of questions in Tessa about how in control he ever was. And how human he was when he was a wolf. How wolf he was when he was a human. They were questions she wasn't sure she wanted the answers to. Tessa blinked, it was too scary. With his shoulder clean and bandaged, Tessa moved onto the less intense wounds and her mind drifted back to the battlefield, he had saved all their lives, monster or no.

"Thank you," Tessa said as she cleaned and bandaged one of his hands. He touched her forearm suddenly, lightly, where one of her own bandages was.

"Looks like I fell short, Hardcore," he said, looking up at her and their eyes catching. Tessa pulled away from the gaze with some effort. She didn't want him using whatever seduction-y Fictional power he had on her.

"No. You were amazing. Without you, we'd all be dead," she said, busying herself with the next wound. Ten minutes later, he was cleaned up and peppered with bits of white gauze. "You should sleep," Tessa said, as she closed the kit.

"Can't," he said. Tessa looked up from the kit, waiting for the rest of the sentence. "If I sleep I'll shift and all your fancy bandages will be for nothing."

"Oh," Tessa said. "Okay, well then, let's—" and before she could finish the sentence, he stood up and she snapped her head to the side. "—Yo!" she yelped, holding up her hands to further block the view of his still-naked body. He looked down at himself but didn't move. Tessa called for Brand.

"Yeah?" he said, popping his head in the room and then snapping his eyes closed and raising his hands. "Jesus, Tessa, you couldn't warn me?"

"Sorry," Tessa said giggling. "Can you grab some clothes from my Dad's room? Nothing will fit, but in the bottom drawer of the dresser, there should be some sweats and undershirts that might sorta work." Brand nodded, his eyes still closed and then visored his eyes and walked through the kitchen with his head down. Fenris continued standing, rather oblivious. Micah came in looking for Brand, saw Fenris, dropped a plate and turned back around without saying a word. Tessa gestured at him.

"Um…could you sit please?"

Fenris smiled. "Of course."

When Tessa felt him sitting again, she looked up. "Shy much?"

"What is there to be shy about?"

"I'll say," Tessa heard Micah whistle from the other room. Two minutes later, a pair of grey sweatpants and a white ribbed undershirt tank came hurtling into the kitchen. Tessa fetched them for Fenris and then left the room. He came out a moment later.

"Christ on a bike," Micah said under her breath, and Tessa smacked her lightly on the arm. Robin sort of glared at both of them. The sweats were slightly too large for Fenris's lean lower body, and the undershirt was far too small for his broad, muscled chest. The result was hilarious but also somehow hot. He and Snow together looked like a weird, perfectly mismatched pair. And they must have known it because they practically growled at one another.

"Everyone get over themselves," Tessa said, rolling her eyes. "We're all lucky to be alive. Or since you don't die, then I guess I'm lucky to be alive, and you three are lucky to have all your limbs…do you lose limbs?"

Snow, Fenris, and Robin all made faces and wavered one hand as if to suggest that the jury was still out, or maybe that it was negotiable.

Tessa groaned. "Well, that's not confusing at all."

Brand raised his hand. Tessa smiled at him and then nodded her head. "Yeah?"

"Um. Can we talk about the fact that you have a magical axe that you conjured out of thin freaking air?! What's up with that?"

Micah nodded beside him. Tessa reached out her hand.

"LA COLOMBE NOIRE!" she shouted and the axe reappeared.

"Yeah, that." Brand said pointing at it.

Tessa turned to Brand. "The Black, what?"

Brand raised an eyebrow at her. "Little Miss European Boarding School doesn't speak French?"

"Listen, I speak a little bit of a whole lot of languages, none of it well…you want me to chop you with this thing?"

Brand raised his hands in mock surrender. "The Black Dove."

Tessa smiled and gripped the axe. "Yeah, that feels right," she said and then looked at Snow. "Do you know anything about it?"

Snow shook her head. "Not really. I heard Bluebeard had a weapon made for himself, but I'd never seen it. *The White Dove'* is, or rather *was* the name for one of the variations of Bluebeard's story, perhaps he named it after that?"

"Are you the only one that can call it?" Micah asked.

"I don't know," Tessa said thoughtfully and put it down on the floor, where it promptly disappeared after a few seconds.

"Badass," Brand whispered.

"Give it a try," Tessa said to Micah who shook her head.

"Oh, no, I didn't mean me."

"I'll do it!" Brand shouted.

Tessa nodded at him. "Go for it."

Brand reached out his hand. "Like this?" Tessa nodded and Brand shouted into the air, "LA COLOMBE NOIRE!" with perfect pronunciation, far better than Tessa's. Everyone waited while absolutely nothing happened. Brand's shoulders dropped. "Damn," he said, and Tessa gave him an apologetic look. After a moment Tessa called the axe again. It immediately crackled and snapped into her hand. Brand smiled.

"I say again, badass."

"How did you get it?" Robin asked.

"She killed Bluebeard with it," Fenris said, and Tessa shot him a look. She hadn't realized he'd seen it.

She looked at Robin. "Yes," she said. "That's right."

"Then I suspect—" Robin started and then trailed off, as if unwilling to finish the thought.

"—That it belongs to you until you're dead too," Fenris supplied, locking eyes with Tessa. She felt a chill run up her spine, yet again. He had a penchant for speaking truth, no matter how unpleasant. Tessa doubted he meant that it would cease to be hers after she passed away at the ripe old age of ninety, sleeping peacefully in her bed.

Tessa wanted to change the subject so she walked back into the foyer where the dead Franken-Dog still laid on the floor, stinking up the whole house. "Thank you, by the way, Fenris, for bringing a giant corpse Franken-Dog into my house. And why exactly did you do that?" Fenris crouched down and turned the dog, wincing from his wounds.

"Wolves have been disappearing. Ever since late summer I've seen, and felt, fewer of them in the woods," he said and pointed to the creature's head, which was clearly that of a wolf. But he continued turning the creature and pointed to the torso and two legs, which looked more like they belonged to a large dog. "But this part, and this, these are dog, not wolf. And most of them were like that, parts of each."

"So the creatures are made of dogs and wolves, so what?" Snow asked.

"I'm the only one likely to miss the wolves," Fenris said, laying the dog back down.

"But people will miss their dogs," Tessa filled in. "Is anyone here good with computers?" Nobody said anything, but Micah looked straight at Brand. Everyone else followed her gaze.

"Yeah?" Tessa said, part question, part statement. Brand folded his arms.

"Okay, yeah, yeah, I am," he paused and added, "But if this is some kind of dangerous solo mission I'm volunteering for, then no, no, I am not."

"It's not," Fenris said and then looked at Tessa. "Where's the computer?"

"My laptop is upstairs," Tessa said and moved to go get it, but Brand put a hand on her arm.

"I've got mine," he sighed, and everyone followed him to the dining room where he pulled it out of his bag. "What am I looking for?"

"Reports of missing animals," Fenris said.

"Wait. From where? *'Good with computers'* is not code for, like, totally able to hack into the Lore PD database, or, whatever," he snapped defensively. And then Micah put a hand on his shoulder.

"Ohmigod," she breathed.

"What?" he asked, still annoyed.

"What if it's not you being good with computers that matters, but you speaking all languages that matters?"

Brand was silent for a moment. And then there was a flurry of typing, and the screen was a blur of changing images, pages moving almost faster than the eye could register.

"Holy crap," Brand said, "I speak computer."

TWENTY-ONE

Half an hour later, they'd marked up a large map of Lore with a red sharpie, trying to find a pattern to the reports of missing dogs. The map was littered with x's. They covered the entire city. Brand continued clicking around his laptop at an almost alarming speed and then stopped. "Um…guys?"

"What?" Tessa asked, looking up from the map.

"It's not just dogs," he said, his face looking a bit green. Everyone crowded around the laptop to see a list of missing people, more than two dozen in just the last month.

The room took a collective breath.

"No," Tessa said quietly, almost to herself, "Does this mean there are Franken-People walking around too?"

The room was silent.

In another half hour, they'd mapped out where all the people had disappeared as well. They all stood back and stared at the map for a long time, absorbing the enormity of what all the red marks meant.

Death, every one of them.

Snow broke the silence. "So, is there a plan in our future? Because it better be superior to the last one. I'm not about to potentially get torn to shreds by killer dogs *again* this weekend."

Tessa looked up, bleary-eyed and stared at the room, everyone looking to her for answers. It was too much.

"A good time for The Advocate," Fenris said.

"Goddammit, stop mentioning The Advocate!" Tessa shouted, and she was gone before any of them had time to respond.

Robin looked at the clock on the wall. "It's almost three, we all need rest," he turned to look at Brand and Micah, "Do your parents even know where you are?" They both pointed at the other one without looking up. "Oh," he said, "Okay, well then, sleep. Regroup once we've done more research."

Snow and Fenris were gone before he even turned around.

The shaft of light from the hall cut out and Tessa looked up to see Fenris standing just outside her bedroom door. She brushed a tear away, embarrassed, hoping his keen eyesight couldn't see *that* well into her dark room.

"What?" she asked.

He pushed the door open slightly, causing the shaft of light to fall across her feet.

"The plan is to re-group once we know more."

Tessa stood up and crossed her arms. "Alright." When he didn't go, she stared at him, trying to make out his face in the shadows. It was impossible. "Something you want to say?"

"Just wondering what happened to the first plan."

"What plan?" Tessa asked, a harsh note climbing into her voice.

"Weren't we going after Robin's tied-up Troll when we were ambushed?"

Tessa's blood ran cold. "Are you implying something?"

"Not at all," he paused, and then ticked his head to the side, examining her in that way he did. She didn't need to see his face to know his expression. "Later, luv."

Tessa sat back down on the bed, winded, like she'd been punched in the stomach.

A few minutes later, Robin knocked on Tessa's door. "Tessa?"

"Come in."

"Snow and Fenris left," he started.

"Yeah, he came by, said he'd be back."

"Of course he did," Robin said under his breath, leaning against Tessa's dresser. When Tessa didn't say anything, he looked at her. "You okay?"

"Um."

"What else did he say?"

"Nothing. It's nothing."

"It doesn't sound like nothing," he said.

"Well, it is."

Silence hung between them. "I'd like to stay," he said finally, but it sounded unsure. Tessa looked up at him for the first time, and there was enough moon from the window that she could see his face. Open and honest. Whatever was going on, it wasn't what Fenris had suggested. She'd been wrong to even think it. And she was mad at herself for letting Fenris so easily push her in that direction. This was what he did.

"I'd feel better if you did stay," Tessa said, smiling.

"Brand and Micah are staying," he said. "I think we should stay close together, at least for the night. All on the same level. I'll put them in your father's room, and I'll sleep on your floor," he paused, now in the open doorway. "If that's acceptable to you, of course."

"I can stay on the floor," she offered.

"Don't be ridiculous," he said, and called out as he went down the stairs, "I'm a hero for hell's sake." Tessa smiled and shook her head. She had a crush on Robin freaking Hood. A serious, full-blown, monster crush. What on Earth would happen next in her life when something like THAT was true?

Robin was so perfect for her it was as if she'd dreamed him up and that frightened her a little. More than a little if she was honest with herself, but she didn't feel like being honest right now. Besides, there were far more important things going on than crushes. She went into her bathroom, and when she came out, Micah and Brand were rooting around in a hall closet for blankets. Tessa went to help and they stopped.

"You okay, Tess?" Micah asked.

"I'm fine," she said, but it sounded sad, even to her.

"Tess," Brand started, "You know what happened with Bishop wasn't your fault, right?"

Tessa pulled down a big blanket from a top shelf and handed it to her friends. "Then whose fault was it?"

"Not yours," Micah said. "Nobody's, I think."

"That's not how it feels," Tessa said, taking down another blanket and a fluffy comforter as well as an extra pillow for Robin. "You guys will be okay in there?" Tessa asked, glancing at her father's bedroom.

"Yeah, of course," they said together.

"Where's Robin?" Tessa asked, looking over the railing to the downstairs.

"He's getting rid of the Franken-Dog," Brand said, "And the blood." Tessa nodded and went into her room to make up a spot on the floor for Robin. She heard Micah and Brand talking in the next room.

Once they were quiet, the house felt eerily still after so much activity. So much had happened in the last week, hell, the last twenty-four hours, Tessa wasn't sure if it was even possible for her brain to process it. And then she decided she liked it better before. When there had been so many emergencies that she didn't have time to think what it all meant. To think about what she was feeling.

To be *so* afraid.

To feel the fear and insecurity closing around her like a shroud. Now, in the lull of the house, the quiet before whatever it was that was going to happen tomorrow, all she could do was worry and wait.

Brand and Micah were in the backyard with Robin, working on some basic training when Tessa got up. She brushed her teeth, washed her face, and then pulled on some clothes and went out to watch. When she did, Brand and Micah looked terribly relived and both made bathroom excuses.

Tessa leaned against the doorframe and watched Robin shoot arrows into a large tree at the end of the yard. They were all clustered tightly on a knot just off-center of the trunk. She tried very hard to think things other than 'hott, double t, hott.'

"How'd they do?" Tessa asked when he was between shots. He looked back at her.

"They have a lot of enthusiasm," he said, a bit grimly. Tessa chuckled and walked over to a wooden picnic table that had a handful of weapons laid out, both hers and Robin's.

"That bad?"

He shook his head no. "Just new. They'll get better. Micah has some promise in hand to hand, some martial arts training from when she was young, she said. It'll come back to her. She's not so fond of the weapons though. I think they frighten her."

"Rightly so," Tessa said, fingering the point of a dagger that lay on the table. "And Brand?"

Robin winced a bit. "He's fast, which is good, but he's still going through a slightly awkward phase. It's getting in his way. He's got a lot of heart though, very 'never give up.' He'll get better," he nodded to himself as he nocked another arrow. Tessa rolled up on him as he drew the string back.

"Teach *me*," she said, standing very close to him, eyeing his target. Robin looked at her and accidentally let the arrow go. It flew over the fence and into the woods. Tessa giggled. "I thought you were supposed to be freaking Robin Hood," she teased, and then turned to look at him only to find his eyes trained intensely on her. Tessa thought that if you could bottle the kind of intensity he had in just his eyes, you could sell it and retire a millionaire. It was bewitching. Irresistible.

He handed her the bow and a single arrow from his quiver without saying a word. Tessa set her feet and raised the bow.

"I thought you were right-handed," he said.

"I'm ambidextrous," she said, shrugging as if it wasn't a big deal.

Robin laughed loudly at the sky. "Of course you are."

"What's funny?"

"Nothing. Just, *of course* The Last Scion is ambidextrous, you come with all the advantages."

Tessa bristled slightly, "Maybe because it's all of you against just one of me."

Robin softened. "Not all of us." He stood behind her and adjusted her form, touching her arms and then legs, little bits of electricity shooting through her when he did. Tessa nocked the arrow.

"Like this?" she asked. He nodded. She raised the bow again and aimed. "Like this?" He was so close to her that she felt him nod his head.

"Yes."

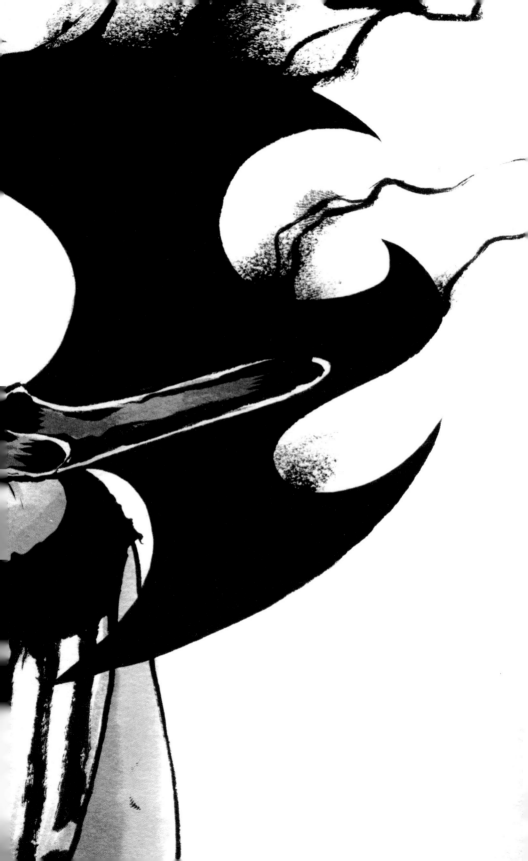

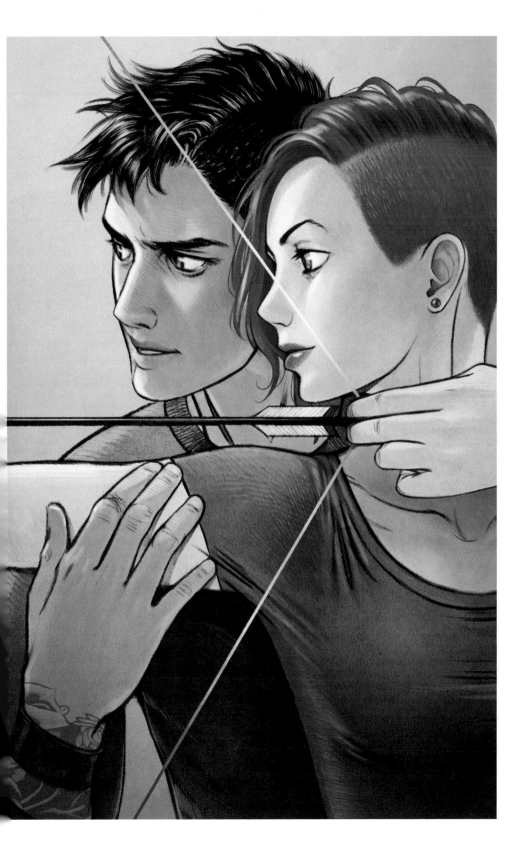

M SOUTHWORTH

Illustrations

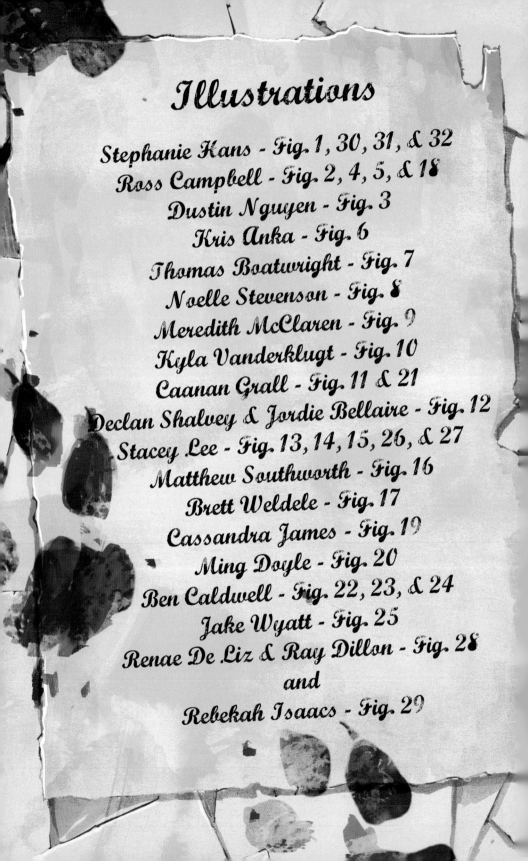

Stephanie Hans - Fig. 1, 30, 31, & 32

Ross Campbell - Fig. 2, 4, 5, & 18

Dustin Nguyen - Fig. 3

Kris Anka - Fig. 6

Thomas Boatwright - Fig. 7

Noelle Stevenson - Fig. 8

Meredith McClaren - Fig. 9

Kyla Vanderklugt - Fig. 10

Caanan Grall - Fig. 11 & 21

Declan Shalvey & Jordie Bellaire - Fig. 12

Stacey Lee - Fig. 13, 14, 15, 26, & 27

Matthew Southworth - Fig. 16

Brett Weldele - Fig. 17

Cassandra James - Fig. 19

Ming Doyle - Fig. 20

Ben Caldwell - Fig. 22, 23, & 24

Jake Wyatt - Fig. 25

Renae De Liz & Ray Dillon - Fig. 28

and

Rebekah Isaacs - Fig. 29

Tessa drew back on the string. She liked the feeling of it, this power, just primed and ready to be released. "What am I aiming for *specifically*?" she asked.

"Let's just start with the tree in general," he said. Tessa smiled and felt his hand move to her hip as he slid to the side to check her aim. "It looks good," he said, his voice quiet.

"Yes," she said, and narrowed her eyes, concentrating. She released the arrow, and the surge of it leaving her was almost as awesome as the sound of it striking the tree with a powerful thwack. Her arrow landed dead center of his already tight cluster.

"Tova lo," he breathed. "You're a natural."

Tessa smiled. "What's 'Tova'?" she asked.

Robin smiled. "It's a swear word."

"One of the big ones?"

"The biggest." He moved to take the bow from her. She didn't let it go. Their hands met and she felt the same surge of electricity. It wasn't lessening with time, if anything it was getting more intense. Tessa looked down at their hands and wondered if it felt the same for him. He was so close she imagined she could feel the heat of him through her clothing.

"Tessa...I..." Robin started, and Tessa could sense there was some speech coming her way, some speech she didn't want to hear just now. Instead, she moved even closer to him.

"Don't say it," she said, her lips inches from his.

Brand and Micah coughed dramatically from the patio stairs and then giggled like schoolgirls as Tessa and Robin separated.

"Yeah, okay, back to it." Robin said, and she could swear he was blushing. She went back inside just as the doorbell rang, several times. It couldn't be Fenris with his inability to use doorbells, but she thought it might be Snow, so she wasn't prepared when she opened the door to find Detectives Wade and Ripley standing there.

"Um. Hi," Tessa said.

"Miss Battle," Wade said. "May we come in?"

"Uh. Sure?" Tessa said, sounding like she was guessing and looking behind her to see if there was anything horribly incriminating laying around. Things looked reasonably together, she hoped the illusion would hold. Wade stepped across the threshold with Ripley following close behind.

Tessa hoped everyone would stay in the backyard until they were gone, and her hopes were immediately dashed when Brand and Micah walked in, fortunately not carrying any weapons.

"Uh. Hey," Brand said. Micah ducked her head and cleaned her glasses on the edge of her sweatshirt. Tessa groaned inside, they couldn't have looked guiltier if they'd tried.

"Miss Chen and Mr. Ellis," Wade said smiling. "How fortuitous, we were just at your homes."

"Kay," Brand said.

Ripley looked at Tessa. "Could I trouble you for some water?"

"Sure," Tessa said, padding into the kitchen, hoping he wouldn't follow her. He did and almost crashed into Robin. Tessa got Ripley a glass and mentally thanked the universe that he'd left his bow outside.

"Hello," Ripley said to Robin, who nodded and did not speak. As Tessa handed the glass to the Detective, she noticed Robin's hands were almost white he was clenching them so hard. "Your boyfriend?" Ripley asked, looking at Tessa.

Tessa shook her head. "Just a friend," she said, smiling politely.

Robin was tense; it was coming off of him in waves, palpable in the room. The word anarchy echoed in Tessa's mind. She worried what being around actual Mortal authority figures would do to him. Judging by the set of his jaw, it was freaking him the hell out. Ripley nodded and turned back to the living room. He sat next to Wade, across from Brand and Micah, who already looked like they'd been put under hot lights for an hour.

"And who are you?" Wade asked as she noticed Robin. Tessa saw Robin through cop eyes and cringed. He had 'troublesome bad-boy type' written all over him.

"Robin," he said flatly.

"Boyfriend?" Wade asked Ripley.

"Friend," Ripley said, smiling. Tessa liked Ripley more than Wade. Wade got under her skin in a way that made her want to itch like mad. That probably made her a good Detective in some ways, but Tessa felt sure she'd confess something to Ripley before Wade if she had the option. Wade wrote something in her notebook.

"Last name?" she asked, without looking up. Robin just looked at her, his eyes sharp in his face. Wade looked up and met his eyes, unblinking.

"Locke," he said, his jaw tightening visibly.

Tessa stepped forward, trying to draw their attention away from him. "So, what brings you here, Detectives?" Tessa asked, taking a seat in a chair across from them.

"It appears your two friends here—Mr. Ellis and Miss Chen—were the last people to see Mr. Bishop alive," Ripley said.

Tessa blinked. "Um…okay?"

"And when did _you_ last see him?"

"In his office that day," Tessa said, stumbling only slightly. It was a lie, she'd never met him before that horrible night at Bluebeard's, but she now had to cover for the book she'd said she'd loaned him when she got caught in his office. This was how people got caught. Lies. Lies stacked upon lies stacked upon lies, until you tripped over one and fell on your damn face.

"But you didn't see him after school that day, in front of your house?"

"No," Tessa said, a bit confused, since she hadn't. That wasn't a lie.

"Because the witness that saw Mr. Bishop with your friends here, saw them right in front of your house."

"Well, I wasn't there," Tessa said.

"She wasn't there. We had been talking to her, but she went in her house and then we were walking home," Brand said.

"And that's when you saw Mr. Bishop?" Ripley filled in.

"Yeah but just for, like, a second," Micah said, and then looked at her feet. Wade's eyes flicked over to Robin, whose gaze could best be described as restrained hatred.

"So can you tell us anything about the last time you saw Mr. Bishop then, Miss Chen? Mr. Ellis?

"He just like, absentmindedly said hi, like he was looking for something, that was it," Brand said.

"And in six hours, he was dead, along with a Mr. Rene Severin," Wade filled in.

Tessa blinked at her and her heart clenched up at the reminder. "Is that when it happened?" she asked, detached, or with a tone she hoped was detached.

"About," Ripley said. "Do you know Mr. Severin?"

"I don't think so, I mean, not the name," Tessa said, trailing off. Brand and Micah both shook their heads. Ripley produced a manila folder and handed Tessa a sheet of paper. Tessa stared at it. It was a series of black and white mug shots. The second from the left was Bluebeard.

"You recognize anyone?" Ripley asked, watching her closely.

"No," she said evenly, handing it back to Ripley, who handed it to Brand and Micah. They blinked at it and shook their heads.

"You sure?" Wade asked. The question was intended for all of them, but Wade looked right at Tessa.

Brand and Micah both said, "Yes. We're sure." Like trained seals. Man, they were terrible at lying. Ripley took the sheet back and smiled at all three of them. Wade followed suit.

"Well then, that will do it for now," Wade said.

Ripley put his water down and nodded at Tessa. "Thanks for the drink."

They stood to go. Wade kept her eyes trained on Tessa, the stare this woman had. "You remember I don't want you leaving the county, right, Miss Battle?"

"Of course," Tessa said, as charming as if she actually meant it. "I've already canceled my highly anticipated world tour." The detectives smiled as if they were charmed, and Tessa walked them to the door. Only when she was sure they'd driven away did she breath a sigh of relief. Robin unclenched, and Micah and Brand finally stopped sweating.

"Great. Just what we need, trips to prison on top of everything else," Brand said. Tessa leaned against the front door and tipped her head back, closing her eyes and wishing she could go back to bed. Just close the shades, get under the covers, and never come out again.

She was pretty sure she had a Trig test tomorrow that she hadn't studied for and even that seemed like a party compared to the rest of her life.

TWENTY-TWO

Indeed she did have a Trig quiz in the morning, and as the teacher passed out white paper sheets of doom, she geared herself up for absolute failure of epic proportions. She had spent the entire day before researching monsters and analyzing data stolen from the damn Lore PD database, not doing Trig.

She was doomed.

"You all right?" Nash asked, leaning close to her while still somehow remaining covert. "You look a little green."

"I, yeah…" Tessa chewed her lip. "I didn't study," she said, which was a massive understatement.

"Busy weekend," he said, nodding, a knowing look in his eyes. Tessa bit her lip again. She had to be careful what she said to him.

"Uh, yeah," she said again. Apparently her witty barbs of last week had now been whittled down to "ums" and "yeahs." Nash slid away as he took his quiz from the student in front of him and Tessa found herself wondering a million things that weren't Trig.

Nash was still as handsome as ever, and anyone in his orbit would feel his warmth, like being near a star. But with what she had felt for Robin over the past few days, his star had waned for her and she was glad.

The only thing that gave her pause was a fear that part of what attracted her to Robin was not in her control. Did he have Fiction-y powers of seduction to go with his archery and swordplay? As Tessa felt herself falling for him so fast, faster than she would have dreamed possible, how much of that was her and how much of it was who he was? How much of what she liked about him was really him and how much was just fancy Fictional magic? At least her affection for Nash felt pure. He was deliciously human and the simplicity of that appealed to Tessa.

Still, it didn't matter.

What was done was done and Nash now seemed like a distant if beautiful star, and Robin a giant glowing sun.

Instead of going to her second period computer lab, Tessa snuck back into Bishop's office to look for more Advocate journals. His office had been cordoned off, so she crawled in the window.

Brand was doing everything he could searching the Lore PD database, but they needed more Story-specific information. Dr. Frankenstein was surely their villain, given what they had fought over the weekend but the locks of stolen hair still plagued Tessa. How did Dr. Frankenstein connect to that hair? And what about The Troll? Was he part of things too? Even with their sights set on a reasonable bad guy and everyone doing everything they could to find him, there were still so many unanswered questions. She was determined to do all she could to protect Brand and Micah, and herself, if it came to that. It was a task that felt impossible when she had no idea what they were up against.

But Tessa hadn't been prepared for the emotions that overcame her in the quiet office. Everywhere she looked was something personal of Bishop's, something that she didn't understand and never would, because she'd not only gotten him killed but had never even known him. In fact, when he'd tried to talk to her, she'd interrupted him. She regretted that so much. Tessa clenched her jaw and wished for the thousandth time that she could go back and do things differently.

There were no more Advocate journals on his shelves, or if there had been the police had taken them. She hoped it wasn't the latter as she couldn't imagine what kind of questions those books would raise. She looked through his desk drawers and found little else. They had clearly already been cataloged and the contents largely seized so most everything interesting was gone. However, among the dregs that remained, clipped to the inside pocket of a spare dress shirt Tessa found hanging on the back of his door, was an iPod Shuffle. Tessa pocketed it without even hesitating. Maybe it was weird to wonder what kind of music he had liked, but Tessa felt she at least owed the man that much.

Tessa was paging through a big volume of Greek mythology when someone yanked open the police tape on the door and walked in on her. And because her life was a very particular kind of screwed, it was Detective Wade.

"Miss Battle," Wade said, crossing her arms over her chest. "I wish I could say this was a surprise."

Tessa sighed and looked down. She seriously doubted her name was in this book too. "Hi, Detective," she said as if she hadn't been caught red-handed.

"Catching up on some more family reading?" the detective posed, nodding at the book.

"Mmmhmm," Tessa murmured.

"Miss Battle," Wade said, sitting down in front of the desk and leaning back in her chair, entirely too relaxed for Tessa's liking. "Let's skip the pleasantries and artful dodging today. My people found something very interesting at Mr. Severin's home this morning, and I was actually coming to look for you, thought you'd get a kick out of it."

"Yeah?" Tessa said, her heart beating in her chest like a trapped dinosaur. She had been there. She had killed him. Her fingerprints could have been on his damn body. Wade slid a small, sealed plastic bag across the desk. Tessa glanced at it and saw several strands of her hair.

"So, it hasn't been tested yet," Wade said, watching Tessa, "But you and I both know that color is Manic Panic, Pillar Box Red, just like yours. And while I'd wager a handful of people in Lore actually use that hair color—"

"—It *is* pretty great," Tessa cut in, trying to throw Wade off the rest of her sentence.

"—Indeed," Wade said, not missing a beat, "But you're the only one with that particular color that I've found twice in this office when you weren't supposed to be. And Mr. Bishop was last seen standing perhaps a hundred yards from your front door."

Wade let the sentence hang out there, and Tessa just left it on the table between them. Tessa's heart was hammering away and her palms were sweating, but this was no different than battling some horrible Story. She had to keep calm and show no fear. When someone asked you if you had the time, the answer was not to tell them what time it was, the answer was to say yes or no. You had to give as little as possible. Giving too much would only get you in trouble. Every time. It wouldn't be any crazy CSI-DNA-hi-jinx that would hang Tessa, she was sure of it, it would be her own stupid mouth. And so she said nothing. Wade let it be quiet for a long time and then stood up. She snatched the baggie with the hair strands from the desk and walked to the door, at which point she turned around.

"I don't care if you are seventeen, kid, you're my number one suspect."

Tessa's heart sank like a stone into her feet, but she kept her face flat. "Uh-huh," she said noncommittally. Wade waited for Tessa by the door.

"C'mon. You can't be in here. In fact, I find you in here again, and you're going to spend a night in holding." Tessa stood up and walked past Wade, into the hallway, and away from her as calmly as possible.

The bell for third period would ring in a few minutes, but Tessa couldn't think straight. No way she could sit through Chem. Instead she escaped outside only to run smack into Nash.

"Hey," he said and then, smiling, "Skipping?"

Tessa nodded and ran an anxious hand through her hair. "I so cannot take Chem right now." She looked him up and down. He was in gym shorts and a tank. She smiled wryly. "Let me guess. Crew?"

Nash all but blushed, "Guilty as charged." He nodded right and Tessa followed his nod. Down a long slope of grass she could just see the flicker of water through grass and tress, the edges of a river she guessed, and at the edge of it, a robust boathouse.

"Pretty swanky for high school," she said.

Nash shrugged. "I guess. I'm just glad it's here. Gives me an excuse to get out of classes. You should come with me some time. Rowing, I mean."

Tessa looked up at him and pushed hair out of her eyes. "Are you asking me out?"

Nash shook his head no slowly, but didn't say anything and his grin was large and carefree and she couldn't help but smile back at him.

"Tessa."

Tessa turned around at the sound of her name and almost fell over to see Robin standing a few feet away from her. She felt instantly guilty even though she hadn't done anything.

"Robin," she said, still stunned but quickly moving toward panic. Him being on campus in the middle of the day couldn't mean anything good. "Everything okay?" she asked.

He nodded curtly and she couldn't tell if it was because things were not good, or something else. Something handsome-Nash-related. Tessa turned and gestured in what seemed to her like a pathetic flail.

"Robin, this is Nash. Nash, Robin."

Nash reached out a hand and Robin flicked his eyes at Tessa for just a second before taking Nash's hand. There was the slightest hint of accusation in his eyes, maybe even hurt. Tessa felt a burn of shame and then reminded herself she'd done nothing wrong.

"Nice to meet you," Nash said, smiling good-naturedly.

"Same," Robin said. There was a pinch of awkward horrible silence that lasted an eternity and then Nash saved them all.

"Well, I'd better get down to the river. See you around, Tessa…Robin."

Robin nodded again and they both watched Nash take off down the grassy slope. When he was out of earshot, Tessa turned back to Robin. "Is everything really okay? You're giving me heart palpitations here."

"Everything's fine. I tried to find the Troll today, but he's disappeared. Trail went dead cold in the woods, he was smart about it, knew I'd be back and definitely didn't want me following him. Doesn't bode well for him being innocent in all this. If he was innocent I don't think he'd have covered his trail so well."

Tessa chewed her lip and shook her head, adding the information to the massive pile of thing she was already worried about.

"I'll keep looking and put the word out, maybe someone can get us a bead on him, but I wouldn't bet on it. Trolls are notorious for doing contract work. I expect that's what's happening here. If it was just the Troll, then nobody would be overly concerned about squealing, but if he's got someone bigger running him…people are less likely to talk." A bell rang in the distance and Robin looked back at the school and put his hand on her arm. Even through her jacket she felt electricity. "You should go."

Tessa stared down at where he was touching her. "I don't *have* to."

Robin smiled at her. "No, you should. I have to go anyway. Just wanted to stop by…give you an update…see where you spend your days." Tessa looked up at him and opened her mouth to say something witty back but for once she didn't have anything so she just smiled like an idiot. Robin mirrored her and then turned away. She watched him go, and when he was a few yards away he turned around but kept walking.

"He's way too clean cut for you," he said, shaking his head in mock disapproval.

She shook her head and rolled her eyes at him. He laughed and then took off running. When she could no longer see him, she turned toward the school, intending to go back in, but as she put her hands in her pockets, she felt the Shuffle and a wave of sadness crashed over her. Instead of going to class, she walked toward the river and the boathouse, hoping the crew team had already left and she could find some quiet corner to tuck herself into. A place to think about what Wade's latest visit meant. There was a chance that the hair stolen from her wasn't for some kind of crazy black magic death curse, it was maybe just about being framed for murder. Then again, her hair probably had been at Bluebeard's so maybe nothing had changed at all? Her head spun.

Tessa peeked into the dark boathouse and when she was sure it was empty she went in, letting the door shut behind her. She climbed up along one of the windows looking out over the river and chewed on her bottom lip anxiously, thinking about what to say to Micah and Brand at lunch about the hair. She felt like she was always giving them bad news.

Tessa reached into her pocket and pulled out Bishop's Shuffle. She fished out her headphones from her jacket and plugged in. The music poured into her ears and she was instantly much more sad than she had anticipated.

She became so consumed with the music, that she didn't hear anyone enter the boathouse behind her. She was even more surprised when whoever it was hit her across the back of the head with a rock.

Tessa hit the ground and her vision was like a kaleidoscope, colors pinwheeling like mad. She groaned and looked up to see none other than Bluebeard standing over her. She rolled away instinctively and while she wasn't sure she could stand just yet, she grabbed a nearby oar as she rolled in the hopes that it would be enough to fend the dead man off.

"I killed you," Tessa said, her voice barely a whisper and more afraid than she would have liked. The man said nothing, just smiled grotesquely. He charged at her and Tessa narrowly avoided him, rolling away and finally managing to get up on her feet. He recovered only a second later and charged her again. This time he stumbled past her, and Tessa was able to bring the oar down on the back of his head as he went past, sending him flying to the ground. As he hit, he seemed to disintegrate, but then she realized his shape was changing.

This wasn't Bluebeard, this was something else dressed up in Bluebeard's shape.

When the shape finished shifting it was an angry red demon looking thing, maybe three and a half feet tall, stocky and strong-looking, with horns, bulging eyes, and a twisted gaping mouth that turned up like a smile but had nothing happy about it. The thing growled at Tessa and swung at her, sharp claws raking lightly across her thigh as Tessa skittered away, a yelp escaping from her. Tessa brought the oar down hard toward the thing but missed it by an inch.

It skittered away into the shadows, hiding amongst the boats and Tessa stood in the middle of the boathouse, breathing hard and listening for it. Two eyes blinked at her from the darkness and Tessa moved toward it, but as she did so, as if materializing out of the dark, it became a Bengal tiger and lunged at Tessa. Tessa dove backwards, screaming in surprise. It advanced, but more carefully, and as Tessa inched backward on her butt she called The Black Dove, hoping the axe's appearance would be enough to keep the thing at bay. The axe snapped into her hand and she swung immediately, barely keeping the creature at arm's length. It roared at her in protest. Outside Tessa heard voices and feet running on the dock.

Nothing was good.

As if sensing that time was running out to eat her alive without witnesses, the thing made a final push, its jaws open, and its massive paws outstretched. Tessa raised her axe and swung it down, landing it in the creature's shoulder with a sickening thud. It shrieked an unholy sound utterly like anything a real tiger might do and Tessa yanked her axe out of flesh and fur and bone. Just as she removed the axe, the tiger morphed into something else Tessa couldn't quite make out. The shape wavered, flickering almost like it couldn't decide on a shape. Behind her, the doors to the boathouse pushed open and Tessa decided to let go of the axe rather than try to explain it. It disappeared just as a shaft of light fell on her.

Tessa heard Nash shout her name, and she blinked in surprise as she saw the creature turn into a human shape, that of a sixteen-year-old boy. Its shoulder was a mess but it backed up into the shadows to better hide itself. Nash reached Tessa and just behind him was Greyson. Nash took one look at Tessa—scratched, disheveled, and generally battered around the edges—and his eyes narrowed dangerously.

"Who did this?" he demanded. Tessa was about to say something, though she had no idea what, when a pair of oars clattered to the floor at the other end of the boathouse and Nash took off running toward the sound.

"No! Don't!" Tessa shouted out after him, afraid he might actually catch whatever she had been fighting. She looked at Greyson imploringly. "I'm fine. Go with Nash—it was a Story—make sure he doesn't find it." She said. Greyson nodded and went after Nash without a word, grabbing an oar on the way. Tessa climbed to her feet and tried to straighten herself up. She tore her jeans so it looked less like claw marks and used a rag to clean up some of the blood on the floor. As she heard them coming back inside she stuffed the rag in her pocket.

Nash looked her up and down when he returned. "Are you alright?"

Tessa nodded. "I'm fine." Her eyes darted to Greyson who shrugged helplessly.

"What happened?" Nash asked.

"Misunderstanding, I think. I mean, I'm sure I'm not even supposed to be in here. It's dark, I startled whoever that was, he turned around suddenly and I got hit with the oar," Tessa leaned forward so Nash could see the bump at the back of her skull. Nash felt it gingerly and Tessa winced.

"If it was just an accident, then why did he run?" Nash asked, looking around the boathouse and then at Greyson who shrugged.

"Well, he obviously wasn't supposed to be here either. Maybe he panicked?"

Nash raised a skeptical eyebrow and then pointed to Tessa's leg.

"What about your leg?"

"From when I fell, I must have caught it on something…maybe one of the boats." She suggested, gesturing vaguely. Nash looked around. He wasn't completely buying it, but he was too polite to call her a liar. "Seriously, I'm fine," she said, putting a hand on his arm, hoping to convince him. He looked down at her hand and then back to her face, concern passing over his handsome face.

"Let's get you to the nurse," he finally said, taking Tessa by the arm, clearly intending to take her there himself even if he had to carry her. Tessa shot a helpless glance at Greyson.

"You know, why don't you let me take Tessa, you should tell Coach about this guy that hit her."

Nash screwed up his mouth. "I barely got a glimpse."

"But I didn't see him at all."

Nash nodded and looked at Tessa again. "That okay with you?"

"Yeah, of course." She nodded.

Nash gently handed her off to Greyson and went off in the other direction. At the doors, he called back to her. "If you remember anything about this guy or see him on campus you'll let me know?"

Tessa smiled. "Of course. And thank you."

Nash shook his head as if he was disappointed in the human race that it had happened at all before disappearing out the doors. Greyson let Tessa go and they walked out the other side of the boathouse back toward the school as a bell rang out across the quad.

"So what really happened?"

"Some goddamn thing attacked me, *of course.*"

"What was it? Anything we know?"

"I don't know what the hell it actually was, but it looked like Bluebeard, and then some kind of angry red demon, then a freaking Bengal tiger, then after I chopped it in the shoulder, a wounded sixteen-year-old kid," Tessa shook her head helplessly. "What a nightmare."

At lunch, Tessa clambered onto the bench beside Micah and Brand who were poring over a black card with elegant silver writing on it. Micah looked up at Tessa and her brow creased in concern.

"You okay? You look a little...rumpled?"

Tessa looked down at herself and tried to straighten herself out. She had thought she'd done a pretty good job, apparently not. "I'm fine," she said, giving them her best, 'I wasn't just attacked on campus' look. "What's that?" Tessa asked, pointing to the card, hoping she could distract them.

Micah pushed the card toward Tessa. She picked it up and started reading.

"You should have one in your locker, too," Brand said. "Everyone from the Sophomore Class on up gets their own invite to The Masquerade Ball."

"Oh yeah," Tessa said, a faint memory prickling at the edges of her brain. "I remember that thing, on Halloween, for Lore High. It's in the park after the Halloween Festival, my parents took me to the Festival a few times – it's like rides and games and food and stuff, right?"

"Yeah," Micah said, and her eyes actually sparkled a little. "During the day, it's the Festival, which anyone from Lore can go to—I've gone every year since I was five—but then at night the park totally transforms for the Lore High Masquerade Ball. It's basically our Winter Formal, but it's like a giant costume ball. It's so cool. Last year was the first year we could go. It was awesome."

Brand nodded. "Yeah, I was skeptical, seemed like chick stuff, but people really went all-out with the costumes, and the food was good, the band too. I'm a convert."

Tessa nodded and pushed the invitation back to Micah. She pictured Robin for a moment, decked out in costume, but it seemed absurd. School dances didn't seem like they'd impress a bad-boy anarchist, let alone a Story who'd seen it all. She gulped and plunged in to her less than stellar news. "So…fyi…I got a visit from Detective Wade." She paused to let the news sink in as her friends both looked up at her, their faces draining of color. "She found my hair at the crime scene."

"We cannot catch a goddamn break!" Brand shouted, pounding his fist into the table and jostling his milk.

"Agreed," Tessa said.

"Did they find our hair too?" Micah asked.

"So far just mine," Tessa muttered.

"It's probably only a matter of time until they find ours as well. Although it's a big house and there were a lot of other women in that house…that will help, I guess," Micah said, as much to herself as anyone at the table.

Tessa took a bite of her apple. "Do you think there's any chance the hair that was taken from us is about framing us for murder instead of some magic death curse?"

Micah shook her head, and Brand spoke, "I doubt it. Like Mike says, our hair probably is there, nobody has to bother to frame us."

Tessa slumped down a bit. "Yeah, I figured that was too much to hope for."

"You know your life is screwed up when you're *hoping* that someone is framing you for murder," Brand said sullenly. "But you know what really burns me about this whole thing? There were bodies—like a dozen headless bodies in that house—stacked like a freaking cord of wood, and yet they're all up in our grill about taking that guy down. Seems instead like they should pull you aside for an award. Yeah, pin a shiny medal to your chest and everything."

Tessa smiled. "That seems unlikely."

"Can't catch a damn break," Brand said again, more to himself than anyone else before taking a swig of his milk. Tessa looked at her two friends.

"I heard Bishop's funeral will be on Saturday—" she started.

"We'll go with you," Brand said before she could even finish her sentence. Micah nodded, and Tessa smiled gratefully.

"Thanks, guys."

"S'what we're here for," Micah said.

At home that afternoon Tessa arrived to find her dad, a day early, reading in their living room. Tessa's heart leapt at seeing him there. It took every bit of her will not to go to him and fall down beside him in tears, tell him everything. But she resisted because she knew better. She'd learned a long time ago that her weakness would not be well received. So she did what she always did.

Shields up.

"Tessa," he said, putting his book down and taking off his glasses as she closed the front door.

"Dad," she replied flatly, standing in the foyer, not moving.

"What on earth happened in the backyard, and to the dining room window?" He asked, searching her face. So much for *'hello'* Tessa thought, along with *'happy birthday,' 'welcome home,' 'I love you,' 'are you okay,'* and a slew of other things it would have been nice to hear before concern for broken lawn furniture.

"You tell me," Tessa said, unmoving.

"Excuse me?" he asked, incredulous but restrained.

"It was that way when I got here," Tessa said shrugging. She didn't like lying to him, but she didn't think the truth was going to be a big winner either. *'Well, Dad, a giant Troll broke in and tried to kill me, Yeah, I know, crazy, right?'* That just wasn't going to fly. He blinked and waited, then acquiesced.

"Okay. What about all my dishtowels?" he asked, without missing a beat. Tessa flashed back to all the blood they'd sopped up over the last week. She'd thrown them out. More importantly, what kind of freak came home and immediately missed dishtowels?

Tessa shrugged again, "Maybe the same thing that happened to the yard? Dishtowel thieves. I hear that's all the rage with the kids these days," Tessa said sarcastically. She couldn't help but add, "Yup, nothing gets kids off like a sweet dishtowel."

Her father sighed and put his glasses back on, resigned, or something Tessa didn't quite understand. "Is this how it's going to be, Tessa?" he asked.

"What Dad? Missing dishtowels everyday? What a travesty. How will we ever go on?" Tessa bit back the last of the words. She and her father had not gotten along since her mother disappeared, but after everything she'd been through, well, she just wanted a damn hug and some part of her hated him for not knowing it instinctively. Clearly, she had been right to assume that hugs would not be forthcoming, no matter how much parts of her were screaming out for one, no matter how long it had been since she'd seen him (and it had been three long years).

"I assume you have homework?" he asked, opening his book back up. This was, of course, rhetorical and Tessa recognized it as his way of ending the conversation. A skill he had always been particularly adept at. Tessa turned without a word and headed up the stairs to her room. "I'm leaving again next week!" he called out as she shut the door.

"Didn't even know you were back," she mumbled to her bedroom door. It was funny, Tessa and her dad hadn't had much of a relationship to speak of for a long time, but ever since the Scion stuff began, she'd been thinking about him a lot more. Who he was beyond just being "her dad," if he knew about any of this craziness, why he'd sent her away in the first place, why he constantly tried to get her to use his name, Daniels, instead of her mother's name, Battle. And why he'd even stayed in Lore in the first place. His job kept him in San Francisco almost all the time, why hadn't he just moved there? Tessa used to think it was because he hoped that her mother would return and that he wanted things to be waiting for her. Why else would he keep the house like some kind of desperate mausoleum, a static monument to her mother? It used to make her feel bad for him, like he was some kind of tragic romantic idiot that couldn't let go of the one woman he'd loved. Now she wasn't so sure. The one thing she had definitely learned in the last few weeks was that things were almost never what they seemed, nor were they simple. Life was more complex than she had ever given it credit for. But she ached for simplicity. And for blissful ignorance.

Already, in her room with the doors and windows closed, Tessa felt claustrophobic. She grabbed her jacket off the hook in her closet and took a piece of paper out of the pocket. Robin's address. He'd given it to her 'in case of emergency.' Tessa didn't think this qualified, but she hoped he'd be glad to see her anyway. Tessa put her jacket on, opened her window, and crawled out onto the roof. She was on the ground in seconds and feeling better with every step she took away from the house.

TWENTY-THREE

When she showed up on Robin's doorstep an hour later, he didn't seem that surprised.

"Tessa," he said, smiling a little. He stood there, shirtless, his eyes sleepy and his hair even more aggressively rumpled than usual. Tessa tried to swallow her delight. He ran a hand through his hair and reached for a white t-shirt nearby. He stepped back to let her inside while he pulled the shirt on.

"Hi," Tessa said, turning her body and edging inside. His apartment was a giant warehouse loft with soaring ceilings. Not one of those fancy refurbished places, this was rough, and Tessa liked it all the more for its roughness. She wouldn't have been surprised to learn the building was condemned. The concrete floors had paint splatters and gashes, and at least twenty of the small, leaded windows that made up most of one wall were broken, letting in the sound of the rain, making it feel almost like they were outside. In one corner of the space was a bed covered in disheveled blankets, a lamp sitting on the floor, and a pile of well-read books, partially toppled over. There was also a flat screen television, a video game console, and some games scattered on the floor. Next to the television were two guitars, one electric, lying next to an amp. A single reading chair was piled high with discarded clothes and in a corner a beat-up rather intense looking motorcycle leaned against the wall. By the front door was a makeshift (probably illegal) kitchen with two stools and a small bar table, and beyond that, a door, which Tessa assumed was a bathroom.

The rest of the enormous space was basically a gym. There was a pommel horse and free weights, a heavy bag and a gymnastics mat, as well as a wall of brutal weapons. Most impressive, however, was the full-sized archery range that took up more than half the apartment and included a variety of targets in all shapes and sizes. A complicated system of ropes and pulleys descended from the ceiling and Tessa stared at it, trying to understand what she was seeing.

"You want something to drink?" Robin asked, stretching his draw arm as he watched her.

"Water?" she asked. He nodded and turned to the small fridge in the kitchen. She looked at him and he tossed her a bottle, uncapping one for himself. Tessa caught it and pointed it at the ropes. Before she could ask, he volunteered.

"You wanna see?"

Tessa nodded and heard a whirring behind her as he flipped on a good-sized generator on the floor. In a moment, it was as if the whole room was spinning. Targets moved throughout the thirty-foot-high space, juking back and forth, up, down, and across, creating three-dimensional moving targets. Tessa smiled.

"Amazing."

"You want to try?" he asked, a now familiar glint in his eye as he picked up a bow off of the counter. "A target that doesn't move, like, say, a tree in someone's backyard is one thing," he said, winking at her slyly. "*This* is a whole other game," he breathed, stepping next to her, his mouth so close she could feel his breath on her neck. Tessa put her hand on the bow.

"I feel like we need stakes, then," she said.

"Ah, the confidence of youth," he said clucking his tongue. Tessa edged back from him.

"Scared?"

He shook his head, "Not at all."

"Then for every miss, we have to answer a question—truthfully. A modified truth or dare, if you will."

Robin pursed his lips and then nodded once, "All right."

Tessa smiled. "Age before beauty," she said, handing him the bow. Robin scrunched up his nose at her but took the bow. He loaded an arrow and released it all in one fluid motion. It stuck in the heart of a thick dummy moving toward them high across the ceiling. He nodded to a second bow on the wall. Tessa picked it up along with an arrow, her hands shaking slightly and, she hoped, unnoticeably. Tessa wondered why she let her mouth get her into such trouble? She had just challenged Robin Hood to an archery contest. She shook her head at her own stupidity.

Tessa raised the bow and pulled back on the arrow, aiming for a target that slid to the left against the back wall. She released the arrow and prayed. The thwack told her, even before she could examine it, that she'd hit the target. But when she did examine it, she realized it was bang on center. Her mouth broke into a wide smile. Robin smiled despite himself and eyed her.

"It seems we have a game here, Miss Battle."

For the next ten minutes, they took turns shooting and never missed. Finally, Tessa put her hands on her hips. "Rule change!" she said, exasperated. Robin raised an eyebrow at her. "From now on, we shoot at the same time, at the same target, whoever gets the better bull's-eye gets to ask the question."

"All right," Robin said again, raising his bow. Tessa did the same next to him.

"Dummy number three," she said, "Between the eyes." Robin nodded, and they both drew and loosed their arrows at the target in perfect unison. Both stuck true, but Robin's had better placement.

"Damn," Tessa cursed and turned to him, waiting for his question.

"Do you really hate it?" he asked, lining up another shot but not releasing an arrow.

"What?"

"Being the Scion. Because you're really, really good at it," Robin said, turning to her and relaxing the bow.

Tessa chewed her lip.

"No lying," Robin said, his voice a tease.

"No lying," Tessa echoed. "I wouldn't lie, it's just not a simple answer. I don't hate it as much as I thought I would," she admitted. "I mean, I miss my boring old life, and I spend a lot of time hating what all of this is doing to me, and I really hate the idea of things being decided for me, but I would be lying if I said it was *all* horrible. There are definite perks," she said, deliberately not looking at him, and then added, "Also, the fighting feels, *natural?*" she added, a question heavy on the last word. Robin nodded.

"I understand," he said. "It's in your blood, just like mine." Tessa turned away and Robin called out the next target. This time, Tessa's arrow had better placing than his. By millimeters. Robin sucked in a breath and turned to face her, a smile curling at the corners of his mouth.

"Do your worst, my lady."

There were so many questions Tessa wanted to ask, but she wasn't sure she'd ever get another shot given his skill. In the end, she went with the question that beat in her heart the hardest. She thought of that moment between them in her yard, so close they were almost one, and there was only one question she wanted to ask.

"Why didn't you kiss me?" she asked, blinking at him and trying not to look away. Robin's eyes fluttered in surprise; he clearly hadn't expected the question.

"I—"

"No lying," Tessa warned. Robin dipped his head.

"Marian," he said, and the word hit Tessa like a bullet. It was the first time he'd said her name, and he said it with a reverence that made Tessa feel she was doing something very, very wrong in even being there with him. She stepped back half a step almost unconsciously. He noticed and winced. "It's not—" he began, raising his hand as if to calm a frightened animal, "—It's complicated, Tessa." Robin looked at her, his expression a mix of both confusion and longing.

"Can you try to explain it?" Tessa asked, picking at the place where the string met the wood on her bow.

"I don't know if you can understand," he said, and then, before she could object, "You're a Mortal, or at least mostly Mortal. You're not Story the way I am, you weren't created as I was, so you don't, you don't understand the compulsion. Marian and me, it's—"

Tessa cut him off with a raised hand, "Please don't say complicated again."

"Well it is," he said, putting the bow down on the counter. "I haven't seen her in nearly a century. It's her choice as much as mine, but she's in here, Tessa," he said, putting his hand on his chest. "She's in here as powerfully as the day we were born. And I don't know that there's room for anyone else, no matter how much I want there to be. And I do want there to be. I've wanted it more in the last few days than I've ever wanted anything. But I can't tell you that it matters. I don't know if it's something I can do anything about, and it's just…well, it's never been an issue before," he was speaking so truthfully, so passionately, it was hard for Tessa to stay cold.

She looked at him skeptically, her mind reeling. But damn if he wasn't convincing. If he was lying, it was the best goddamn lie Tessa had ever heard. And that was the thing, Tessa didn't even know if he *could* lie. He was a hero, right? Wouldn't he be compelled to speak the truth about something like this? He mentioned compulsion, wasn't that part of it? Wouldn't Robin Hood feel *compelled* to tell the truth?

"That's pretty good," she finally admitted. Robin looked at her blankly. "You did a good job of explaining it," she said, shrugging, and then added, "But does it have to be all that right now? Can't it just be this? Can't it just be us seeing if there's anything here first?" Tessa stepped closer to him and linked her fingers through his. Robin looked at their hands together.

"I don't want to hurt you," he said.

"And maybe you won't, but you're a romantic hero, love stories always have hurt in them, right?" Tessa smiled at him, trying to lighten things.

Robin shrugged. "I wouldn't really know, I mostly get happy endings."

Tessa laughed, "Then no wonder you're scared." She leaned forward into him. Their bodies pressed together lightly in places, and Tessa swore she could feel his heart beating inside her. She tilted her head up to him. She wanted to melt into him, everything inside her was crying out for it. But she was resolved. She knew she had to let him make the move. She had to wait for him to decide, it was important that he choose. Even if that meant he never kissed her. And there was a sudden and empty ache inside her at that idea.

His hand found her neck, and she shivered as he drew his thumb across her jaw. When his lips finally touched hers, it was as if he was tasting her, tentative at first, sweet and tender, like finding his way in the dark. Tessa sighed involuntarily. He pulled back slightly and smiled and then tasted her again, more hungrily. This time there was no reservation, no hesitation, just the pure decadence of giving in to what you've wanted since the moment you saw it, the excitement of finding out it tastes even better than you imagined.

Everything was so perfect in that moment that Tessa thought she might just be Fiction too.

TWENTY-FOUR

Every day that week, Tessa helped Micah and Brand with research in the afternoons. Trying to find Dr. Frankenstein, trying to figure out what he might want, what the master plan might be. Brand was eclipsing them all when it came to the research; his mind absorbed the Stories they read like a sponge, and he made connections as if he had been born for this life. More than once, Tessa thought that "destiny" had all gotten it wrong and Brand should have been The Scion. It was hard to tell what was just Brand and what was his Story gift, but it didn't matter anymore, they were one and the same now.

In the evenings, Tessa escaped to train and patrol with Robin. And it was then that she felt at home. Like maybe destiny *did* know what it was doing. She got better everyday, making fewer mistakes, learning what did and what didn't come naturally for her. What didn't come naturally, she and Robin worked on until she felt confident. What did come naturally was *a lot.*

They also spent a good deal of time making out.

As a result, Tessa was some giddy version of herself she never would have recognized a few weeks ago. As tough as Tessa pretended to be, as aggressive as she played, she'd never had a boyfriend before, and though she'd kissed a few boys in her travels, she was less experienced than she would ever let on. But with Robin everything felt so right. Like the fighting, it felt natural. It felt like she *should* be with him. Like she had just been waiting for this moment in her life for everything to snap into place.

But it frightened her how fast it was happening. How much she felt, how quickly, how deeply, how out of her control it all was. Sometimes when she thought of her and Robin, the image that sprang to mind was that of a speeding train that she had neither the power nor the desire to stop. Had that train been headed for the side of a mountain she would have been powerless to stop it, and she wouldn't have cared.

Scary.

All week, they'd found no real leads and it left Tessa anxious, as if they were missing something. But she was also happy. For the first time in her life she had real friends and a boyfriend of sorts. She also had a purpose that felt big and important. If she could have just eliminated all the death and destruction from the equation, she might have been headed toward something resembling a real life, a good one.

Then Friday happened.

Tessa's dad had left the night before (and four days early) on the red-eye to San Francisco, leaving her with another white envelope of money, this one, sans a note. And in the morning, well before an hour fit for humans, or at least for humans named Tessa, the doorbell rang.

Tessa dragged her sword down the stairs with her, wondering what new hell awaited her. She opened the door, rubbing the sleep from her eyes, to find Robin standing in the rain in his faded hoodie and black leather jacket. He also had a reasonably full duffle bag slung over his shoulder. Tessa's shoulders dropped. This couldn't be good.

"It won't be for long," he said, before she could even say anything.

Tessa moved to the side and gestured him in. "Where?" she asked, monosyllabic.

"I have a lead I have to follow. It might help."

"You have to go today? Tomorrow's the funeral," she said.

"I know, I'm sorry."

"Why does it have to be you? Why can't Fenris go?"

Robin laughed loudly, and Tessa made an annoyed face at him. "Tessa. You must listen to me about Fenris. You're not taking his threat seriously enough. He is more powerful than you can imagine."

"Why is he so powerful? I don't understand. His story is old, but not older than others like Snow, right? What makes him so special? Why are you all so afraid of him?"

Tessa bit her tongue. She hadn't meant to say afraid, she didn't think he'd like that, but to her surprise he blew right past it. He crossed his arms and looked out the front windows and then looked back at her.

"You're referring to *Little Red Riding Hood*," he said. Tessa nodded. "Well, that's 14th century and a fair bit older than Snow, but that's not his original story. Tessa, I thought you understood," Robin put his bag down and paced the living room for a minute as if he was deciding what to say and what not to say. "Fenris is not just The Big Bad Wolf from *Little Red Riding Hood*, he is every big bad wolf EVER. Any non-specific 'bad wolf iteration,' *that* is Fenris. He is the goddamn cautionary tale in the oldest of stories. He goes back thousands of years—to Aesop and your B.C. He is one of the oldest of us, and thus, one of the most powerful and feared. He walks through stories like a god. He has been made one by Mortals."

Tessa looked at him and blinked. It was a lot to process all in one shot. "Oh," was all she could get out. Robin watched her as she turned away from him, trying to gauge her reaction. Tessa turned back to him and smiled wryly, trying to make light of it. "Dude looks good for his age, yo?" Robin shook his head and grabbed her roughly by the shoulders.

"Tessa, you can't trust him."

"Don't say that," she said, shaking him off. "You're always saying that. I don't want to hear it," she held up a hand. "It's freaking me out."

"It should freak you out. You need to—"

Tessa gestured at him, cutting him off. "No. He's been loyal. He's saved lives, including mine, including *yours*."

"It's an act, Tessa."

"You can't know that," she said bitterly.

"Tessa, it's in the damn name. BIG. BAD. WOLF. For thousands of years. You think he's a good guy?"

"I think people, even Stories, can change," Tessa said.

"They don't," Robin said, a hard edge to his voice.

"If you believe that, then you're a thief and an anarchist with a *very* serious love story, You want me to judge you solely on that?"

"It's different," he said, lowering his head.

"Really?" Tessa said sarcastically, crossing her arms.

"Yes. For starters, I'm still a hero. At my core, I was written to be a hero. It's in my DNA. I'm also sometimes a screw-up, or an asshole, a flake, a terrible son, a failure, a playboy, an anarchist, any number of iterations shade me with other aspects, but I always default back to hero, because that is ALWAYS part of my story. Fenris was built, *literally* built, to be the bad guy. The *original* bad guy. The bad guy to *represent* all bad guys. He is designed to seduce and kill you. Nothing more. Are you telling me you haven't heard that in his voice? I've seen you feel it. I've seen you shake it off, the almost hypnotic quality it has."

Tessa blinked but didn't look at Robin. That was true, and she couldn't deny it. She didn't even like Fenris, but there were times when he spoke that she felt herself changing her mind, being lulled into thinking something else. She shook her head.

"No. That's not his fault any more than you being able to hit any target with an arrow is your fault."

"Dammit, Tessa," Robin breathed, frustrated. "Listen, I get it. You're not destiny's bitch. You've made that very clear. You believe, right or wrong, that we all have free will, even Stories, but I'm telling you, Fenris can't fight his Fiction, not forever. Even if he wants to, which I doubt, it's a battle he cannot win. Yes, there are parts of me that are dark and dangerous, even non-heroic, there have been many interpretations of my Fiction over the years, which give me layers and room to maneuver within my Fiction, if you will, but at the end of the day I am designed to be a big goddamn hero of epic proportions. I'm the guy that comes through. I save the day. I show up. It's what I do, it's who I am. I don't say it to brag, I say it to draw a contrast.

"At the end of the day, no matter what you see them do, Snow and Fenris are the big bad tovaien villains. They will stab you in the back in the final act. Every time. Fenris will eventually show you who he really is, and if you're not ready for it, if you don't anticipate it, it will be devastating." He took a breath and forced her to look him in the eyes. "You're a hero, Tessa. They're not on your side. But I am. I always will be."

Tessa pinched the bridge of her nose to head off an oncoming headache. "He's saved my life, Robin. If nothing else, I owe him. He's in for now, and I don't want to hear about it anymore."

"There's something else," Robin said and Tessa could tell he was anxious about saying it. She sighed heavily.

"What now?"

"I think…I think part of what you need to be concerned about is that he's a pack animal."

Tessa blinked stupidly. "Excuse me?"

"I mean, traditionally, Fenris is not actually a pack animal. He's the single wolf, which is an aberration in and of itself, but put him in a pack and he is the alpha. He's the ultimate alpha."

Tessa shrugged. "Great. Seems like that will work to our advantage in case we come upon any werewolves…which…hell, werewolves are real, wow…anyway, yeah, I mean, how is that not an advantage?

"Because, Tessa, YOU are the alpha here."

Tessa stepped back from him half a step. "Huh?"

"Listen, I don't have time to argue about this, I didn't even want to bring it up, but ultimately in our worlds—Story *and* Mortal—The Scion, the only person with the power to kill us? YOU are the alpha. And more than that, you specifically are particularly strong and adept. I have met other Scions over the years, I haven't known them well, but I've seen them and my opinion is that you're nothing like them. You're much stronger than they were. In just a few short weeks, you…I mean, you simply *command* a battlefield when you're on it, and with almost no training; you boss around ancient and powerful Stories without a second thought; and you inspire people to join your cause. You don't do these things deliberately or with malice, they just come naturally to you. You're the ultimate alpha. And as a result, I think there is no way for him to see you as anything but a threat that must be taken out."

Tessa stared at him. What he had said was incredibly kind, and it spoke volumes about how he respected her and maybe even how he felt about her, but it was hard to believe it and part of her didn't want to because it was scary. She didn't recognize the person he was describing. It didn't sound like her. How could it? She was failing Trig, she couldn't be in a room with her dad for more than five minutes without getting in a fight, and she selfishly thought all the time about making out with Robin Hood instead of saving the world. How could that be the same person he was describing?

"I…" Tessa had no idea what to say. Robin looked anxiously at the window.

"Tessa, I have to go."

Tessa blinked, and started to get mad. "Wait. You're going to say all of that, some of which is just amazing, and some of it so scary I can't even process it, and then you're just going to leave?"

"I'm sorry. I don't have a choice. My window for leaving is very narrow." He looked at his watch. If I don't leave in the next two minutes, I'm going to miss it."

Tessa felt angry, and even more annoyed that she had nowhere to direct it. "Okay, well then, thanks for the revelations."

Robin looked away, both hurt and angry, and more than a little exasperated. "Have you even seen him recently?"

"No," Tessa admitted. "Not since he disappeared the last time."

"Convenient," Robin mumbled.

Tessa cut him a sharp look.

"Okay, listen," he said, clearly trying to make peace. He put his hands on her shoulders, gently this time, but she shook him off anyway. He gave up and sighed. "I didn't want to fight with you before I left. That's not why I'm here," he said. Tessa crossed her arms again and looked at the carpet. Robin moved toward the door and picked up his bag. "Just do me a favor. Don't see him while I'm gone. It shouldn't take more than a couple days," he said.

"And what if something comes for me while you're gone? You want me to not see him, to not accept his help, to maybe get myself killed—all because what—you're jealous or something?"

"I'm not jealous," he said flatly.

Tessa arched a skeptical eyebrow at him.

"I don't like him around you, for a whole slew of reasons, but it's nothing as simple, nothing as petty, as jealousy," he said.

And Tessa could see that he meant it, even if she didn't entirely believe him.

"Tessa," he started, and then, looking at his watch, got a pained look on his face. He walked back a few steps toward her. "I have to go, I'm sorry." He kissed her on the cheek and then walked out the door.

Tessa immediately regretted letting him go, despite her anger. Not only because it was a stupid fight, but also because anything could happen to her, to him, while they were apart. They didn't live normal lives. They lived horribly violent aggressive lives. That could be the last time she was ever going to see him. The image of Bishop's lifeless face snapped into her mind. Tessa threw the door open to chase after Robin, to apologize, but he was gone.

A little stone of dread settled into the pit of her stomach. She didn't know what it meant, but she felt suddenly sure it would stay there until he returned.

Robin hiked about a hundred yards into the forest behind Tessa's house and checked his watch. He looked around to make sure he was in the right spot, but before he could verify it he felt that familiar snap of electricity that preceded a dimensional rift. A flash of blue illuminated the leaves all around him, and a moment later Tal materialized.

She smiled at him and conflict rocked around inside him.

It was a smile she gave to few and he knew he should cherish it, but it was a smile that wanted more than he could give and so there was guilt attached to it. She saw his hesitation and slipped back into her trademark stoicism, sighing, annoyed with him.

"I'm sorry," he said, trying to cut her mood off at the pass.

"You don't have to apologize to me," she said flatly.

"Your expression says I do."

"Don't punish me with bullshit drama just for liking you more than every other worthless thing in the worlds."

Robin smiled. "Oh, Talia. You have such a way with people. You should have looked into customer service instead of bounty hunting."

Talia's stony expression cracked, a smile peeking out.

Robin beamed at her. "So, I'm here. You were very adamant about me being on time, so let's go."

Just as he finished he heard a sound behind him and he spun, loading an arrow as he did, to see Snow, not remotely blending into the forest in a glittery white dress and a massive white fur coat, angrily pushing branches away from her. She stumbled in her heels as they sunk into the moist earth.

"Tovaien kiaane, Tal. Did we have to meet in the simane tashla feeata!?"

"You would prefer Main Street?"

"Yes. Yes, I would," she seethed, joining them, the air dropping in temperature just based on her proximity alone.

"If you'd just warm up the air a bit you probably wouldn't need to lug around that huge animal carcass," Robin said.

"Do you mean this *magnificent* animal carcass?" Snow asked, scrunching herself down into it even deeper.

"Enough. Let's go," Tal said, all business now that Snow had joined them.

"Wait. I didn't sign on for a trio," Robin protested.

"Not my call," Tal said, and she caught Robin's eye for just a moment, something dangerous flashing in them.

"I've been summoned," Snow said matter-of-factly.

"Let's hope it's a one-way trip for you," Robin said, trying to ignore her and catch Tal's eye again, but failing at both.

"Oh gods, yes, let's hope," Snow replied, genuine excitement in her voice. Tal rolled her eyes as she took out a dimensional pebble and threw it into the air. It hovered midair as words slipped from her mouth and the forest flared up into a shock of blue light.

"Well, let's make sure to drop me off first then," Robin said as the doorway opened.

When Robin emerged on the other side of the dimensional doorway to find himself in a remote part of the Story castle that housed The Court he knew something had gone horribly wrong.

School was a blur of noise and bright colors that Tessa had trouble feigning interest in and the next time she felt conscious of herself (and slightly less miserable) it was night, and she was patrolling Northside Park.

It frustrated her that she felt more aware of herself—more alive, even—in her "Scion Tessa" persona then in her "Normal Tessa" persona, but she pretended it was just because one made her feel closer to Robin and that she missed him.

It made her feel a bit better about things.

The park was just as quiet as it—and everything—had been all week. When she was done patrolling Northside, she headed to Woodlawn Cemetery. Woodlawn bumped up against the woods on three sides, which made it prime grounds for things that went bump in the forest as far as Tessa was concerned.

It was also where Bishop's funeral would be tomorrow afternoon and Tessa wanted to make sure his funeral was peaceful, even if his death had been anything but.

Tessa walked through the Woodlawn gates and left the auto path to wander among the graves. It was silent and still, and it probably would have been nice except her mind was in overdrive. All the silence did was provide a nice blank landscape for her brain to go crazy on.

Robin had not even been gone for a day and she missed him like a phantom limb. He had somehow managed to crawl into all the corners of her mind. Even places he didn't belong. She had been unprepared for how quickly she had become attached to Robin. The intensity of her feelings continued to frighten her, but her fear was nowhere near as strong as her longing. She wanted him back, safely at her side.

Ten minutes into her sweep of Woodlawn, she heard, or perhaps felt was more accurate, something following her. She abruptly circled a decrepit crypt and looped back in the hopes of coming up behind whatever was following her. When she turned the last corner of the crypt, she almost collided with Fenris, leaning against the stone, arms crossed, waiting for her.

"Dammit!" Tessa shouted, jumping backwards and clenching her eyes shut reflexively.

"Sorry, luv," he said, a funny smile on his face. Tessa clenched her fists almost unconsciously, all of Robin's warnings echoing in her brain.

"What are you doing here?"

Fenris shrugged noncommittally and looked around the dark cemetery. "Thought you could use a hand on your sweep, with Robin away," he said, turning his gaze back to her, a bit hungrily, she thought. Tessa turned away from his look and began walking again but in a different direction than she had originally been headed.

"Thanks, but I'm fine. I'd rather be alone," she said, not sure if she really meant it. Fenris jogged a few steps until he was keeping pace with her.

"Lots of bad things in these places, Scion. Doesn't hurt to have an extra pair of eyes," he said, his voice rough.

Tessa arched her eyebrow at him. "I have seen a whole lot of nothing on the bad front," she said and then thought better of it and added, "Not that I'm complaining."

Fenris looked toward the trees surrounding them. "Just because you don't see it, doesn't mean it isn't there," he said. Tessa stopped walking and turned to face him. Robin's speech must have gotten under her skin more than she realized, or maybe she'd just had enough cryptic crap to last her a lifetime.

"Oh, yes, of course, yet another cryptic response. I see a lot of smoke from you, Fenris, I've yet to find the fire," she snapped.

Fenris continued scanning the woods around them. "There's nothing cryptic about it, Scion. You've just barely scratched the surface."

Like everything he said, Tessa could feel the multiple meanings.

Some made her squirm inside more than others.

She climbed a small hill, chewing on her lip and thinking about how she should respond. As she neared the top, she turned to face him and stretched out her arms. She continued walking backwards and looked at the quiet all around them. "So show me something beneath the surface," she said.

And as she did so, she fell into an open grave.

TWENTY-FIVE

Tessa hit the bottom of the grave with a thud.

But she wasn't just in an open grave. She was in an empty coffin. She shuddered, hoping it wasn't some terrible, prophetic sign of her imminent death. By the time she looked up, Fenris was standing at the top of the grave.

"You alright?" he asked.

"Yeah," Tessa said, standing up and brushing herself off. "Why the hell is this all open and empty?" she cussed.

"We've got bigger problems than that, Hardcore," Fenris said, and she noticed he wasn't looking at her, but out across the graveyard.

"What?" she asked, scowling and wishing she didn't have to know the answer. He looked down at her and shook his head, then knelt to give her his hand, pulling her up out of the hole.

"Look," he said, pointing. Tessa followed his gaze. Before her, across the rolling dark grass, she saw dozens of graves, all dug up, all empty. They laid there like open, black, festering sores, piles of dark dirt lying next to them.

"Balls," Tessa said under her breath. "Well, that's not good."

Fenris shook his head at her side. "I'd say not."

Tessa and Fenris examined a few of the empty graves and the not-so-subtle trail that led into the woods behind the cemetery.

"They don't look like they rose on their own," Tessa said.

"Yes, when something rises from the grave it tends to not leave a neat pile of discarded dirt." Fenris moved to the edge of the woods, sniffing, and then turned abruptly back to Tessa. "Let me walk you home."

"What?" Tessa asked, surprised and more than a little annoyed. "I mean, first of all, *'no, I don't need an escort, thanks'* and secondly, aren't we going to follow the trail?"

Fenris shook his head. "No."

"Explain."

"We can't, just the two of us, follow a trail of dead into the woods, who knows how deep and with who knows what waiting for us."

Tessa mocked him. "I'm sorry—is the BIG BAD WOLF—*afraid*???"

"Not afraid. Just smart. You think you get to be this old by just running off half-cocked at the first sign of trouble, Hardcore? You're smarter than that."

Tessa grumbled, but inside she knew he was right. He put a hand on her arm as if to guide her home, and she shook him off. They walked in silence for nearly ten minutes before Tessa couldn't take it anymore.

"Good God, man, don't you know how to make polite conversation?"

Fenris shifted his eyes at her, one eyebrow raised. "Is that what you want?"

"It's better than walking in silence," Tessa said and then clarified, "Wait. Nothing prophecy-related, nothing horrifying, we're talking casual light conversation, yeah?"

Fenris smiled. "I think you have me confused with Robin."

Tessa now raised her own eyebrow, "How so?"

"Robin's the all-business type. I'm anything but," he said, his smile curling deeply into his face.

"Oh yeah, you're the picture of Mr. Funtime," Tessa said sarcastically, and the look on his face was almost like she had hurt his feelings. "How about this," Tessa said, throwing him a bone. "Tell me something nice. True and nice."

There was a long pause, and Tessa wondered if he was having trouble coming up with one good thing. Jeez.

"I like Mortals," Fenris said finally.

Tessa chuffawed (and nearly snorted). "What, to *eat*?"

He stopped walking and looked at her, as if offended. Tessa stared back at him, unsure what was happening. He frowned. "Not to eat. To be around. To spend time with. They're—" he trailed off, almost like he was embarrassed. "They're funny," he said finally. Tessa opened her mouth to speak and then shut it. She felt like she'd slipped into Bizarro world.

"You're, you're being serious."

Fenris nodded.

"You like mortals because they're *funny*?" Tessa asked, not even trying to hide her surprise.

"Stories aren't very funny on the whole. It's all 'dire this' and 'tragedy that.' Big stakes and prophecies and damsels in distress—"

"—From *you*," Tessa cut in.

"Sure, whatever," he said dismissively. "And it's not like there aren't funny Stories. There are. They exist but even then it doesn't feel *organic*?" he looked at her, a question in his expression as if he wasn't sure that was the right word. Tessa shrugged her shoulders. She had no idea how to help him with his puzzlings; she was so floored by the entire line of conversation she couldn't have made a helpful suggestion if her life depended on it.

"It's all, *telegraphed*," he said. "Or that's how it feels to me after being here for a few centuries. Mortals surprise me all the time. Stories almost never do. And I like surprises," he said, shrugging. Tessa blinked and said nothing. It was funny that he thought Stories couldn't be surprising because this whole conversation was surprising the hell out of her. Also? This was now, officially, the weirdest conversation of her entire existence. Which was saying something.

She took a chance.

"Do you know where I come from? What Story The Scion line is descended from?"

There was too long a pause for the answer to be no.

"You wouldn't know him," Fenris began, and before Tessa could interrupt, he continued. "A Scion killed him long ago and thus he no longer exists."

The information was like a bucket of ice water poured over her. "Wha—? Why would a Scion kill our own ancestor?"

"I don't know," Fenris said, and it had the frustrated sound of truth.

"Can you, I mean, even if I wouldn't know his Story—what was his name?"

"His name was Xavier. He was very old and very powerful," Fenris said.

Tessa thought it sounded like he had known him well. "Why is everything so goddamn complicated? It feels like for every question I ask or new thing I learn, there are infinite layers. I mean, what else don't I know?" she opined, more to herself than Fenris.

He was quiet for a long time and then stopped walking and said, "I will tell you something that I think you should know, Scion."

Tessa trembled a little despite herself and stopped so that she could look at him. They turned to face each other on the empty street, and Tessa could feel he was going to say something horrible, something that would make her life even more difficult. She took in a deep breath. "Okay. Shoot."

"The Story world is at war with itself. It's one of the many reasons that your appearance right now is both important and dangerous."

Tessa was stunned. "War? What kind of war?"

Fenris considered his words. "Like everything else, it's complicated, but think of it this way, Scion, in the Mortal world, you have all manner of disagreements when it comes to God. Religion and God here, it frequently means nothing less than war, right?"

Tessa nodded. "Sure. I mean, yeah, of course."

"It's no different for Stories. Story has all your same Mortal problems. Where do we come from? What are we, really? Why do we exist? Why are we created? Why don't we die? Who was the first? Why can't we have children? How did the Scion line come to be? Where do we go if a Scion does manage to kill us? And for all the answers that we come up with, just like Mortals, we don't all agree."

"God."

"Exactly. And just like for you Mortals, it's caused war. A very old one."

"Is it, is it something I need to worry about? Something I need to do something about?" Tessa stared at him, floored. She hadn't even imagined such complications. She wished she'd never asked him anything at all.

Fenris began walking again, and Tessa noticed it was a casual way of avoiding her gaze. "If you live long enough, I suppose you should worry about it very much, yes."

"Well, that's comforting," Tessa said, feeling exhausted all of a sudden. "So, who is the war between? Like good guys and bad guys or something?"

"No such thing," Fenris said, a sharpness edging into his tone.

"Huh?" Tessa asked.

Fenris looked at her, his dark gaze piercing through her, and she could tell something was dancing on the tip of his tongue, just aching to be said. Instead he looked away, dismissing her. "It's a bit above your pay-grade, Scion."

"C'mon. You started this."

"The lines are not so clearly defined as you would like to believe, luv. There is no black and white, it's all rather muddy and mostly grey. In the simplest of terms, I would say that some of us believe in fighting our Fiction and some of us believe in accepting it."

Tessa blinked twice. It was the exact same phrasing Robin had used. *Fighting our Fiction.* She shook her head. "You were right, it's complicated and I don't understand." After a moment, she looked back at him, trying to catch his eyes again. "Which side are you on?"

He didn't hesitate. "You don't know me well enough to ask that question."

And it was as if a metal curtain had been drawn between them. So abrupt and absolute was his tone that Tessa could almost hear the clang that separated them, perhaps permanently, drawing lines she didn't yet understand.

TWENTY-SIX

The funeral, which should have been a grim affair, was unbearably sunny.

A small crowd, *just enough'* Tessa thought to herself and then quickly wondered what that meant, had come to Bishop's graveside ceremony. Tessa had noticed police tape roping off the northern quadrant of the cemetery when she'd come in, and at least a dozen emergency vehicles were parked along the winding road, checking out the empty graves she and Fenris had discovered the night before. She hoped she didn't leave any more hair at the new crime scene. That was the last thing she needed.

Fortunately, Bishop's ceremony was well away from the chaos, situated on a slight bluff at the western edge of the cemetery. Lush grass surrounded his site and a large old tree sat not far away, casting deep shadows across the lawn. It was the kind of gravesite Tessa had thought existed only in Stories. It must have been a family plot, for the headstones all around his read Bishop as well. Snow had not come, which Tessa was grateful for. The crowd was a strange mix of what looked like students and teachers, some of them surely friends and family, and of course Detectives Wade and Ripley. Tessa wondered if they'd planned to come all along or if they'd been here for the empty graves and decided to stop by anyway. She hoped it was the former. It seemed less crass.

Tessa didn't listen to the words very closely. She was too tired and sad and worried about everything. She thought a lot about how wasteful Bishop's death had been, how useless she'd felt having it happen while she was right there, how she should have been able to stop it, and now he was just gone. And she barely knew him. How many words had they said to one another? Whatever it was, it hadn't been enough. She could count the number of minutes they'd spent together on one hand. Micah linked her fingers through Tessa's. It relaxed her, but only a little.

When the ceremony was over, it started to rain a little, which Tessa appreciated. It should have been raining all along.

People scattered in the rain. Micah pulled on the arm of Tessa's jacket and Tessa resisted. "Go ahead, I want to stay for a bit."

Micah hesitated and then thought better of it. "We'll wait for you by the entrance," she said. Tessa nodded. Detectives Wade and Ripley had watched her intently during the ceremony. Tessa had tried to ignore them, but it had been difficult. Now they hung around like vultures, and she ached to shake her fist at them, to scare them away.

Tessa bowed her head and closed her eyes. She tried to picture Bishop's face before he had died. It was his face after death that haunted her, and she wanted to remember the man, what little she knew of him, not the empty body. When she opened her eyes she was alone at the grave save a handsome older man in a sharp dark suit standing next her in the rain, covering them both with his excessively large umbrella.

"Well, you don't look like a murderer," he said, almost jovially, and not even looking at her.

Tessa squinted up at him and clenched her fist unconsciously. "Excuse me?"

"Captain West," he said, and they turned to face one another. "My detectives, or at least Detective Wade, likes you for murder in this unsavory business, Miss Battle,"

"Yeah, well, she's not real bright," Tessa said, running a hand through her wet hair and flinging the excess water on the ground.

West smiled a charming, irresistible smile. "Actually, she's one of my best." He stared at Tessa a moment and then added, "But I think she may be wrong about you."

"Can you get her to back off then?" Tessa said, more than asked.

"Ohhhhnoooo. I've never been able to get Wade to do much of anything."

"You're a Captain, doesn't that make you her boss? Isn't that, like, your *job*?" Tessa wanted to be annoyed with him, but something in his demeanor put her at ease. He was an imposing figure at six foot two and broad shouldered. He should have been intimidating but he was also kind of devastatingly handsome and absurdly charismatic, even at a funeral, which made him imminently likable at the same time.

"A good detective follows her instincts, regardless of what the brass says. Wade would be a better employee if she did what I said, but a lesser detective. Besides, sometimes being a good leader is knowing when to get out of the way, let others lead, do what they're best at. Wade can close a case like nobody's business. I'd be a fool to get in her way." He paused and smiled at Tessa. "Still, I'll put in a good word for you."

Tessa squinted up at West, trying to figure him out. "Why? I mean, you don't know me, so why would you do that?"

"I was once a detective myself. I've got plenty of instincts left, or at least a few, and mine say that you're no murderer. But you're clearly a girl with serious secrets, I suspect that's what's tripping up Wade."

"Everyone has secrets," Tessa said defensively.

"Indeed. But I wouldn't bet on holding onto them, Miss Battle."

"Great," Tessa muttered miserably.

"You hiding something I should know?"

"Just because I didn't kill Mr. Bishop doesn't mean I have nothing to hide. Just because I'm innocent doesn't mean I want her rooting around and messing up my life."

"Well, I'd learn to live with disappointment, Miss Battle. Secrets have a way of unraveling when people start digging. You're in a tough spot."

Tessa met his eyes. "You have no idea, Captain."

He was taken aback by her directness and his playful smile faded. "Do you need help, Miss Battle?"

Now it was Tessa's turn to be taken aback. "Yes, I mean, no, no, I'm fine, Captain. But thank you for asking. Been a while since anyone offered me help without strings. It's nice."

"Well, the offer stands." West reached into his pocket and drew out a business card. He handed it to Tessa. "Here's my card if you want to talk. And please, call me West."

He turned to go and when he was a few feet away Tessa called after him. "You should still be a detective," she said, "If I *was* guilty I'd confess to you before either of them."

West turned back to face her and gave her a slight bow. Tessa laughed a little. She liked West, he had a charm to him that set her at ease. She wished she could trade him for Wade.

When Tessa looked again, there was a tiny old woman, shrunken and pruned but with sharp eyes like tacks, standing not far from where West had been, dwarfed by another massive, black umbrella. Where did people get these huge umbrellas?

"You're Battle," she said, and it was not a question so much as a statement. Tessa looked up, her eyes a bit wide.

"Yes ma'am," she said.

"I recognize you," the woman said, squinting at her.

Tessa shook her head, confused. "How's that, ma'am?"

The woman examined her across the grave. "You have the look of all Battles," she said, doing a fine impression of a wise sage, and then added, "Also he told me you had very weird hair in your passport photo." The woman cackled aloud. Tessa smiled briefly before it all fell away.

"I'm sorry," she said.

"It's all right," the woman said. Tessa shook her head and looked down, she was too embarrassed to even look her in the eye now that the woman knew who she was.

"It's really not," Tessa said. "It's my fault he got killed."

"Don't be silly, dear. It's dangerous work, things happen. Benjamin knew that since he was a small boy. He never feared the risk and always loved the job, or at least the idea that he might someday get to actually do the job."

"Benjamin," Tessa murmured to herself. She hadn't heard anyone except Bishop actually say his first name until now. The woman reached out to take her hand. "It's an honor to meet you ma'am," Tessa said, shaking her small hand carefully.

"Call me Maeve, dear. I was once an Advocate myself and hearing you call me ma'am makes that feel like a dozen lifetimes ago, instead of just the one."

Tessa nodded but she wasn't sure she could use her first name. "I'm sorry," was all she managed a second time. Maeve tsked her.

"Battle, the day he finally found you, was the happiest day of his life. He had almost given up hope that a Scion would be called in his lifetime, and to find out that it was you, that it was 'The Last'…well, when he called to tell me, it was pure joy I heard and nothing more." Tessa choked out a thank you, and Maeve nodded. She then reached into her coat pocket, drawing out a silver chain with a charm at the end and holding it out to Tessa.

Tessa fingered the charm, drew in a surprised breath. It was a modified tree of life. Tessa had a version of one tattooed on her shoulder.

"You know what that is?" Maeve asked.

Tessa nodded. "It's a tree of life," she said staring at the charm, which sparked a feeling of memory though she was sure she had never seen one exactly like this before.

Maeve nodded, "It is based on that, yes, but it's the mark of the Advocate." Tessa looked up from the charm to meet Maeve's eyes. "It's been with Benjamin since he was a child, but you should give it to your new Advocate, when you find them."

Tessa examined the charm. It had a solid silver center resembling a tree, intricate silver branches bending off of it, above and below, so that all the branches connected together into an endless circle around the tree. However, in this version, one of the branches was a vibrant green. It edged out of the tree at the center and wound its way around the tree and back again, creating its own distinct circle within all the silver ones. Tessa assumed it was meant to represent The Advocate line, or perhaps The Scion line. It was wholly unique and precious. Tessa blinked back some tears threatening her.

"Thank you ma'am. It, it means a lot." Maeve nodded at Tessa and a sharp clap of thunder rang out followed almost immediately by a bright flash of lightning. The raindrops became bigger suddenly and fell faster. The sky darkened dramatically all around them. Maeve squeezed Tessa's arm and then began shuffling down the wet hillside. Before she had gone too far, she turned to look back at Tessa. "Be careful, dear. If you really are The Last then you're more important than any of them have been. And that is a thing, indeed."

Tessa watched her go. By the time she was a little black dot in the distance, the rain had soaked Tessa through and the sky was brutally dark, almost like night. Lightning and thunder came more and more frequently, as if stacking on top of one another. Tessa turned to leave, but as she did something caught her eye in the woods. Something big and brownish green.

"No…" she breathed, and froze, narrowing her eyes, trying to be sure that what she saw was not what she feared. That the shape was *not* the Troll.

But of course it was.

It was because Tessa's life was 100% suck.

"Dammit," she cursed under her breath before running toward the woods where the shadow moved almost elegantly through the thick trees. As she ran, she crested a small hill, and from there she could see the entrance to the cemetery. Brand and Micah were standing there, huddled under a tree, and she saw Brand notice her running toward the woods. They didn't even seem to think about it, let alone discuss it, before coming after her. Tessa cussed again. They were too good of friends, and it was going to get them killed.

Tessa entered the woods and followed the relatively wide swath of destruction that most certainly had been the Troll. She was running after it at a good clip when she came around a large tree and pulled up short to avoid the giant shape standing in the path. She swore and backed up a few steps. A brown shape that was not the Troll she had been expecting stood on the path. Tessa blinked at it, and before her eyes, it shifted into a Bengal tiger. *Her* Bengal tiger, complete with a slight scarring on its shoulder where her blade had landed. The tiger roared and Tessa blinked at it again, stunned. It took two menacing steps toward her, and she shouted out "LA COLOMBE NOIRE!" The Black Dove snapped into her hand with a satisfying, wet smack.

Tessa pointed the axe at the tiger. "You remember this? Well, I've about had it with you," she said. The tiger seemed to almost smile at her and then shifted effortlessly into a monkey. Not a big one, but a fast, tricky one, and it scampered partway up a tree before Tessa could even register it. Tessa heard Micah and Brand in the woods somewhere behind her, and she saw the monkey hear it too. "You leave them out of this," Tessa growled. The monkey, still with its shoulder scar, even in this new form, cackled and then clapped its hands three times in a decidedly human gesture. Thunder broke open the sky with each clap, and as it finished the last clap, another flash of lighting popped, the rain slowed, and all of a sudden Tessa couldn't see.

It wasn't like it had gotten darker, or her vision went blurry, it was like she didn't have eyes. She was plunged into a blackness so complete she couldn't even begin to comprehend it. And yet everything else remained the same, the sounds of the woods, the feel of rain occasionally hitting her jacket, the smell of wet dirt. Tessa reached up with her free hand to touch her eyes and drew back horrified.

They were gone.

Her eyes were gone.

TWENTY-SEVEN

Tessa felt the terrifyingly smooth skin where her eyes used to be and a strangled cry escaped her throat, pathetic and feeble. She drew in a breath and prepared to let out a scream she hoped would rip the universe in two but heard Micah scream instead. It was a sound that curdled her blood, every damn inch of it. Tessa moved toward the sound but stumbled on a branch immediately and only kept from falling over by clutching at the trunk of a nearby tree.

"TESSA!!!!!!!!!!" Micah cried out desperately. Tessa swung The Black Dove all around her, trying to find the wide path the shape shifter had carved for her.

"MICAH!" Tessa called, "KEEP TALKING SO I CAN FIND YOU!!!" Tessa stumbled forward, tripping and falling again. It was quiet for a long moment and so Tessa stopped, but then she heard Micah again.

"THIS WAY!"

Micah kept calling "this way" until Tessa was quite certain that she was all but upon them. "Ohmigod, Tessa! Your eyes!"

Micah drew back, horrified to see Tessa's face, exactly the same as it had always been, except as though she had never had eyes, as if smooth pale skin had always been there instead of those piercing blue eyes ringed in heavy black eyeliner. Brand, his mouth looking the same as Tessa's eyes, clutched at the edge of Micah's sweatshirt. He met Micah's eyes, and she could see tears spilling across his cheeks as he shook his head in horror and fear. Micah choked out a sob for both of them and clutched her glasses in her hand nearly snapping them in two.

Tessa groped blindly for her friend's arm. "Where's Brand?" Tessa asked, and then felt his hand. He was right there. "What…what's wrong?" Tessa asked. Brand was never this quiet, it was almost more disturbing than not having eyes.

There was a long pause, and then Micah spoke, too loudly, considering that they were all standing there together. "Brand can't talk, his mouth, his mouth is gone. It's like your eyes. God, it's horrible. What are we going to do?!"

Tessa felt tentatively up Brand's arm and then touched his face, her thumb gently gliding over where his mouth should be. Sure enough, just like her eyes, where his mouth used to be was only flat smooth flesh. Like it was a third cheek or something.

Tessa choked back a sob.

She clutched Micah's hand. "Are you okay?" There was another long pause and Tessa heard a faint scratching sound, and then Micah spoke again, again far too loudly.

"I can't hear, Tessa. I, my ears, it's the same for my ears as your eyes and Brand's mouth, just swallowed up by flesh. Oh, God," she wailed, breaking down again, fear pitching her voice wildly. Micah caught her breath and tried to continue. "Brand had a pen and a notebook in his bag. He's writing down what you're saying so I can read it, but I can't hear you, I can't hear anything." Tessa reached for Micah who guided her hand up to where her ear should be and Tessa's fingers slid over the smooth skin. "My glasses won't stay on," Micah said, rather hopelessly. "So I can barely see, too…unless I hold them up to my face." Tessa could hear Micah spiraling and worried her friend was going to just outright lose it. "What are we going to do, Tessa?!"

Tessa shook her head. "I don't know, but for starters, let's get out of the woods. There's something in here with us." Tessa waited for Brand to write it down for Micah.

"Okay," Micah said, taking a deep breath, and then added, "This way." Micah placed Tessa's hand on her shoulders, so that she could follow them out of the woods. But just as they started to move forward, a clumsy little caravan, something big ran past them in the woods. Tessa stiffened and Micah shouted out "WHAT?!"

"Shhhh," Tessa warned, and then heard some scratching, which she thought was Brand again.

"Brand says he saw it, just a bit of it. He said it looked like a monkey."

"Dammit," Tessa cursed.

"What is it?!" Micah asked, still too loud.

"Mike, you have got to calm down, I can't see anything so I have to be able to hear."

Tessa assumed Brand did the translation because Micah said only *Okay* quietly to herself. Something passed by them again, even closer. Tessa was certain it was circling them, the circle becoming tighter each time. Tessa shouted out for The Black Dove. It came to her faithfully, and she felt only slightly better. She had no interest in accidentally decapitating her best friends instead of whatever this thing was. She heard it again, to her left, even closer than last time, followed by the furious scratching of Brand on his pad of paper.

"He said it changed shape," Micah said, as if she was reading. "He says it looks like—" she paused and then Tessa heard her elbow him, "—you idiot, write more clearly, I can't read it!" The scratching continued and Tessa listened for the monkey, or whatever it had changed into. "He says it looks like one of those Japanese demons—red, with the horns and the big mouths and eyes—" There was another long pause. "You mean an Oni Demon?" Micah asked Brand. He must have nodded because she drew in a sharp breath.

"What does that mean, Micah?" Tessa asked, still listening for the thing. More scratching, the circle growing ever tighter around them.

"I don't know," Micah said, unsure. "They're Japanese folktales, my mom used to tell me stories about them—but they don't usually shift, not like this one seems to. But it could be—" she got very silent. And as Tessa waited for Micah to finish the sentence, something hit her from the side and she went flying off the path and into the trees. Tessa had sensed it an instant before it happened, but not quickly enough to defend herself. She landed in the dirt and leaves, off the path, and away from her friends. The thing was on top of her, tearing at her. She twisted madly, trying to get away from it, but it drew sharp claws across the side of her face and the scratches burned enough that Tessa knew they were dangerously deep. She felt warm blood pour off her face, down her neck and into her tank top.

She could hear Micah and Brand not far away, freaking out. Tessa managed to kick the thing away from her finally and scrambled to her feet. She stood, with the axe in hand, listening for it, trying to pinpoint the sound, which was nearly impossible with all the dead leaves and rustling branches.

Suddenly Micah yelled out, "Six o'clock!"

Brilliant girl, Tessa thought. She turned her body so that she could swing at something coming at her from behind. She didn't hit it directly with the blade of the axe, but she still managed to clip it, deflecting it away from her. She adjusted her grip on the axe and waited for Micah's next instruction.

A moment later, Micah shouted, "Eight o'clock!" Tessa obeyed and The Black Dove whizzed through the air, glancing off something ineffectively. Tessa reset herself and waited, listening. But then Micah shrieked and shouted, "Twelve o'clock!"

Tessa hesitated. "YOU'RE at twelve o'clock!"

Micah screamed at the top of her lungs, "Twelve o'clock!!!"

Tessa raised her arm and threw the axe end over end at twelve o'clock and prayed it wasn't going to land in one of their heads. She heard the axe bury itself in something not far away and then heard the familiar pop of it disappearing. She called for it again and as she did she heard Micah shriek an unholy sound. Tessa stumbled in the direction of the blood-curdling screams and tripped over something on the path. She reached down and immediately knew it was Brand. Her heart skipped a beat and she felt for his neck. He still had a pulse. Micah continued to shriek, and it was an inhuman, unfathomable sound. Unbearable. Tessa felt helpless and had to curb the urge to cover her ears with her hands to make it stop.

It was the sound of someone being killed.

TWENTY-EIGHT

Robin paced the small room, his skin itching and hot and desperate to be free of the confined space and rules that he knew bound this place.

Story was everything and anything a person could imagine, quite literally, but there were things about it that felt so restrained to him. In Story more than anywhere else in the worlds, he was painfully aware that he was someone else's creation. That he was bound by things utterly out of his control and forever beyond his reach. It was deeply ironic that he should keep trying to impress upon Tessa the way in which the rules of Fiction could not be broken, when in fact, he was, at his core, nothing but a rule breaker. The fact that he had been written as a rule breaker, and yet still had to—on some base and fundamental level—obey what was put to paper made him want to tear off his skin. And the fact that it was in fact rules of a sort that wrote him as a rule breaker was enough to screw with anyone's head.

Tessa thought him jealous of Fenris, and he was, but not for the reasons that she suspected, or mostly not for the reasons she suspected. The man was monumentally self-possessed. It was something Robin had never managed and Fenris seemed so at ease with that aspect of his life, had accepted it, or was exceptional at faking it. Of course he'd had a good fifteen hundred years on Robin, but it was cold comfort, a reminder that Fenris was ahead of him. And Robin often wondered if Fenris truly felt the weight of those years the way Robin did. He didn't exactly come of as a tortured soul.

The man infuriated him.

And there was no comfort.

Every moment they kept him here against his will was another moment that something might come after Tessa. Another moment that Marian might find out he was back in Story. It wasn't that he didn't want to see her. Quite the opposite. In fact, huge swathes of him wanted it so badly he could taste it. He wanted to see her and do nothing else. But he honestly didn't know if he'd be able to leave if he saw her, and Tessa needed him, and he needed to know what it was they had. It was somehow like what he and Marian had, and also utterly different. Both things terrified and excited him.

The heavy wooden door to the cell masquerading as guest room creaked open and Robin sprang to life, lunging for the door and his escape only for the door to be filled with someone entering. When the cloak fell back off her head and he saw Morgana, he had to forcibly stop himself from hissing like a cartoon villain. Still, she saw the restrained hatred on his face and was unmoved by it. She stepped deeper into the room and looked him up and down, appraising him openly. "You're looking different these days."

"Well, you know the Mortal world, quite colorful," he said, his voice clipped as he tried to restrain his hatred for authority and for Morgana especially.

"Mmmm," Morgana mused, unclasping her cloak and draping it over a chair. She sat on a stone bench and pushed her inky hair behind her shoulder. "Deception has never been your strong suit, Robin. Let's just be frank with one another, shall we?"

Robin doubted that was remotely possible, but he wasn't going to be the one to say it. "Fine. What in the name of all that's holy gives you the right to keep me here? I was promised safe passage and there are people I must see."

"Don't be an idiot." She sighed, adjusting the threaded gold cuff on the sleeve of her dress. "I have saved your stupid life by keeping you here."

"Explain."

"Midas guaranteed your passage, yes?"

"Yes."

"And you trust him?"

"Of course not."

"Well then," she said, as if that was the end of the conversation.

Robin clenched his fists open and closed in frustration, "Well, I don't trust you either, so I don't see where I'm at an advantage here."

"Do you trust, Tal?"

He hesitated. "Yes."

"And you think she would have just dropped you into my 'evil clutches' if there wasn't a reason, if she had other options?"

"So explain."

"There's a bounty on your return to Story."

"There's *always* a bounty on me. It's how Tal and I became friends in the first place."

"But Midas hasn't always been in charge and now that he is, he's made some promises to powerful people for your safe return home. After you and Snow were deposed by The Court, there was to be a vote about whether you would be able to return to the Mortal world. That vote was not going to go your way. I had Tal bring you here in secret instead."

"If that's true, Snow knows I'm here. She can't be trusted."

"She can. On this at least. Besides, she's so busy trying to argue her way back home she'll barely give you a second thought."

Robin couldn't help but smile. That was probably true. "So why bring me at all then? Why not just have Tal warn me and avoid all the theatrics?"

"I need you to do something for me."

"No way."

Morgan looked at him, exasperated. "You don't even know what it *is* yet."

"Well, it can't be *good*."

"I have a message for The Scion. A warning. You see, you have no idea what you're dealing with, who your enemy *really* is."

Tessa stumbled away from Brand's body and toward Micah's shrieks coming from the trees. She seemed to get no closer, as if she was walking through quicksand. And then the cries stopped as quickly as they'd begun.

The silence was powerfully deep.

And far more terrifying than the shrieks.

Sound at least meant life.

A moment after the screaming stopped, Tessa felt a shockwave of some kind, like the blowback from a small bomb, the force of which knocked her flat on her back. There was a painfully bright pop of light all around her. Her vision had been restored. Her eyes were back! She could feel them blinking in her face, devouring oxygen greedily. She narrowed them and peered into the trees, trying to find Micah, but there was nothing, just a dense layered mess of green and increasing darkness. Brand moaned some distance behind her, still on the path, and Tessa ran back to help him up. His mouth was back, he was making glorious noise.

These were wonderful things.

"Your face," Brand said, his own looking pained. Tessa reached up to touch the side of her face, which had three brutal cuts running across it, one of them especially deep and stretching from her cheek all the way through her lips, stopping halfway down her chin. She drew back a bloody hand.

"Yeah," she said. "C'mon," she pulled him with her toward the trees. "I think she's this way." And no sooner did she say it, then Micah began walking to them through the brush. Tessa looked at her and furrowed her brow. Something was different. Something had happened. As Micah neared them, Tessa saw her friend, entirely intact, though looking rough, her neck a nasty shade of red. But when Micah looked at them, a little glint of green light flashed in her eyes. "Micah?"

"I'm fine, Tessa," she said, her voice rough and raw from screaming.

"What happened, where is that thing?" Tessa said, looking around them and adjusting her sweaty grip on The Black Dove.

"Shikigami," Micah said flatly. "Or Shiki. They're familiars of Onmyoji. This one was sent by his master to put a spell called 'See No' on us."

"Who was its Master?"

"Circe," Micah said, brushing some leaves and dirt off her jeans and sweatshirt.

"Circe the Greek goddess?" Brand said, open-mouthed.

"The same," Micah said.

"So, how did you—?" Tessa started, and then stopped and tried again, anxious. Something was definitely wrong. "—Where is it?"

Micah whistled and the thing came out of the woods, almost shy. Tessa raised her axe. "You don't need that," Micah said.

"Why not?" Tessa asked.

"Because I'm its master now," Micah said, her voice flat and emotionless, her eyes glinting the greenish-gold again for just a moment.

Tessa blinked at her friend, "You're its what?"

Micah blinked back at her, almost as if she herself was under a spell, "I'm its master. I defeated it and thus the Onmyoji that controls it. It is now bound to me, like it or not," Micah said, casting her eyes down to it. The Shiki shuddered a little as if it was as displeased with the situation as everyone else.

"Um, how?" Brand asked.

"I think," Micah started and lost her voice. She started again, slowly. "I think it's my 'change.' Remember Snow said that it could latch on to latent heritage or traditions? Well, my parents are both steeped in ancient Asian culture, even if I couldn't give a damn, so I don't know. I think on the brink of death…I think that something kicked in and allowed me to exert my will over the Shiki. Defeat it and thus control it," Micah said, and her voice was filled with both relief and concern. She shrugged at the two of them after a moment.

"Fierce," Brand breathed finally.

"Fierce?" Tessa repeated, "Are we still saying fierce?"

Brand shrugged, "What do I know?"

Tessa eyed the Shiki, still in the form of an Oni demon, the form it had taken for a time in the boathouse—bright red, with horns and bulging eyes, a grotesquely large mouth that seemed like it was smiling. It was small, no more than two and a half feet tall, but powerfully built, and it stood next to Micah, breathing loudly, small fists clenched, as if it was fighting her.

"What, what do we do with it?" Tessa asked her friend. Micah looked at Tessa like she had asked an absurd question.

"*We* do not do anything with it. It's my responsibility now."

"Okay," Brand started more cautiously. "What are *you* going to do with it?"

Instead of answering, Micah looked down at the Shiki, which looked back up at her. It seemed like it both hated and loved her, and she it. Some kind of silent communication bounced between them. It was almost palpable to Tessa and Brand, who touched hands while watching the surreal sight. After a moment, the Shiki seemed to lose whatever mental battle they were having. Before their eyes, it shifted into a black crow. It let out a caw, flew into the air, and then landed on Micah's shoulder. Micah looked back at her friends.

"We should get out of here. Just because I was able to get control of the Shiki doesn't mean that Circe herself is defeated," Micah said, walking toward the edge of the woods. Tessa and Brand looked at one another, shrugged, and followed her out.

The three friends walked to Tessa's home from the cemetery. Micah's Shiki flew not far in front of them the entire way, stopping periodically to stand on branches and caw at things. Tessa and Brand said nothing and watched their friend. Tessa wasn't entirely convinced it *was* their friend.

At the house, Micah went to the kitchen and got a glass of water. When she looked at Tessa over the glass, she opened the drawer that held the dishtowels and handed her one.

"No," Tessa said, rejecting the thin, checked one Micah had extended to her. "Give me that expensive-looking grey one," she said. Micah shrugged and gave Tessa the one she requested. Tessa pressed it against her face and grimaced. "Are you alright?" Tessa asked Micah pointedly.

Micah looked up at her and for the first time she seemed to Tessa like she was herself again. "Yes," she said. "It's just, it's a strain," she said, nodding toward the Shiki, which shifted into a grey striped housecat and jumped onto the counter. Tessa blinked at it, shocked, but Brand brightened.

"It's like the greatest pet ever!" he said and came up to it, intent on petting it.

"Yeah," Micah said warily and Tessa could tell she certainly did not agree. The Shiki hissed at Brand's hand as he reached for it and then turned to Micah, who looked back at it intently. After a moment it went to Brand, as if in apology, and sat, almost content, as Brand pet it.

"How are you shifting its shape?" Tessa asked.

"You're doing that?" Brand asked, amazed.

"Yes, I'm doing it," Micah nodded and then looked at Tessa. "As far as I can tell, it's bound to me and changes shape based on my will," she paused and rubbed her temple. "Do you have an aspirin?"

Tessa went to the cupboard for the bottle. Micah refilled her glass and took a few, certainly more than the recommended dose, but Tessa held her tongue. "So, what now?" Tessa asked, eyeing the Shiki.

"About the Shiki?" Micah asked, "I don't know. For now, I've got it, it can't do any harm. But we need to talk about Circe."

"What about her?" Tessa asked, watching Brand stroke the Shiki, which seemed to be softening ever so slightly on the idea of being pet.

"The Shiki had to share what it knew with me. It didn't know everything Circe knows, but it knew a lot. It knew that Circe was working with someone. That she was tasked with keeping you busy. The Shiki was instructed to get the hair from each of us for this spell, he called it 'The See No.'"

"See No…" Brand mused, "Is that…" he trailed off and then smacked his head as if something had just occurred to him. "Of course!"

Tessa and Micah looked at him, "What?" they asked in unison.

"*See No Evil, Hear No Evil, Speak No Evil,*" he said, looking at them pointedly.

"Oh hell," Tessa said, marveling at its simplicity. Micah nodded. Her face had relaxed a bit, and she smiled at Brand.

"Keep petting it, it must like it. Despite the pretense, it's fighting me less," she said, touching her head and closing her eyes for a moment. And it did look as if the tension and energy she was expending to keep the thing in line had lessened slightly. Tessa wondered what would happen when Micah needed to sleep but didn't say anything out loud.

Brand glanced at Tessa, "I think maybe we need to go to the hospital for your face, it's not healing as quickly as I would think," he said, his mouth twisting in concern. Tessa pulled back the towel and looked at the mess of dark red, almost black blood.

"Yeah, I know," she said. "But I don't think I should go to the hospital, how would I explain it? And what if they can tell I'm healing faster than normal? No. It'll be okay, we've got some butterfly bandages in the kit, right?"

Brand nodded and went to the cabinet for the kit, which he brought back to the table and pushed to Micah who began fishing for bandages. "There was more," she said, without looking up from her search. Tessa and Brand waited and then Micah looked up to meet their eyes. "Kill everyone except The Scion."

"And indeed that is what I was hoping for," said a voice from inside the house.

Tessa sprang up to see someone standing in her dining room.

Dr. Frankenstein wasn't the mastermind.

It was *The Monster.*

And he was in her dining room.

TWENTY-NINE

Tessa sucked in a breath and backed up a step.

It was strange, he was instantly recognizable for what he was—The Monster of *Frankenstein* legend—and yet he looked nothing like the monster movies Tessa knew so well. His skin was yellow, not green, and the stitching that held him together was fine and almost subtle. But the pieces didn't fit right, they were stretched taut in places and then too loose in others giving an uneven appearance to his flesh, as if his skin could barely contain what lurked beneath. He was massive in size, nearly eight feet tall and perfectly proportioned, not awkward. But the shoulder span of an eight-foot man is more massive than you can imagine. Not to mention the length of his arms, his hands the size of cookware, his feet like boats. His hair was longish, dark, and almost absurdly lustrous while his mouth was a black inhuman slash that made Tessa shiver.

She supposed this was your fate when you were assembled from spare parts.

But his eyes. His eyes haunted Tessa. Intelligence and humanity. This was no mindless monster. This was a cursed man. And yet his actions marked him clearly as a monster. Tessa felt conflict surging inside her over these unexpected revelations and with that conflict, a despair she didn't yet understand.

Three large figures loomed behind him in the dining room. They were similar but different, like corrupted reflections of The Monster. Inferior smaller copies, but still large and powerfully built, scary. Tessa's brain was so busy calculating what it all meant that she had almost forgot to respond.

"Well, since we're all still alive, then I guess you'll have to mark that one down as a failure," she finally said.

"I suppose, but even in failure there are things to be learned," he replied. Tessa saw a tiger standing next to her in the kitchen, and she slid away from it with a gasp.

"Tessa, it's me," Micah said. "It's the Shiki." Tessa looked at Micah like she was insane.

"Yes, very impressive," The Monster said.

"What do you want?" Tessa asked.

"Well, if no offer of beverages will be forthcoming, then you are right that we should get down to business. I'm here to correct my mistake." He looked at the copies behind him. "Kill all but The Scion or don't bother coming home," he said almost casually before disappearing out the dining room window, broken, yet again. Her dad was going to lose it when he saw that.

The first one hit Tessa with the back of its hand, and she bounced across the room like a rubber ball. Before she could get to her feet it lunged at her and she felt like a house had been dropped on her. The weight and the speed of the thing shocked her. How could it be so big and heavy and still move so fast? Out of the corner of her eye, Tessa saw the Shiki leap at a second monster, knocking it back into the dining room. But the third made a beeline for Micah and Brand. Micah shouted and the Shiki tried to come to her aid, but the one it had knocked into the dining room was already back up, and it grabbed onto the tiger and pulled it to the ground. Tessa struggled with hers as she watched the third creature corner Micah and Brand in the living room.

Ten more seconds of this and her friends were going to be dead.

Tessa launched her monster away from her and into the foyer with her legs, trying to scramble free, to get to them, but as she did so she saw a streak run through the room, so fast she almost missed it.

It was Fenris, but in his human form, leaping at the third creature, knocking it to the ground mere inches from Micah and Brand. Tessa breathed a sigh of relief. The man had impeccable timing if nothing else. Tessa saw the Shiki tear off the arm of the one it was fighting in the kitchen and thought that seemed like a pretty damn good idea. When hers came back at her, Tessa called The Black Dove and then swung it into the thing's shoulder, neatly severing the arm. It didn't scream out but it did seem *concerned*. Tessa smiled. With Fenris here and this new Shiki as Tiger, these creatures didn't stand a chance. When a blue-white flash of light illuminated the room and an arrow came flying out of the glowing doorway pinning a monster's hand to the wall, Tessa couldn't help but laugh.

These things were toast.

And they knew it.

Before Robin had even finished glowing blue from the doorway, the Franken-copies were stumbling over one another to escape out the dining room window.

When Tessa saw Robin, she was flooded with relief. Not because the cavalry had arrived but because he was here and all in one beautiful, living, breathing piece. As he stepped away from the glowing blue doorway Tessa was struck by the true depth of her feelings for him. Until this moment, on some level it had all been play. A powerful lusty crush. And who wouldn't have a crush on Robin Hood? But seeing him now, his face creased with concern for her well-being, Tessa knew that her feelings had nothing to do with 'Robin Hood' and everything to do with *Robin*.

He was no mythical hero, no sexy bad-boy anarchist, no Fiction she had made up. He was just Robin, and that was better, so much better. He was the person in the room that couldn't take his eyes off her. The person that worried for her with every breath and who would fight by her side, no matter what. He couldn't be her whole world because there were people depending on her, and important things for her to do, but an ache inside her told her that she *wanted* him to be her whole world, and maybe just knowing that was enough to make her sure of everything she'd been afraid to admit to herself since meeting him.

Robin reached out to touch Tessa's bleeding face with concern. It must have looked even worse than she thought. She pulled him to her and kissed him deeply, Shiki wounds be damned. She hoped the kiss would tell him everything she was thinking. Tessa didn't care if it was gruesome and bloody, or public, and he must not have either because he kissed her back with the same intensity.

"Welcome back," Tessa said, their mouths still touching. Tessa embraced him, hard, and ignored the pain of her face rubbing against his jacket. She noticed that they were alone in the room, the others having escaped to the kitchen.

Robin pulled back from Tessa and turned her face to examine it. "What did this?"

Tessa nodded at The Shiki, lying on the kitchen floor not far away, and watched as it shifted from ferocious tiger to a sweet, grey-striped kitten. "It's a long story though," she said.

And then she saw that Tal was standing in the kitchen with Brand, Micah, and the Shiki, and she was looking at Robin with a sour, possessive look on her face. Tessa looked at Robin and then back to Tal. She could feel some tension, a strain. There was something undeniable between them, and Tessa's mind raced at what exactly it might be. A tremor of fear ran through her unlike any she had ever felt before.

Different than fighting monsters.

Scarier.

Maybe in part because at least she was good at fighting monsters, *this*, she had no idea what to do with, how to fight, how to win.

Robin shook his head at Tessa, seeing the confusion and suspicion taking over her face. "I needed Talia to get back," he said quietly. Tessa nodded at him, trying to let the practicality of it soothe her and trying to ignore the fact that he had just called her Talia when everyone else called her Tal. She told herself that she had misread what she'd seen between them. What had she even seen, anyway? Nothing. A look, a gesture, nothing.

Tessa opened her mouth to say something but the Shiki meowed plaintively, drawing their attention. Micah fussed over The Shiki, clearly concerned. It was the only one hurt badly from this latest encounter and it mewed pitifully. Robin walked Tessa into the kitchen and then sat her down at the table, reaching for the pillaged first aid kit.

Tessa looked at Micah. "Does it hurt you too?"

Micah nodded. "A little," she said, wincing. Brand picked the Shiki up carefully and laid it on the kitchen counter. He dabbed at the wounds with a wet cloth while it protested.

Tessa turned back to Robin. "It's not Dr. Frankenstein, it's The Monster."

Robin nodded. "Yes, we discovered the same thing. I got back as soon as I could."

"How did you find out?"

He hesitated and it seemed almost as if he was going to a lie for a moment and a bite of fear pricked at Tessa. "Actually, Morgana told me."

"Morgana?"

"Yes. I wasn't entirely sure she was telling the truth. Obviously she was."

Tessa bit her lip. "I wonder why," she said more to herself than Robin and then, looking up, "Did she tell you anything else?"

"She told me about Circe, that they're working together."

"Hmph," Tessa said, "I didn't think she was an ally."

Robin shook his head back at her. "I'm not so sure she is. She could have known what was happening here. She could have told me knowing full well that you were about to learn it for yourself anyway, in the hopes that it would work in her favor later."

"So she's an enemy?"

"I honestly don't know, Tessa. Here's what I do know. Morgana is like Fenris. She's the slow knife."

"The slow knife?"

"A blade that is able to penetrate and kill because it takes its time. It succeeds where others fail, because it asserts itself slowly over time, often unnoticed, so that it has killed you before you realize what you have let in."

"Jesus, Robin."

"We're playing a serious game, Tessa."

Tessa blinked and opened her mouth but before she could speak the Shiki cried out nearby and Brand raised his hands helplessly, stepping away from the creature. "I—I don't know what I'm doing."

Tal, who had mostly been glaring at Tessa, glanced at Brand with the Shiki and then sighed dramatically.

"Do you have something to add?" Tessa asked. Tal glared at her again and then walked over to where Brand was standing and held out her hand for the towel. He put it in her gloved hand, and she shooed him to the side with a flick of her wrist.

"Do you know what you're doing?" Micah asked nervously, as Tal examined the Shiki. Tal looked up at Micah and her eyes softened.

"I've patched up Hecuba many times in the field," she said. Tal took off her jacket and unstrapped a leather belt that had a small pouch attached to it. From the pouch she removed a syringe and bottle as well as a needle, thick black thread, and gauze. Tal uncapped the syringe carefully and filled it with some of the liquid from the bottle. Micah inhaled sharply. "It's just a local anesthetic," Tal said, and injected it into the Shiki without waiting. The Shiki hissed and then relaxed.

"Deep," Robin said, touching the side of Tessa's face, turning it to better see the largest cut that refused to heal.

"I know," Tessa said, watching him.

Robin held a damp towel to her cheek. "This one cut is bad, I'm afraid it might scar," he said and Tessa winced both from pain and at the thought of a permanent scar on her face. *That* would make life extra awesome. Then again, the Shiki seemed to be permanently scarred no matter what shape it took thanks to Tessa's blow with her axe, so maybe this was only fair. An eye for an eye and all that. Robin went about cleaning her wounds without further comment. At the counter, Tal handed Brand the needle and thread.

"What?" Brand asked, confused.

"I'll walk you through it," Tal said, her voice clipped.

"Why can't you just do it?" he asked, pushing the needle and thread back at her. In answer, she held up her gloved hands with the thick metal fingertips that would make fine work—like stitching a wound—nearly impossible. She clicked them together rather than saying anything. "So take them off," Brand said, pushing the tools back at her again.

"She shouldn't," Robin said from the table, without looking up from Tessa's injuries. "She's Sleeping Beauty," he said. Everyone looked at Robin in slow motion, their mouths hanging open. "She pricks her finger on anything sharp and she'll be asleep for a *very* long time, possibly taking a bunch of us with her," he added almost matter-of-factly.

Heads turned from Robin back to Tal, drinking her in. Now that he'd said it, it seemed obvious, the perfect princess-like beauty, the crazy long, golden hair, the figure that supermodels would kill for. Of course, the leather and hunting gear, not to mention the surly attitude, didn't fit Tessa's preconceived image of her, but the steel tipped gloves should have been a dead giveaway. The room was perfectly still for a moment and so quiet that you could practically hear hearts beating, and then Brand cleared his throat and pulled the needle carefully away from Tal.

"Okay, tell me what to do."

Half an hour later, Tal prepared to leave and Tessa tailed her into the living room. She noticed that Robin made a point of not saying goodbye. "Tal?" Tessa called, walking over to her.

"Scion," she said.

"I just wanted to thank you."

"Sure," Tal nodded, stuffing her hands into her jacket pockets. She closed her eyes and chanted the now familiar words and disappeared in a snap of blue light and energy.

"So friendly," Tessa muttered, and then looked back at Brand standing in the doorway. "Did you get it?"

Brand looked up from a small notebook he had in his hand. "I think so."

"Good," Tessa said, nodding and heading back into the kitchen. She looked around at the group, realizing just now that Fenris had disappeared, again. "Does anyone know how to reach Fenris?"

Everyone looked at her blankly.

"Why?" Robin asked, doing a half decent job of concealing his rage at the mention of the name.

"Because I think it's time I finally agreed to find The Advocate. And he seems to think he knows how to do that."

THIRTY

In the morning, Tessa woke to find Robin gone from her room. She slid on beat-up bunny rabbit slippers and walked to the end of the hall to peek in on Brand and Micah, asleep on her father's bed. Micah was curled into a ball in one corner of the bed while Brand was splayed across two thirds of it, snoring softly. The Shiki, still a sweet, striped grey cat with a few bandages, slept inside a two-foot diameter ring of salt on the floor. Tessa shook her head at the incredible weirdness of her life.

Downstairs, Tessa looked out the broken dining room window to the backyard and saw Robin shooting arrows into the tree. He seemed decidedly un-calm. She wished he could understand the depth of her feelings for him, but she supposed that was impossible since she was just beginning to understand them herself.

Brand entered the kitchen and poured cereal into a bowl. He yawned and waved a hello at her and then held up the box, silently asking if she wanted to partake. Tessa nodded, and he poured another. They ate for a minute before speaking at all.

"Where's Micah?" Tessa asked between spoonfuls.

"Still sleeping," Brand said, looking up from the kiddie puzzles on the back of the box.

"And the Shiki?" Tessa asked, looking at him.

"Sleeping in its *circle of salt*," Brand said, looking back at Tessa.

"You know anything about that thing?" Tessa asked.

"No," he said, but she could tell from his tone he'd been thinking the same thing.

"Can you find out?"

"Yes," he said, and she knew they were on the same unpopular page. A moment later, Micah walked in the room. Tessa and Brand looked up, their mouths simultaneously dropping open.

"What—" Tessa started

"—Is that?" Brand finished.

"It's Jeff," Micah said, looking at the Shiki and reaching for the box of cereal and a bowl.

"Jeff?" Tessa and Brand repeated, staring dumbfounded at what appeared to be a green dragon about two feet long flying about the kitchen, occasionally yawning.

"Yes, the Shiki. He wants to be called Jeff," Micah said, pouring milk in her bowl as the Shiki (Jeff, apparently) tittered lightly and landed on the kitchen island. Tessa couldn't take her eyes off of it.

"Ooookay. Why—" she started.

"—Is it a dragon?" Brand finished, and Tessa nodded in agreement.

"He changes shape based on my mood," Micah said, shrugging as if this was completely normal information to be sharing.

"And you're feeling—"

"—Dragon-y?" Brand finished for Tessa a third time.

"I guess so," Micah said, taking a bite of cereal.

"Mike," Tessa said, trying to look at her friend and not the dragon on her kitchen counter. "This thing, it's not a pet, it's dangerous. You saw what it did to, well, *us*."

"I know," Micah said, looking at the Shiki.

"So…" Tessa said, trailing off uncomfortably.

"I'm not killing him," Micah said.

"Who said kill?" Brand asked, unable to look away from the thing.

"I know what you were thinking," Micah said, casting her eyes clearly at Tessa.

"Okay, okay, not kill. What about release?"

"I can't," Micah said, shaking her head. "You said it yourself, he's dangerous. At least this way, he's under my control."

"And you're sure you have it, er, *him* under control?" Tessa asked, unsure.

"Yes," Micah said, her tone flat and certain. "Jeff and I have an understanding. Don't we, Jeff?" She looked at the Shiki. The dragon tittered again as if agreeing. There was a long pause, during which Tessa and Brand exchanged a glance while Micah ate cereal. Brand shrugged helplessly at Tessa.

"Okay," Tessa said. "For now. But Brand is going to look into this further. This is not a closed topic."

"Fine," Micah said and picked up her cereal bowl. "C'mon Jeff," she said, heading into the living room. Jeff lifted up and flew after her, landing on her shoulder as she disappeared around the corner.

Fenris walked in the front door, skipping the doorbell, and Tessa rolled her eyes. He must have her house bugged, how else did he always know exactly when to show up? She would have Brand look into it later. "Are you ever going to get the hang of the whole knocking thing?"

Fenris threw a languid smile in her direction. "No."

Tessa threw up her hands and walked into the backyard. Fenris cast his eyes at the dragon and then at Micah.

Micah shrugged casually. "He's called Jeff," she said.

Fenris nodded appreciatively. "Nice." He sat down on a couch and they watched cartoons, chuckling occasionally. Brand shook his head at the surreal sight and returned to his cereal in the kitchen mumbling to himself.

"The Big Bad Wolf is watching cartoons with my best friend and her pet dragon. Everything is fine, everything is fine, I'm not freaking out, *I'm not.*"

Tessa stood on the porch stairs and waited for Robin to finish his shot.

"What?" he asked as he released the arrow.

"Fenris is here," she said. "Will you come in?"

Robin hung his head and then put the bow and quiver down on the picnic table nearby.

"Are you mad at me?" Tessa asked as he walked to her. After realizing the intensity of her feelings for him, suddenly the idea of him being mad at her was devastating. And that made her feel a little uncomfortable. Standing on the step to the house, she was a bit taller and he looked up at her as she touched his face. "Please don't be mad at me," she whispered before he could answer.

"I'm not mad at you," he said. "I'm worried. They're entirely different."

Tessa nodded and bent her head down and kissed him. "Then don't worry either," she said, and led him into the house by the hand. In the living room, Tessa felt Robin tense just at the sight of Fenris. But he then noticed the dragon and balked.

"Jeff," Micah said, seeing his expression.

"The Shiki," Tessa added, as way of explanation.

"So, how does this work?" Tessa asked Fenris, still holding Robin's hand

"There's someone I can take you to. She can help you find The Advocate," he said.

"Where?" Tessa asked.

"We can drive partway and then it's about half a day's hike. We'll have to camp overnight, as we can only call on her at dawn and sunset," he said. Robin shook his head, clearly hating the plan. Tessa squeezed Robin's hand.

"Robin comes," she said, and before Fenris could protest, she added, "It's non-negotiable."

Fenris sighed. "Fine." He stood up. "Gather your supplies, we should leave within the hour. I'll be back." Tessa watched him go.

"I hate that fucking guy," Robin grumbled.

Tessa squeezed his hand again. "I know." Micah and Brand looked at Tessa. "You guys are staying. And Snow is the babysitter. I don't even want to hear about it." They both looked down, but after yesterday's horror show they seemed less inclined to complain. Tessa looked at Robin. "There's some camping equipment in the basement. Will you start putting together what we need? I'm going to call Snow and get her over here." Robin nodded and left the room.

Forty minutes later, everything was ready and Snow was in the living room, looking like a grouchy supermodel, as per usual.

"You do know I'm not *actually* Heckle and Jeckle's babysitter, right, Scion?"

Micah and Brand looked at one another. "Heckle and Jeckle?" the asked, confused. And then Brand lit up.

"We've been given minion names!" he said, clapping excitedly.

"Upgrade!" Micah shouted, her fist vigorously pumping the air. Then they stopped abruptly and cut mean sarcastic looks at Snow, who looked away, bored.

"Snow," Tessa began, "I greatly appreciate your help. That said, you owe them both for saving your life the other night. You will return that favor by taking them to your home. They will stay with you tonight, you will drive them to school like a good babysitter and pick them up at exactly 2:50 p.m. tomorrow. They will stay with you until I return, and if they have so much as a scratch on them when I pick them up, I will take it out of you in pounds of flesh." Snow crossed her arms and sat down huffily without a word. Tessa turned to Brand and Micah. "For your parts, you will behave like angels, get in zero mischief, and do nothing that puts you in any kind of insane Story jeopardy. Grey has agreed to watch out for you during classes tomorrow and to go with you to Snow's after school."

"We need *two* babysitters?" Brand said incredulous.

"Yes," Tessa said without missing a beat, and then added, "We also need as many allies as humanly possible." Brand shrugged in acceptance, and Micah looked at Jeff as he crawled into her lap, shifting effortlessly from a dragon into a cat. "When I get back, we're all at a table and puzzling this out. The more research you can do between now and then, the better." Someone knocked on the door and, for a moment, Tessa marveled that Fenris had actually knocked. She opened it without looking and then turned to see Detectives Wade and Ripley on her porch. Again.

Wade looked at the pile of camping equipment on the floor of the foyer, "Going somewhere, Miss Battle?"

"You guys ever take a day off?" she asked.

"No," Wade said, stepping inside without being invited. Ripley followed her, looking slightly apologetic about it. "Seriously, Miss Battle," Wade said, kicking at the tent on the floor. "I thought I asked you not to leave the county."

"I'm not," Tessa said and then looked at the two of them pointedly. "Is there something I can do for you two?"

"Where's your father?" Wade asked.

"San Francisco again. On business," Tessa said, irritated.

"What's the phone number?" Ripley asked. Tessa walked into the kitchen and returned with a business card. She deliberately handed it to Ripley while staring down Wade.

"And now you know as much as I do," Tessa said.

"Not close to your father, Miss Battle?" Wade asked.

"Yes, years of boarding schools have made us the best of friends. And if that's all, please leave my house."

The two detectives turned and walked to the door. Ripley was halfway down the walk when Wade turned back around. "I'll be coming for you this week, Miss Battle," she said.

"If you bother me again, it better be to charge me with something," Tessa said.

Wade smiled thinly. "Don't worry, it will be."

Tessa shut the door on Wade and leaned up against it. She watched her friends staring back at her, silent and anxious. Jeff meowed. "I cannot catch a goddamn break," Tessa said, and the room nodded in agreement, even a begrudging Snow.

THIRTY-ONE

The long drive and the hike to the campsite had been absurdly uncomfortable. The tension so thick you could cut it with a giant freaking magical axe. Half an hour into the drive, Tessa had given up on trying to lighten the mood and settled into a somber pout that put both Fenris and Robin to shame.

Fenris had, naturally, disappeared not long after reaching a small clearing where he said they should camp, and Robin and Tessa pitched the tent in silence.

"It would be great if you could let up just a little bit," Tessa said.

Robin looked at her over the tent. "I'm sorry but I can't. I don't trust him. And I don't understand why you do."

"For the record," Tessa said, unzipping a flap on the tent, "I never said I trusted him."

"You keep letting him in," Robin argued.

"I do not. He keeps coming in. There's a big difference," Tessa said. "And when he comes in, he saves lives and offers valuable information. So, I don't see as I have much choice."

"There's always a choice, Tessa," Robin said flatly. "You're taking the easy road, and the ends are not going to justify the means."

"Interesting philosophy, coming from you," Tessa said bitterly. She was grouchy and frustrated. She wanted to be swooning and in love. Not fighting. She didn't understand why he was being so difficult or why she was so offended by it. The whole thing made her feel out of control, which she hated.

"What does that mean?" he asked, his tone sharp.

"Are you kidding me? Your whole entire bit is stealing from the rich to feed the poor, how is that not the *definition* of ends justifying the means?!"

"It's different," he said, frustrated, running a hand through his hair and looking away.

"Oh, of course it is," Tessa said. "Conveeennnnient."

"Listen, there are means and then there are means. Sometimes the risk is worth it, sometimes it's not. In this case, I believe there are other ways," Robin said.

Tessa turned angrily on him. "Really?! Bishop is dead, Robin. Micah and Brand nearly died yesterday too. Micah is now bonded with some incredibly dangerous demon that could turn on her, or any of us, any second, and look at my goddamn face!?! Circe, a freaking Greek goddess, and seriously powerful witch is possibly working with the Frankenstein Monster to build a zombie army in order to kill everyone around me, do God knows what with me, and probably take over the world, and you think I'm just going the easy way for the hell of it? I'm going with the only options I see!"

Robin walked around the tent and took her hand. "I'm sorry."

Tessa snatched her hand away. He reached for it again and pulled her into him. "I'm sorry," he said again, quieter, "I'm scared."

"Me too," she said, into his jacket. "But I need you with me, not against me. And every time you question my choices it just, it makes me even more afraid that I'm doing the wrong thing, making the wrong call, over and over again. It only—"

"What?"

"It just reminds me that it's my fault Bishop is dead—"

"It's not your fau—"

"—You weren't there, Robin. It *was* my fault. And I can't bear it if I get someone else killed. Someone I know, someone I lo—someone I care for."

He finally got it. He nodded and held her tighter. "Okay. I'll try. I promise."

Tessa saw Fenris watching them from the edge of the woods and pulled back, startled. Fenris smiled and stepped into the clearing.

"Sorry to interrupt," he said smoothly.

"No, you're not," Tessa said.

"True," he agreed, tilting his head to the side. He watched Tessa for a long moment and then moved to the fire Tessa and Robin had started. He took out a map that he'd marked up. Tessa and Robin crouched down to examine it with him. "You should leave no later than five a.m.," he said.

"We should?" Tessa interrupted. "Where will you be?"

"Around," he said.

"What the hell, Fenris?" she sighed.

He ignored her. "You follow this path," he pointed to the markings on the map, and then pointed to a dense, barely visible path leading out of the clearing they were in. "That way. Push hard and it will take you less than 90 minutes to get to the lake," he began, and Robin interrupted.

"There's no lake on the map," Robin said, pointing to the dense trees at the end of Fenris' marked path.

"Trust me, it's there," Fenris said. Robin made a huffing sound at the word trust. Tessa cut him a look.

"Once you get there, you have to call The Lady forth. Spill your blood in the lake, Scion, and that should do it."

Tessa scrunched up her face. "I'm running out of blood, man."

Fenris looked at her. "You have plenty left yet to give."

Robin went to the tent first, probably because it was hard for him to sit still *and* be close to Fenris for so long. Tessa wanted to go too, but she was feeling fidgety and unsure. She sat with Fenris, thinking about The Monster, thinking about everything. When she finally spoke, her voice was a whisper.

"Why doesn't he want to kill me?"

Fenris gazed at her and said nothing.

"He said *'kill everyone but The Scion.'* Is it just because he doesn't want the border to close? Could that be it? Is there some big plan? Is there something big coming through, what?"

"I suspect that is all true," Fenris said, his sentence sounding unfinished.

"But what?"

"But I suspect there's more. I think he wants something very specifically from you."

"Like what?"

"I don't know, Hardcore."

"Stop calling me that."

"Have you read his Story?"

"The Cliffs Notes," Tessa said, blushing. Fenris tsked her and she shrugged.

"The Monster is a miserable outcast. He fits in nowhere. He belongs nowhere. A foot in both worlds, welcome in none."

"That's grim," Tessa said.

"It's life for some of us," Fenris said and then stood up unexpectedly. Tessa stood too and was taken by surprise when he reached out to touch her face. Tessa grabbed his wrist, stopping him.

"What are you doing?" she asked. He removed her hand from his wrist and continued to reach for her, pushing her hair out of the way so that he could see her face. Her injuries had gone a long way toward healing, but from the looks of it she was going to have at least one big scar.

"Tch," he said, clucking his tongue. "Too bad," he said, his voice rough, and then he touched her cheek near the wound lightly. Tessa bristled and pulled away from him.

"It's fine," she said, but her voice was uncertain and he knew it. He lowered his hand and she relaxed. "It's not really my primary concern," she said, wishing the statement was as true as it should be.

"Where will you sleep?" Tessa asked.

"I'll be around," he said, disappearing into the woods.

In the tent later, with Fenris gods knew where, Tessa couldn't sleep. She lay in the crook of Robin's arm and listened to his heartbeat. "Are you asleep?" she whispered.

"No."

"I don't know what I'm doing, Robin," Tessa said, biting back tears.

"You're doing great, you're doing your best," Robin said, stroking her hair.

"I don't think that's enough."

"It will be. It has to be. And I believe in you," he said.

Tessa sighed into him. "I'm so tired. I feel like, I feel like this whole thing was a mistake."

"What whole thing?"

"This Scion business. Me being The Scion—all of it."

"It's not," Robin said assuredly.

"How can you say that with such conviction?"

"Because I've seen you in action."

"Seen me in action? I've gotten at least one man killed, permanently scarred my friends and my face, destroyed an ancient Story, and I'm scared *all the time*, all in a matter of weeks. What's so great about that action?"

There was a long pause before he continued, "Do you know what your name means?"

"Means?"

"I find the meanings of names interesting, especially for Fiction," he said.

"I'm not Fiction," Tessa said, a little too hard.

"Well, you sort of are," Robin said, a little too matter-of-factly.

"I'm not," Tessa snapped.

"Okay, fine," he said, backtracking. "Regardless, your mother, she knew who you were, who you might be, who you might become. And her name, you told me it's Sophia, right?"

"Yeah."

"Sophia means Wisdom."

"Are you sure it doesn't mean 'she who abandons'?" Tessa joked bitterly.

"I'm sure," Robin said, smiling into Tessa's hair.

"So what's it mean, my name?"

"It means Reaper. Harvester."

"Well, that's awesome," Tessa said sarcastically.

"You should think about it," Robin said. "It means something. It's no coincidence that The Last Scion has this name."

Tessa was quiet for a long moment. "These destiny conversations with you are always so cheery."

"You're destined for great things, Tessa. Your mother knew it, and you should know it too."

Tessa sat bolt upright and stared at him in the dark. "How is being a Harvester—a Reaper—and the last of something violent and dangerous, a "great thing"?"

"Because you have the opportunity to do great things with it, Tessa. Save lives and set right wrongs."

Is it really that easy for you? That black and white?" Tessa asked, still frustrated.

Robin sat up. "Yes. It is. I know it makes you uncomfortable, but I believe in my Fiction. I believe in my destiny."

"I thought you were fighting yours too?" Tessa said, wary.

"In a way, I am," Robin said, and Tessa noticed they both went out of their way not to say Marian's name.

"Well, maybe you should make up your damn mind," Tessa snapped, and then scooted away from him and rolled over. "For someone so sure of their place, you are full of contradictions."

"Tessa."

"Leave it," she said, suddenly insanely tired. "We should sleep. Five a.m. will come fast." Tessa slid deeper into her sleeping bag, her thoughts clouded and confused. This had all been easier before she realized she was falling in love with him.

Doubt loomed larger in her mind than ever. Not just doubt about being the Scion but doubt about their future. When it was just a crush she didn't have to worry about where it was going, or if it would end, if he would choose her, if one of them would die.

Love sucked.

She felt cold without him close, a cold that ran much deeper than the physical, a hollow chill that frightened her.

In the morning, Fenris was nowhere to be seen.

'Typical," Robin muttered. Tessa ignored him, determined not to get in another fight. "Are we sure this isn't some elaborate trap?"

Tessa didn't answer.

"I mean, he has been trying to get you out here since you first met, right?"

Tessa continued to ignore him and picked up one of the small backpacks. She didn't want to give him the satisfaction of being right, but she felt nervous. Fenris *was* impossible to trust, even with the good he'd done. And he *had* been angling for this since the first time she'd found him in her house—uninvited.

They headed up the path Fenris had marked almost wordlessly. They pushed hard, only talking once when they had to consult Fenris's map. Tessa took the lead after that, against Robin's wishes.

They hiked for over an hour without stopping. Tessa could tell they were close, and she knew Robin could feel it too.

There was magic in the air.

THIRTY-TWO

In the distance, as if it was a mirage, watery and faded, and would disappear if one were to squint too hard, Tessa saw the edges of what must be the lake through the trees. She could just make out the water, but more easily seen was the gauzy mist laying above it.

Tessa could hear Robin behind her, keeping his distance, walking on eggshells ever since their last argument. As if he was trying to both be there and not be there. She didn't want them to fight, but it was becoming more obvious with every conversation they had that they had some serious disagreements on some pretty fundamental stuff. When it was just a crush, none of that stuff had mattered much, but now? Now she wasn't so sure. She had even caught herself once wishing he was just a simple high school boy like Nash so she could spend time making out with him and going to the movies, not arguing about the intentions of wolves, the meaning of names, and the philosophies and politics of another dimension. Then again, part of what she loved about him was his passion and belief.

Yeah, she was really confused.

Robin watched Tessa cut through the trees and tried to be honest with himself.

The truth was this: from the moment he'd first seen her, Tessa had him in her thrall.

And, with that, he'd known a certain doom.

She sparked in him something he hadn't felt in a very long time. More than a century. At least. The kindness buried beneath all that sarcasm. The brutality of her passion, even as she tried to dodge it.

Everything about her was palpable.

It reminded him of being new, of all he had felt when *he* was new. Watching her fight, he couldn't help but wonder if those things that she conveyed as naturally as breathing were part of her Scion "superhero package." If they were part of the power she had been given—the power to enthrall, the power to enchant, the power to draw others to her side like a deadly siren song—she *was* part Story after all and many Stories had powers like that.

He wondered how anyone could look at her, be in her presence, see she what she was capable of, how hard she fought, and *not* fall in love with her, with everything she was. Like a bright shining star, destined to be great. Like a warrior and a king rolled into one magnificent package. At other times, times when she made him laugh with her sass and her entirely unique way of looking at things; the way she fought against her destiny while at the same time embracing it, he knew it had nothing to do with Tessa being The Scion, and had everything to do with her just being Tessa.

It was a funny thing to fall in love with someone new after centuries.

And so fast.

He wished he could deny it, but it was pointless. It lay there in his heart and mind as honestly as anything true that he'd ever felt or known. How could he have let it happen?

He blamed Fenris.

If not for The Wolf, he would have been whiling away his time somewhere far away from here, pointlessly, but safely. Instead he had come here to help her, to train her, to put someone just on the path of righteousness and give them the tools they'd need to not die, or at least not die right away. He hadn't wanted to hear about The Last Scion getting killed because she'd never been trained, let alone because Stories, his own people, were all gunning for her. And so he'd come.

And only now could he see that moment in his life as the point when everything changed.

When his life went veering insanely off course to become something else.

Forever.

It threw so much he'd always believed into question. It was both terrifying and exhilarating. But if he'd known he'd fall in love with her, he would have stayed far away. Love was a complicated thing for a Story, especially one like him. He and Marian were tied together in ways that both lifted them up and chained them down. Equal parts pleasure and damnation. Tessa couldn't possibly understand it. Hell, half the time he and Marian didn't understand it.

And why had Fenris sent him?

It pricked at him constantly, but he wasn't smart enough to figure it out. Whether Tessa wanted to deny it or not, The Wolf was the most clever of enemies and he played a long game. He was patient. He laid out pieces at a great distance and it required a mind that could take the long view to see his endgame. It was a particularly hard thing for Robin to do. He wasn't dumb, but he was impatient, impulsive, reckless. There was nothing reckless about The Wolf, and Robin could not see the why behind sending him to Tessa's side. It kept him up nights.

Ahead of him, the faintest glimmer of a lake sparkled as Tessa broke through the edge of the trees. Despite the mist, the morning sunshine cut through the trees and glinted off of her skin—making her appear as if she was lit from the inside—she looked back at Robin, triumphant, smiling. She glowed. She was indescribably beautiful. His heart lurched.

He was in trouble.

Tessa pushed through the last rows of trees, and the lake didn't pull a Houdini as she half-expected it to. There was no shore to speak of, the trees were nearly in the water they sat so close, as if they just happened to crawl up unto shore and then take root there, too tired to move further inland.

Robin was still a fair distance behind her, and from the lake's edge, she looked back at him and called out, half triumphant, half surprised. "It's here!" She covered her mouth, feeling as if her exclamation was breaking some unspoken peace of the magical place. Robin nodded and smiled at her. It was devastating to even look at him, like being punched in the stomach with rainbows or something. God, what was happening to her?

But as she watched him hike toward her, she suddenly had this very strong feeling, almost like a premonition, that she was going to get hurt, very very hurt. She supposed that was your punishment when you tried to break up a love story that had been going on for hundreds of years. Her smile faded as she watched him but she shook her head, trying to clear it, she couldn't think about that now. Now was the time for work, now was a time for magical nonsense.

The mist was clearing quickly, burning off as the sun rose, lightening everything around them. The lake was not as large as she first thought but far more beautiful. The surface was still as glass and almost as reflective. At first it was dark, almost black, but as the sky grew lighter, it appeared green all around the edges where it reflected the trees, and a pristine blue in the center, reflecting the cloudless dawning sky above. It felt like a place nobody had ever been before. Untouched by Mortal or Story. Tessa wondered for a moment if they were really in the right place. She saw no evidence of anyone else ever having been here at all.

Robin continued toward her. When he was close enough that she could speak to him without further disturbing the scene, she asked, "What now?"

He moved subtly and Tessa glanced over at him. He had out the short blade that he generally kept in a knife sheath on his belt. Tessa eyed the blade with a cocked eyebrow. "Something you want to discuss?"

He smiled at her and then tried to hide it. "Be serious," he said. "Your blood, in the water." He handed her the blade, grip first. She took it from him, sighing.

"Why is it always blood? We're only doing this for a few weeks now and already I'm sick of blood." He tried not to look at her cutting into her arm. She did it casually and with barely a wince, though it surely hurt. Superhero powers didn't mean no pain, just quick healing.

"Get used to it," he said, trying hard to sound unaffected by the sight. Tessa held her arm out over the glassy lake and watched as dark drops of her blood collided with the water. Instead of just disappearing as she expected, the drops of blood overwhelmed the massive body of water. They spread, infecting the entire lake, taking it over and turning it an unnatural crimson from shore to shore and thus changing the entire feeling of things. The color shifted the scene from idyllic to something closer to what a lake in hell might look like.

Tessa sucked in a breath. "Balls. That can't be good."

Robin put a hand on her shoulder as she folded her arm back against herself to stem the bleeding. He took the knife and sheathed it but kept a hand on his bow, anxious. They were both thinking the same thing. *Fenris had screwed them.* Tessa cursed as something at the center of the lake began to bubble, sending gentle ripples through the entire lake. When the ripples increased and reached the shore before them, Robin's hand pressed harder on Tessa's shoulder.

"Tessa," he began, but before he could finish she reached out her hand and shouted.

"La Colombe Noire!" The Black Dove materialized from the ether, or wherever it was that it lived whenever it wasn't in Tessa's hand, and snapped powerfully into her grip. The now-familiar hilt had begun to feel like home to her, and Tessa set her feet and prepared herself for whatever non-delightful surprise might rise from the boiling, red lake. But then there was a flash of bright white light, hot and irregular like lightning. It spread out across the lake, bathing everything in a white so pure and powerful it was difficult to look directly at it. Tessa visored her eyes with her hand to protect against it, and Robin turned his head and squinted. The light then faded to a pale, soft white, easier on the eyes and more serene than the electric of the lightning. A woman stood before them, mere feet in front of them, in fact. She was currently submerged to the waist but continued rising up from the water, not walking, but *rising.*

"Scion," she said, her voice somehow both warm and cool, her eyes still closed. Tessa lowered her axe without realizing it, and though Robin still had his hand on his bow at his shoulder, she could feel the tension leaving him. The woman in white opened her eyes, which were pure white, with no pupils or irises and looked at Tessa. "Ah, The Last." she said, unsurprised, her voice trailing off. It was nice for once, Tessa thought, to have someone unsurprised that she was a chick. That particular brand of shock was wearing very thin.

"Yeah. The Last," Tessa said, unsure if she should be talking at all. The woman smiled.

"I am The Lady," she said.

Tessa arched her brow. "'Kay."

"And what is it you seek?" The Lady asked.

"I'm—" Tessa began before faltering. She wasn't sure what she should be asking, how much she should say or not. She tried again. "I'm Tessa Battle, and my Advocate, Bishop—he died, in a fight. It was my fault. Bluebeard killed him, but it was my fault."

"Bishop was destined to die, child, there is nothing you could have done to prevent it," The Lady said matter-of-factly, but not unkindly. Tessa steeled her shoulders and felt Robin stiffen beside her.

"No. I don't believe that," Tessa said. "I make my own destiny. I don't want to hear any more of that prophecy crap." Tessa winced as the words came out of her mouth. She'd just said "crap" to some kind of magical witch deity that rose out of a bloody lake in a flash of lightning, what the hell was she thinking? She'd also basically just told some all-powerful witch that probably bought her summer home off the proceeds of prophecies that she didn't believe in them. But The Lady only smiled.

"Fair enough, Scion. Living one's life by prophecy is not easy. Certainly The Scion, above so many, has reason to doubt," she said. "I can more than understand your resistance."

Tessa softened. "So, someone told me, er, us, that there are other Advocates that could guide me, that in Bishop's place a new Advocate should have stepped forward, or whatever. But nobody has showed up and, I…I need help. I was told you might know who the Advocate is, where the Advocate is, or maybe why they haven't showed." Tessa stopped her rambling and waited uncomfortably for The Lady to respond.

The Lady closed her eyes, and her head rolled back as if she was feeling the whole world. Her eyelids fluttered so that Tessa saw inside them, beneath her papery lids as the same glowing white-hot light that they had seen upon her first arrival burned beneath them. Tessa silently hoped that she wasn't about to open her eyes and laser the two of them into ash. Her grip on The Black Dove tightened. The Lady looked back at them.

"Interesting," she said, pausing. "Your Advocate is under a spell. A powerful one. They have been cloaked not only from others but from themselves. It has been weaving for a long time now," she paused, and closed her eyes again, her mouth flickered into a frown and then became neutral again. "And it is not just Story magic, it is Mortal magic as well. Stories and Mortals working together to keep you both from one another."

"Can it be undone?" Robin asked, speaking up at Tessa's side. The Lady fixed her gaze on him, as if seeing him for the first time.

"Robin of the Hood," she said, smiling as she had when she first said 'Scion.' "Yes. The spell is simple to undo. The spell itself is doing all the work, hiding the truth. It takes much power to hide the truth, to keep things from being in their natural state. It requires an incredible amount of weaving and will to maintain a spell that intricate for that many years, which is one of the many reasons this is so interesting. Someone must want the two of you apart a great deal."

"Can you see who?" Tessa asked.

"No. This I cannot see," The Lady said.

"Can you tell me who The Advocate is?" Tessa pressed.

"No, Scion, the magic cloaks them from me as well."

"Not even a hint?" Tessa prodded.

"I am sorry, Scion, it is not within my power. What I can do is to unweave the spell from your eyes, so that should you find The Advocate, you will be able to see the truth."

Tessa chewed her lip, thinking that it was better than nothing. "But The Advocate still won't know who it—he or she—is?"

"I can give you the necessary tools to remove the deception from The Advocate's eyes as well, should you find them. It will not be difficult. It is as if simply removing a veil."

"Okay, well, how do I remove the spell, I mean, if I want to?"

"If?" Robin asked quietly at her side, and she pressed her hand against him to stop his question.

"I will give you some words, that is all it will take. It will unravel easily, like thread pulled from a sweater," The Lady said.

Tessa nodded, "Okay."

The Lady smiled and then paused, "Scion, I must warn you, I see no other Advocates beyond this one. The line is dead, not unlike the line of Scions appears to be. It has come to its natural end. Should you choose to lift the veil on this Advocate, you must protect them with all you have, because like you, they are the last. Close your eyes, Scion."

Tessa shuddered almost imperceptibly, but she knew Robin noticed it. This was the worst thing The Lady could have said to her. The Lady reached out to Tessa and placed three fingers on Tessa's forehead, whispering some words. There was a cool flash of light and then Tessa opened her eyes and everything looked…exactly the same.

"Your eyes are clear now, and you possess all the tools you need," The Lady said, smiling beatifically. "Be well, Scion."

Tessa offered a small smile back in return. "Thank you."

Tessa turned away, returning to the path. Robin did not immediately follow her and she looked back to see him speaking with The White Lady. Tessa paused and waited for him. She sort of wanted to eavesdrop, but if anything was being said, she couldn't hear it. After a minute, he moved to join Tessa on the path, but he looked stricken.

"Are you alright?"

He nodded, curt, and she could tell by his face he was lying. "I'm fine."

She stared at him as he passed her on the path and then looked back toward the lake. Tessa did a double take. It had disappeared, leaving behind only an endless forest. Tessa blinked and shook her head.

She would never get used to magic.

Back at the campsite, Fenris sat in front of the small fire. Tessa emerged first from the trees, and he tried not to smile at her but found it impossible. Such a strange creature she was. Young everywhere, except in her eyes which seemed as old as time. Her hair an obscenely bright red, shaved into nearly a mohawk, all long in the front, shaved in the back and on the sides. It was a look that tried so hard not to be feminine, to be tough and edgy, yet it somehow made other parts of her seem even softer. He didn't know if the Shiki scar was going to be permanent, although he suspected it might. Some part of him hoped it would, as it made her strange features even more interesting.

She was lethally beautiful.

All long limbs and power, vintage t-shirts and big black boots, sass and brutality, warmth and sarcasm, compassion and unyielding force.

She would lead armies.

Men would follow her to death and glory. She would not even have to ask. They would fall on swords for her.

She possessed this rarest of powers and somehow it wasn't because she was The Scion. He had met Scions before and she was unlike any of them. He didn't quite understand it but she was something else. Something he had been waiting for a very long time.

She had to go.

But when was key.

When was all that mattered.

"Back so soon, Hardcore?" he asked.

"Why didn't you come?" she asked him, not stopping for pleasantries. And her insight surprised him even now. He answered her plainly.

"Because I have no interest in The Lady knowing my mind," and as he said it, Robin emerged from the trees, his face a look that told Fenris all he needed to. It was all he could do not to pat himself on the back. He smiled, the look of the cat that has finally caught the canary, and Robin looked back at him, his hatred barely restrained.

"Can the two of you finish packing up the gear?" Tessa asked. "I have to do something."

"Of course," they both said in unison, never taking their eyes off one another. Once Tessa had disappeared into the trees, Robin drew his dagger and, in a flash, held it to Fenris's throat.

"Tell me how you really feel, hero," Fenris drawled.

"When we get out of these woods, you are going to leave Lore and never come back so long as Tessa is there, or I swear to the gods I will gut you from head to furry fucking tail, Wolf."

"Bit extreme, no?" Fenris said, edging his neck back ever so slightly from the blade as the point drew a spot of dark blood on his flesh.

"Not from where I'm standing," Robin said. "I don't know what your game is, but it can't be good for her and I will end you before you touch her."

"Try to keep it in your pants, Robin," Fenris growled, knocking Robin's hand roughly away from him so that the dagger flew off into the dirt.

"Like you? You're not fooling anyone, Wolf. It's obvious what your intentions are."

"You forget yourself, anarchist. I'm the one that brought you to her in the first place. Don't bloody cross me in the process or it'll end badly for you. I've no fear of you or your two-bit arrow," Fenris snapped, and then cut the comment with a smooth smile. "What are you so threatened by anyway? You're the guy in the tent. What scares you so much about me just being here?"

Robin said nothing, and Fenris knew he'd hit his mark. "I'll see you destroyed the same as any wolf. Even in your own story, the Huntsman wins, old man."

"Depends on the version," Fenris said, his eyes flashing.

"Yes, you're right. Sometimes the girl just plain outwits you."

"It's true. And sometimes I devour everyone. I wonder if Marian would even bother to cry if I devoured you."

"Leave her out of this."

Fenris laughed boldly. "Make up your mind, hero. Which one are you in love with?" Fenris pushed Robin away with exceptional force, and as Robin stumbled backward, he drew his bow as effortlessly as if taking a breath. Robin rolled to the side while nocking an arrow and was on one knee, with his arrow pointed between Fenris' eyes, faster than the Mortal eye could process it. Fenris stood, stoic and unmoving, his eyes bright and narrow, a low growl emanating from his chest. He smiled at Robin. "Touched a nerve?"

Robin released his arrow.

Brandon Ellis had stayed up half the night looking for information about Circe in the hopes that it would help him understand what was happening with his best friend and the incredibly dangerous Shiki now bound to her.

He'd found out almost nothing about The Shiki, but he had stumbled upon what he was almost certain was a business Circe owned in town. A Greek restaurant, of all things, named Nightshade (terrible name for a restaurant, considering some kinds were poison). Nightshade was a plant from the genus Circaea. Named that *because* of the Circe myth.

And that could not be a coincidence.

Well, okay, it could, but the owner a—*Cathe Greta Dushe*—which was an anagram for *Hecate's Daughter*, and Hecate was sometimes said to be the mother of Circe, could NOT be a coincidence.

And all these facts together were impossible to ignore.

Now he just had to get someone to listen to him long enough to agree.

THIRTY-THREE

Less than an inch from Fenris' face, The Black Dove knocked Robin's arrow off course. The arrow and The Black Dove embedded in a tree beside Fenris, the axe disappearing a moment later. Tessa glared at Robin, her face furious.

She walked to the tree and yanked Robin's arrow from it, flinging it back at him with a rage she didn't even try to conceal. They both looked at her but didn't speak. "Are you two idiots—who apparently forgot I have goddamn super-hearing—done pissing all over yourselves yet? I'd like to leave." She grabbed one of the large backpacks, walked out of the clearing to the original path, and began hiking back to the car. Fenris and Robin took up the rest of the gear in silence and followed her down.

They stopped once to eat and again when they reached the jeep, and at no time did anyone speak. One of them tried to speak as they climbed into the car. Tessa didn't even know which one.

"Shut up!" she shouted, slamming the door.

No sooner did they begin driving, then the sky darkened dramatically, feeling almost like night, and it began to rain.

It was going to be a long way down the mountain.

It took all of first period to convince Micah of Brand's evidence. But it took even longer—three periods of constant text messaging in fact—to get her to agree to his plan to go to the restaurant after school. And even then she wouldn't agree to "go rogue" with him unless they could convince both Snow and Grey to go with them. Something about safety in numbers and not getting kidnapped again.

Brand could tell she really didn't want any of it to work since she hated Snow and would never argue for something that meant spending *more* time with her.

But it had worked anyway, and Brand knew this because as they walked toward him after school, Grey had the look of someone that really did not want to have been convinced of something but knew it was too late to go back to being unconvinced. Brand slapped him good-naturedly on the back as they ran across the school parking lot through the dark afternoon rain.

Snow was easier to convince than Brand thought, maybe because they made it clear that they were going with or without her and Tessa's "pound of flesh" speech was still ringing in her ears.

Unfortunately, the restaurant did not open for dinner until five-thirty p.m. and so the four of them waited it out in Snow's icy condo, watching the clock and sometimes glaring at one another. Go team spirit!

As Tessa, Robin, and Fenris neared Lore, still in the woods but perhaps only ten minutes from Tessa's house, and after more than three hours of nothing but pounding rain on the roof for company, Fenris shouted from the backseat.

"STOP!"

Robin swerved and nearly crashed his jeep into a tree, then skidded in the rain as he overcorrected. They came to a halt in the middle of the small, fortunately deserted, wet road.

"What in seven hells, Fenris?!?" Robin shouted.

Fenris yanked on the door handle but the door didn't open. He looked at Robin, incensed, "Do you have the goddamn child locks on?!"

Robin looked at him, still confused about what was happening.

"I don—"

"Unlock the door, Robin, or I will tear it from its TOVAIEN HINGES!" Fenris roared the words, becoming less intelligible and more animal with each syllable. Tessa had never heard him use the Story language before, something was really wrong.

Fenris never lost his cool, something was really really wrong.

Tessa turned in her seat as Robin, clearly as thrown as she was, pushed on the door locks while Fenris pulled on the handle, thus keeping the door firmly locked. It would have been hilarious if Tessa hadn't been worried that Fenris was going to devour them in single bites if he didn't get out of the car immediately. Fenris slammed himself against the door in mindless frustration while an inhuman and uncontrolled growl shot out of him. He narrowed his eyes at Robin, and though they were usually grey, they now glinted yellow in the catches of light. Tessa feared he was going to shift right in the back seat.

"Stop pulling on the damn handle!" Robin shouted, trying the locks again. Finally the door popped open, and Fenris sprang from the car, disappearing into the woods almost instantly.

Tessa stared wide-eyed at Robin, who looked more shocked than pissed for the first time ever when it came to Fenris. "Do we wait for him?" Tessa asked.

Robin shook his head, unsure and looked in the rearview mirror for traces of Fenris.

After ten minutes of anxious waiting, they were both fed up.

"Tessa, we're close to Lore, he knows these woods better than anyone, there's no harm in leaving him."

"What if it's harm to us, not him?" Tessa ask.

"Meaning what?"

"Meaning he tore out of here like I've never seen him—he never loses control—what if there's some kind of danger?"

"But even if that's the case, we've no idea where the danger is—we could just be sitting here waiting for it."

Tessa sighed. "You're right. Let's go."

But before they had a chance to go the car was literally covered, as if from out of nowhere, with zombies.

Except, these weren't the same as what they had seen before.

These were different.

Some of them were wearing armor and helmets like Vikings would wear, like Norse soldiers except the undead variety. They gave the impression of being ghosts, although the force with which they slammed against the car proved them anything but. In fact, only moments after surging against the car, one smashed its hand clean through Robin's window. Robin reacted with pure instinct, driving his knife through its face.

They moved about as fast as the others they'd encountered, but more importantly, they moved almost as if in coordination with one another. The others seemed mindless in comparison to these.

Even worse, the one that Robin had just killed stood back up, very much alive, or what counted for alive when it came to zombies.

"Yae Simane," Robin said. "They're Stories. I can't kill them."

All the color drained from both their faces.

"Oh, God."

Fenris slowed his pace. The rain was confusing his senses. All of them.

He tasted sulfur on his tongue and came to a stop, looking for the source. A residue of static was in the air, pricking at his skin. But before he saw anything, he smelled it again. A smell that both haunted him and that he ached for. Things that should not have been the same but were.

Fresh cut grass. Baking bread. Wood nymphs. Lavender.

Red Riding Hood.

Robin and Tessa scrambled over the front seats and into the back. Tessa punched at every fleshy bit that came at them while Robin reached over the seat and into the back to draw out his bow and a sheath of arrows stored where the spare tire should have been.

"What happens if you get a flat?" Tessa asked.

"I'm screwed," he said, and then smiled, trying to keep things light. "So, if this even works, we're going to have to run," he paused. "For a long time. Like, until we can find shelter or lose them, long time."

"Yeah, I get it. I may not have the best endurance, but I'm the freaking Scion, Robin. I'll get it done."

"That's what I wanted to hear," he said, smiling and kissing her on the mouth briefly as another ghost-zombie hand went through the back window. Robin popped open the sunroof and they both climbed through, yanking their clothes free of grasping hands. Tessa called her axe and chopped away at arms and gaping jaws while Robin loaded a bow. He shot a tree far away, high and deep into the woods. He pulled the attached cable tight and grabbed Tessa around the waist.

"This is very Batman of you," Tessa said, as she kicked a zombie in the face and linked one arm around Robin's neck.

"I was thinking more Skywalker, but yours is better," he said. They leapt and swung over and away from the zombie-covered car, landing roughly in the woods.

"Go," he said, as they landed hard and immediately scrambled to their feet.

Tessa made the mistake of looking back.

They were already chasing them.

"Ryder," Fenris said, unable to stop the smile that spread unbidden across his face. The words had long been absent from his tongue, and he had missed them.

"Wolf," the beautiful redhead said from a stand of thick trees. She nodded her head at him to follow her, and he did, until they were standing under a canopy that shielded them from most of the rain. Once there, Ryder pushed back the scarlet-colored hood from her head, shaking her long red curls free. She smiled a layered smile, one perhaps understood by Fenris alone.

Fenris stepped toward her but she side-stepped him easily and wagged her finger at him playfully. The sight of her brought back a powerful want he had long been trying to forget, had sometimes thought he might have.

"She's young," Ryder said, clucking her tongue disdainfully.

Fenris didn't blink. "All Mortals are young, as are all Scions," he said, circling her, an old dance that they were well-versed in.

"Your interest in her insults me," Ryder said, moving away from him, dipping into a deep shadow.

"It's a complicated matter, Ryder."

"It seems decidedly simple from here."

"Then you're not looking hard enough," he said.

Ryder caught his eyes for the first time since arriving. "I looked pretty hard."

"The long game has never been your strong suit," he said, and it had a bit of meanness he hadn't intended. He changed gears. "Enough, Ryder. What brings you to Lore?"

"You, Devourer," she said innocently, before breaking the stare. "It's always you."

He watched her, his eyes flicking around her face, trying to find truth. He was trying to remain composed, but he could feel his edges fraying. Ryder always caused his edges to fray, and he wished it didn't make his skin feel alive.

She changed gears this time. "So why *did* you send Robin to her? You are right, I cannot see the play."

"Because there isn't one."

"There's always a play with you. Centuries of knowing you, there's always a play, no matter how long the view."

"There isn't," Fenris said, moving closer to her.

Ryder allowed him to close in, and then tightened the distance between them herself, laying her body against his carefully, touching him lightly. "You never change," she purred. He didn't resist her.

"You're rather lush yourself, Ryder," he breathed, trying to slow his heartbeat.

Ryder sighed into his neck, like an old lover, but when she spoke her words were anything but sweet. "You stink of her. Of Mortal."

Fenris didn't push her away but didn't breathe her in as he wanted to either. "Hard not to. When you live here for centuries, it's bound to rub off eventually."

"So come back," she said, her voice barely a whisper in his ear. Fenris tried to hide his surprise and failed, edging back to look her in the face.

"Really?"

"Maybe," she said, her eyes light, dancing around his face.

"All you have to do is say the word, Red. You're the one that decided Story wasn't big enough for us both. I exiled myself to this place for you. I'll undo it for you just the same."

Ryder eyed him skeptically. "I think you're lying." She spun away from him, suddenly quite sad and no longer playful. "I pushed you away and now I've driven you into the arms of the enemy."

"Is that it? You want me to come back, not for love, not because you've finally missed me, but because you believe I'm on a side you don't approve of?" He turned away from her. "Talk about taking the long view," he said, a snap of bitterness to his voice. He softened it and reached for her but she evaded him. "I have been in love with you since you took breath, and so long as you do, I'll love you still. I'm a slave to my Fiction and I've never wanted to be free of it, not the part that touches you leastways." He reached for her again, and once again she slid away.

'You're deluding yourself, Wolf. Your feelings about these things are clear."

Fenris tried to change tactics. "Weren't you the one that said I was incapable of love?"

"No, I never said you were incapable of love, I just said for you it's the same as devouring. Someone always get devoured, and somehow it's never you."

"I'm happy to be devoured by you, Ryder," he said, finally pulling her to him. She took his hand and placed something inside it, closing his fingers around it.

"I guess we'll see."

Fenris looked at what she had put in his hand.

It was a life preserver, and it spoke volumes. About how she felt for him, about how dangerous things had become, about the choices ahead of him.

An ancient ache shuddered through him, and he thought that part of him might rip out and go back to Story all by itself without his permission. He put away the life preserver because looking at it was making him feel torn in two. Instead, he looked at her, alarmed. "What aren't you telling me?"

"The Monster has had Circe raise The Draugr," she said flatly.

Fenris looked at her, wide-eyed. "He wouldn't."

"He has," she said. "He has not only raised them, but he has sent them and as we speak, they hunt her down."

THIRTY-FOUR

Tessa thought she was going to die. She had never before run so hard, so fast, or so long. She might have been able to handle the first two, but the third was killing her. There were only three things keeping her going: the horrific sound of a horde of zombies crashing behind her, somehow moaning *"Scioooooonnnnn"* as they ran; the humiliation of being proven wrong—that she didn't have the endurance to keep up with Robin; and the sight of Robin's ass as he ran, which was more than enough reason to keep living and thus, running.

When the trees began to thin a bit and Tessa saw the edge of her house's gabled roof poking through, she had never been more relieved in her life. Tessa and Robin jumped her back fence and ran across the yard.

"The damn window!" Tessa shouted as she heard the first of the zombies collide with the fence behind them. The fence wouldn't hold against the stampede for long.

Robin and Tessa broke through the plastic sheeting over the broken dining room window. Robin tossed his bow and arrows to the ground. "The table," he said, pointing to the dining room table. They lifted it and pushed it up over the window. It was big enough to cover the hole, but not heavy enough to keep a wave of zombies from pushing through. Robin pointed to a massive hutch. Tessa winced. It was full of expensive china. But he was right, it was the best, closest, heaviest thing. She helped him shove it across the floor and up against the table. Tessa grimaced, thinking it wouldn't be enough.

And as the first zombie hit the flat side of the table in the yard she knew she was right as the china shuddered inside the hutch, clinking softly. Tessa and Robin looked around and finally dragged the living room couch into the dining room. It was just long enough that they could wedge it between the far wall and the hutch, a fulcrum of some sort, which seemed like it might actually work. Tessa peeked out the window above the back kitchen door and watched the zombies stream across the lawn, piling through a section of the fence already flattened. Most of them collected against the 'table as window,' not entirely mindless, but seemingly out of ideas. Or at least that's what she hoped.

Tessa had no idea how long it would hold.

In the Nightshade parking lot, Brand, Micah, Snow, Grey, and Jeff, again looking like a dragon, watched the patrons coming in and out for five solid minutes from Grey's car before anyone said anything.

"So what do we do?" Grey asked.

"We go in and, uh, look around," Micah said and Jeff tittered nervously next to her.

"Okay, what are we looking for?" Grey asked.

Everyone kind of shrugged.

"Clues," Brand said, uncertainly, and then more definitively, "Let's go. Now," he said, as if urging them all to action. By some miracle, they all listened to him and opened their car doors. He couldn't have been more shocked if he tried. Was he in charge?

The thought terrified him.

"If we end up pigs, I am going to kill *everyone*," Snow hissed as they neared the entrance.

Once inside Brand stepped forward and opened his arms wide to embrace the host, a mountain of a man, "Αχ! Φίλος μου! Έχει τόσο καιρό!"

Micah gave Grey the side-eye, which he returned. Brand continued chattering in Greek, and the rest of them looked around the restaurant trying to be casual, trying to look like they belonged. An impossible task.

"Well, I'll be damned," Snow breathed icily and slid away from the group.

"Snow!" Micah hissed, clutching Grey's arm, watching her go, Jeff shifting into a slightly larger animal inside her sweatshirt pocket. Snow moved gracefully across the long room and rolled up to a table filled to overflowing with delicacies.

Snow reached out to a tall blonde woman clad in green, standing next to the table, and tapped her on the shoulder. The woman turned around, and there was a momentary flash of recognition across her face as Snow said, "Circe."

Tessa slumped against the floor and covered her ears, her back against the couch-as-fulcrum. She was suddenly very sure she was going to die. Here, in her house, at the hands of relentless Story zombies. Her adrenaline was pumping like mad, and her mind raced.

She reached suddenly for Robin and kissed him. A serious kiss that made its intentions clear.

Last kisses.

Kisses that come at the climax, before people died horribly.

Tessa put thousands of unspoken words into it. It was amazing how the brink of death could make you forget everything else. Her brain was so swelled with lust and desire she couldn't even remember why she'd been angry with him this morning.

Everything was meaningless. Everything except *this*.

Robin answered in kind, pulling her tightly to him, his hand on her neck, his thumb roughly against her jaw and then moving into her hair, holding her mouth firmly to his. He kissed her deeply, powerfully, differently than before. There was more persistence than there had been before, more urgency, as if he understood every silent declaration in her kiss. It probably should have scared her, but she liked it, wanted it, needed it.

Tessa grabbed the edge of his jacket and pulled it off him. His hand slid up under her tank top, warm and electric, and Tessa sighed into him. She ran her hand up into his hair and drew him down lower with her, so he was on top of her, pressing on her in startling ways that made her mind race. She reached underneath his shirt and edged it up, her hands drifting across his hot skin. Robin paused in kissing her just long enough to strip his t-shirt off and then returned to her mouth, insistent. He kissed her neck, and Tessa groaned. She pulled off her tank top with his help and then he returned to her mouth, the intensity of it leaving them both breathless. She wanted him, and it was stirring something primal in her that she feared she wouldn't be able to turn off. But if she was going to die, what would it matter if she couldn't turn it off? She reached for the belt on his pants and unbuckled it, and then, as she unbuttoned his pants, passing some invisible line in the sand and not caring, something slammed against the front door with far more force than one of the zombies.

Robin shot up off of her, and Tessa instinctively reached for her tank. They edged around the corner of the dining room, staying low, watching the door as something repeatedly smashed into it. Tessa slid her shirt on and winced as she heard the frame splintering. Robin buckled his belt and reached for his T-shirt. He looked at Tessa.

"What do you think?"

Tessa was about to shrug helplessly when the door gave inward, and Fenris crashed through it, hurtling into the foyer.

"Fenris," Tessa said, equal parts relieved and irritated.

"Scion. You're alive," Fenris breathed, still more out of control than Tessa had ever seen him. She walked toward him while Robin put on his shirt.

"Look what you did to my damn door, Fenris."

"I'll replace it," he said, breathlessly without missing a beat. Tessa tried to shut the splinted door and as she did so, she saw Robin's jeep, windows all broken, generally torn up, and covered in mud, parked haphazardly in front of the house, one wheel on the sidewalk. She looked at Fenris, surprised. Had he really been concerned? Or maybe just afraid he'd miss out on the show. He *had* taken them out into the woods and abandoned them just prior to being attacked. But there would be time for that later. Right now one of the zombies had figured out how to get out of the back yard and was heading for a front door that wouldn't shut.

"Help me," she said, trying to push the door shut. Fenris saw the zombie and put his shoulder against the door with her. They got it closed, but there was nothing to lock it and the door shuddered against them as the first zombie slammed into the splintered wood.

"Robin!" Tessa shouted, as one started to climb through the door falling apart under their hands. Another put its arm through the glass window next to the door.

They would be inside in moments.

THIRTY-FIVE

Circe smiled at Snow and opened her mouth to say something, but before she could, Snow's fist came flying at the woman's face and knocked her out in one punch.

Circe fell backward into the table of food, sending much of it clattering to the ground. Patrons looked on, shocked, and several waiters and busboys headed over. Snow turned, and glowing brightly with her bluish-white light, cast a hand widely over the restaurant. It was as if everyone paused mid-thought. She then looked at Brand, Micah, and Grey, dumfounded near the door, while she massaged her punching hand. "I'm not going to carry her too, make yourselves useful, minions."

Brand, Micah, and Grey rushed over dutifully, and Grey and Brand tried to untangle Circe from the table and food. Micah gaped at the frozen restaurant patrons.

"Will they...will they be okay?"

"Yes, it won't last long. It's a soft freeze, there's too many to do anything more elaborate or longer lasting. We should get out of here, now."

Micah nodded and reached absentmindedly for an olive from Circe's table but Jeff, back to his cat form, leapt forward and knocked it from her hand. Micah looked at him, confused. Brand looked at her as he draped one of Circe's limp arms over his shoulder.

"Don't ever eat anything from Circe's table, Mike," he said. Snow nodded in agreement. And then, seeing a busboy near her moving a little as if the frost was already fading, nudged the both of them.

"We need to go."

The group hustled to the car, inelegantly dragging the unconscious Circe with them.

Two more had started to come through the kitchen window, and three more pounded on the front door, a relentless thudding sound that made Tessa's head hurt.

Then all of a sudden it stopped.

They didn't disappear, but it was as if they turned into mindless husks and a moment later they slumped to the ground together, a hive mind with the plug pulled. Tessa nodded to Robin and Fenris and they all moved away from the door (which was now barely a door and more just some slats of wood that looked as if they might have once been bound together). As they did so, one of the zombies fell face first into the house.

Tessa reached toward the figure, aware it was a classic mistake, but unable to resist. Just as she was about to touch it, her phone rang shrilly in her pocket and she fell backward onto her butt. Robin and even Fenris leapt backward and then held their chests as if holding their racing hearts inside their ribcages. Tessa breathed a relieved sigh, dug into the pocket of her jeans, and picked up on the third ring.

"Brand? Is everything okay?"

"Yes! We got Circe!"

"What?!"

"Yes, just like two minutes ago. I mean, I know you're going to be mad, but I like, figured out where Circe was, and we went on, like, a recon mission, but then she was there, and so Snow just, like, walked up to her in the restaurant and knocked her out. It was the single greatest thing I have ever seen!"

"Snow knocked Circe out? She's still unconscious?"

"Yes, we have her with us, we're driving to the condo."

"No. Bring her here," Tessa said, and looking at the ghost-zombie on her floor, added, "And make sure she doesn't wake up."

Tessa and Robin were standing in the backyard, staring at the pile of re-animated, now unconscious dead in a pile on her grass. They'd dragged the handful that had made it to the front yard into the backyard again. Altogether there must have been nearly four dozen.

"The Draugr," Fenris said from behind them, and they spun around, startled.

"Jesus, Fenris," Tessa breathed. "Can you be less goddamn stealthy, please?"

"The Draugr," Robin said breathlessly and looked at the pile again. "He wouldn't."

"He has," Fenris said solemnly. Tessa looked between the two of them. It was nice that they were finally on the same page and not fighting, but she would have appreciated being in the loop.

"Helllloooo? Care to fill me in? What's a Draugr?"

"*The* Draugr," Fenris corrected. "They're Norse Mythology—loosely translated it means 'again walker.' They're like zombies, but also a bit like ghosts, they have much more power than your average zombie."

"Power?"

"In the past, in their Stories? They can exhibit superhuman strength, change their size and weight, they're, well, they can be very powerful," Fenris said.

"But these, they lost consciousness when Circe did—is it possible she's controlling them?" Tessa asked.

Fenris bent down to examine one of them. "I don't know," he said, unsure. "Perhaps—"

"Perhaps what?" Tessa urged.

"Perhaps if they have been called against their will, if Circe and The Monster have raised them and are controlling them, it would explain their behavior."

The sound of a car in front of the house and Brand and Micah screeching at the sight of the house actually made Tessa smile. In all this madness it was easy to forget how much she was cared for, and how much she cared back.

Tessa went to the car, where the group stood gaping at the house.

"Yae Simane," Grey said, stepping out of the car, his face shocked and concerned. Tessa moved to the car and took Circe from Brand who was struggling with her limp frame. Tessa threw the woman over her shoulder and took her into the house.

Tessa set Circe in a living room chair. The woman looked like some kind of ethereal blonde sex goddess. A mane of impossibly thick, flowing blonde hair, flawless skin, curves to kill, and legs so long and shapely that they practically caused Tessa to blush. She was wearing a low-cut, fitted, glittering green dress, appropriate for nothing short of the red carpet and an amount of expensive jewelry that on anyone else would have looked wildly excessive.

Tessa rolled her eyes. She was getting tired of beautiful. It was exhausting to be surrounded by so much of it. She felt like an unfortunate looking extra on a movie set. Just as Tessa turned to speak to Brand and Micah, the woman stirred in the chair.

"She's waking u—" but before Brand could finish the sentence, Tessa spun around and punched her in the face, knocking her out again. Brand and Micah giggled.

"Nice," Micah said, nodding. Tessa smiled at them.

"Watch her for a minute, would you?" They nodded. Tessa walked to the backyard. On the way she ran into Snow, standing in front of the open freezer and drinking ice water. "Thanks for knocking her out," Tessa said to Snow. Snow nodded.

"We're even now, Scion," she said back, her voice calm. Tessa shook her head, disappointed. Of course that's what it was about. Couldn't have just been Snow doing the right thing. Tessa went into the backyard to find Grey standing with Robin and Fenris, staring at the pile of bodies.

"So what do I do?" she asked them. They turned and looked at her as one and then looked back at the pile.

"I think you have to kill them," Fenris said. Grey shuddered a bit but didn't comment.

"Robin?" Tessa asked.

"I agree," he said. "We can't risk them re-animating when Circe wakes up," he said. "Especially since you're the only one that can kill them. It would be nearly 50 against one, impossible odds."

Tessa nodded. "Will killing these—will it erase them—their Story? Their Myth?" She stood on the other side of the pile and stared at the three of them. They all avoided her gaze. "C'mon guys, zombies or not, we're talking about your people here—what are we talking about?"

Grey shrugged, conflicted. "I don't know, Tessa, I'm new to all of this. I have no idea."

"I doubt it will erase the myth of The Draugr by killing these," Robin said.

"I agree," Fenris said. "I think, to kill The Draugr as a Story you would have to kill them all. It's not like with Bluebeard, where he is the central character of his Story. The Story cannot exist without him, but these are just part of a concept, none are integral to the story itself—in theory, at least."

"I'm not hearing a lot of confidence," Tessa said, turning to look at the bodies again.

"Because I'm not," Fenris said.

"My fucking kingdom for a rule book!" Tessa shouted at the sky.

"Tessa—" Grey began, and stopped, seeming to have second thoughts.

"What Grey?" Tessa asked. "Now's not the time to be shy, there are no stupid questions today."

"I just wondered if you wanted the answer to be yes, or no," he asked.

Tessa balked. "No. I want the answer to be no."

"But—" he began again.

"But what?"

"But if you don't eliminate their Story, then even if you kill these, Circe can likely just call more," Fenris supplied. "The Draugr, they are, I don't want to say infinite, but that wouldn't be an unreasonable estimate." Grey nodded his head and shoved his hands in his pockets. Tessa got even quieter.

"Well, if they're infinite then at least it makes my job tonight easier," she said, and threw out her hand. "La Colombe Noire!" The Black Dove materialized into her hand, and she looked over her shoulder at them watching her. "Go inside and watch Circe. I'll be there in a bit."

Tessa moved toward the line of bodies and began the messy business of disposing of them one at a time. At the door, Fenris and Robin looked back just once before going inside.

"She'll be fine," Fenris said, and it almost seemed comforting to Robin. He looked at Fenris and tried to read his face. But he couldn't.

"I know," he said, going inside.

Tessa hadn't just sent them inside because they couldn't help her, she'd also sent them inside because she didn't want them watching her do it. She wasn't sure if she was going to straight up have a mental breakdown chopping the heads off of fifty people, zombies or not, but it seemed like one of the worst things she could imagine. She felt like some kind of medieval executioner, and she puked three times before she was done. When Tessa came back inside twenty minutes later, she was messy and exhausted, spent both emotionally and physically.

She returned to a heated discussion about drawing straws to see who got to throw a glass of ice water on Circe to wake her up, but given that Circe had almost killed Micah, in the end everyone agreed Micah should do the honors. The Shiki seemed particularly pleased about it, prancing around happily and almost grinning, even in his house-cat form. Tessa got the distinct impression that he had not enjoyed being Circe's Shiki, which, she had to admit, made her like him more. For her part, Micah seemed to find the biggest cup in the house and filled it with the coldest possible water, Tessa suspected she had Snow work a little magic on it as well. Micah threw it in Circe's face with a joyous abandon and Circe sputtered to life under the deluge and opened two big, beautiful green eyes right at Tessa and then smiled easily, too easily.

"Scion," she said, and it was more a purr than a word.

"Bitch that blinded me," Tessa said in response.

Circe's smile spread. "None other, darling."

"And raised The Draugr?"

"Guilty as charged."

"And sent The Shikigami after us."

"Mmmmhmmm."

"And The Troll."

"Mmm, no," she said, and Tessa blinked in surprise.

"No?" Tessa asked, unconvinced.

"No," she said again, and Tessa had the distinct feeling that she wasn't lying.

"But everything else?"

"Correct," she said.

"Why?"

"California," Circe said simply.

Tessa opened her mouth to speak and then did a double take, "Huh?"

"I have been promised California. And Maine, actually. When this world is covered in the dead, ruled by him alone, California and Maine will be mine to do with as I choose. I'll probably have to build some big fences, but that's a small matter," she mused, as if she was also thinking about what wedding china she would register for.

"That's it? That's so…random," Tessa said. "He'll have all the world and you'll have California and Maine?"

"I'm not greedy. And I'm fond of both California and Maine."

"You're nuts," Tessa said, looking down at her.

"I'm not fond of that expression," she said, almost demurely and then slid her eyes off Tessa and directly at Micah. Tessa saw this and placed herself more directly between them.

"Don't look at her," Tessa said quietly. Circe flicked her eyes back at Tessa and then strained a bit to see Micah again.

"Come now, Scion, I'm only curious. Curious to see what was so powerful in that little one that she could best me and my Shiki in battle. There must be power there—let me see it."

"I'm all the power you need to worry about just now."

Circe sent a disdainful look her way. "Please. Your power doesn't interest me," she said dismissively. "What are you going to do? Punch me again?"

Tessa arched an eyebrow as if to say 'hell yes', and Circe's lips curled up at the edges.

"Ah, Scions. All brute force. Crude and unrefined. All sharp edges and no nuance. All arrogance and superiority. Bulls in china shops. I have no interest in you. But your little friend—*that's* something else," she said, sliding her eyes to Micah again, who shifted uncomfortably. Next to her, Jeff shifted into a tiger and roared. "See?" Circe said. "Complex and delicious. I can almost taste her."

Tessa smacked Circe so hard across the face she was shocked that she didn't knock her unconscious again, or just take her head clean off. Circe looked back at Tessa, one hand on her face, a trickle of blood at the corner of her mouth. Her eyes flashed a glowing green for a split second before returning to normal.

"You look at her again and I will end you," Tessa hissed. Circe pulled back her hand, bloodied from her mouth and showed all her teeth.

"I *did* say crude and unrefined, didn't I?"

Tessa was unnerved by her control. She was captured, surrounded by enemies, and yet she was clearly unimpressed. And wholly unafraid. Tessa couldn't tell if it was an act or not. If it was an act, she deserved the Oscar she looked like she was dressed to receive. If it wasn't, then they were in big trouble. "What's the plan and where is The Monster?" Tessa said abruptly, hoping, if anything, to draw her focus away from Micah.

"Ah, Scion, you ask the wrong questions. I think The Doctor may have overestimated your worth."

"Nice try," Tessa said, crossing her arms. "We know we're dealing with The Monster, not Dr. Frankenstein."

Circe laughed. The sound unnerved Tessa to no end.

"Yes, you are right, Scion. Dr. Frankenstein has nothing to do with this."

Something was going on, and Tessa didn't understand what she was missing. She looked to Robin who shook his head lightly. He was lost too. Fenris looked slightly less lost but he wasn't sharing if he knew something.

"Then who are you talking about?"

"It's nothing for you to worry about, my lamb. You'll find out in time."

"You're not working for The Monster?"

"I am."

"Then what am I missing?"

Circe smiled at her, fixing her gaze deeply on her. "Oh, so very much, Scion."

"Are you telling me that The Monster is not my enemy?"

"He is."

"Goddamnit!" Tessa shouted and had to curb the urge to strangle her to death. "Who am I fighting?"

Circe tsked and smiled widely again. The bitch pretty much hadn't stopped smiling since she'd arrived, and Tessa was at the end of her rope. "You ask the wrong questions, Scion. The Monster *is* your enemy and I am indeed in league with him, But what is beyond him? You haven't even begun to scratch the surface, darling." She paused and addressed the room. "You're all going to die. Some of you more gloriously than others, and all of you at the side of this petulant child with delusions of grandeur. A worthless waste, if you ask me."

A hush had fallen over the room.

Whether anyone believed her or not, she had gotten their attention.

"He has raised an army that is going to crush you and your little band of misfits, Scion," Circe said, raising a dismissive hand to the crew of Stories and Mortals standing behind Tessa. "Even you," she said, fixing her big green eyes on Micah.

Tessa searched for her voice, afraid it would come out an ineffectual squeak, "I've killed all of your Draugr."

"There's more where those came from," Circe said, unconcerned, and then narrowed her eyes at Tessa. "There's always more when you're trading in the dead."

"Well, it ends now," Tessa said, reaching for the broadsword on the nearby table and raising it to Circe's throat.

"Oh, darling," Circe sang. "It ends when we say it ends."

And before Tessa's eyes, she disappeared in a snap of golden light.

THIRTY-SIX

After Circe disappeared, Tessa went into the backyard and cursed for roughly ten minutes without taking a breath. "I hate magic!" (along with every expletive in the book) was the general theme.

When Tessa rejoined the group in the kitchen, Fenris had disappeared again. "Typical," Tessa muttered, and then directed her attention at the rest of the crew.

The group looked back at her and Tessa blinked.

She was so tired.

They must be too. They must be scared. Who wouldn't be with her leading the charge? She had no idea what she was doing and Circe had called her on it.

She had been right.

Tessa released a long sigh and looked at the clock on the wall, it was late. "Everyone go home. Get some rest. We'll regroup later." As a unit, they hesitated and looked at one another and then started to get up without a word. As he walked past her, Tessa pulled Brand aside.

"After you get some rest, do your hacker thing, search for other places Circe might be hiding, scour the city for her, okay?"

Brand nodded and put a comforting hand on hers. "It'll be okay, Tess," he said, and for a moment Tessa almost believed him. After everyone had left, Tessa went to the backyard, filled with zombie bodies and heads. She began piling them up. Robin joined her after a few minutes.

"Do you want me to stay?" Robin asked, unsure.

Tessa didn't look up. "Yes. Very much. Which…is why you should probably go," she said, resigned. He nodded.

"I agree. I don't want to and it may physically kill me to leave, but I agree." He smiled at her and she smiled back. He moved forward to kiss her and then, seeming to think better of it, just kissed the palm of her hand. "I have to go now or I'm never leaving."

"Yeah," Tessa said, thinking that she was going to need the coldest shower ever later. Of course, dragging headless zombie bodies around a yard and burning them in a huge funeral pyre was a good way to kill the libido too. She got back to work.

Halfway through, she stopped. "Fenris," she said, standing up straight but not turning around.

"See, less stealthy," he teased, sliding up beside her.

Tessa ignored him and tossed another body on the pile. He helped, wordlessly, and she was glad for it, both his help and his silence. Half an hour later, Tessa lit them on fire. She would be lucky if the smoke didn't bring the police and the fire department. Tessa stood, watching the blaze of the mythical Norse zombies with the Big Bad Wolf at her side, and her head spun yet again at the utter absurdity that was her life.

She honestly couldn't stop to think about it. Her life looked so foreign to her that she had started to forget who she had been a few short weeks ago. Some other person she now hardly recognized. And were all her friends going to die because of it? She stood with Fenris in silence for a long time, until the fire started to die out.

"It ends when we say it ends," Tessa repeated, and then quieter, "Is she right, Fenris?" she asked never taking her eyes off the faint glow of the dying fire and the ashes, mounds of them, so much that it made her throat clench up.

"No."

"You sound very sure."

"I am," he said, and Tessa was grateful, because as usual with Fenris, his words had a decided ring of truth. This time she actually wanted to believe him.

"Do you know who she's talking about? The Doctor she's referring to?"

Fenris didn't speak for a long time. "Here's the thing, Scion. She spoke the truth. But she did it deliberately. Everything she said was true but well calculated. She didn't lie because she knows that the truth can be more powerful. There is a much bigger world out there, and there are forces much more dangerous than The Monster, but it doesn't change the fact that The Monster is who you are fighting right now. You cannot allow her to draw your focus to other things, or he will kill you and it won't even matter what those other things are."

It was a huge answer that Tessa hadn't expected and was not sure she knew how to process. "The slow knife," Tessa said to herself. Fenris pricked his head up.

"What did you say?"

"Something Robin said before. The slow knife. That it's what would kill me. A slow blade. That I wouldn't even know it had already begun to penetrate. It's already begun, hasn't it? And I didn't even notice." Tessa felt a wave of desperation fall over her, everything seemed oppressively dark. Fenris didn't speak, which didn't make her feel any better. His lack of protest seemed like tacit agreement. Tessa turned and blinked at him. "The war you mentioned before."

"Yes."

"So who is he, The Doctor?"

"I'll make a deal with you. I will tell you as much as I can after we take care of The Monster."

Tessa chewed on her lips and looked back at the fire, now just embers being devoured by ash. "Alright," she said, and nodded her head resolutely. She moved toward the house and then paused. "Thank you."

Fenris reached out to her as she headed up the porch stairs.

"Give me your hand," he said.

She looked at him, her brow furrowed. Her thankfulness did not extend to hand holding. "No."

He did something between a growl and a sigh of annoyance and took her hand anyway. He held it open between them and put something in her hand, then closed her fingers around it.

"I'm giving this to you. It could help," he said. Tessa opened her fingers and blinked at the thing in her palm and then looked up at him, unsure. "Take care of it. They're hard to come by. But it could be the difference," he said. Tessa's mind reeled with possibilities.

"Yes," she said, understanding his meaning.

He started to go and then turned around. "I think Circe is controlling the Mortal zombies as well."

"Why?"

"I killed something, back before you came to Lore. It confused me at the time because it was Mortal, but it stunk of Story magic. I think she has raised those mortals and turned them into zombies. It also might explain why we don't have an actual zombie apocalypse on our hands," he said.

"Right, like, if they weren't being controlled, we'd have more victims and random attacks. A town overrun by a literal zombie apocalypse."

"I'd think so."

"But why wouldn't she want that? Wouldn't it just grow her army?"

"My guess is she's spread a little thin."

"And maybe adding to the army means she can't control it."

"Perhaps."

"So you think killing her will take out both The Draugr and the Mortal zombies?"

"It can't hurt," he said. Tessa looked back at her hand and when she looked up, he was gone again. She sighed. When it came to Fenris she could not see straight, and she never understood what he was doing. He had all but led her and Robin to their death today, abandoning them just before the shit hit the fan. And yet, he had seemed concerned for their (or at least her) well-being when he arrived, driving like a madman and breaking down a door to get to them.

And now he spoke with her truthfully, gave her sound advice, and this gift. And it *was* a gift.

She might never figure him out.

THIRTY-SEVEN

Things were quiet.

Too quiet.

It was killing her.

It was so obviously the calm before the storm that would probably actually kill her, that she was going crazy. Her thoughts and fears, and most especially everything Circe had said plagued her. Fenris had been right to focus on The Monster, but with no Monster to actually fight her mind was consumed with horrible 'what ifs.' She was wound so tight she sprang at the slightest noise, the slightest aggravation. Hell, she didn't even need aggravation, she'd freak out at *nice* things. She'd even cussed at Fenris when he showed up with construction dudes to fix her house.

It was like without a monster to hit, she would hit anything.

In the bustling hallway after the final bell, Tessa fidgeted with her locker, deciding if she even cared to bring any of her books home. Would she do her homework? She couldn't imagine it. It sounded drastically unimportant. Why do your homework when you probably weren't going to get to finish your junior year?

While still tuned out to most everything around her, whatever superhero power she had that warned her about shitty things about to happen kicked in and gooseflesh broke out over her arms.

Tessa's locker slammed shut at a blinding speed, and only her advance warning and lightning quick reflexes helped her get her hand clear of a blow that probably would have broken her hand.

"Hey, freak," said a handsome jock in a letterman's jacket with his arm around a perky blonde. Tessa turned to look at him and found he had a whole little attractive group with him.

"Do you actually want something?" Tessa asked, "Or is this just some kind of a *'you're bored so you're trying to drum up something interesting to do'* kind of thing?" She kind of hoped he started something, it would be good to take out her aggression on someone that deserved it, even if she did have to pull her punches. Her response was clearly more aggressive than he was used to and so he turned around, the rest of his entourage following suit.

The group slid back toward her, menacing and less pretty with every step. Just as Tessa was balling up her fist and wondering how to gauge the appropriate amount of superhuman force needed to take down a non-Story, seventeen-year-old jock in one punch, they all stopped and shifted their gaze to something just behind her. Tessa blinked and turned. Nash was standing behind her, leaning against the lockers, his arms crossed, his jaw set.

"Hey, Nash," the jock said.

"Hey, Tyler," Nash said. "Can I do something for you?"

"No, no problem here. See you around."

"Yup," Nash said. And the group walked away. Tessa couldn't decide if she was pissed or thankful. But since her emotions had been all over the map, she went the wrong way.

"What was that?" she snapped. Nash, of course, took the high road.

"Just trying to help out," he said.

"I don't need a hero," Tessa said, sulking.

"There was nothing heroic about that," Nash said. "That was just being a good friend."

Tessa hung her head, feeling like an even bigger jerk. "You're right," she said and then, "Thanks."

"I'll take what I can get," he said and then touched her chin gently, tipping her head up so he could look her in the eyes. His eyes flitted to Tessa's scar, still red and angry, like Tessa herself. "You okay?"

Tessa pulled back from his hand and let her hair fall back across her face. "Oh yeah. That. Totally fine—fell in the, um, shower," she said pathetically.

"Your shower have claws?" Nash asked, skeptically, but not unkindly.

"Guess it does," Tessa said, trying to make it sound like the end of the discussion.

He got the hint and lowered his hand, but kept her gaze. "I'll see you later."

Tessa nodded and went looking for Micah and Brand. They could calm her down if anyone could.

On the bus, Tessa listened absently to Micah and Brand's chattering. Tessa nodded occasionally but it was obvious she was just placating them. Micah finally jabbed her in the ribs.

"Are you going to ask Robin to The Mask?" Before Tessa could answer, Micah answered for her, practically swooning in her seat, "You should *totally* ask Robin."

Tessa chewed her lip. She still wasn't sure Robin Hood would be into going to a high school dance. Micah picked up on Tessa's hesitation. "Or, I mean, we could all just go together, make a night of it."

She elbowed Brand. "Right, Brand?"

"Yeah, sure. Micah and I went together last year and you know what they say, 'Three's Company,'" he smiled.

Micah elbowed him again. "Dumbass, that's not the saying."

"Sure it is, that old TV show."

"Yeah, it's the TV show, but the saying is 'two's company, three's a crowd.'"

Brand scrunched up his face. "Well, that's stupid," he said. "Three is totally company."

Micah rolled her eyes. "Whatever. So what do you say Tessa?"

Tessa nodded. Maybe a dance was just what she needed. "I'll ask him. It would be fun."

It turned out that despite the possible end of the world just about everyone was indeed going to The Mask. Micah and Grey had decided to go stag, together, which seemed to contradict itself, but Tessa wasn't going to ask. Brand was somehow going with Snow, which nobody wanted to know about, and for once he didn't seem anxious to tell a story. And Robin had been surprisingly on board.

Once Robin had agreed, Tessa had to admit she was getting really excited about it. She and Robin had kind of skipped right over dating what with all the training and life-threatening violence. This wasn't only her first date with Robin, it was actually her first date ever.

After school the day before the dance, Micah realized Tessa didn't have a costume or dress and dragged her (quite literally) to the mall to shop for something to wear.

"I don't understand," Tessa said, running her fingers over the brightly-colored dresses. "I thought it was a costume party."

Micah shrugged. "It's a Masquerade, so some people do really elaborate costumes, others do dresses and tuxes with masks, it's a pretty good mix usually. We can hit the costume shop next," Micah said. "But I bet the costumes will be pretty picked over at this point. Still lots of good dresses though," she said, pulling out a pretty lavender dress and holding it up to Tessa who shook her head no.

"No pastel," Tessa said. Micah chuckled and put it back on the rack.

While Tessa tried on a simple short black dress, Micah sat outside the dressing room, letting Jeff, currently a small green gecko, run over her fingers.

"So how's it going with Robin? You guys seem pretty googly for each other."

"Googly? That doesn't sound like me," Tessa said from inside the dressing room.

"Then you haven't seen you and Robin," Micah teased.

"Haha," Tessa said sarcastically. After a long pause, she opened the door. "It's too tight," she said, and turned so that Micah could see it wouldn't zip up.

"I'll get you another one," Micah said, and Tessa looked in the long mirror.

"No. I don't like it, it feels too—somber," Tessa said, leaning against the wall of the dressing room. She picked at the edge of the dress. "Things are getting pretty serious," she said, and then closed the door again.

Micah perked up. "Like *how* serious?"

There was a long pause behind the door. "I hate this one," Tessa said finally and opened the door. "It accentuates the scar." She gestured to the edge of the dark purple dress and self-consciously raised her hand to the Shiki scar, faded now, but permanently fixed on her face. Micah cringed a bit. The scar made Tessa no less beautiful, but Jeff had made it and it was a permanent reminder of that terrifying day.

"I thought you'd come to terms with the scar," Micah said, tentative.

"Some days are better than others," Tessa said, drawing her finger across it. She shifted gears again and said, "Like, serious, serious."

"Hott." Micah said under her breath.

"HEY!"

"Sorry," Micah said, shrugging. "What do you expect? Dude is freaking hott."

Tessa closed the door again, pulled the purple dress off and threw it over the door. "What about that blue one—the strapless with the short skirt?"

Micah put Jeff in her sweatshirt pocket. "Yeah, I'll bring it to you."

"Thanks." Tessa gave up on a third dress halfway through pulling it on. The blue dress and two others, both red, came sailing over the door a minute later.

"Nice," Tessa said, looking at the two others. Tessa unzipped the blue one and stepped into it. "What do you think of this whole Snow and Brand thing?"

"I think it's fucking weird," Micah said aggressively. Micah never cussed.

"He wouldn't tell you how it happened either?" Tessa asked, zipping the dress up on the side.

"No, which I find highly suspicious," Micah said. Tessa peeked over the door to see Micah slumped down in the big chair.

"You're not jealous though?" Tessa asked.

"What? No. I mean, that he has a date? Maybe. That it's not me? No way. That it's a borderline super-villain, non-borderline complete bitch? No way. I just, I don't know what he's thinking and I'm not used to that. Also, have you read *The Snow Queen* story recently? I have, and her whole thing is like kidnapping and becoming obsessed with this innocent young boy…Kai is his name in the story."

"That can't be good," Tessa said uneasily.

"Yeah. I mean, I know she's been helpful to us, but I'd feel better if we all, Brand most of all, didn't forget who she is, *what* she is, and what she may be up to. I mean, as much as I hate her guts, even *she* might not realize what she's doing, right? Like she might not be aware of it. If it's a compulsion, if it's just her acting out some part of her Story, that's how it works, right? Man, this is confusing," she trailed off, scowling. Tessa opened the dressing room door and Micah brightened "Hey—that one's brilliant." Tessa smiled and looked back in the mirror, adjusting the dress.

"Yeah, it even has pockets," Tessa said, jamming her hands into them.

"Awesome."

"What do you think Snow will wear?" Tessa asked, crinkling her nose and looking in the mirror again.

Micah rolled her eyes. "I'm sure she'll just go as her fabulous self. That's already a costume, right?"

Tessa laughed and then spun around, wide-eyed. "Ohmigod."

"What?!" Micah asked, alarmed, sitting up and looking around, her sweatshirt pocket bulging as Jeff shifted into something larger and more dangerous simultaneously with her heightened fear.

"That's it!" Tessa shouted. She grabbed her clothes and ran toward the front of the store. "C'mon!" By the time Micah was out of the dressing room the store alarms had sounded and Tessa was running back into the store and to the counter. Rather than stripping off the dress, she just paid for it and a blue-feathered mask hanging near the counter. By the time Micah got to her, the clerk was taking off the security tag.

"Tessa?" Micah asked.

"C'mon!" Tessa shouted again, grabbing Micah's hand and dragging her forward with her, out into the mall and toward the parking lot, yelling as they ran. "It's The Mask! He'll do it at The Mask, on Halloween—when he can blend in with everyone else!"

THIRTY-EIGHT

Since Tessa's dad was recently back in town, everyone met at Snow's condo. Ever since Tessa had had her revelation in the dressing room, a plan had been forming in her mind.

But she was going to need everyone, and a lot of damn luck.

Micah had brought excellent Chinese food from her father's restaurant, and if they hadn't been planning for a battle that was maybe going to kill them all, it would have seemed like a pretty good time. Tessa felt guilty dragging Grey into this, but she needed as many people with her as possible.

Fenris was conspicuously absent, as per usual.

When the food was finished, Tessa stood up and laid out her plan to the group. She talked for what felt like forever, and at the end, took a deep breath and turned to face them. "So what do you think?" A sea of blank faces blinked back at her. She got nervous. "No?"

Micah shook her head. "Tessa, it's kind of brilliant, but there are a lot of ifs. And some of us have—surprisingly large roles to play. I'm not sure, I mean, *should* some of us have such big roles?" she asked, panic creeping into her voice.

"Someone recently told me that sometimes as a leader you have to get out of the way, let others do what they're good at. I think he was right."

Micah nodded and breathed like she was trying not to pass out. Tessa put a comforting hand on her shoulder and looked at the rest of the group. "One of the biggest 'ifs' in this plan is one we have to solve tonight." Tessa stood up and drew seven small circles on the map spread out on Snow's dining room table. "Brand has been searching the city for traces of Circe or The Monster, and we have several good leads for potential hideouts."

"Based on?" Grey asked.

Brand leaned over the map. "First we used the missing people reports to narrow our search to smaller areas of the city. Then I searched for large properties in the area owned or leased by corporations or individuals with names that fit Story profiles, or were anagrams of Story profiles, that sort of thing. I then cross-referenced that list with city utility bills, looking for anything unusual, like spikes in usage," Brand finished.

Robin nodded his head. "Impressive."

"Story upgrade," Brand said tapping the side of his head.

"So we need a hard target search of those locations tonight to pin her down." Tessa said.

"So what, exactly, are we looking for?" Snow asked.

"Just Circe," Tessa said.

"Not The Monster?" Micah asked.

"Just Circe. And whoever finds her calls everyone else to their location. This is locate only." The group nodded. "If this works, then we go into The Mask tomorrow night with a serious ace up our sleeves."

"Why not take her out now? Why wait for The Mask?" Micah asked.

"Well, we don't know where The Monster is, for starters. I want him to get comfortable, think it's all going to plan. If I spook him now by taking out Circe early who knows what he might do instead, if we'll ever even find him, and maybe he'll just continue killing, maybe he'll never stop." Tessa took a breath and made sure they were all still with her. They either were or they were doing a good job of faking it. "Okay, so three teams. Snow and Brand, I want you to take the first two locations. Micah, The Shiki, and Robin, take three and four, and Grey and I will take these three."

"What about me?" Fenris said from the other room, leaning against the wall, as if he'd been there all along.

Tessa looked him up and down. "Good to have you." She turned back to the group. "New groups. Brand, Snow, and Robin together. Fenris, Micah, and The Shiki for locations three and four, Grey, you and me still for the last three."

Everyone nodded and nobody spoke. Tessa tried to smile. Leaders needed to instill confidence, right?

As everyone geared up to leave, Snow pulled Tessa aside in the foyer.

"Scion," she said, her voice serious. "If I do this tomorrow, I'll be out. That will be it for me for the fight, you know that, right?"

Tessa nodded, "I know. But you *can* do it, right?"

Snow looked away. She seemed more unsure than Tessa was used to seeing her but also more serious. "I can. I'll have to prepare, and someone will have to get me out of there after, but I can do it."

Tessa looked at her. "I'm counting on it."

At the door, Tessa passed Fenris.

"You'll watch out for her," she said, giving him a hard look.

"Of course, luv," he said, unmoving, a handsome but complicated smile on his face. "Just glad I wasn't paired with boy wonder."

Tessa rolled her eyes. "Oh yes, I was going to pair you two together so that you could pull each other's hair like bitchy rival cheerleaders."

Robin stepped beside her. "Who's a cheerleader?"

Tessa looked at him. "Nobody. What's up?"

"Everyone's ready."

"Good," Tessa said. She looked across the room and called to Grey from the hallway. "You ready, partner?"

"Yup."

Grey tossed her the broadsword and picked up his own sword.

"Let's do this." Tessa said to the room.

Robin put a hand on Tessa's shoulder. "Be careful." He kissed her and then drew her into a hug, his hand in her hair.

"You too," she breathed into him.

In the parking lot, Grey pointed to his car at the far end of the lot. "So you and Robin are getting pretty serious," he said, as if waiting for her to fill in the blanks.

"Why is everyone so interested in me and Robin?" Tessa asked, exasperated.

"It's hott. Double "t" hott," he said, echoing Micah and smiling. "Plus there's a pool going," he added as he unlocked the car.

"Oh God." Tessa said, her mouth falling open, her cheeks turning red.

"Oh yeah, I'm surprised there isn't a chart, maybe some sexy diagrams," he said, laughing.

"You guys are the worst."

"Whatever, I'm pretty sure I'm winning," he said confidently. Tessa cocked an eyebrow at him.

"What do you have?"

"Actual dating, making out, headed for happily ever after," Grey said.

Tessa groaned. "Uggghh. What does everyone else have? Wait. Never mind, I don't want to know!"

Grey laughed and after another long pause continued, "So is it? Happily ever after?" Tessa didn't say anything, and after a moment Grey filled in the blank. "Marian," he said and the word cut through Tessa like a knife. She and Robin had done a great job of avoiding her name, but she was always there, floating in the background.

"Subtle you are not," Tessa said.

"Sorry, I just get it," he said, shrugging.

"Well, can you explain it to me? Because nobody else seems to be able to."

"He's got a powerful Fiction driving him, Tessa. It's not like there are Robin Hood stories with a different love interest. It's never Robin Hood and Elizabeth or Kate or some other nonsense. It's Marian. She's it, y'know? Every. Single. Time. It reinforces that power—the connection they feel, over and over again," Grey paused before going on, choosing his words carefully. "Imagine never dying and being with the same person forever—and really, you didn't even pick this person. Someone picked for you. You *feel* like you love them, you know you're supposed to, and sometimes you even do, because everything you are tells you that that's how you feel. But sometimes it feels like, well, sometimes it feels like someone laid it all out for you and maybe it's not actually what you would have chosen. And you can't deny the truth of that feeling, because once you're aware of what you really are—a Story—then you know that that's exactly what actually happened. Someone else chose for you."

Tessa arched an eyebrow at him, "Are you sure you're talking about Robin?"

"I'm talking about a lot of us," he said somberly. "Even you."

At Tessa and Grey's second location, a large modern house set on nearly two acres of gated land just off Northside Park, was Circe's new hideout. Tessa could feel something strange as she and Grey crept up the long winding road toward the stone walls that surrounded the place and, on the heels of that, as they got closer, a smell that could not be ignored.

They found a fallen tree that allowed them to reach the top of the wall. Tessa pushed aside a mass of heavy leaves and branches to reveal the expansive lawn leading up to the gleaming, well-lit house.

The grounds surrounding the house were teaming with Mortal zombies and The Draugr.

There must have been hundreds.

Tessa drew back and looked at Grey.

"Tessa," he breathed, his eyes fixed and wide.

"Balls," Tessa said. Her mind racing. "Call everyone."

THIRTY-NINE

"It smells like death," Fenris said when he and Micah arrived. Tessa nodded. They of course both had super-senses, but she suspected you didn't need any special senses to smell the death if you were this close. It was thick in the air. Tessa jutted her chin at the partially fallen tree.

"Take a peek," she said. Micah and Fenris both climbed up and then back down immediately. Micah was pale as moonlight. Fenris seemed unsurprised.

"More than I thought," Fenris said. Tessa nodded.

Micah shook her head as if trying to shake the image out of her mind. "Are they on their way?"

"Yes," Tessa said, chewing her lip nervously and checking her watch.

"Then we wait," Fenris said and stripped off his shirt. "I'll do a pass around the grounds, make sure there are no surprises." Tessa nodded again and looked away as he unceremoniously took off his pants. Grey, caught unaware, did not look away.

"Whoa," he said, part surprised, part impressed, as he got a peek at naked Fenris before he shifted. Tessa chuckled.

"Yeah, you gotta watch out for that," she said.

Grey shook his head. "Or y'know, have my camera ready."

Tessa stifled another laugh.

Twenty minutes later, Robin emerged from the trees with Snow and Brand stumbling awkwardly behind him.

"Smells terrible," Brand said, covering his nose with his shirt-sleeve. "What is that?"

Tessa nodded at the tree and they climbed up, even Snow in her four-inch heeled boots, and then back down. Snow was already as pale as a body could get, but Brand's face was giving her a run for her money. Even Robin looked wan. Tessa looked at Micah.

"Are you sure you can do this?"

Micah shook her head. "No." Tessa smiled at her friend's honesty. "I can't promise," she said. "But we'll do everything we can." Micah pulled The Shiki as green gecko from her sweatshirt pocket.

Tessa and Micah climbed up the tree together, and Micah set The Shiki on the top of the wall. They seemed to mind meld for a moment before she let him go and he scrambled down the wall. Tessa narrowed her eyes, watching the grounds, and a few moments later she saw a zombie shape materialize out of nothing. It turned and looked back at them for a split second before blending into the teeming mass. Micah shuddered and Tessa put a hand on her back.

"Are you okay?" Tessa asked.

Micah gritted her teeth and squinted. "It's scary," she said. "It's like I'm in there, and he's afraid," she said, trailing off. Tessa looked into the horde and couldn't make The Shiki out from the others. She looked back at her friend.

"Should we stop? If you can't do it, we'll find another way."

Micah shook her head. "No, this is the best way. I—we can do it," she said. Tessa climbed down and then helped Micah too. Fenris returned, and everyone looked away as he put his clothes back on.

"It's done?" Fenris asked.

"Yeah. Phase one, complete," she said.

Grey dropped Tessa, Micah, and Brand at Brand's house, since Tessa and Brand had the task of keeping Micah up all night. She would be monitoring the situation at Circe's via Jeff. Micah also needed to be sure she didn't lose control of him, which was likely to happen if she lost consciousness.

They ordered pizzas while Brand pored over movies, looking for the perfect comedy to keep things light. Tessa tried to enjoy her first sleepover since she was seven. She wasn't sure what you were supposed to do at a sleepover (other than the aforementioned pizza) but she was pretty sure that this one had extenuating circumstances, what with keeping one member up at all costs, and the threat of impending doom in under twenty-four hours.

It was fun anyway, which Tessa thought spoke volumes.

Around two a.m. Brand took the first sleeping shift, and Tessa stayed up with Micah, who was already somber and quiet. They'd tried not to talk about it, to distract her from what was really going on, but Tessa wondered if it might help her to talk about it.

"Are you okay?" Tessa asked, tentative.

Micah nodded subtly.

"What's it like?"

"Usually? Or now?"

"Both," Tessa said.

"Well, at first it was horrible. It was like trying to hold onto a wriggling snake with my mind, constantly. When he stopped fighting me, it got better. At some point we got in sync, made an agreement of sorts really. Promises about mutual freedom or something like that. And so then it became like being on a team, all the time. Which is not so bad, although a bit crowded. But I…" Micah trailed off.

"But what?"

"But now, with him in there, I'll be honest Tess, it's horrifying."

"I can't even imagine."

"No, not just that. I mean, yes, pretending to be the walking dead, brainless amongst enemies, at anytime they could swarm him—us, it's terrible. But that's not the scariest thing."

"What's scarier than that?"

"I love him, Tessa. Like, we're bonded on a mental level I can't even explain to you, it's like having a beloved pet but times a thousand. I mean, I shouldn't even refer to him as a pet, that seems insulting, that seems beneath the way we're connected. He's like a pet and a best friend, a brother, he's like everything. It's, I can't explain. I love him and I'm terrified I'll lose him, and I don't think I really understood how I felt until he went in there."

"Whoa." Tessa said, blinking and trying to imagine the breadth of what she was saying. She would have to stop referring to him as 'The Shiki,' he was clearly more than just some creature to Micah.

"So while I'm terrified something will happen to him, I'm trying to be calm, the way were connected, if I panic, he will too."

"So, we shouldn't watch this raunchy comedy then," Tessa said, trying to lighten the mood and holding up a brightly-covered DVD case.

"Yeah, probably not," Micah said, grinning. "Focus, calm, these are good things. Of course, those things also rhyme with boring, though not literally, I guess."

"So, also no rambling period pieces," Tessa said, holding up a more subdued movie case.

Micah laughed, "No. Maybe something in-between?"

Tessa nodded and dug into the shelf, looking for something soothing but not boring. It was harder to find than you'd think. Plus, movies weren't as comforting as they used to be. Not when you knew that everything you watched was out there somewhere.

Real, breathing, and maybe coming to kill you.

 FORTY

Tessa woke up on Brand's bed with a storm of emotions rushing around inside her. The two that rose to the surface however were intense anxiety and some kind of bottled adrenaline. Swirling around in there somewhere was a little pebble of dread. Some innate knowledge that no matter what happened, no matter how successful they might actually be, that something bad would come, too.

Tessa passed by Brand and Micah, watching their millionth movie and eating cereal and drinking cans of Red Bull in his living room, and just nodded at them before heading out the door. They returned sleepy nods. There wasn't much to say, and if they were as churned up inside as she was, it was better to keep quiet. No sense in everyone freaking out at once.

When Tessa showed up back at home, there was another white envelope of money waiting for her. The sight of it depressed her to no end.

What if she died? When would he even find out? Would Detectives Wade and Ripley come to deliver the news? Would he even care? He'd barely acknowledged her presence in his life after all these years.

Her mother wouldn't even know what had really happened to her.

Nobody would know what really happened.

Tessa went upstairs and brought down a huge box. She put the box on the kitchen counter. She'd ordered a gross of her dad's favorite stupid dishtowels online. If she never came back to the house, at least he'd have plenty of dishtowels to keep him company.

She had meant it as a nice gesture, but now it just seemed grim, and kinda mean.

A few hours later, Tessa answered the door in her strapless blue punk rock number, 20-eye Docs, and leather jacket, the feathery blue mask hanging around her wrist.

"Wow," Robin said, unable to take his eyes off her. "I never thought I would say this, but formal wear somehow suits you." He paused before adding, "Of course, the leather helps."

Tessa smiled and then pulled at the top of the dress. "I should have gotten something with straps," she complained. "I wasn't thinking but at least it's tight," she continued, looking at her reflection in the window. "I think it'll stay up."

"Better if it doesn't," Robin said. Tessa laughed and then took in his own costume, looking more like a true Story than ever. He had at least partially embraced the "costume" part of The Mask and was dressed up as a more literal Robin Hood than usual in leather pants and a hooded tunic, as well as a complete weapons package, all highly suitable for the battle to come. She slid into his arms and kissed his neck. He groaned a little and found her mouth. It wasn't until she pulled back and saw his eyes that she knew something was wrong.

"Wait, what's wrong?"

His face fell and then recovered. "First the good news."

"Okay—?"

"I've called in some help for us tonight. Mini-reinforcements."

"That *is* good news. What's the bad?" she asked, trying to kill the tremble in her voice.

"Wait. There's still more good. There are presents."

Tessa smiled faintly as he handed her a smallish box with a big shimmery blue ribbon tied around it. Tessa took it from him and sat down on the couch. He sat next to her. She untied the box and lifted off the lid. Inside was a silver box about half a dozen inches wide and half a dozen inches long, and a few inches deep. The box was delicately latched. Tessa took the box out and moved to open it.

"Careful," Robin said, wincing a little.

Tessa unlatched the box and opened the lid. Inside, lying on a dark blue velvet lining, were seven tiny winged creatures, some curled up and others splayed out, as if sleeping. And they looked exactly like what every child in the world imagines a fairy must look like. Naked and lovely, like beautiful miniature shiny women with wings, they were all different glowing sparkly colors, a red one and a blue one, a pink, a purple, a yellow, a green, and an orange one. Tessa gasped.

"Are these Fairies?!"

"Sort of," Robin said. "You mean Fairies, like F-A-I-R-I-E-S, and that's what these are based on, the design, I mean. But these are something called Ferries, like F-E-R-R-I-E-S. They were created by Fairy Godmother and The Blue Fairy, with a little help from others, I suspect. They were created to send messages between Story and The Mortal World. They're extremely rare, and basically illegal. I can't tell you how many favors I had to call in to get just these seven."

"They're amazing." Tessa felt like she was five years old, she wanted to take them out and play with them for hours. It was like seeing a Unicorn, even if they weren't the really real thing. "Can I hold them?"

Robin shook his head. "No. They're not to be played with. You should only take them out when you want to send a message to Story. You take one out, you hold it in your hands, make your hands like a cup around it and then you whisper who you are trying to reach and what your message is into your hands. When you open your hands, the Ferry will disappear, and they won't stop until they have found the person you are seeking and delivered your message. They'll come back with a return message, always. When they return, hold them in your hands as you did when you sent them off, put your ear to your hands and you will hear a message back from the one you seek. How long it takes is dependent on how hard your receiver is to find, it can take some time. After one trip, they will expire."

"They die?!"

"They're not real, Tessa. They're not real Fairies. Think of them like fancy but very fake carrier pigeons made of science and magic."

Tessa stared at them, beautiful and sleeping in the box, and then suddenly realized why he was giving her this present. She closed the box, latching it carefully and put the box down on the table. "You're leaving me."

"I've been called back to Story, and I have to go. Tonight. After the fight."

Tessa stood up and walked away from him. Then, realizing she had nowhere to go, she sat down on another different couch, deflated.

"I'm sorry, Tessa. It's something with Marian, and I can't say no to her."

At the sound of Marian's name, Tessa flinched. "Can't or won't?"

"Both," he said.

Tessa took a calming breath and tried to make things light. "Okay. How long will you be gone?"

Robin came and sat by her on the new couch, taking her hand. "I don't know. I don't know how long it will take, and more importantly, I don't know if they'll let me come back."

"So, you're saying not only is this *not* a quick trip, but it might be permanent?" He didn't want to say yes, but she could tell that was the answer.

"The change in power of the Story court means that I may have trouble getting back through," he said. "You don't understand some of the politics, it's—"

Tessa cut him off, "—Don't you dare say complicated."

Robin pressed his lips together.

"So, you're choosing her over me, even though it's a choice that might be made permanent."

"I'll do everything in my power to come back," he said, touching her cheek, turning her to face him. "There are lots of ways back to the Mortal world, even if Story tries to stop you."

A couple tears rolled down Tessa's cheek. "That's not what I'm worried about."

"You're worried about Marian."

Tessa nodded and chewed her lip. "You love her, you've always loved her, and when you see her again, you'll remember how much."

Robin shook his head but didn't actually disagree with her. After a long time he said, "I don't know what will happen. Nobody does."

"That doesn't sound like you."

He pressed her hand between his. "Well, you're very persuasive." She threw her arms around his neck and then saw the clock.

"We have to go," she said into his neck.

"I know," he said. Tessa released him and stood up. In this moment, she decided that to get through the night she had to pretend there wasn't going to be anything after the fight.

Just an open abyss.

Which sounded terrible, but somehow seemed more comforting than Robin leaving her.

FORTY-ONE

Northside Park was dramatically transformed. Tessa and Robin parked his jeep a long distance away thanks to the number of people and cars already there, and as they got closer to the entrance, Tessa was caught up in the spectacle so much that she almost forgot the more nefarious reason they was there. Twinkling white lights strung in trees everywhere gave it a surprisingly sweet and almost Christmas-y feel but the rest of the decorations, which were decidedly grim and legitimately spooky, resulted in a cacophonous, decadent spread of food, people, lights, and music that felt surreal and fantastic. It felt magical and not at all like the Mortal world.

When Tessa got over the sight of it herself, she realized that it truly was a rare event in which The Monster, and all sorts of other things, might be able to slip by unnoticed. People headed for The Mask were decked out in everything from elaborate monster costumes to decadent ball gowns and eye masks. It was just dusk, and the day activities were wrapping up just as the night festivities were getting underway. The crossover meant a stream of people, mostly families with children in tow, leaving the grounds for their cars while The Mask attendees funneled toward a giant tent on a hill in the distance.

The massive tent, lit from within and glowing softly, was set at the top of a hill in a large clearing surrounded by woods. Wild, tall grass filled the field surrounding the tent. It was stunningly beautiful, but Tessa couldn't help thinking that the hill was good for her as it would mean anything attacking would have to climb. However, the woods literally circled the tent and field, which made Tessa feel dangerously exposed and simultaneously surrounded. Tessa looked closely at the crowds coming and going, trying to see if she could make out monsters from people, but it was difficult. The time of night made it hard to see well, and the tiny white fairy lights made everything lovely and soft but not clear. She ached for a well-lit room or a bright summer day. She did manage to see both Detective Ripley and Captain West in the crowds, though Wade was thankfully nowhere to be seen. It occurred to her suddenly that maybe she'd be arrested for murder before she could even charge into battle.

From the inside, the tent appeared even larger. Sparkling white lights were strung throughout, and there was even a lavish chandelier hanging in the center. A segmented floor that doubled as a dance floor was laid throughout the space, and at the far end of the tent was a massive stage, too large, in fact, for the band there that had already started playing, something with a heavy sexy beat.

Toward the front of the tent was an area for pictures to be taken, and a series of long tables lined the entire left side, filled with food and drinks. The first half of the tent was crowded with medium-sized round tables and chairs, and the second half, closest to the large stage, was for dancing. Many chairs lined the side of the tent and Tessa cursed, for if they hadn't been there it might have been easier for people to get out if (when) there was a problem.

As it was, most of the people were going to be funneled through the entrance or would panic and run for the sides and pull the entire thing down onto everyone. But maybe the one entrance could work to their advantage as well, minimizing the bad guys efforts to get in. There was only one entrance since the stage covered the entire back of the tent.

It was a terrible set-up, though she supposed that those setting it up had not had a massive battle and minimizing collateral damage in mind.

The tent was already packed with what looked like the entire school. She found Micah easily enough, tired and looking it, standing with Greyson and pouring more Red Bull into her glass of red punch on the right side of the tent. Micah wore a bright green dress with small, white polka dots on it. She looked lovely, despite her furrowed brow. A mask shining with green and silver costume jewelry was pushed up on her head. Grey wore a sharp black suit, but with a faded green t-shirt instead of a dress shirt, and Tessa had to admit that he was rocking it. He also had a green mask, though a much simpler one, and his was on his face. Dress-up suited him. She hoped Ian would notice.

Handsome Nash, looking very 007, glided past her toward the dance floor, a pretty cheerleader-type on his arm.

He caught her eye and winked, "Save me a dance."

Tessa smiled and watched him spin the blonde girl around elegantly. He looked happy, and Tessa hoped she could keep it that way. Just as she was about to look away he caught her eye again and smiled a devastating smile, so open and honest, so uncomplicated. Tessa caught herself, for just a moment, yearning for that lack of complication. How nice would it have been to be dating simply good and handsome Nash and just be on a lovely fairytale worthy date with not another care in the world. He probably wasn't going to abandon his date at the end of the night for parts unknown. She smiled back and then looked away. It was too tempting to imagine a totally different totally easy life with someone like Nash. But there was no going back. Not from the things she hadn't chosen, like being The Scion; and not from the things she had chosen, like loving Robin, even if he was going to abandon her (assuming she didn't die). Tessa felt a wave of fear roll through her and she pushed away all her dark thoughts. She had to stay focused.

Tessa nodded at Micah, not far away, who offered a weak smile that Tessa took to mean that all was as well as could be. Micah inclined her head to the right and made a face Tessa didn't quite understand.

Tessa followed the nod to find Brand, looking quite handsome, his hair less disheveled than usual, in a traditional black tux and simple black mask. He was smiling broadly, and a moment later Tessa understood why as she caught sight of Snow moving through the crowd in a glittering long silver dress, with a high slit. It plunged dangerously low in both the back and the front, showing off all her pale skin and slender curves. She had a decadent white fur boa draping partially off her shoulders and glittering diamonds adorned her neck, ears, and hands, her hair swept up into an elegant but complicated bun that was topped off by an actual freaking crown. She looked like she belonged at a high school dance about as much as a decked out supermodel belonged at a laundromat.

Tessa groaned. She looked back at Micah who shot her a knowing look and then shrugged her shoulders helplessly. Fenris was, typically, nowhere to be seen. And thus everything was as in place as it would ever be. To be fair, there was nothing suspicious about the dance. It seemed like a typical dance, not that Tessa would actually know, since she'd never been to one before. She considered for a moment that she'd gotten it wrong, that The Mask was not The Monster's intended target.

The idea both horrified and relieved her.

The sudden notion that she could just go to the dance and not fight for her life was intoxicating, but then what? Then she would have made a huge mistake and people would die and maybe the Mortal world would eventually become a zombie paradise? No, she was sure this was it, if only because the little pebble of dread was still in her stomach. In fact, it had about doubled in size. As if sensing her increasing dread, Robin touched her back and guided her effortlessly onto the already-crowded dance floor.

The heavy beat reverberated through the air and into Tessa's bones. Tessa and Robin had never danced together before and yet there was something familiar about it. She notched into him like they had danced a thousand times before, and as she breathed him in she realized why it seemed familiar and laughed into his neck.

"What's funny?" he asked, pulling back.

"I felt like we'd done this before, danced, I mean," she said. He waited for her to finish. She ran her hand across his shoulder, down his arm, and looked at him. "Dancing, it's choreography—" she said and he locked eyes with her, pulling her closer.

"—Like fighting," he whispered, finishing her sentence, and then kissing her. Tessa tried to memorize the kiss, what it felt like to be in love with him, to feel like maybe he was falling in love with her too. When the kiss ended, she nuzzled into his neck and for a couple minutes, almost a whole song, she managed to forget just about everything else. Her dad, Bishop, The Monster, Circe, zombies, Franken-creatures, The Draugr, Bluebeard, The Troll, and even Story itself faded into a bad, very weird dream. Like this, Robin was a perfect haven from all of it, and she wanted to just be lost in him and this moment for as long as possible.

But it shattered a few moments later when Tessa felt a tap on her shoulder. She hoped it was just someone cutting in (someone she would punch in the face for cutting in), but instead it was Micah, a pained expression on her face.

"They're coming," she said.

FORTY-TWO

Tessa looked from Micah up to Robin. "Okay," she said. Robin smiled sadly, resigned, and followed Tessa out of the tent, where Micah, Grey, Snow, and Brand joined them.

Tessa scanned the nearby trees. She didn't see any zombies or The Draugr, or the Franken-creatures in the darkness that surrounded them, but she could feel Micah was right, something was coming, it was palpable in the air around them.

"They're spread out in the woods around us, but only below," Micah said, looking around, a weary but frantic look in her eyes. Tessa nodded and the group made their way to the edge of the woods and then tracked through it a little until they reached a small open grove in the trees, keeping an eye out for anything that might be lurking in the shadows. In the grove, Robin went after their weapons, stored in the hollow of a large fallen tree along with the rest. Grey knelt down and handed Micah the hatchet and Brand the Katana. To Tessa, he passed a small arsenal including a modern crossbow, a short dagger, and her broadsword. Tessa strapped a holster with a sheath to her thigh and put the short dagger in it. She filled her jacket pocket with crossbow bolts and set the crossbow down.

Fenris walked nonchalantly out of the trees, as if he had been there all the time. Tessa was both relieved and irritated. She looked at Robin.

"Your mystery guest?"

Robin checked his watch. "Any minute."

Tessa looked around at her friends standing in a half circle, dressed in eveningwear, and ready for battle. "Everyone know what they're doing?" The group nodded as if one. Tessa knew it was the moment for a rousing battle speech, a call to arms that would inspire them and quell their fear. But her mind was both racing and blank. She looked at Brand and Micah, inspired by them, their lack of fear, or rather their bravery in spite of fear. They were so vulnerable, despite their gifts, and their bravery filled Tessa with pride and guilt. The two emotions wrestled inside her. "I know I'm probably supposed to say something encouraging here. Some great call to arms or something about how all of you are doing the right thing or some other nonsense, but I just…mostly I just feel grateful to you and I hope…I hope you don't get dead."

The group blinked at her. Brand coughed. "Maybe you work on that speech for next time, yeah?"

Tessa smiled, embarrassed but relieved that he thought there would be a next time. "Deal."

The air around them crackled with blue light. Tal emerged from the transport sphere with Hecuba at her side and Tessa stepped forward. Fenris growled almost imperceptibly, Grey got tense. Tessa felt he might dash away at any moment.

"Tal," Tessa said coolly.

"Scion," Tal said, narrowing her eyes slightly at Tessa. Grey stood up from where he had crouched, and Tal looked at him, bored. "I'm not here for you, kid. Not today leastways," Grey still looked like he wanted to bolt, but he held his ground, and Tessa was thankful for it.

"You're the reinforcements?" Tessa asked, taking two more steps forward and crossing her arms.

Tal smiled thinly. "Robin convinced me it would be good to have The Last Scion owing me a favor." Tessa glanced at Robin.

He shrugged. "We need everyone we can get, right?" Tessa nodded. He was right. Tal and Hecuba were formidable and when your numbers were as small as theirs were, adding two fighters was huge. Maybe they actually had a chance here.

"Can I trust you?" Tessa asked Tal plainly.

"For today," Tal said, looping her bow over her shoulder.

"Then I'll take you."

Micah looked up at the group, her face a sickly green that clashed with her dress. "Good," she said softly, "Because it's started."

And no sooner did she say it than they heard a piercing shriek from the direction of the clearing.

When they hit the tree line, they saw a massive horde of The Draugr, Mortal zombies, and Franken-creatures, both men and dogs, headed toward the tent. A few people who had been outside must have seen them and then run inside. None of them had yet reached the tent, and The Monster was nowhere to be seen, however leading the charge of the miscellaneous undead army was Circe, dressed in her same inappropriate, glittering green gown. She and Snow could have had an outfit inappropriate-off. Tessa looked right and left at her friends and allies, and her gaze fell on Micah.

"Are you ready?" Tessa asked. Micah nodded weakly as Tessa turned to Snow. "And you?"

"I'm ready, Scion," she said, and she bent down to lay her hands on the grass before her. Tessa looked at Robin, her face tense. He smiled easily and her confidence surged, she had to say yes in this moment before it ebbed.

"Do it, Micah," Tessa breathed, watching the scene before them anxiously. Micah closed her eyes, and as she did so, a zombie figure lurched forward and clocked Circe on the back of the head with a massive branch. The woman fell in a pile of golden hair and green glitter.

No sooner did she fall than The Draugr stopped in their tracks and then sank to the ground like wilted flowers. The Mortal zombies shuddered and convulsed and then, with no magic powering them, fell uselessly to the ground with The Draugr. Taking out Circe had felled perhaps seventy five percent of The Monster's army in one brilliant move. And Tessa smiled, happy, if only for just a moment.

Maybe this was actually going to freaking work.

The zombie with the branch, which was Jeff The Shiki, then shifted into Circe's form and stepped over Circe's unconscious body and continued toward the tent without missing a beat. It looked flawless, but Tessa could hear Micah straining next to her. She worried about her friend, worried that she had asked too much of her.

Tessa nodded to Snow, who crouched with her hands buried in the earth, and began glowing, less the pale bluish-white that she usually did and more a bright shimmering white, cold and clear. She gritted her teeth, and everyone watched as crackling white energy poured down her arms and out of her hands and into the earth. The white snaked its way across the field, and then up into the constructed monsters and Franken-dogs that marched up the hill toward the tent, stepping over their fallen comrades as if they were blades of grass. Snow groaned as the white light crept up into the legs of the creatures, slowing them, then stopping them entirely, freezing them where they stood. Snow managed to grab perhaps thirty immediately. But already Tessa saw Circe stirring and she looked at Snow. Those thirty would have to be enough.

"Snow, focus on Circe!" she hissed. Snow gritted her teeth and poured even more power into the ground, directing it all at Circe's collapsed figure. The icy light enveloped the woman, lightly at first, binding her like a shimmering spider-web, and then more tightly and thickly until she appeared frozen in a solid block of ice.

In a matter of minutes, Snow had felled a good deal of The Monster's remaining army and trapped Circe. The woman was a Queen for a reason. But it had taken its toll and when Tessa looked at Snow again, she was passed out. She lay splayed across the grass like a pale grey statue. Brand looked at Tessa, panicked. And Tessa nodded her head. "In a minute," she said. She looked to the rest of her army. "You know what to do. Keep the creatures from the tent at all costs." Tessa nodded her head at Brand. "You're with me."

Tessa began running, her friends on her heels, armed and about to dive into insane battle.

It was completely surreal, even for *her* life.

Tessa, with Brand in tow, headed straight for Circe. Snow had done well and the goddess *was* well and truly frozen, but Tessa was taking no chances on The Draugr and Mortal zombies coming back into play. She removed a blue transport pebble from her pocket, precious as gold and knowing that she and Brand only had one shot.

She didn't know how Fenris had gotten it or why he had given it to her, but in truth, it was when he gave it to her that this plan had started to form. Tessa set the pebble on the frozen ice-block that was Circe, and Brand recited the words he had been learning and perfecting every time Tal arrived. He had learned them well because the sphere appeared as soon as he began speaking, and it swallowed up Circe with a flash of snapping blue light.

Tessa looked at Brand and smiled, it was working. It was actually working.

She nodded at him to go back and take care of Snow and then joined Fenris, Robin, Tal, and Hecuba in battle. Robin and Tal had run to the top of the hill and taken positions there defending the tent, sending volleys of arrows into the creatures as they climbed. Fenris, still in his human form, tore through the creatures like they were paper. Hecuba was only slightly less vicious cutting them down. Tessa glanced at the tree line to see Micah there, leaning against a tree, concentrating, as Grey stood watch over her, his sword drawn. Tessa smiled. Less than a hundred creatures, both those that had once been animals and humans, and The Monster of course, were all that stood between them and victory. She could almost taste it, and chided herself for the thought. Tessa moved toward the tent where she suspected she would find The Monster, but as she did so she looked down to see one of the frozen Mortal zombies.

It was Bishop.

FORTY-THREE

Tessa went rigid. His face, decomposed and now frozen was almost unrecognizable. But she would never forget. It was burned into her brain. Tessa stared into his lifeless eyes and was overcome with doubt. Why did she think any of this was going to work when she was staring at the corpse of her first Advocate, at her ultimate failure. All he had tried to do was help her and look what she had rewarded him with? Tessa looked across the field at her friends, fighting for their lives.

They were all going to die.

What had she been thinking?

A creature slammed into her from the side, and Tessa went down.

Her mind went blank.

The creature brought down its fist, and Tessa didn't move. A second before impact, the arm was stopped and then the arm and the creature attached to it went flying off into the darkness.

Fenris looked down at Tessa, a curious expression on his face. "Scion?" Tessa shook her head and took the hand he offered to help her up. "What happened?" he asked.

"I don't know," she said, unable to look away from Bishop's frozen face. Fenris followed her gaze.

"Your Advocate," he said, nodding, and then moved to continue on his way. When Tessa didn't move, he punched a creature closing in on them and turned to face her again. "Scion. Time to move."

Tessa shook her head hollowly. She couldn't stop looking at Bishop. She was crying. The middle of her own damn battle and she'd lost it. "I don't know what I'm supposed to be doing," she said.

Fenris smashed his fist into another creature. "Supposed to be doing? You do that a lot do you, Hardcore?"

Tessa blinked and then looked at him, her eyes clearing. "No. No, I guess not."

Fenris slammed his fist into another creature, and a growl tore from his throat. "It's the best damn thing about you. So get back to it."

Fenris walked away, stripping off his shirt and beginning to change shape. Tessa blinked and then drove her sword into the head of a dog creature in front of her, decapitating another before beginning her way toward the tent again.

When Tessa reached the top of the hill, Robin and Tal were still there, relentlessly loading arrows and hitting everything they aimed at. Tessa looked behind her to survey the field. They were doing well, comparatively. But there was a long way to go yet and Tessa had no idea what awaited her in the tent.

Tessa pulled back the door flap on the tent and Robin put a hand on her arm. "Let me come with you," he said, his voice rather desperate.

"No," Tessa said. "That's not the plan. You're here to take these out, to lead the rest of the team, to make sure we win and that nobody dies. God knows what will happen if those things get past you. That's what I need you to do."

Robin looked back at the field, his expression not particularly optimistic.

"When you finish, then sure, come on in," Tessa said smiling, her voice full of false cheer. Robin gave her a look and squeezed her arm.

"Okay then," he said loading another arrow. Tessa ducked inside, expecting to find chaos, a teeming mass of panicked teenagers in costumes, maybe being held captive by who knew what. Instead, she found only deadly silence.

It was so much worse.

Bodies littered the floor, some slumping over one another, others splayed out like art. Tessa reached down to the body closest to her and felt for a pulse. Asleep. They were all asleep. Not far from her was handsome Nash, gorgeous even while unconscious. Tessa swallowed hard. She had to be careful or who knew what would happen to him and all the rest.

In her peripheral vision, Tessa saw something move toward the back of the tent and turned her head to see The Monster emerge from behind a curtain on the stage. He had Circe (aka The Shiki) by the throat, and he was squeezing hard, if the way The Shiki was squirming under his grasp was any indication. Tessa didn't know why Micah wasn't having him shift out of Circe's form, into a snake or a bird, something that could slip away, or even a fire-breathing dragon that could burn his damn face off. And then she remembered Micah drinking the punch. She must be asleep, like the rest of them.

"Very clever, Scion," The Monster said. "Taking out Circe was indeed wise, and using her own familiar against her, ingenious. It does make things a bit more difficult for me. Of course, I do have The Shiki now, so perhaps you'd be interested in a trade?"

"For what?" Tessa asked. "I don't have anything of yours."

"You have Circe," he said, although there was a hint of a question in his voice.

Tessa shook her head. "No, I don't. I sent her back to Story. She's gone."

The Monster blinked. "Yes, very clever. Although, rather unfortunate for The Shiki," he said, squeezing more tightly and causing Jeff to let out a mangled cry. Tessa winced, it was a terrible sound. "I guess I could take you, instead."

Tessa watched The Shiki wriggle in pain, desperate and afraid. The Shiki had been her enemy not so long ago, but if things worked the way Micah said, it hadn't ever been his choice. He was part of the team now and had proved himself more than once. Besides, Micah loved him like he was part of her, which Tessa guessed he was now. She couldn't let anything happen to it, to him, to Jeff. Micah would never forgive her.

"Fine. Just let him go."

The Monster looked down at her through partially lidded, heavy eyes. "Come closer, and drop the weapons, please."

Tessa dropped her sword and the crossbow slung over her shoulder. She unstrapped the leg holster and dropped it to the ground with the rest. The Monster watched her. "Lose the jacket," he said, and Tessa shrugged it off. The Monster nodded in tacit agreement, and Tessa began walking toward the stage, stepping over and between the bodies carefully. When she was perhaps a dozen feet from the stage where The Monster stood watching her, he pulled the cord on the curtain and it fell back to reveal a huge metal wheel. Some kind of machine that was equal parts dark ages and futuristic. An elaborate mess of dials and levers, wires and tubing, but its horrible center was unmistakable—there was a place for a human body to go.

To go and be strapped in.

"Get in," he said, as if he were offering her a ride home. Tessa eyed the machine. She could guess what it did. What it would do to her and, she'd wager, to the bulk of Lore High School, unconscious at her feet. "Second thoughts?" The Monster asked, eliciting another round of cries from Jeff's throat.

"No," Tessa said evenly, swallowing her fear as best she could. She climbed the stage and stepped over the sleeping bodies of the band members, including Ian. She approached the machine tentatively. She wasn't even sure how to get inside it. The Monster eyed her.

"Perhaps you need a little help?" he offered. "My assistant can aid you." He gestured as another figure stepped out from behind the machine. From the looks of him, he could only be Dr, Frankenstein.

"Yes, he has been here all along. He's not happy about it, but a son wants his father there for his final moments of triumph."

Tessa looked at the doctor, who looked back at her rather helplessly, his hands and feet bound in heavy chains, wearing a tattered, once-white doctor's coat that someone had written "assistant" on sloppily in black marker across the pocket.

"Are you all right?" Tessa asked.

Dr. Frankenstein nodded. "But you cannot get in this machine," he said.

"Oh, but she will," The Monster said, squeezing Jeff again, who squealed.

Tessa looked at him, hard. "I said I would." Dr. Frankenstein opened a hatch-like door and Tessa stepped inside, fitting herself into the person shape at the center of the machine. The Doctor positioned her against the metal slab and locked her feet into steel stirrups, pulling her arms away from her body to lock them into position.

"Father is very proud of my work, even if he likes to pretend otherwise," The Monster said.

"I'm in. Release him," Tessa said, nodding her head at Jeff's squirming Circe form. The Monster seemed to consider it for a moment and then let go.

"I am a man of my word, if nothing else."

Jeff shifted out of Tessa's view, and Tessa could not see into what. She didn't know if Jeff would even be on her side anymore, now that Micah was likely unconscious.

This had maybe been a bad idea.

"I have been transforming my dead slowly, using corpses to create my creatures. You see this machine needs a battery, if you will, to power it. And one mortal life gives me a decent charge. But a Mortal life is limited, and I can only get perhaps half a dozen creatures from one. But you, Scion, are so much more than Mortal, and I'm excited to see how many *your* battery can transform." The Monster gestured to all the costumed, unconscious figures crowding the floor of the tent. "I'm willing to bet it will be quite a good number."

FORTY-FOUR

Brand's sole tasks for this battle had been to transport Circe back to Story with the transport bead and to get Snow out of the line of fire and into the cold to heal after she did her work. He had accomplished the first, but the second was proving to be far more difficult. She was almost too hot to carry and getting hotter by the moment, not to mention alternately delirious or unconscious and Brand was panicking. His arms burned, both the muscles inside from the effort of carrying her through uneven terrain in the woods and also quite literally where she laid across his skin. Her skin had long ago burned right through his jacket, and now her flesh seared his wherever they touched. He suspected his tux deposit would not be returned. He was afraid to put her down for fear he'd be unable to pick her up again. There was no way they were going to make it back to his house, or her penthouse, as originally planned. Brand collapsed against a tree, and her eyes fluttered open.

"So innocent," she said, trying to raise a hand to touch his face and failing.

"Snow. What happens if I can't cool you down? You can't die, right?"

Snow nodded almost imperceptibly. "Can die, just not forever," she said. Brand chewed his lip and looked around.

"How long? How can we get you back? What happens?

Snow blinked sleepily. "Few decades is all…" she said, before her head lolled to the side and she passed out again. Brand closed his eyes and laid his head back against the tree.

And then he heard it.

A slight trickle somewhere behind him. He spun and followed the sound. It was the sound of a river. He raced toward it, stumbling over branches and rocks and almost dropping Snow twice before he reached the river's edge and laid her down beside it. He plunged his hand in and yanked it out. It was cold. Very cold. He lifted Snow, groaning at the pain in his hands as they grazed her bare flesh and plunged her in the river. He held her in the stream, fully underwater, hoping she wouldn't, or couldn't, drown.

"C'mon, Snow." he said, his heartbeat loud in his ears, his arms throbbing from burns.

Grey had been slapping Micah for a full minute trying to get her to wake up when he finally remembered what he had in his pocket. He always had it with him. Ever since Juliet and he, well, ever since always, he supposed. As he cradled Micah's head and moved to uncap the vial, a small red figure came running at them, horned, with bulging eyes and a grotesquely large mouth twisted into a bizarre grin. Grey dropped the vial and picked up his sword, pointing it at the creature. The creature shuddered to a halt and then paused, as if thinking, before shifting its shape into the grey-striped tabby cat. Grey lowered the sword, and Jeff ran to Micah's side, licking at her limp hand while Grey searched the ground for the vial he'd dropped. But then Jeff hissed, his fur standing on end, and Grey turned to see two Franken-dogs stalking toward them, guttural growls rumbling about their chests.

Tessa looked at the levers as Dr. Frankenstein pulled on them and occasionally eyed The Monster, who watched them closely, never more than a few feet away. Nobody saw Fenris until he was within striking distance from the stage, in his handsome man-shape (and inappropriately naked, yet again). Tessa had never been so glad to see him, naked or not.

"Monster," he said, his voice even and charming.

"Wolf," The Monster said, nodding his head in greeting. Tessa looked from one to the other.

They didn't seem like strangers.

This didn't seem good.

The Monster narrowed his eyes at Fenris. "Do not interfere."

"I'm afraid I must," Fenris said, and Tessa's heart raced. Something was happening that she didn't understand, but the pebble of dread in her stomach was rattling powerfully.

"And why is that, Wolf?"

"I'm afraid it doesn't suit my purposes for the border to close at this moment, and so The Scion must live, for now," he mused, licking his lips and glancing at Tessa. Tessa tried to catch his eye, to read his expression, but it was as unreadable as ever. "I, of course, respect your needs, but I urge you to reconsider this course of action," he said evenly, looking back to The Monster. "Perhaps you can try again later, when our goals more closely align?"

The Monster paused, as if seriously considering the request. "No," he said finally. "You are an old and respected Story, and I've no wish to be your enemy, but I have waited long enough. A century and a half alone just for her to be born. Though I hoped to have a larger army at my disposal at this point, nothing is so ruined that I cannot still get what I desire."

"I think you'll find that is untrue," Fenris said, stalking closer to the stage. "I have been working beside her and she is—preternaturally talented, even for a Scion."

"And you've known many Scions have you?"

"Known? No. But I have killed more than my share," Fenris said, looking directly at Tessa who looked back at him, wide-eyed. She was struck by the distinct feeling that he was, as he always seemed to be, telling the truth. Tessa felt sick to her stomach and feared she might throw up. She turned her head away from both of them and clenched her eyes shut trying to ratchet down her fear.

"Truly?" The Monster said, impressed.

Fenris nodded and looked away from Tessa and back to The Monster. "This girl will be the end of you, Monster. Retire now and fight with me another day."

The Monster seemed to consider it but then shook his head. "No. The offer is tempting, Wolf, you are ever the silver-tongued beast of legend, but I'll have my will done, and I will have it now."

"Have it your way, though it will be the death of you."

"Indeed," The Monster said, turning to Tessa and staring at her. "We shall see." And Tessa watched as Fenris shifted back into his massive Wolf form and left.

He actually left her.

She couldn't believe it.

The Monster nodded his head to Dr. Frankenstein. "Do it," he said and Tessa turned to see The Doctor throw the switch on the machine forward.

FORTY-FIVE

Robin, Tal, and Hecuba were overwhelmed.

Fenris, who had been brilliant, even in Robin's estimation, sometimes literally tearing through the opposition, had of course disappeared. And with his absence the battle had shifted. Brand had escaped with Snow, as planned, but Micah was in distress and Grey was needed to protect her, so they were already down in numbers. Fenris's absence had simply tipped the scales too far. Tal cried out as she saw Hecuba suddenly buried by dog-creatures, and the terror in her voice was palpable. She ran to Hecuba's aid, leaving Robin alone near the tent. The creatures saw opportunity in it and instantly overran him. They grabbed at him, clawing and pulling him down.

And at that very moment, an unholy scream erupted from the tent, tearing through the air.

The scream was Tessa, and the creatures everywhere seemed to smile.

"Tessa!" Robin shouted, pushing toward the tent, straining valiantly but pointlessly against the wall of creatures. With nobody to left to help, he was buried under them and Tessa was left to scream.

Brand's hands, now burning from the cold of the river, from holding Snow under the water, were starting to look blue. He hoped he was imagining it, but he doubted it. And then Snow's eyes snapped open and she smiled as her face broke through the surface of the water.

"Brilliant boy," she purred, and reached out an icy hand to touch his face. Brand helped Snow out of the river, her skin now a crystalline white and almost frosty. She perched on the edge of a small boulder and pushed some hair from her face. Brand shed his burned up jacket and handed it to her, averting his eyes diplomatically. Snow looked down at her mostly naked body, her once elegant dress in tatters, and smiled at Brand as she took the jacket.

"Thank you," she said, putting it on and then clutching it closed with one hand.

"Are you all right?" he asked, hovering around her. Snow nodded and reached for his exposed arms. He watched as she laid her hands on his burns, soothing them. Both the pain of the burns and the redness receded like magic.

"I am fine," she said, her voice back to its even, almost bored tone. Brand looked back toward the battle. He had heard screaming, which he didn't think was a good thing.

"We have to go back," he said.

Snow shook her head. "No," she said. "I told the Scion that I was out after that stunt. She knew it and she agreed."

"But you're okay, you just said," Brand argued.

"I have fulfilled my obligation, Brandon," Snow said flatly, wringing out her hair.

"Snow. Please come with me. What can I do? Talk at them? I'm borderline useless in a fight, good maybe only for getting killed. You have real power, you could be the difference here. Please," Brand said, his voice plaintive but passionate. Snow looked up at him for a long moment and then stood.

"I do this for *you*, Brandon Ellis," she said, staring at him, her big blue eyes unblinking. Brand pulled back, the power of her gaze intimidating, intoxicating.

He reached out his hand to her and she took it.

Grey watched Jeff run at the Franken-dogs, and as the creature ran he shifted effortlessly from the grey housecat into a massive tiger, roaring wildly as he did so. The dogs, less dumb than they seemed, skidded to a halt and tried to reverse course, but it was too late. Jeff jumped on one, and they rolled together, a pile of orange and black, flashes of white. The second dog jumped into the mix and Jeff bellowed as it bit into his shoulder. While Jeff wrestled with the creatures, Grey located the vial and held it under Micah's nose. He waved it there for a few moments with no effect and then her eyes snapped open, big and dark and somewhat horrified.

"Jeff!" she shouted, panicked, sitting up and looking at the Shiki as it fought the dogs less than a dozen yards from where she and Grey huddled.

FORTY-SIX

As Dr. Frankenstein threw the switch on the machine, a searing pain tore through Tessa and the scream she had told herself The Monster would not get from her escaped her throat at a decibel she thought impossible. Her thoughts swam and her vision blurred, and all around her an orange glow fanned out, bathing the room in pale amber light. It took only moments for it to drift over the crowd. Even through her tears, Tessa could see her classmates changing. Bits of them fusing to their costumes, some of them fusing to one another. As the light poured over them, they undulated, transforming into something horrible and mindless.

The Monster watched, not with any kind of glee but more a clinical eye. Tessa's mind raced, but it was hard for it to land on anything except pain. She closed her eyes and begged her throat, her mouth, to be still, to be quiet. After a moment she was able to be silent, her teeth grinding together in pain. The Monster looked at her, one stitched eyebrow raised with vague interest.

"Impressive, Scion," he said. "Both what you hold and that you've managed to stop screaming. I've not seen that before."

In her peripheral vision, Tessa saw a greenish brown figure that could only be her damn Troll, but her brain was too consumed by pain to understand what it meant. She heard a shout, and then The Troll threw something at the stage. Tessa felt a small impact followed by the slightest give in the right cuff restraining her arm. Whatever The Troll had done, it had loosened the restraint. The Monster roared at The Troll, easily as confused as Tessa was, and The Troll escaped through the side of the tent, leaving a Troll-sized hole in the fabric, like a cartoon.

Tessa pressed her eyes closed and concentrated with everything she had. "LA COLOMBE NOIRE!" she screamed, her voice ripping at the air. The Monster blinked at her, as the crackle and pop of The Black Dove bathed the room in blue for just an instant. The axe snapped into her hand and Tessa squinted her eyes, sending all her remaining strength to her right arm. She wrenched her wrist free of the cuff in one horrible yank. In that same movement, she hurled the axe at The Monster. It landed in his chest with such force that it sent him stumbling backwards. He blinked at it, sticking out of him for just a moment before it disappeared, and then he fell backwards off the stage.

Dr. Frankenstein leapt to his feet and turned off the machine. Tessa nearly fell out of it, she was so weak. She felt like passing out as he un-cuffed her left arm, but as she looked at her classmates on the ground, a cold fear gripped her. It was too late for many of them, already transformed and strangely inhuman. They were now some abominable blend of science and magic, Mortal and Story that Tessa couldn't even understand.

The new creatures started to move, undulating like a living, monstrous carpet. As Tessa tried to stand, her legs gave out. Even if she could fight them she didn't know if she should, they had been human and innocent mere moments ago.

Tessa looked at Dr. Frankenstein who also stared at the crowd in shock, horrified and guilty. Tessa turned to him. "Can you reverse it?"

"What?"

"Can you change the machine to reverse it?"

The Doctor looked down stupidly at the machine, "Yes. But—"

"But what?!" Tessa demanded.

"But it will still have to be powered by…something," he said, casting his eyes to the side. Tessa got up the rest of the way.

"I know," she said, climbing back into the machine. "Just do it."

The Doctor leaned over the machine, adjusting levers and wires.

"You've got to strap me in, otherwise, I don't think I can stay still." Tessa warned, looking at the restraints.

"Are you sure about this, Scion?"

"There's no other way. Just do it, or all these people are going to die."

Dr. Frankenstein leaned down and locked in her feet and then her left arm. The right cuff was broken, so she'd have to leave the one arm free.

"Hurry." Tessa said, unable to take her eyes off her inhuman classmates.

The Doctor looked up at her, his eyes wild. "It's ready," he said.

"Then do it," she said.

The same pain ripped through Tessa, and she was a second time unable to resist screaming. A bluish light poured out of the machine this time, rolling over the frozen crowd. Seconds turned into agonizing minutes, and Tessa managed to swallow some of her screams.

Tessa squeezed her eyes shut and clenched her jaw. And then the pain stopped. As quickly as it had begun. Tessa opened her eyes to see The Monster standing above her, his gaze drifting across the crowd as it returned to normal again, falling into little unconscious, but human, piles.

"What have you done, father?" he asked, his voice cold and sad, defeated. Tessa reached over and unlocked her left hand with her right and then called her axe and chopped at both leg braces, hoping she didn't miss and chop off her own damn foot. She stepped out of the machine, placing herself between The Monster and Dr. Frankenstein.

"Back up," she said as The Monster advanced on them. She didn't know if she had the strength to lift the axe above her head, but she wasn't about to let him know that.

"Father, were you not proud? Not even a little?" The Monster asked, as if Tessa wasn't even there.

Dr. Frankenstein hung his head in shame, and Tessa looked between them.

"Sorry, Doc," she said, shrugging, and then punched Dr. Frankenstein in the face, knocking him out.

The Monster hadn't wanted to do any of this without Dr. Frankenstein here to witness it. Tessa didn't think knocking Frankenstein out would stop The Monster's plans, but maybe if he was attached enough to the idea of his father watching the master plan unfold it would at least slow him down.

Tessa shrugged as The Monster looked at her, a glimmer of confusion in his eyes.

Suddenly, The Monster reared up and caught Tessa under the chin with his massive, frying pan-sized fist. She flew a dozen feet in the air and at least as many backwards, landing on the edge of the stage. Tessa crawled to her knees just as a giant black boot came at her midsection, lifting her several feet off the ground. Tessa landed on her stomach, gasping and trying to catch her breath. Every hit was like being hit by a truck. Tessa rolled over just as he brought his black boot down toward her face. Tessa caught it mere inches from her face and pushed him backwards. He stumbled off-balance but righted himself before Tessa could get to her feet.

She was not feeling her usual superhero self thanks to the machine, although with his strength, she wasn't sure it mattered. Tessa heard gunshots in the distance and worried for one moment what was going on outside the tent before his giant palm connected with her face and sent her sliding across the stage like a rag doll.

FORTY-SEVEN

Brand and Snow stumbled to the edge of the trees.

Things did not look good. Though they'd whittled the army of creatures down impressively, a still formidable army remained and it surrounded Micah and the others. Brand looked at Snow in desperation. She looked back at him and shook her head.

"No," she said as if reading his mind. "I don't have enough left to help, I'm sorry." He could tell from her eyes and the flush in her skin that she was tapped. He thought she might even actually be sorry about it.

"I have to go," he said, and she nodded in understanding. He didn't have any weapons though; he'd lost his Katana somewhere between sending Circe away and carrying Snow off the battlefield.

"Here," Snow said. She held out her hand, and it glowed a fierce white for a few moments. When the glow subsided she was holding a long blade of ice. Brand reached for it but it was so cold that touching it was like touching fire. He tore off the sleeve of his shirt and wrapped it around the hilt so he could carry it. "Be careful," she said, "It's sharp," before passing out on the grass. He looked at her for just a moment and then ran toward the circle where his friends were surrounded.

Though there were only perhaps a dozen creatures left, which should have been manageable, they had just been pushed too far, fought too long. And the result was a badly injured Shiki that could not maintain its dangerous tiger shape and kept shifting back into a housecat, a giant limping dog, two marksmen out of arrows, a tragic hero with a critical stomach wound, and a sublime, barely conscious, unarmed drummer.

But all they needed was a final push to get through to the end, and who knew that would be in the form of a nerdy storyteller with a sword of ice? Brand crept up behind the largest of the creatures and sliced its head off with his ice sword before anyone on either side knew what was happening.

That was all it took to galvanize them to a final battle cry, whether to their deaths, or glory, or both.

Tessa regained consciousness as The Monster lifted her off the stage floor as if she weighed no more than a few blades of grass. He threw her across the stage where she bounced once before stopping. Tessa looked up at him as he walked toward her. "If you kill me now, you're just going to be trapped in *this* world," Tessa said, her voice wavering.

The Monster stopped quite suddenly and looked down at her, puzzled. "Scion, I'm afraid you've rather missed the point."

Tessa's muscles shuddered as she tried to get up. "Oh yeah?" she asked, her voice far more confident than the rest of her.

"I don't want your world," he said. "I mean, yes, I would have taken it, that was Plan B, but do you know how complicated that would have been? I couldn't create the zombies fast enough to get a real apocalypse going, and really, they're mindless, soulless things. Who wants to live in a world of only that? Plus, Circe? I couldn't trust her. No. If you hadn't undone my plan tonight, someone would have eventually, maybe even your Mortal military. They would not have been able to kill me, but as you said, with you dead it would have just left me trapped in your world, more alone than ever. And I'm sorry to say, but your world looks very much like my own, though your technology is quite enjoyable."

"Then, what?" Tessa asked confused, her muscles still refusing to obey her.

"Silly child. Plan A was simply death. My own. I want sweet oblivion and in it, the freedom of final release. But you are no killer, not really. I knew I would have to push you to the absolute edge. You would never grant me the death I seek without me driving you there. You needed to believe that I would take your world, would kill all that resided here, including all your friends, only then would you release me."

"You've wanted me to kill you all along," Tessa said, the enormity of it washing over her.

"Yes. In my own Story, I am granted the promise of death. But there is no hope for me, really. It's all just artifice. A cruel trick of creation. I have no power over my destiny, I remain forever an outsider, shunned and feared, with no place to call home, no respite from being hunted, a monster to all who encounter me. Though you are beautiful and not at all hideous, you are saddled with many of my same challenges, especially for one so young.

"I thought you of all creatures might understand my plight, that you would grant me my release. See, like me, Scion, you live in two worlds but will never be accepted by either. If the Mortals ever find out who you are, you will never be safe from them. Stories already know who you are and fear you for the unholy creature you are. It's the same for me, with the living and the dead.

"Of course you are very pretty. You can pass, unlike me, for a time at least. But it won't last. And you know that the truth. You know inside that you will never again fit in, if you ever did. So have some mercy. Free me from my prison. Can you say you wouldn't want the same?"

Tessa heard the shots before she saw them, but they ripped through his chest as ineffectually as if they were shooting a paper target. They must have hurt though, because he turned in a fury and lunged at Detective Wade, standing less than ten feet from him on the stage. He smacked her with one of his pan-sized hands, and she instantly went down.

"No!" Tessa shouted, and willed herself up and moving toward them. The Monster held up a hand.

"She's alive, Scion, but I can easily change that," he said, turning to face Tessa and placing one of his tree-trunk-like boots precariously on Wade's neck. All he had to do was step forward and he would crush her like warm butter. Tessa's heart hammered in her chest, and she choked on a cry of pain and disbelief.

Detective Wade was her Advocate.

FORTY-EIGHT

Tessa looked from Wade's unconscious form under The Monster's boot and tried to meet his eyes. She couldn't stop the tears that rolled off her cheeks at the thought of The Monster killing Wade, of failing to save another Advocate in the same way she had failed Bishop.

"Please don't do this. I, I need her."

The Monster looked at Wade's peaceful face and then back to Tessa. "It is your move, Scion." His face softened. "This is a simple thing."

"But it's not," Tessa cried. "I read your Story. It's beautiful, it's important. If I kill you, that will disappear. And it will damn your people."

"What do I care about important novels? It's my *life*. And not just my life, it's the ability to be in charge of my own destiny. What happens to me—a person, even a Story—we should all be allowed to make that call ourselves."

Tessa shuddered and looked down at Wade. Somehow his answer was more horrifying for sounding like something she believed in. Tessa looked back up at him, her eyes sad and conflicted.

The Monster looked down at Tessa's beaten and bloody frame. "You have taken away the privilege of having my father look on as I surpass him, as I create a new world for myself, one he can never again touch, but I do not blame you. You're full of honor and goodness. These are things to be proud of. I wish I had more of them myself. But still, you must release me. You must free me now. Your own code demands it. I have killed many of your Mortal people, and I will kill this one too."

Tessa bowed her head. "I can't…"

The Monster blinked at her. "You must, Scion. It's not a choice."

"It is!" Tessa said, angry now. "Don't you see, you do have choice, you have it right now. To *not* do these things, to go on, as you are, to be better despite all that has been set against you. You have the power to prove them all wrong." Tessa stepped closer to him, her voice desperate.

"No. It's not possible. It's too long. It's too hard. It's too lonely. You are seventeen, you have no concept of centuries, let alone the idea of infinity. You are kind to want to spare me despite all I have done, but the kindness I would ask for is a quick death. Release me from my suffering."

"You don't know what you're asking," Tessa said.

The Monster laughed, a strange lonely sound. "A quick chop with your lovely axe should do it, girl."

"That's not what I mean," Tessa said, looking up at him. "This isn't just about you. If I give you this, it changes the Mortal world in important ways that

I don't fully understand, it leaves everyone from your world stranded and homeless, wandering for eternity, the same fate you hope to escape. And for me—selfishly for me—it's like admitting that I can't ever win in this."

"I see what you mean," The Monster said, and reached out toward Tessa's face as if he wanted to touch her, but he pulled back before he did. "I'm sorry about the scar," he said, his voice genuine and terribly human. "That was a mistake, I didn't mean to scar you."

Tessa brushed tears from her cheek roughly. "I won't do it."

"Then I will kill this one," The Monster said.

Tessa looked at Wade again, still unconscious under The Monster's boot. He could snap her neck with a simple twist of his ankle. Just like Bishop. There was a long silence between them, and The Monster moved slightly.

"Don't," Tessa said quietly, choking on the word.

"Then give me what I crave, Scion."

Tessa closed her eyes. "LA COLOMBE NOIRE!" she shouted, and The Black Dove materialized in her hand. She looked at The Monster and gripped the axe with both hands.

Tessa pulled the axe back and swung it with all her strength at The Monster, never breaking the gaze between them. The axe sailed through him, almost as if he wasn't there.

There was a flash of bright light and then he was there before her on the stage.

Undone.

Split in two, and never to be put back together again.

It was done. He was gone. And with him, an important Story, a tragic figure that no one would ever know. Tessa felt the loss like she had cut off one of her own limbs. He had taken so much more from her than she had imagined.

She knelt down next to Wade to feel her pulse. She was unconscious but alive. Tessa looked at the far end of the tent to see her friends, badly banged up, but alive—Micah, Brand, Robin, Grey, Shiki Jeff, even Snow, Tal, and Hecuba.

But Tessa couldn't bring herself to feel like they had won. Everything inside her was hollow.

FORTY-NINE

Inside the tent, some people were starting to come to and Tessa and her friends hobbled outside, aching and bleeding,

Outside was a bloody battlefield, the aftermath of nothing less than a small war.

"Oh God," Tessa said, looking at the mess. "How are we—" And as if to answer the unasked questions, a crackling blue doorway appeared. Tessa's heart sank with an inner cry of 'What now?!'

Morgana stepped out of the doorway but did not close it. Tessa narrowed her eyes at the woman. "What are you doing here?"

"I was urged to come, to clean up your mess," Morgana said.

"Yeah, thanks for showing up *after* the last curtain call," Tessa snapped.

"It is in the best interest of Story that the Mortal world does not know of our existence, but you have made quite a mess, Scion, and so we offer our help. Do you want it or not?"

"Yes," Tessa said, gritting her teeth and swallowing both anger and pride. "What can you do?"

"For starters," Morgana said, casting a hand over the field. "A decent glamour. It will hold up to the casual observer." And Tessa watched as the scene before her became a perfect green field again, free of blood and bodies, appearing as it had been just a couple hours ago. Innocent and clean. Tessa blinked at it.

"And?" Tessa urged.

"The Draugr I can call home now that Circe is out of the picture. They do not want to be here, and have been unnaturally brought here, so that will resolve itself naturally," she said, closing her eyes and lifting one hand that glowed faintly with power. The mindless Norse husks reappeared on the field, reanimated once again, and walked as if sharing one mind toward Morgana's doorway, looking like weary soldiers headed home.

As the last of The Draugr disappeared through the doorway, a small, unarmed army came through. Tessa gripped her axe more tightly, but they merely scuttled about the field cleaning up the creature's bodies and taking them through the portal too. Tessa winced because some parts of those creatures were Mortals, but she couldn't explain what had happened to them and she didn't think seeing what they had become as corpses would bring anyone peace, so she bit her tongue.

"The human zombies should stay here," Tessa said, thinking of all the empty mortal graves throughout the city. Thinking of Bishop.

"I agree," Morgana said stiffly, and then adjusted her stance. "This is more difficult. It takes much power, and I must take it from somewhere. To ask something so great of magic, you have to give something as well. Magic is nothing if not a transfer of energy." Her face set into a hard line and Tessa looked at her anxiously. She sensed she was about to be asked for something. Morgana stared Tessa down. "Fortunately for you, Scion, you have, much to my surprise, made a few friends along the way, and someone has offered to share her energies, to make such an ask possible."

Tessa opened her mouth to ask who but knew it was The White Lady, and so she closed her mouth again and whispered a silent thank you in the hopes The Lady could hear her.

Morgana's brow creased and sweat broke out across her pretty skin. Story words came out of her mouth in a series of melodic and then clipped sentences. Some of them sounded beautiful, some cruel. The bodies began to reappear gradually on the field, some grotesque and maimed, some as they had always been. And then slowly, one by one, they vanished, as if they had never existed.

"What did you—" Brand said, his mouth hanging open.

"I returned them to where they belong," Morgana said, her voice breathy.

The effort had clearly cost her, even with help. Now, instead of looking power-hungry and mean, she seemed kittenish and almost sick. She raised her hand to the sky a last time and clouds gathered, fast and furious above them. "You have five minutes before a downpour the likes of which you have never seen fills this field. A cleansing rain, if you will," she said simply, and then, turning to Robin. "I understand you are returning to where you belong." Robin nodded curtly. Morgana didn't answer him and only turned away. She looked at Tessa as she walked with noticeable effort to the doorway. "Don't make such a mess next time, Scion. We will not always be able, or willing, to clean up your messes."

Tessa felt a silent rage that Morgana was so powerful and yet had let them flail and struggle, alone. "Unbelievable," she said under her breath.

"Excuse me, Scion? Something to add?" Morgana asked, seeming to gather her strength back to her.

"Damn right," Tessa seethed.

"By all means," Morgana said, clearly steeling herself for whatever was to come.

"Look at the power you have! Why didn't you help us? You clearly could have made all the difference. Instead people have died while you, what? Did nothing?!?! I can't believe you!"

Morgana hooded her eyes at Tessa. "You know why I didn't help you, Scion? Why we all didn't? Because it's not our job. It's not our destiny. It's yours. And if you would take it more seriously, if you had let others help you when they first offered, maybe your body count would be lower."

Morgana turned to go again. Tessa lunged forward, but Robin reached out and put a hand on her arm and then just wrapped her up into an embrace.

"You did so good," he whispered into her hair.

Tessa opened her mouth to speak, to beg him not to leave, but nothing came out. Robin pressed something into her hand. She looked down to find a silver talisman on a heavy silver chain. An unfamiliar coat of arms was engraved on one side with some Story words on the other.

"What's this?"

"You can use it to call Talia while I'm gone."

Tessa scrunched up her face. "Talia?"

"Tal. Call her when you have a Story you need her to take home. Promise me. She won't like it, but she'll come because it's the right thing to do."

Tessa breathed deeply and then nodded in agreement. He pulled her into him again, kissing her head, breathing her in. "Please don't leave me," Tessa said, and a sob lodged in her throat made her voice sound awkward and strange to her.

"You'll be okay, I know it," he whispered.

"It's too fast," Tessa said, her voice breaking, "Way too fast."

"I'll come back. I promise."

"Because you're a hero," she said, almost sullen.

"Nah, for love," he said, smiling and squeezing her more tightly, burying his face in her neck. Tessa swallowed another sob. When she pulled away from him, he drew her back closer again and kissed her.

She tried so hard to pretend it wasn't the last.

Tessa closed her eyes as he let go and when she opened them she caught a last glimpse of his face as walked backward through the glowing doorway. It snapped closed once he was inside with a finality that physically pained Tessa.

No sooner had the doorway disappeared then people started to come out of the tent, disoriented and confused. Detective Ripley and Captain West were trying to calm everyone down but looked easily as confused as the crowd even though they tried to hide it.

A roll of thunder sounded far away.

"Gas leak, everyone! Please remain calm," West shouted.

Ripley nodded, adding, "There are ambulances on the way to check everyone out."

Tessa did, in fact, hear ambulances in the distance.

She looked at her friends. They were badly banged up. Brand was missing one of the arms to his dress shirt and was half-holding up Snow (wearing only Brand's tuxedo jacket, which Tessa was definitely going to have to get the story on later); Jeff was curled up possessively on Micah's shoulder as the tiny green gecko, and Micah held her broken glasses in her hand, her pretty dress torn rather to bits; Grey's clothes weren't in much better shape and he held his hand over a stomach wound that was healing with impressive speed.

"Can you guys get home?"

Grey nodded, "We have my car."

Tessa gestured to his wound. "Do you need a hospital?"

Grey smiled thinly and held up his hand. "No, it's almost healed."

Tessa looked at Snow and then up at Brand, "You can take care of her?"

Brand nodded and Micah joined him. "Yeah, we got it," she said. "What about you? Aren't you coming with us?"

"No, I—" Tessa looked back toward the tent. "I want to go check on Detective Wade."

"Wade?" Brand wrinkled his nose.

Tessa kicked at the ground. "She's the Advocate."

"Holy shit," Micah said, and everyone looked at her and smiled.

"Yeah. That's about right," Tessa said.

Everyone stood in shock for a moment, and then Micah reached up and hugged Tessa. "I know you did good. I know we can't understand it all, because we don't remember everything, because there's a big black hole now where a bunch of knowledge used to be, but I know you did the right thing," she whispered.

"Thanks, Mike," Tessa said. Lightning flashed in the sky followed by a clap of thunder and Tessa looked up at the heavy low clouds. "Get out of here before it starts," she said.

They nodded and headed down the hill toward the park entrance, Snow balanced between them. Brand turned the three of them back to Tessa before they had gone too far.

"Pancakes at your house, tomorrow," he said.

"Okay," she said, smiling.

"Tomorrow," they all said, again.

Tessa watched her friends until they were out of sight. How she could feel simultaneously so lucky and absolutely jinxed she wasn't sure.

"Battle?"

Tessa turned around to see Detective Wade standing in front of her. Just great, just what she needed tonight, to be arrested for murder. That would really cap the night off perfectly. Tessa wanted to snap at her, but now that she was her Advocate, she just couldn't bring herself to do it.

"Hello, Detective."

"I—" Wade stopped short, as if unsure. Tessa looked at her more closely. She was different. Less aggressive. Maybe the unexplainable stuff she'd seen tonight had frightened her. Maybe she remembered that Tessa had saved her life. That seemed like too much to hope for. Wade examined Tessa, bruised and bleeding. "Are you alright?"

Tessa nodded, "I'll live. Thanks for asking."

Wade shook her head, and her face returned to bewilderment. "I think maybe we need to talk."

"Okay," Tessa was cautious.

Wade looked around uncomfortably, Ripley and West not far away. "Not here. Can I come by your house sometime?"

"Will you be arresting me when you do?"

"No. This will be about something else," she said.

"Okay then." Tessa said. She reached into the inside pocket of her jacket and pulled out the necklace Bishop's grandmother had given her. "This is yours," she said, holding it out to Wade.

Wade shook her head. "That's not mi—" and stopped short, her eyes flashing with something that was almost recognition. She reached out and let Tessa put the necklace in her hand. She stared at it. "You sure this is mine?"

Tessa watched her examining it. "Feels like it is," she said. Wade nodded and started to walk away.

"Get home Battle, looks like it's going to storm," she said, walking away, staring at the necklace linked through her fingers.

"You have no idea." Tessa said.

Wade looked up at the sky just as the rain began to come. She slipped the necklace into her pocket and ran the rest of the way to Ripley, West, and the crowds, slipping easily back into "cop mode."

Tessa had decided after seeing The White Lady that she wasn't going to foist this life on The Advocate when she found them.

It had to be their choice.

But Tessa really hoped that Wade would *want* to know, would *want* to have her eyes opened. Tessa sure could use the help, not to mention another friend and ally, especially one that didn't have complicated Story allegiances.

An adult that knew what was going on with her and cared about things other than disappearing dishtowels couldn't hurt either.

Fat raindrops hit Tessa's jacket and seeped into her scalp through her hair.

Tessa turned to go home, but as she did she saw a pair of flashing yellow eyes in the woods.

Fenris.

 FIFTY

The Troll beside Fenris drew back further into the trees.

"Go," Fenris said.

The Troll hesitated, looking between The Wolf and The Scion in the distance. Fenris growled a warning at him, and The Troll disappeared into the brush. Fenris watched Tessa as she walked to him in the rain, and he noticed that she did not let her axe disappear but kept a tight hold on it.

"So I guess you really are The Big Bad Goddamn Wolf," Tessa said when she was a few feet from him.

"I never said otherwise, luv."

"True enough. But now that you've left me to die, or perhaps worse, we're going to have a new relationship, you and me," Tessa said evenly, trying to control her rage.

"That's too bad," he said, and Tessa shot him a look. His eyes were calm, warm even.

"I don't know why I ever trusted you," Tessa whispered.

"I never told you to trust me."

"But you saved my life. A few times. Why?"

"It suited me at the time."

"And now?"

"It still suits me," he said, ticking his head to the side, watching her.

"But you left me there, to be tortured, for those people to be transformed, for The Monster to kill me," Tessa said, her voice wavering.

"I knew he couldn't kill you," he paused, and then smiled broadly. "And I was right."

What made you so sure? You've seen other Scions die, you said you killed them."

He didn't respond.

"How many Scions have you killed?"

He looked away from her for just a moment and then back. He caught her eyes and spoke clearly. "Six."

Tessa's stomach flip-flopped and a wave of dread passed over her.

Six.

"That's it," she said. "You're out."

"Out?" Fenris asked, feigning innocence.

"Skulking around, acting like one of the gang, it's over. I've been defending you to Robin, Snow, even Micah and Brand. All this time I've been on your side when I should have been shutting you out, listening to my friends."

"You're kidding yourself if you don't think every single Story in your life doesn't have an agenda, Scion," Fenris said, edging a half circle around her, something more animal than usual about his movements and that always annoying hypnotic truth to his words.

"I'm not concerned about everyone else right now, Wolf, I'm concerned about you," Tessa said, hard and flat.

Fenris bristled. It was the first time she'd called him Wolf. Others, especially Stories, used it freely, but she never had.

It unsettled him.

And it further unsettled him that it unsettled him.

He pushed toward her, so close that they were touching. This time she didn't back down or step away. She held his gaze and didn't blink.

"You shouldn't be so judgmental, Scion," he breathed, drinking her in. "You do realize, of course, that for Stories, *you* are The Big Bad Wolf. The monster that lives under the bed. The horror story that they tell to their children. We're the same, you and me. Outcasts, villains, cautionary tales, the things that go bump in the night, creatures that can never fit in, never be accepted. I've been waiting for you for a long time, and here you are. We're exactly the same you and me."

Tessa didn't edge back an inch, though his words felt like they were cutting her to ribbons inside. "I'm not killing you today because I owe you. Despite your betrayal, you've saved my life, the lives of my friends, and for that you get a pass. *Today.*"

"Today," he echoed, amused.

Tessa turned from him and walked away. "I see you again and *this* cautionary tale is going to end yours." She paused and looked back at him over her shoulder. "You've killed six Scions, but I'm the fucking Storykiller, and I will grind you into dust."

Tessa didn't look back.

She walked through the cold relentless rain as crowds scattered in the distance.

The Monster had forced her to abandon all her beliefs, Robin had deserted her, Fenris has switched sides or maybe just revealed who he had been all along, and her new Advocate was someone that mostly hated her.

Though she had ultimately saved the day, Tessa felt raw and exposed. And more alone than ever.

Fenris's words reverberated in her head. As always, they had the painful weight of truth.

It wasn't a cleansing rain she walked through. It was a clarifying one.

She was a monster.

FIGHT YOUR FICTION

EPILOGUE

Sophia's ability to view the battle in Lore ended abruptly as her daughter cut off The Monster's head in one smooth stroke.

Sophia cried out as the picture that floated before her in the pool vanished. The Monster was dead and thus her temporary link to the Mortal world had been severed. She closed her eyes and let out a breath she didn't realize she had been holding.

Tessa was safe.

The Monster, working from his own playbook instead of theirs for a long time now, had worried her. He had been sent to test The Scion and to bring her back to Story alive, but it had become clear almost immediately that he'd always had his own plans.

Sophia whispered thanks to the gods that his plan had been to take his own life and not Tessa's.

None of this would please The Doctor though.

Sophia would have to think of a way to tell him. She would accentuate the positive—Tessa was still alive and thus their plans had not been thwarted—only delayed.

She would have to offer him something to draw his focus though.

Sophia wrung her hands together and went to her desk. She pored over some of her books that laid open, piled on top of one another, scrolls rolling off the desktop and onto the stone floor.

She would have to give him Tessa's father, or at least promise that she could finally get him. He was hidden with powerful magic, but her spells had been slowly chipping away at that magic and she felt sure she would have him within her grasp in a few more weeks. And then she could send something, something powerful to bring him back here, even if he didn't want to come.

The Doctor had nothing but horrors prepared for the man, but if it meant saving Tessa's life then she would give up his without a thought.

"Jagan!"

Sophia shot upright and closed one of her books. She picked up another and hurried from the room toward his voice, the book pressed protectively to her chest.

"Jagan!" He called again and then turned to see her in the doorway. He reached out his arm to her. "Ah! There you are. How are things going with our little project?"

Sophia's voice wavered a moment and then she found it. "A failure, I'm afraid. The Monster is dead, The Scion beheaded him as he demanded. Circe was returned to Story, though I doubt they could hold her. She'll make contact soon, I'm sure. The Scion lives, as do all her friends."

He closed the distance between them and put a hand tenderly to her cheek. She nuzzled into him.

"Ah, Jagan. She is still alive. That's good. And we must take our small wins when we can. Failure is what we deserve, I suppose, for trusting a Monster to do our work. We will be more careful next time."

"About that," Sophia began. And then noticed his clothing, stained with dark blood though his hands remained clean. "I didn't think to ask…*your* work?"

"A failure too, I'm afraid," he said, shaking his head and returning to his desk, the white hair around his face glowing in the light almost like a halo. Sophia swallowed her fear and waited for what she knew was coming. "We're going to need your daughter soon, Jagan."

"What about her father instead?"

He turned back to her. "You've found him?"

"Almost," she said, clutching at the book.

"Excellent," he said, nodding.

Sophia breathed a sigh of relief tinged in guilt. How had things become so complicated? She had come to Story with only her daughter's future in mind, and everything had gone so wrong.

There were no paths left to her now that were not bathed in blood.

"Jagan."

Sophia looked up at him. He took the book from her, set it on the operating table and embraced her.

"Don't be somber, Jagan," he said, softly and without malice. "You are Jaganmata. You are the mother of the world. Your daughter is a triumph. She is a credit to her race. With our help she will be the god she was always intended to be, you and she, mother and daughter, gods. She will be but the first of many, the martyr that gives rise to something so much better, so much stronger, so much more beautiful than any of us could ever imagine. But these things cannot be rushed. We must take the long view. Patience is our greatest weapon."

Sophia smiled. When he said it like this, it was easy to believe that he was right. His vision was so clean and clear, she had once believed it with all of her being. But finally seeing Tessa these last weeks, and after so many years, it had become harder to think about killing her daughter, no matter what beauty it might bring into the world, no matter how it might assure Tessa's role, her place in history.

"I know you're right. We are on the side of righteousness."

"We are indeed. And because of that we will triumph. Righteousness is always destined to triumph." He took her face in his hands, "We will write our own history, Jagan. And it all ends when we say it ends."

ACKNOWLEDGMENTS

First and foremost to my family – Mom, Dad, Scott, and Dave, who are kind of like winning the lottery when it comes to families. Also to Shelti, the best sister-in-law one could hope for and of course Luke, my nephew, who is clearly a brilliant adorable genius far better than any other child on Earth. Infinity, no backsies, etc.

Thanks to Miriam Kriss, Susan Solomon, and Christine Cuddy who all stuck with me even when others "didn't get it." I'm eternally grateful for their belief and encouragement at every crossroad.

As always, you would not have this book without the astounding help of my good friends and writing group "The 33rd Street Writing Collective" (we remain fancy!)—Sarah Ulicny, Marta Ficke, Jon LaPearl, and Rob Bieselin. Big thanks are also due to exceptional beta readers outside of the collective: Erin Jade Lange, Ross Campbell, Lewis Smith, Matthew Branin, and Arturo Diaz.

Editor Kristy King with her sharp eyes and brilliant suggestions was a godsend in whipping this puppy into publishable shape. To the fine people at Four Colour Print Group (especially Bekah and Sean!) that helped put the gorgeous printed edition into your hands, and Max Bliss who did the e-book formatting.

Artist Stephanie Hans for a second time brought me the most striking and powerful cover a writer could dream up for her book. And impossibly huge thanks to the illustrators of Storykiller: Kris Anka, Thomas Boatwright, Ben Caldwell, Ross Campbell, Renae De Liz & Ray Dillon, Ming Doyle, Caanan Grall, Stephanie Hans, Rebekah Isaacs, Cassandra James, Stacey Lee, Meredith McClaren, Dustin Nguyen, Declan Shalvey & Jordie Bellaire, Matthew Southworth, Noelle Stevenson, Kyla Vanderklugt, Brett Weldele, and Jake Wyatt. All were so generous in giving their time to this project, I'll forever be in their debt.

To stalwart advocates and friends: Jose Rodriguez, Keegan Xavi, Ross Campbell, Meredith McClaren, Rebekah Isaacs, Josh Chaplinsky, Sue, Nick Moceri, Jason Grimes, Kyle Smith, Paige Adamczyk, Jessica Kuiken, Karen Mahoney, Brian Wood, Scott Snyder, Alexa, Oona, & Alasdair, The Hahn, The Miner Clan, Karen Gache, and Brooke Gardner.

Spelled right! YES.

Special thanks to Richard Cameron, former boss and always friend. Even on my worst day in New York I have to be glad I came here, because otherwise how would I have known you?

Last but certainly not least, thanks to Adam, my best friend and partner in all things, I'd say he's my rock in stormy seas or some such nonsense but that's just a cliché, right?

Still, it's true.

THANK YOU KICKSTARTER BACKERS

A Borst, A. E. Rhynes, A.I. Ruiz, A.K. Leonard, Aaron, Aaron Costello, Aaron Egely, Aaron Hunter, Aaron Lime, Adam Kennedy, Adam Massimiano, Adam Nadeau, Adam Snowball, Adam Sypnier, Adam T, Adam VDL, Adam Whitcomb, Adrian Lilley, Aerynn Viruet, Agentrose, Ahmed Bhuiyan, AJ Howard, AJ Jordan, Ajdan Adem, Al-X Melchor, Alain Atxa, Alan Evans, Alan Ralph, Albert Lei, Aleksandar Jankovic, Alessandra Ribeiro, Alex Amos, Alex Girard, Alex Hunt, Alexander L Martin, Alexander von David, Alexandria Gray, Ali Grotkowski, Alicia K., Allan Park, Allen Wilkins, Allison "alliartist" Thomas, Allison Wisniewski, Allyson P, Alvin Dantes, Aly Cat, Aly Caviness, Alyssa Eng, Alyxandra O'Brien, Amanda Clare Lees, Amanda Evans, Amanda Johnson, Amanda Leigh Sauter, Amanda Lodi, Amanda McPeck, Amazon Lea, Amber Loveless, Amethyst246, Amy Chop, Amy Chu, Amy Lewis, Amy N Diegelman, Amy Jay & Zoe, AN Bengco, Ana Freseman, Andrea Raptor Smith, Andreas Bodensohn, Andreas Gustafsson, Andreas Hegemann, Andrew Belding, Andrew Bomberry, Andrew Corbett, Andy Haigh, Andyv112, Angela Capel, Angela Graham, Angela O., Angelo "Bubba" Gray, Angie Batgirl, Anika Guldstrand, Ann Lemay, Anna Daniell Annabeth Leong, Anne Haney, Annie Fitzgerald, Annie M., Annika Quint, anonymous, Antonio Dickerson, Anyika Butterfly, April Daniels, Araceli, Aram Zucker-Scharff, Ardid, Ariana Maher, Arysta, Ashley Berry, Ashley M Kingham, Ashley Miller, Ashley Peckford, Ashlie Foreman, Ashlie Witherspoon, Aspasia, Atalaya, Audrey Schroeder, Aunt Mary & Uncle Laird, Austin Bantel, Austyn Nelson, Avery "Rad Dude" Evans, Aymeric P., Ayo B., Parran, B. Pressly, Bailey, Barbara Paier, Becca Read, Becky, Becky Cloonan, Becky Marie, Bel Tomov, Ben Cohen, Ben Meginnis, Benedict Durbin, Benny Singh, Beth A. Lawhead, Beth Damone, Beth Revis, Bethany D., bibi faith, Billie Barker Pritchard, Billy Chiam, Blair Mason, Blair Mueller, Blake Michaud, Blake Skidmore, Bob Cairns, Bobby Hazelton, Bogdan Coman, bonnie may, boxscorehaiku, Brad Nicholls, Brad Richardson, Bradley Grehan, Braeden Jones, Brandon 'Link' Copp-Millward, Brandon Eaker, Brandon Lee, Brandon Schatz, Brandon Thomas, Brandon Vessey, Brenda Le,

Brenda Sohn, Brendan Sheehan, Brendan T., Brent Day, Brett P., Bri Rudd, Brian Baggett, Brian Burston, Brian Caffrey, Brian Cronin, Brian G., Brian Groth, Brian J., Brian K. Pittman, Brian Keohan, Brian Lyons, Brian Truitt, Brian Wood, Briana Riggs, Bridget A. Natale, Britt M Jernigan Jr., Britta Rogowski Brittanie O., Brittany Miller, Brodie Powter, Brontis Shane Orengo, Bruce Howat, Bryan Q. Miller, Budarbot, C. Adams, C.R, Cacau M. Grando, Caitlin Eve Rosendorn, Caitlin Walker, Callum James Francis Espie, Calum Chisholm, Cameron D., Camryn Neilson, Candice Casas, Caritas89, Carl Rigney, Carly Kocurek, Carmen Plumb, Carol Darnell, Carol Sheldon-Ybarra, Caroline Sharp, Carolyn Kniga, Carolyn Reid, Carson Rizor, Carsten Immel, Cassandra Hipple, Cassandra Rose, Caterina Pryde, Catherine Dobbs, Catherine Moran, Cat Young, Catie Coleman, Cavan Leigh, CC, CJ, Cecilia Hudson, Ced Pharaoh, Chad Bale, Chad Canterbury, Chad Carlson, Channing Ellison, Charibdys, Charles Crowe, Charles Lynch, Charlie Ruggiero, Charlie Wilkins, Charlie Zimmerman, Chel Maxfield, Chelan Sweeney, Chi T. Nguyen, Chizzle Bear, Chloe Turner, Chris, Chris Bachalo, Chris Beatty, Chris Bird, Space Hero, Chris Brunner, Chris Gile, Chris H, Chris Helsabeck, Chris Hull, Chris Knadler, Chris L. Kimball, Chris Segal, Chris Soule, Chris Vance, Chris Vincent, Chrissandra Porter, Christa Seeley, Christian Smith, Christian Steudtner, Christina Kerndt, Christine Clukey Reece, Christopher Fokken!, Christopher Mansell, Christopher Wilde, Christy Wood, Cindy Nakano, Claire E. Adams, Claire Ory, Clare Mitchell, Clark Pacheco, Claudia, Clint Jenkins, Coby Schouten, Cody Black, Cole Amezcua, Cole Jack, Pittman, Colin Brennan, Colleen Tyhurst, Colleen Vanderlinden, Comics Bulletin, Corky LaVallee, Cory Sherman, Craig, Craig Blackwood, Craig Hackl, Craig Johnston (flash_cxxi), Craig Oxbrow, Craig Van Collie, Craig Welsh, Creatrix Tiara, Cristin Grothaus, Cristin Hipke, Cristina Lazala, Crystal D Hill, Crystal Lynn, Cullen Bunn, Cynthia Anne Cofer & Mark Buckmaster, Cynthia Ramey, Cyphermage, D-Rock, D. Elan McAtee, D. Miles Martin, D. Paul Leiba, Damien Swallow, Dan Grove, Dan Mattson, Dana Rae, Dani Daly, Daniel A. Campisi, Daniel Chant, Daniel Chuhna, Daniel Dellinger, Daniel Higgins, Daniel Komis, Daniel Phillips, Danielle Van Gorder, Dark-Ape, Darla Riccetti, Darrah Rippy, Darren Davis, Darwin Pierce, Dave Hampson, Dave Rezak, Dave Thompson, David (neko), David Alex Shepherd, David Allyn Galvan, David & Stephanie Jones, David Golbitz, David Harris, David Lover, David M., Kay, David R. Sanderson, David Ramsey, David Salazar Jr., David Small, David Tai, David Ting, David Zurek, Dean A. Hacker, Dean Trippe, Debi Linton, Deborah G Wilbur, Delia Gable, Denise Pirko, Derek "Pineapple Steak" Swoyer, Derek Dockendorf, Derek Handley, Derek Helton, Derrick Korto, Devin L. Michaels, Diadathie, Diana "on3w1nged4ngel" Lalitsasivimol, Diana Garcia, Diana Volta, Diandra Mae, Diane Dooley, Diane E., Diego Guanzon, Dillon Huang, Dina

Nguyen, Dinnsdale Piranha, DMS, Doctor Q, Dominik Pich, Donald E. Claxon, Dorothy P., Doug Bissell, Doug Dorr, Douglas Alexander Cuzner, Douglas Yee, Dre Lasana, Dylan Tate, E.J. Mellow, Ealasaid Haas, Eamon R. McIvor, Eddy Whiteside, Edward_D, Eileen M. Priboy, el diabetico, Eddy, Eleanor Russell, Elena Rivera, Eliana Vornov, Elisabeth de Grandpre, Elise Roberts, Elizabeth Brandow, Elizabeth Brown, Elizabeth C., Elizabeth Parmeter, Elizabeth S. Sevey, Elizabeth Williams, Elle Chen, Elle Skinner, Ellen Brigham, Ellie Danielle Lovasz, Elliott Sawyer, Emily Goodrich, Emily Mishler, Emily Moran, Emily Noto, Emily R., Emily Ramos, Emma Axelson, Emma Engel, Emma Finken, Emma Haich, Emma Levine, Emma W., Emmanuel Colvin, Eric Bacon, Eric S., Eric Smith, Eric Tilton, Erica McGillivray, Erica Packington, Erica Pantel, Erik Singer, Erika L Guidry, Erika Terriquez, Erin Subramanian, Erin Symonds, Esther Jiwon Kim, Eugenia M. Pinzón Balam, Eva, Evan Cruser, Evan Johnson, Evan Ritchie, Evans Creative Studios, EvilTwinBrian, F Chen, F.Dunne, F.Vijfvinkel (nl), Fan, Fan of Words, Farah Ismail, Fawndolyn Valentine, Felomena Li, Ph.D., Ferebee/Canfield Family, Fiona Wood, Forrest C. Helvie, FozzieB, Franchesca Ruiz, Franny Jay, Fraser Simons, Frauke P., Frederick Melhuish III, Frederick Ostrander, Freeman Danger Kelly Donatelli II, Fu Chilima, Gabri M., Gabriel Schlesinger, Gail de Vos, GALVelociraptor, Garrett Pauls, Gary A., Gary Owen, Gavran, GBE, GeektoEnglish, Geoff Wong, Geoffrey Ford, George Trello IV, Gerard Gunnewijk, GermanCityGirl & GermanCity, Gerry Saracco, GhostRelic, Gillian Dawson, Ginny Quaney, Giovanni Velazquez, Girls With Issues Podcast, GJ Kruijff, Glenn, Glenn M Carrere Jr., Glenn Turner, Gord Tremaine, Grace Park, Grant Hayward, Greg "schmegs" Schwartz, Greg & Julie Hatcher, Greg Burgas, Greg Cimilluca, Greg Evans, Greg Matiasevich, Greg McElhatton, Greg Rucka & Jen Van Meter, Gregers Sode-Pedesen, GriffinFire, Gryvon, Gucky, Guido A Sanchez, GuiOhm, Gunnar Hildebeutel, Guy "Couchguy" McLimore, Hae it's Jacob, Haley, Hanna Paquette, Hao Wu, Haviva Avirom, Hayden, Hayden Jones, Heath White, Heather Crane, Helen Mc, Helmut Lindermann, Heng Wee Tan, Henri Patricio, Henri Patricio, Henry Jones, heycraig, Hilary Friesen, HKMouse, Iain Bex, Ian Clarke, Ian Cyr, Ian Sawlor, Imani J Dean, Impling, Inuminas, Ira & Susan Kalina, Isaac Yañez, Isabelle Melançon & Megan Lavey-Heaton, Isabelle Potier, Ivan Yagolnikov, Ivy B. Gladstone, J. Mitchell, J. Tew, J. Alva, J. E. Tetzloff, J. Kenneth Riviere, J.C. Hutchins, J.M.G., Jackie Shekell, Jacob Haronga, Jacob M Sandoval, Jacob Pauli, Jacob Richards, Jacob Wittenberg, Jaime C., Jake Pickthall, Jake the board gaming robot from the future, Jamal Campbell, James Abels, James Blanton, James Coniglio, James E., James Leask, James Leech, James Leung, James Morris, James Whatley (Whatleydude), Jamie Keenan, Jamieton Nooney, Jamilla Emerson, Jammies, Jammrock, Janet Armentani, Janine Krüger, Janna

Hochberg, Jaroslaw Ejsymont, Jasmine P., Jason Bender, Jason Best, Jason Enright, Jason Grimes, Jason Hutter, Jason K Averill, Jason Light, Jason Oren, Jason Roop, Jason Verdugo, Jasper Ramirez, Jasper Zagaet, Jay Emond, Jayjay Ferro, Jeanne, Jeff Dyal, Jeff Hitchcock, Jeff Metzner, Jeff Roberts, Jeffrey Dodd, Jen MB, Jen Moseley, Jenn Simonovich, Jennifer Chen, Jennifer Corbett, Jennifer Imus, Jennifer Joseph, Jennifer Konikowski, Jens Eschholz, Jere Manninen, Jeremy Farber, Jeric Pereda, Jerome Lim, Jerry Walter, Jess Meyer, Jesse McClusky, Jesse Richards, Jessica Andersen, Jessica Homer, Jessica Jones, Jessica Kuiken, Jessica Lewenda, Jessica Watkins, Jessie Basham, JHG Hendriks, Jim Waters, JLRoot, Joachim Ziebs, Joanna Doberstein, Joanne Mackellar, Jodi Chromey, Joe Cannizzaro, Joe Glass, Joe Wagstaff, Joel Denyes, Joelle Platz, Joey Lindsey, Joey Oakes, John & Anna Winocur, John Hague, John Idlor, John Larison, John P Wales, John Woollard, Jon Christianson, Jon Nilsen, Jonathan "ChessboardMan" Barrett, Jonathan C., Jonathan Farber, Jonathan Petersen, Jonboy Hancock, Jonna Hind, Jonny Mark Young, Jonny Rice, Jordan Buller, Jordan Duletzke, Jordan Johnson, Jose Rojas, JoSeph Balderas, Joseph Fong, Josh Bazin, Josh Candia, Josh Eklund, Josh Schroeder, Josh Shaver, Joshua Chaplinsky, Ju Li Khaw, Judith Carney, Judyt Guzman, Julia Linthicum, Julia Sullivan, Julie E. Rubin, Julie Ko, Julie Krzykwa, Julie Martel, Julie Ray, Julie Scheina, Juliette Capra, Julles T, June St.James, Justin Brownell, Justin Dorr, JW, K. D. Bryan, K. Jeffery Petersen, K. Van Dam, Kacee D. Eddinger, Kady O'Malley, kaerze, Kahlil Chu For, Kai B, Kaia Gavere, Kaitlyn B., Kaitlyn MacKay, Kaizoman, Kapu Snow, Kara Barrett, Karahkwenhawe H. Stacey, Karen Feldman, Karen Gache, Karen Mahoney, Karen Monaghan, Kari Sanders Merritt, Kari Torson, Karl Foster, Karl Hailperin, Karl Schmidt, Karon Flage, Karsten Franke, Karyn Pinter, Kat Martine-McEvoy, Kate Holloway, Kate Kirby, Kate N., Kate Sargent, Kateri Tyre, Katherine Aragdon Reyes, Katherine Bell, Katherine Lin, Katherine Malloy, Katherine Schramm, Katherine Suarez, Kathleen Foley, Kathryn O'Farrell, Kathryn Tom, Katie Ingram, Katie Logan, Katie McCamey, Katrell Faison, Katrin Liang, Katrina Goodwin, Katrina Kieman, Katrina Lehto, Kaul, Kaydalia, Kaye Spivey, Keith Bowden, Keith Potempa, Kelly Babcock, Kelly Gorman, Kelly Ratliff, Kelly Sue DeConnick, Kelly V. Rothstein, Kelseigh Nieforth, Kelsey Liggett, Kelsey Rar, Kelson Vibber, Ken Chin, Ken Zeng, Kenneth Cuyugan, Kenneth Hayes, Kenneth Kalchik, Kenneth Nida, Kenny Stull, Kermit O., Kevin Bates, Kevin E. Walker, Kevin F. Maye, Kevin Halstead, Kevin Lilley, KGBeatnik, Kiel Cross, Kika Green, Kim Faulk, Kimberly Baker, Kimberly Elaine Keating, Kin Wong, kindofstrange, King Jimmeh, Kirk Greenquist, Kirk Jorgensen, KM Strawser, Kris Panchyk, Kristel Mobley, Kristen, Kristin Brooks, Kristy Baker, Kristy King, KV Taylor, Kyla Blythe-Prahl, Kyle Cardona, Kyle T. Schoonover, Kyle Tierce, Kylie Wells,

304

Lady Seraph, Lara Margarida, Larissa Haluszka-Smith, Lars Kellogg-Stedman, Lau Sivertsen, Laura Burns, Laura Cabral, Laura Cudahy, Laura Gramlich, Laura MacDonald, Laura Newburn, Laura Wesley, Laurel Amatangelo-Whitten, Lauren Burke, Lauren Michniacki, Laurent Lehmann, Lawrence "Lawdeala" Bryant, Lawrence McClurkin, Lawrence Recio, Leah Webber, Leandro Sousa Fazio, Leashelle Miller, Lee Cross, Lee Hume, Leisha Hussien, Leonce Bowie, III, LeRoy K., Lesley Butler, Lewis Smith, Lexi, Lexie C., Liam Dinneen, Lianne Burwell, Lily Ann Montemayor, Lily Jones, Lindsay Day, Linn Song, Lisa Forlow, Lisa Heermann, Lisa Higgins, Lisa Hunt, Lisa Rabey, Lito Hernandez, Liz, Liz Aleshunas, Liz Colombo, Liz Duong, Liz Pagani, Lizzie S, LM, Logan Marlowe, Logan Riley, loudlysilent, Louise Williams, Luis Jaime Pena, Luis Quevedo, Luke Eperthener, Lyle Skains, M. Chan, M. Foster, M. Scharmack, M. Walk, M. Anthony, M.T. Wells, Macario Reyes, Mackenzie Williams, Maddy Beaupré, Madis Sillard, Maelynn Drescher, Maleghast, manda brown, Mara Wood, Marcel Beaudoin, Marco Strupat, Marcus Liddle, Margaret M. St. John, Mari, María Eugenia Reimunde, Maria Ey. Luihn, Maria Larraga, Maria Sandmo, Marielle, Marikka, Marina Müller, Marina Pereira, Marissa Dakay, Marita Jackson, Mark Ceasar Thaddeus Diza Blancaflor, Mark Hirschman, Mark L., Markus Magnitz, Marlys, Marshall & Tamme Thompson, Marta da Costa, Marta Fleming, Mary Spila, Marykate Jasper, Master Guy, Mat Groom, Mathilde Sachiko Bouhon, Matt Adams, Matt Ashcraft, Matt Benter, Matt Connolly, Matt Hurlburt, Matt King, Matt Loman, Matt Riggsby, Matt Smith, Matthew "MADrobo" Dolan, Matthew Bogart, Matthew Brodie-Hopkins, Matthew Chin, Matthew Ellison, Matthew Kyle Branin, Matthew Laurier, Matthew Lowe, Matthew Walker, Matthew Walker, Matthew Welch, Mattias Johansson, Maverick Man, Max Bliss, Max de Jonge, Maya Haller Urschel, Maya K., Meagan Damore, Meaghan Fitzgerald, Megan Congdon, Megan Irving, Megan Sullivan, Meghan Ansbach, Meghan Asaurus, Meghan Smith, Meidara, Mel Tong, Melanie Stapel, Melia Parsloe, Melisa S., Melissa Dominic, Melissa Faith Berman, Melissa Newlin, Mellisa Hannum, Melody L, Melody Thompson, Melyanna, Meredith Jeanne Gillies, MG, Mia De Seram, Michael, Michael "CodingMerc" Henke, Michael Ball, Michael Barbour, Michael Busuttil, Michael C. Fedoris, Michael D. Blanchard, Michael Feldhusen, Michael J Hinojosa, Michael J. Sullivan, Michael Kaplan, Michael Lane, Michael Ring, Michael S., Michael Son, michael stermer, Michael Weaver, Michelle Maxson, Michelle Nosal, Michelle Senderhauf, Miguel Antonio Alderete, Mike Bunch, Mike Cassella, Mike Di Salvo, Mike Kitchell, Mike Meltzer, Mike Miller, Mike Scigliano, Mike Skolnik, Mike Spencer, Mike Weldon, Mikey d., Mintchip, MissKat, Mitch n Ritch, Mittie Paul, MJ Kwiatkowski, Mollie Walker, Molly Cady, Molly McNeeley, Monica Caples, Monica Piluso, Monika MHz, Mr. Dancer, Ms. Jennity, Munchezuma, Namige, Nancy Xu, Narciso Espiritu,

Natalie, Natalie Catania, Natasha Forrester, Nathalia Panesi, Nathan & Heather, Nathan Olmstead, Nathan Soderland, Nathaniel Skiba, Neil Cameron, Neil Kapit, Nicholas McIntyre, Nick Elias, Nick Lapeyrouse, Nick Marino, Nick Miller, Nickole Lewis, Nico "The Chosen One" Kolstee, Nicole Cannon, Nicole D. Teague, Nicole Hall, Nicole Oweger, Nicole Paine, Nicole Rivera AKA Apples, Nightscooter, Nina Raoof, Noah Lockwood, Nora Hailey, Norma JMB, Noviny, Olav Beemer, Oliver Schwarz, Olivia Luna, One-Shot Gallery, Paige Pozan, Pamela Gutman, Pamela Zaniewski, Paolina Barker, Patricia J.V. Clark, Patricia Sanvictores, Patrick Battaglia, Patrick O'Donnell, Patrick O'Shea, Patrick Reitz, Patrick Tran, Patrick Whalen, Paul Allor, Paul Castillo, Paul F. Lerman, Paul Johnston, Paul K., Paul Was, Paula Zimmerman, paulidin, Pawel Martin, Pensmith, Pete Hurley, Peter Campbell, Peter Hospodka, Peter John Kamikawa, Peter Marinari, Peter Souter, Petter Wäss, Phil Wait, Philip Sellin, Phloyd, Pippa Ashton, Priscila Tchorbadjian, R. K. Bentley, Rachael Kubikowski, Rachael Stephen, Rachel Atwood, Rachel Barsness, Rachel Clair, Rachel J. Kirkendall, Rachel Preston, Rachel Trout, Rachel Yeomans, Rachelle Stein, Rae Grimm, Rae Wood, Raelyn Nieves, Rafael Diaz, Rafia Mirza, Ramon Yvarra, Randy Heath, Randy Johnson, Randy Reitz, Rasmus Durban Jahr, Reba Jacobs, Rebeca, Rebecca NM, Rebecca Woolford, Rebekah Isaacs, Reina L., Ren & Mally Cappelli, RexCelestis, Rey Morales, Reymundo Garcia, Rhiannon K., Rhiannon L Crothers, Rhiannon Tripp, Richard Billings 2, Richard D. Llanton, Rick Jones, Riley F Skender, Ringo, Ripley Marvin, Rob Loxterkamp, Robert B., Robert Bieselin, Robert Duckworth, Robert E. Stutts, Robert Hähnel, Robert Hedley, Robert J. Plass, Robert McDonald, Roberta Miller, Robin Babe Draper, Robin Hetzel, Robin "The Darg0" Hartmann, Robyn L., Rochus Wolff, Rodney Carter, Rodrigo Kern, Rohan Graetz, Ron, Ronaldo Jackson, Ronny H. Ringen, Rosalia Millan, Rosetta Lediard, Rowan McCormick, Rubiee Tallyn Hayes, Rusty Rowley, Ruth Bedder, Ruth Krabacher, Ryan Capriglione, Ryan Hill, Ryan Hull, Ryan K Lindsay, Ryan Kennedy, Ryan Kertai, Ryca Rein, S.A.J Jenkins, Sabine Sapia, Sally Jacka, Sally Jane Thompson, Sam Reece, Samantha Cote, Samantha J. Sargent, Samantha Leigh, Samuel Hansen, Sara 'Bagel' Nagel, Sara McCardle Blunk, Sara Nelson, Sara Pyle, Sarah Adair, Sarah Boyle, Sarah Bryars, Sarah C Jackson, Sarah Coldheart, Sarah Dory, Sarah E Hall, Sarah Gardiner, Sarah Greybeck, Sarah Jacobson, Sarah Kingdred, Sarah Kuhn, Sarah Littlehales, Sarah Rice, Sarah Robertson, Sarah Williams, Scott Beveridge, Scott Carlson, Scott Hyman, Scott J. Wilson, Scott Rives, Scout Johnson, Sean & Lauren Richmond, Sean Brandt, Sean CW Korsgaard, Sean Hockett, Sean Jensen, Sean Liu, Seeley James, Senyee Lee, Sergio Talavera, Shanleigh Lauren, Shannon Lynn, Shannon Wright, Shaun Richens, Shauna Kosoris, Shawn Belton, Shawn Prince, Shean, Semeicha & Sapphira Mohammed, Sheepofheight, Sheila Barnes,

Shelby Norris, Shelley Garnet, Snow Wildsmith, Sonja Hase, Spencer Brint, Squid Widget, SSL Thompson Powers Activate!, SSZee, Stan Yamane, Stefan Radermacher, Stefan Wagner, Steffi Marschall, Sten Sondre Johnson, Steph Davi, Stephanie, Stephanie Forbes, Stephanie Ford-Scheimer, Stephanie Gunn, Stephanie Sears, Stephanie Sherman Stephanie Wood Franklin, Stephanny McQuillian, Stephen Blanzaco, Stephen Conway, Stephen Dalton, Stephen Hunter Roberts, Stephen J Byrnes, OD, Stephen Mellor, Stephen Paradis, Stephen R. Walli, Stephen Ward, Stephi Graf, Steve Brady, Steve Pieper, Steven Morris, Steven Petersen, Stuart Bailey, Stuart Telfer, summervillain, Suri Ratnatunga, Susan Adami, Susan S., Susanne Fischer, Suzanne Dawson, Suzanne Richardson, Suzanne Samson, Sven of the Dead, Sy Bram, Syd Lindblom, Sydnee Allen, Sylvia Vale, T. Pillar., T.C. Vulpes, T1mco, TabbyHayfever, Tabz, Talia Earle, Talisha Harrison, Tamara Brooks, Tamara McAuley, Tamara Wharton, Tammy Graham, Tania C Richter, Tanner Pomerleau, Taylor R. Martin, Ted Slater Jr., Teddy J. Justice, Tegan & Isabelle McCarty, Tegan Pyke, Terry Dodson, tess, Tessara Ahlin, Thai N., The Amazing Space Tako Overlord, The Beans, The Brush family, The Cherrybomber, The Hahns, THE Kevin, The Miner Family, Theo Fredrik Hauk Luiggi-Gørrissen, TheZMage, Thilo Mothes, Thom Cuddihy, Thom Heaton, Thomas, Thomas Giles, Thomas Krech, Thomas Polok, Thomas Sowell, Thorsten Claus, Tiago Ferreira, Tianita, Tiffany Reynolds, Tiffany Rumfelt, Tiffany Togoto, Tili Sokolov, Tim D. Moon, Tim Hanley, Timothy Donohue, Tina Kim, Tisha, TJ Rockwell, Tk Appleton, Tlegg, TM Bangalore, Tom B, Tom Canavan, Tom Ladegard, Tom Leahy, Tomas Burgos Caez, Tommy Svensson, toni pizza, Tony Contento, Tony Peterson, Tori Brochu, Toyota Clan, Tracy Jasper, Travis Bramble, Travis Dunn, Travis Pelkie, Trowby Brockman, Trystan Rundquist, Tsutako, Tyler 'Doc' Barnas, Tymothy Peter Diaz, Tyson Elmer, Unreluctance, Valentine, Valerie Gillis, Valerie S., valeriepica, Vampress Luxura, Vanessa Gabriel, Vanessa McKinney, Vanessa Satone, vbunny, Victor Fuste, Victor Hung, Victoria Fletcher, Vince Thomas (Swansea), Vincent Morano, Vinisa Brown, Vladimir Duran, Wade Woodson, Walt Parrish, Walter Sand, warmist, Wayne Turner, Wendy A. B. Whipple, Wendy Hathaway, Wendy Smith, Will Harrison, William E. Baker, William L. McKeon, William R. Karr, William Valentine Zajac III, Winnie W. Kwan, Winston Mapa, Xavier Bolanos, Yulia, Yve Budden, Zach Smith, Zach Zimmerman, Zachary Clemente, Zache, Zack Caton, Zak Bryson, Zakelro!, Zero DragonLord, Zimbabwe Birnbaum, ZMiles, zombieundergrnd, Игорь Студенков

EXTRA SPECIAL THANKS

Anis Mojgani, Becky Cloonan, Brett White, Brian Cronin (CSBG), Brian Wood, Chris Sims (Comics Alliance), Corrina Lawson (Geek Mom), David Aja, Eric Smith (Book Riot), Erin Jade Lange, Greg Rucka & Jen Van Meter, James & Brandon (Comics! The Podcast), Jill Pantozzi (The Mary Sue), Karen Mahoney, Katrina Hill (Action Chick), Kelly Sue DeConnick, Lauren Davis & Rob Bricken (io9), Meagan Damore (Gif Soulmate!), Nick Marino (AudioShocker), Paul Allor, Scott Snyder, Sue (DC Women Kicking Ass), & Tim Hanley!

and
Angela Chatha, Daniel Bélanger, Fred Leggett, Maeve K. Cahiwat, M.P., Richard Cameron - Atelier & Company

KELLY THOMPSON'S first novel *The Girl Who Would Be King* was a breakout Kickstarter success, and an Amazon best seller. Kelly's teenage love of superheroes compelled her to pursue a degree in Sequential Art from The Savannah College of Art and Design, and roughly a million years later, she has a graphic novel forthcoming from Dark Horse Comics with artist Meredith McClaren. Currently living in Manhattan with her boyfriend and (still) no damn pets, Kelly dreams of returning to Los Angeles where she can have a pet, less frizzy hair, and one day a swimming pool. You can find Kelly all over the Internet where she is generally well-liked, except where she's detested.

www.1979semifinalist.com
www.storykiller.com

WRITER PROCESS

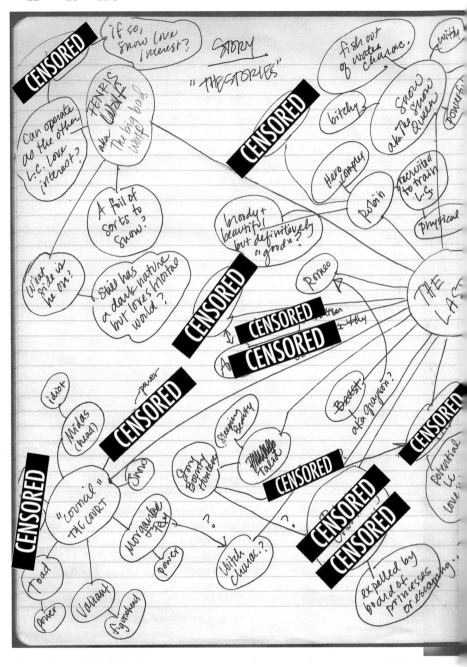

Kelly: This is the brainstorming technique I use for everything. And this is the scan of the first one I ever did for Storykiller (then called The Last Scion). I learned the technique in high school creative writing and it has stayed with me ever since. I find lists really restricting, as you feel compelled to keep them neat and organized. The brainstorming process should not be neat. It should be chaos!

WRITER PROCESS

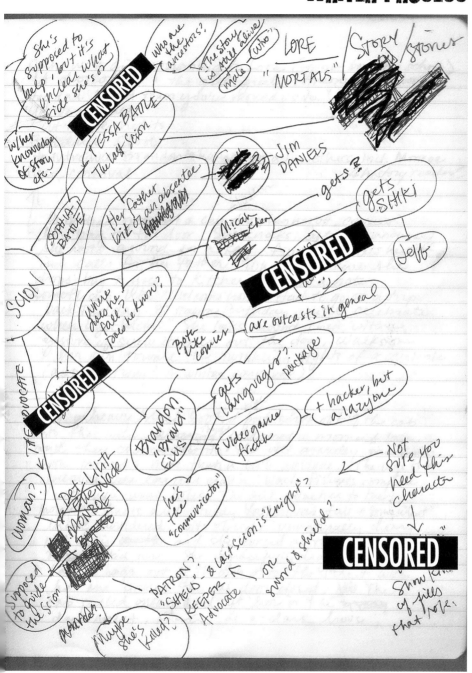

She's supposed to help, but it's unclear what side she's on?

who are the ancestors?

The story is still alive? Who

"male"

where knowledge of story at?

LORE

"MORTALS"

STORY / STORIES

CENSORED

TESSA BATTLE
The last Scion

JIM DANIELS

gets?

gets SHIKI

Her father isn't it? an absentee

SOPHIA BATTLE

Micah

Jeff

CENSORED

SCION

Where does he fall? Does he know?

Both like comics

are outcasts in general

gets languages? package

+ hacker, but a lazy one

CENSORED

THE ADVOCATE

Brandon "Brand" Ellis

Video game freak

he's the "communicator"

← Not sure you need this character

woman?

Det. Lilith ETHELWADE MONROE

CENSORED

Supposed to guide the Scion

PATRON? "SHIELD" & last Scion's "knight"?
KEEPER
Advocate

or sword & shield?

Show kind of fills that role.

Maybe she's killed?

Kelly: This way the ideas can flow freely & you can more easily see character and plot connections. A thought or idea you have can go down and instantly be tied to dozens of other things, with just a line. It's more organic and feels more the way that life actually works, as opposed to a neat and orderly list, which is not like life at all. That said, I admit that the above looks pretty wild. They don't all look like this one. Storykiller is by far the most complex version I've ever done. Well, so far.

WRITER PROCESS

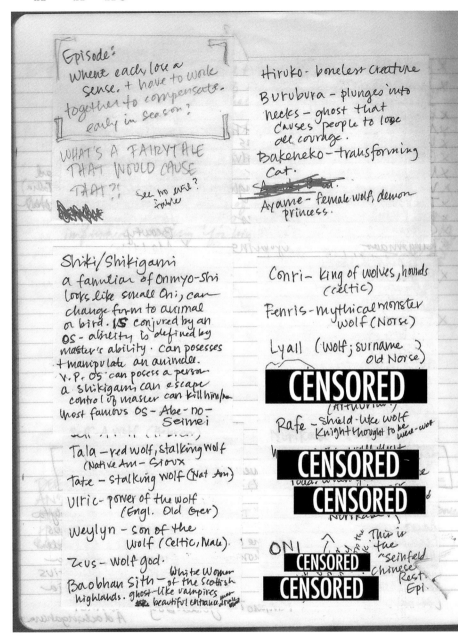

Episode:
Where each lose a
sense. + have to work
together to compensate.
early in season?

WHAT'S A FAIRYTALE
THAT WOULD CAUSE
THAT?! see no evil?
hear no evil

Hiruko - boneless creature
Burubura - plunges into
necks - ghost that
causes people to lose
all courage.
Bakeneko - transforming
Cat.
~~Shk~~~~~at.~~
Ayame - female wolf, demon
princess.

Shiki/Shikigami
a familiar of Onmyo-shi
looks like small Oni; can
change form to animal
or bird. IS conjured by an
OS - ability is defined by
master's ability. can posesses
+ manipulate an animal.
V.P. OS can posess a person.
a shikigami can escape
control if master can kill him/her
Most famous OS - Abe-no-
Seimei

Tala — red wolf, stalking wolf
(Native Am - Sioux
Tate - stalking wolf (Nat Am)
Ulric - power of the wolf
(Engl. Old Ger)
Weylyn - son of the
wolf (Celtic, Male).
Zeus - wolf god.
Baobhan Sith — White Women
of the scottish
highlands. ghost-like vampires
beautiful entrance

Conri - king of wolves, hounds
(celtic)
Fenris - mythical monster
wolf (Norse)

Lyall (wolf; surname ?
Old Norse)

CENSORED

Rafe - shield-like wolf
knight thought to be
were-wolf

CENSORED

CENSORED

ONI ← the This is
the
"seinfeld
CENSORED chinese
Rest.
CENSORED Epi.

Kelly: So this is a far less deliberate technique than my brainstorming system. This is more a function of "falling down the web wormhole." You go to the web researching some small item. You find said item. You grab a post-it note and jot it down. But wait, what's that link, that seems interesting. You click it. You learn more and it's something you can use, something that warrants more research. You grab another post-it. And the next thing you know you've got 20 damn post-its. I work at this point either on the computer or in a moleskine notebook (I used to use lined - like above - but I've moved to the graph paper, which I prefer). Eventually all these post-ts find their way to that notebook.

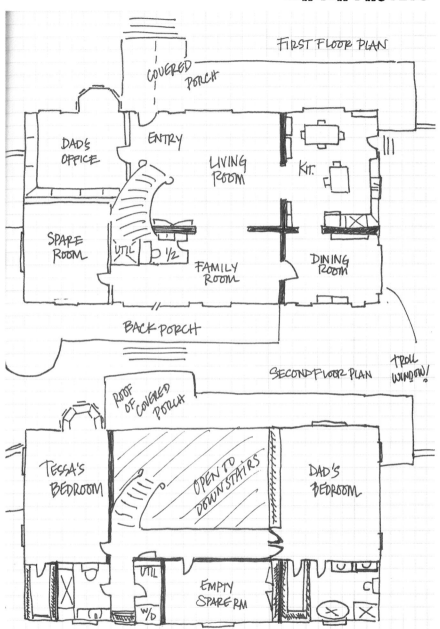

FIRST FLOOR PLAN

COVERED PORCH

DAD'S OFFICE

ENTRY

LIVING ROOM

KIT.

SPARE ROOM

UTIL

1/2

FAMILY ROOM

DINING ROOM

BACK PORCH

SECOND FLOOR PLAN

TROLL WINDOW!

ROOF OF COVERED PORCH

TESSA'S BEDROOM

OPEN TO DOWNSTAIRS

DAD'S BEDROOM

UTIL

W/D

EMPTY SPARE RM

Kelly: So, this is exactly what it looks like – The floorplan(s) to Tessa's house. I'm no architect so it's horribly flawed, and certainly not to any real scale, but doing stuff like this for heavily used locations really helps me to focus – especially when it comes to action – on the movement and choreography of a scene - rather than getting hung up on small details and worrying about where things are for consistency. This way it's burned into my brain and really frees me up to get creative in how I use the space. I also just like drawing floorplans!

STEPHANIE HANS: I wanted to do a classic "team" illustration. Somehow I always start that kind of work thinking and aiming for Drew Struzan but finish as far away as imaginably possible!

STEPHANIE HANS: The challenge in the "team" picture is to have a general composition that works as a whole but also in its individual pieces. The characters have to each stand out on their own, while interacting harmoniously with each other without weighing on the main character.

STEPHANIE HANS: In the end I lightened the black tones on the characters in the background to push Tessa to the front of the image.

PROCESS SKETCH by STEPHANIE HANS   **ARTIST PROCESS**

STEPHANIE HANS: I wanted to have a simple single characer image with Tessa, confident, strong, and full of wild power, with her calling her axe, The Black Dove.

STEPHANIE HANS: I wanted Tessa to not even be looking at the axe because she's damn sure it will be right where it belongs, in her hands. And nothing is more confident than that. I also didn't want her posture to be girly or frail. I wanted her to be all power.

ARTIST PROCESS

PROCESS SKETCH by STEPHANIE HANS

MEREDITH MCCLAREN: I chose the Frankendogs piece because I wanted a subject that potentially had a lot of movement.

MEREDITH MCCLAREN: It was fun working on a larger size (necessary since we were doing a large print). It let me narrow in on a bit more detail. But I wanted to keep the colors fairly simple, so the piece didn't become too difficult to read. All in all, a great deal of fun.

PROCESS DRAWING by MEREDITH MCCLAREN ARTIST PROCESS

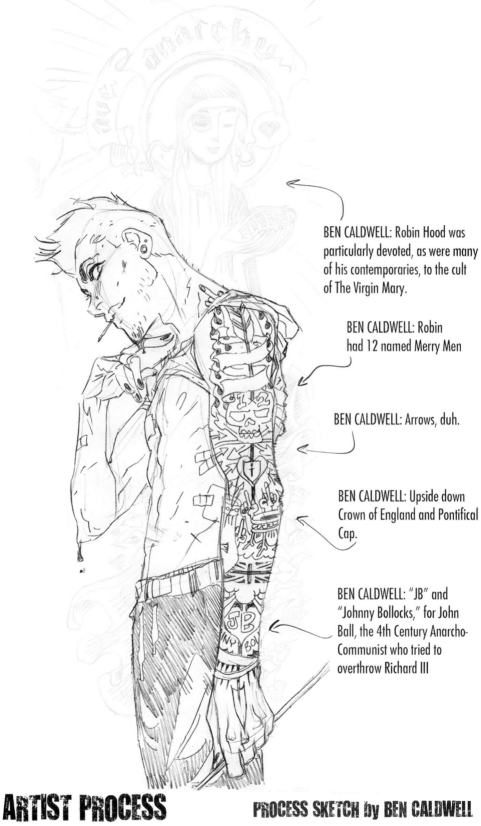

BEN CALDWELL: Robin Hood was particularly devoted, as were many of his contemporaries, to the cult of The Virgin Mary.

BEN CALDWELL: Robin had 12 named Merry Men

BEN CALDWELL: Arrows, duh.

BEN CALDWELL: Upside down Crown of England and Pontifical Cap.

BEN CALDWELL: "JB" and "Johnny Bollocks," for John Ball, the 4th Century Anarcho-Communist who tried to overthrow Richard III

ARTIST PROCESS

PROCESS SKETCH by BEN CALDWELL

CASSANDRA JAMES: I honestly couldn't choose a character to draw so I decided on doing the main three: Tessa, Brand, and Micah. I also wanted to try to incorporate some of the imagery from the book and Jeff's various forms (the dragon below Tessa, the gecko, raven, and tiger on the wall behind Micah and the cat in her arms).

CASSANDRA JAMES: To evoke a storybook-type vibe I chose to work with markers and watercolor paints for the shading after I finished inking the piece, adding a few colors in photoshop afterward. The paper textures were added as a final touch.

LINE WORK by CASSANDRA JAMES   ARTIST PROCESS

KRIS ANKA: When I read the descripton of Snow, I knew there was no way I could pass on drawing her...

KRIS ANKA: As I went through the chapter there were so many specific moments and items I wanted to draw that I couldn't settle on just one, so I worked out a kind of character sheet montage where I could squeeze in all the elements I wanted to show off about her. Really making it about the characterization rather than the events trasnspiring.

ARTIST PROCESS

LINE WORK by KRIS ANKA

DELETED SCENES

Kelly: So this was, for a long time, the very first chapter of the book. And frankly, I still like it even now for a whole slew of reasons. I like the tone it sets right out of the gate - mysterious and dangerous, a large and varied world, it establishes magic early on and that nothing is really what it seems. I also liked starting not with Tessa as it was a good primer for readers that this would not be in her POV but would jump around to focus on a variety of characters.

DELETED SCENE No. 1

The wolf had been hunting it for nearly half an hour. This was entirely too long even in the rain, considering the speed of the thing. There was something wrong with the smell, something he couldn't quite figure, some mix of death and magic and Mortal and Story that didn't quite make sense, not in a way he could put into Mortal language at least.

Finally he got a bead on it, and certain of its direction, he began running after it in earnest. The trail seemed like a thing somehow in a hurry but not hurrying and he added it to the list of things that didn't make sense about it. But soon enough he was upon it. From behind he could see that it was large and heavy, lumbering as if injured. It was male and tall, long limbed and once even powerful perhaps. But now it was his. Under the faint shafts of a pale half moon he jumped it from behind and it let out a cry that seemed human enough. Biting into its neck however, the flesh was strange.

It tasted just as it had smelled: wrong.

And for a thing to both taste and smell wrong was a worrying thing indeed. He'd be around a long time and tasted and smelled many different things in that time. This was not quite like any of them.

All of this concerned him, but not as much as it probably should have.

It would bother him more much later when he was better able to think what such a thing might mean. For now there was just the hunt and the kill, and some haze of bewilderment.

CONTINUED

DELETED SCENES

He tore at it some more, and when his prey continued to shake and shiver he took the head off entirely.

That was the end of it.

Under normal circumstances he would have eaten it now, but there was nothing normal about this thing he had killed, and in truth there was nothing normal about him of late, either, so instead he left it, silent and still, in the thick trees.

As he left it, he also left the woods. Heading toward the edge of the city that lived outside the forest. As the brush grew thin around him he changed his shape until he was nearly Mortal looking. He was naked and strong, handsome and powerful, exactly as he desired. He looked back into the woods only once, wondering if there was someone he should tell about the thing he had found.

And then he remembered that there was no one to tell.

There had no been anyone for a long time.

Kelly: In the end, though I still love this scene, I felt starting with anyone other than Tessa was a mistake. I hoped to find a place to add this scene that felt natural and warranted, but it just never happened and though I liked it and thought it added a nice bit of texture, it wasn't necessary and so it was lost to the editing gods.

Kelly: And this was the first sketch I ever did of Tessa Battle back in 2010

I'm not much of an artist, never was and these days especially I'm rusty as all get out, but I always liked this sketch. It well captured the essence of Tessa, and of course look at that awesome hair.

DELETED SCENES

Kelly: This is an excerpt from an alternate opening to how Tessa, Brand, and Micah meet as well as how they all first meet Snow, Tal, and Hecuba. This scene is definitely an example of killing your darlings. There are still elements here I wish I could have found a way to keep - the carnival, the bullies, Tessa's first fight being a non-powered one, and the encounter that comes just after this - Tessa's fight with Tal. Unfortunately this old beginning took too long to get to some of the key elements and had too much exposition. This version also didn't build the suspension of disbelief for the characters in an ideal way.

DELETED SCENE No. 2

She was about to put her buds back in her ears and go back to her book when a shout followed by a loud bang came from the same direction the pair had come in. The boy and girl both jumped to their feet almost like prey. Like rabbits or small birds. Four big teenagers (the kind nobody ever wanted to see late at night) appeared in the doorway. Three boys and a girl, the boys all big and broad shouldered with dumb dangerous faces, the girl lanky and sharp looking. The biggest of the boys was also the most handsome, but as he took in the two friends a mean smile slid across his face. He focused on the girl with an intensity that Tessa found alarming.

"Hey Chen," he said and it rolled off his tongue as if coated in slime. Flash Jr. stood in front of the girl, which made Tessa smile a bit, a very gallant gesture, even though it was clearly going to get him pummeled. The alpha jerk grabbed Flash Jr. by the neck of his t-shirt roughly. "Hey Ellissssh...I'm talking to your little double half-breed girlfriend here, not you, so just step to the side." And with that he flung him aside as if he weighed no more than sheets of paper. Flash Jr. was back up on his feet almost instantly, living up nicely to his t-shirt promises.

"I told you not to call me that, Chad," he said, his voice surprisingly steely, though Tessa could hear the faintest tremble underneath it.

"It's your name Elllisssssh," Chad intoned, slurring the word Ellis strangely, almost like he had a lisp, or was pretending to. As he talked his gaze was still locked on the small dark-haired girl, who for her part was staring right back at him, rather than cowering with a lowered head as most would. But Tessa's heart was hammering as the tension in the room continued to build upon itself.

CONTINUED

DELETED SCENES

"My name is Brandon," Flash Jr. said, his fists clenching. "You want me to call you Weener?"

"It's WINE-er," Chad said, finally pulling his focus from the girl and looking at Brandon. Brandon shrugged and crossed his arms across his chest defiantly and then cocked his head to the side. It looked great, but Tessa cringed inside. He shouldn't be tying his hands up like that.

"Sounds fitting either way then you doucheba-," Brandon said and before he could finish the 'bag' part of douchebag Weiner was on him. They went crashing to the ground. Weiner was straddling him and about to throw a brutal-looking punch when Tessa shouted out from the darkness of the balcony.

"HEY!"

The sharpness with which her voice pierced the room shocked all of them enough to stop them in their tracks, even Tessa. Weiner looked up into the darkness, narrowing his eyes and trying to get a bead on who had intruded, one fist still raised in the air, the other clutching a handful of Brandon's shirt.

Tessa had no idea what she should do now. She had been in her fair share of fights in life (or perhaps more than her fair share) but she certainly couldn't take all four of them, and even though Brandon was clearly gallant as all get out, in truth, it didn't look like he could throw a punch to save his life. Hell, he was already down. But she stood up anyway. It was too late for second thoughts. Besides what better way to ring in her birthday than with fresh bruises? Tessa stepped out into the light and began her way down the stairs. When Weiner saw she was a girl, a giant grin broke out on his face and spread to the others like an infection. On the upside, he stood up off of Brandon and walked over to her, and the groups' focus shifted to Tessa. On the downside, Tessa saw the dark-haired girl, Chen, dart out the back exit, which surprised her, though she couldn't fault her for it. This meant they were only two now instead of three.

CONTINUED

DELETED SCENES

"Well, well, seems Ellllisssssh has a bodyguard. A goth-y chick bodyguard, but still," Weiner said, drinking in Tessa from boots to cherry colored hair. Tessa rolled her eyes, irritated at the goth moniker, it was where guys like Weiner always went with her, like clockwork. She found it incredibly tedious. Weiner went to open his mouth, surely to drop more brilliance on them all, but Tessa had had it. She balled up her fist and swung it, connecting nicely with his jaw in a satisfying smack. Weiner went down. In her experience the cliché about how big they were and how hard they would fall was painfully true, and she was glad to see it hold here as Weiner went down like a sack of mean potatoes.

Unfortunately the rest of his crew took the opportunity to rush her, although one of them held back, and laid a heavy foot on Brandon's chest. Brandon struggled valiantly to unpin himself, but it was never going to happen. The girl was fastest and got to Tessa first but she was also the least intimidating strength wise and so Tessa held her ground and took a swing. She connected again, though less accurately, and she clipped the girl, pushing her back, but only briefly. She came at Tessa again and this time grabbed at her awkwardly. A second too late Tessa realized the girl wasn't trying to hit her, but to hold her, and the misjudgment cost Tessa as the girl got her long skinny arms around Tessa like a vise. Guy number three came at Tessa and punched her hard in the gut. The breath came out of her in a whoosh and she had to will herself not to throw up the cotton candy and corndogs she'd devoured. He wheeled back and took another swing, this time at her face. His aim was poor though and the impact of the punch was blunted, but her lip broke open and trickled red just the same. He lost his balance in the wake of the awkward punch and Tessa used the blissful second he needed to recover to slam her head backward, cracking the girl in the face with the back of her skull. The girl screamed out and released Tessa instantly, her hands flying to her face where the gushing blood told Tessa she'd maybe broken the girl's nose, or perhaps taken a tooth.

CONTINUED

DELETED SCENES

The girl screamed out and released Tessa instantly, her hands flying to her face where the gushing blood told Tessa she'd maybe broken the girl's nose, or perhaps taken a tooth. Guy number three was turning back around when Tessa jumped at him, both feet in the air and landed them firmly on his chest. He fell back, but so did she (an always-fatal flaw in the double kick to the chest maneuver).

Tessa crawled to her hands and knees and tried to get back up, but before she could manage it a pair of boots stood in front of her, dangerously close.

"Oh yeah, please get up," the boots said, and Tessa looked up to see Weiner standing over her, touching his own busted lip. He raised his fist, clearly planning to imbed her head in the wooden floor. Tessa squinted her eyes and tried to imagine how she was going to look in a full body cast. Just as she almost had the picture in her mind a loud male voice (one that sounded decidedly and blissfully adult) shattered the room.

"What's going on here?!"

Tessa looked up from her low vantage point and saw a tall broad-shouldered older man (the kind that lifted heavy things for a living) with a head full of salt and pepper hair, standing at the back entrance to the theater, Chen next to him. She hadn't run away, she'd gone for the cavalry. The cavalry was apparently one dude, but still.

The group of bullies sprinted for the other exit, led by alpha bully coward Weiner. The man, surprising everyone, actually ran after them. Tessa struggled to her feet, and midway through her struggle Brandon and Chen came to help her up. Standing there together, Tessa was the tallest, and the most pummeled by a good distance. They exchanged looks for a moment and Tessa leaned against the edge of the stage, her head throbbing, Brandon spoke first.

"So first 'whoa!' and second...who are you?!" He paused, but not long enough for anyone to actually answer and then added, "And if you say Wonder Woman I'm going to KNOW I'm dreaming." Chen rolled her eyes and pushed him lightly.

CONTINUED

DELETED SCENES

"Yeah, *wet* dreaming," she said, seeming almost embarrassed on his behalf. She looked up at Tessa, dug her hands out of her big hoodie pockets and reached out to Tessa. "I'm Micah Chen."

Tessa shook her small hand and felt her split lip with the other. "Tessa Battle. Definitely NOT Wonder Woman," she said, holding up her bloody fingers as proof of her lack of invulnerability. Brandon smiled broadly anyway and Micah rolled her eyes again, but less intensely. She thumbed her finger at him.

"This is Brandon Ellis."

Brandon rubbed his palm on his jeans and reached out to shake Tessa's hand. She obliged and he added, "People call me Brand. Well, except them," he said, referring to the group of thugs. Tessa smiled slightly and then nodded her head in the direction the bullies had run.

"Who were they—what's the story?"

"Same story as anywhere," Brandon began, "They're just jerks with big muscles and tiny—"

Micah elbowed him hard in the ribs and he glared at her.

"Ow! MINDS. I was going to say MINDS," he said, elbowing her back. "Jeez, give me some credit. I do have SOME decorum," he said, sniffing his nose with a superior air. Micah put her hands up in surrender and opened her mouth to apologize, but then he added, "They also have tiny dicks."

Micah shut her mouth and hung her head, slightly shamed. Brandon continued, undaunted, "I suspect this is why they're so unhappy and try to take it out on everyone," he finished with a professorial tone. Micah cast her embarrassed eyes up at him. "You *know* this is why we never have any new friends right?" she threw her hands up helplessly. Tessa couldn't help but chuckle at the whole thing. She liked these people. They clearly adored each other. They also seemed undeniably good to Tessa. And good was something she had seen precious little of lately. Good was *good*.

CONTINUED

DELETED SCENES

"So um, nice use of the double foot kick to the chest," Brandon said. "You've really got to be committed to use that move," and then, again without really pausing to let Tessa respond he said, "You've got to let us buy you pancakes."

"Pancakes?" Tessa asked, her eyebrow cocked. She looked at Micah for approval who was nodding her head vigorously. It was such a strange offer but she found herself liking it all the more for its strangeness. Tessa felt a little flutter of something inside her but dismissed it as too many corndogs and despite that fact she realized she was going to agree to the pancakes. Hell, it *was* her birthday (about thirty seconds ago actually) she *deserved* pancakes. But as Tessa opened her mouth to say yes a noise from where the bullies had run spun the trio toward the door. Neither the bullies nor the man appeared in the doorway but a faint bluish white glow bobbed up and down in the hallway, growing steadily in intensity. The trio instinctively backed up a few steps. Tessa remained in front of the others, her hands splayed out protectively. She threw a glance at the other door, their way looked clear should they need to make a run for it. From what, she had no idea.

The bluish white light pulsed brightly and then faded to barely a glimmer and a woman stepped into the otherwise dark doorframe. She seemed almost lit from within by the same bluish white light, her skin glowing and bright, flawless and almost sculptural in its perfection. She was tall and shockingly slender, a long impossibly white dress clung to every bit of her body, except where it splayed out at the bottom laying in a way that looked like it was actually floating above the grime, too good to bother touching it. The dress sat dangerously low on her pale shoulders, and it glittered as she moved. It was an absurd outfit, but it somehow seemed anything but absurd. It seemed divine. But even the outfit somehow paled in comparison to the mountains of ethereal white hair that was both piled artistically on her head and spilling down her shoulders in waves. Not blonde hair, not even

CONTINUED

DELETED SCENES

platinum, but white. A soft white with an almost bluish tint that seemed to radiate its own light in the same way that her skin did. Her eyes were a cold blue, and despite their color being quite pale, they appeared shockingly bright in her face, which was otherwise nearly colorless. She was the kind of beautiful that didn't seem real. Like she had been shaped from stone and born of imagination, not the messy business of flesh and reality. The trio blinked at her and Tessa almost remembered that this wasn't a dream when she heard Brand whisper under his breath "ohmigod." She didn't know if it was meant in admiration, shock, or denial, but if Brand was feeling what Tessa was then it was all three combined into some very confusing but potent elixir. Just looking at the woman had the tiny hairs on the back of Tessa's neck standing on end, she felt her every sense primed. Primed for what she didn't know. When the woman finally spoke, what came out of her mouth was an even bigger shock.

"Battle. Step forward and come with me. I am your escort to Story." Her voice was as icy as her appearance suggested and seemed almost formal. But the three stood still, as if they themselves were stone. The woman looked at them, with all their lack of moving, and her facade broke almost immediately. She dropped her formal air and cocked her hip to the side dramatically, her face a look of exasperation even though she'd been there no more than two full minutes. "Seriously? Battle. Step up man." Something about the woman, even now, suddenly and strangely informal, continued to panic Tessa. Down deep in her stomach, no, lower, somewhere lower than that, she felt a kind of dread and horror that she couldn't put into words. But everything in her was telling her to run. It was primal.

"Run," Tessa hissed at Brand and Micah under her breath. Micah darted her eyes in Tessa's direction and said "What?" so quietly it was nearly inaudible.

"Run!" Tessa half hissed, half shouted. And the trio took off, as if they were one, for the door behind them. The blue-white woman watched them go, her mouth open in surprise.

CONTINUED

DELETED SCENES

"What the...? Oh hell. I do *not* run," she said examining her nails in an effete gesture. After a minute she sighed and turned her head toward the dark hallway behind her. "Tal? You LOVE to run...so be a dear and fetch them," she said flicking her hand dismissively in the direction the three had run.

Tal emerged from the shadows like dark mist. Even taller than the woman in white, she was clad in luxurious dark brown leather from her knee-high boots to a fitted motorcycle jacket. She wore thick brown leather gloves with steel fingertips that glinted in the pale light as she pushed a stray strand of hair from her face. A longbow, made of rich brown wood was slung over her shoulder, and a quiver of arrows was strapped securely to her back. A mass of shiny golden blonde hair bound loosely in a thick braid hung down her back. She was as impossibly beautiful as the woman in white, though her skin was the color of a vibrant rosy peach and her eyes were a much darker, stormier blue.

The woman narrowed her eyes and removed the longbow she was wearing. Beside her in the darkness, a massive dog emerged. It looked half wolf, and its shoulder nearly reached Tal's hips. The dog's fur was black as night, thick and beautiful, its paws large and powerful. But even the size of the thing was not what stood out, what stood out were the eyes, glowing a steady orange red that looked not unlike two tiny fires in its face.

The woman in white flicked her bright blue eyes at Tal. "Meet me there," she said and walked back into the dark hall, her internal brightness temporarily lightening the hallway. Tal met eyes with the dog and then wordlessly ticked her head lightly up and forward to indicate that it could go. The dog took off running after the three teenagers and Tal followed, her bow clutched lightly in her right hand.

Kelly: Sorry to leave you in on a cliffhanger there, but not like this really happened. Besides, I suspect Tal and Tessa will eventually trade punches at some time in the future - so I might want to recycle some of their first great (now never happened) fight. Speaking of recycling, the eagle-eyed among you likely noticed that I did use some of what's here in the final version - especially when it came to descriptions of Snow, Tal, and Hecuba. As always with killing darlings - save what you can! In fact, when I edit I keep an "excerpts" file, and put everything I'm cutting in that document that way it makes it easier to cut mercilessly, because nothing ever feels truly lost.

DELETED SCENES

Kelly: There are, quite frankly, never enough Fenris scenes. He and Tessa have a natural uneasiness and both common and conflicting goals tat are always fun to play with. Fenris is also a "truth teller" character, which are often my favorite, but he's also highly mysterious while Tessa is very direct and no-nonsense. It makes them oil and water in a way that is fun to write. This is one of the few scenes of them that I had to cut. But even when I found ways to pare back his role, Fenris always seemed to find a way to worm his way back in with new scenes. He's clever that way.

DELETED SCENE No. 3

Tessa and Fenris examined a few of the empty graves and the not so subtle trail that led into the woods behind the cemetery.

"They don't look like they rose on their own," Tessa said.

Fenris nodded. "Yes, I'd say they had help. When something rises from the grave it tends to not leave a neat pile of discarded dirt." Fenris moved to the edge of the woods. "What say you, Scion?"

Tessa looked at him, "What? Follow the trail?"

"Why not?"

Tessa could think of about a hundred reasons why not, including Robin's warnings from this morning, but she didn't want to share any of them with Fenris. "You can follow the trail?"

"Yes," he said, looking again into the woods. "Even if it becomes obscured there's no way to hide the scent of death they're leaving behind."

"Okay then," Tessa said standing up. Fenris looked back at her.

"Stay close," he said, before he took off running into the woods.

"Shit," Tessa said under her breath, rushing after him, tired before they even began.

Fenris ran hard and it was all Tessa could do to keep up with him, especially as the woods became more dense and dark around them, moonlight shifting through the trees their only light. About ten minutes into the run Tessa remembered Robin trying to get her promise not to spend any time with Fenris while he was away. She hadn't actually promised but a slip of guilt twisted painfully in her belly anyway. Twenty minutes into the run Tessa realized that she was following The Big Bad Wolf deep into the woods, in the dark, and there was no way that she knew where she was or how to get back. She cursed under her breath some more,

CONTINUED

DELETED SCENES

calling herself all kinds of names. When they stopped about five minutes later Tessa was so winded she thought she'd pass out right in front of him. Fenris was breathing barely harder than normal. Had Tessa needed to defend herself with The Black Dove she wouldn't have been able to raise her damn arm. Fenris looked back at her and made no mention of her rib cage expanding and contracting as if about to burst.

He breathed in deeply and turned to the right. "We go quieter from here," he said his voice barely a whisper. "Say nothing."

Tessa nodded and followed Fenris as he began a short but steep climb up the face of a rock. Tessa had to drop The Black Dove in order to do so and she was none too pleased about it. At the top of the short climb, Fenris led Tessa through a small down slope of densely packed trees. The branches tore at Tessa and as she yanked her way ungracefully through, she collided with Fenris who spun around and clasped a large hand over her mouth before she could say anything.

Tessa couldn't even be mad at Fenris. She'd made it so goddamn easy for him. She was a trusting fool, she thought to herself as he held her, his hand tightly across her mouth, shaking his head lightly at her. Only, he wasn't killing her. Or anything else. He was just trying to communicate something to her via intense eye contact. If he'd been less intractable and she'd been less pissed and disappointed in herself, perhaps she could have figured it out. But instead she bit his hand—hard. He grimaced and bit his own lips as he tried not to shout out and she felt the parts of him that touched her trying to shift into a wolf in reaction to the pain. He glared at her when he got control of his scream and shifting. After a moment he turned his body, still holding onto her tightly and turning her as well, to reveal some commotion below them. He looked back at her and raised his eyebrows. She nodded her head that she understood and he released her.

CONTINUED

DELETED SCENES

They turned as one and crouched together as one behind a mass of rocks so they could watch the small area below them unseen. Perhaps 50 feet below them there was a large break in the trees, and just beyond it, a house. All alone, but well lit in the otherwise dark woods. Fenris made a motion toward some trees to their left. Tessa followed him, even as he climbed out onto the thick branches of one of the trees. When they finally stopped she could see they were positioned out over the house, a large skylight below them. The room below them was large and strange, and seemed to take up the bulk of the house. In the middle of the floor lay a pile of dead bodies, at least a dozen all in various stages of decomposition. Beyond the bodies, there was a huge metal wheel. Some kind of machine that was equal parts dark ages and future. It was a mess of dials and levers, wires and tubing, but at its horrible center was unmistakable, a place for a human body to go. To go and be strapped in. Tessa shuddered involuntarily and the leaves on the tree danced dangerously. Fenris shot her a cautious look.

Below them a figure moved, all grace and not at all what Tessa had expected. A woman by the size and shape, but covered in a black cloak and hood. Some blonde hair fell from the hood as she leaned forward to adjust one of the bodies. She then disappeared from the room, or at least the parts of the rooms that were visible. Tessa and Fenris exchanged a glance and she think he recognized her either.

And then, from wherever the woman had gone, emerged another figure. Hulking and monstrous, it was something Tessa hadn't even considered.

Kelly: So this was not the original way that Tessa discovered the real villain she was dealing with, but an interim version. I like the idea of Tessa and Fenris going on a dangerous action adventure of sorts, but this never quite worked for me, although I confess I do like the reveal of the wheel coming earlier in the book, and the subsequent scene (also cut, obviously) showing how the wheel works, was a much better introduction to that idea than what I ended up with - which is to say introducing it and what it could do, earlier, was better. But the book generally moves so very fast, especially toward the end, there was just no natural place to insert a scene that introduced it earlier. Still, in the end I much prefer the walk home and the complex conversation we get between Fenris and Tessa to this scene.

HOME OF THE MIGHTY MANTICORES!
GO MANTICORES! GO!